THE NIGHTMARE THIEF

MEG GARDINER

ISIS

LARGE PRINT

Oxford

First published in Great Britain 2011
by
Blue Door
an imprint of HarperCollins Publishers

Published in Large Print 2012 by ISIS Publishing Ltd.,
7 Centremead, Osney Mead, Oxford OX2 0ES
by arrangement with
HarperCollins Publishers

British Library Cataloguing in Publication Data
Gardiner, Meg.
 The nightmare thief.
 1. Adventure games - - Fiction.
 2. Wilderness areas - - California - - Fiction.
 3. Suspense fiction.
 4. Large type books.
 I. Title
 823.9'2–dc23

ISBN 978–0–7531–8962–7 (hb)
ISBN 978–0–7531–8963–4 (pb)

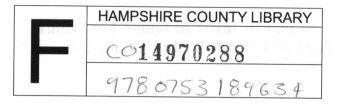

For Nancy Fraser

THE NIGHTMARE THIEF

CHAPTER
ONE

The young trader stumbled from the trees like a scarecrow running on legs of straw. Her suit was muddy, her blouse torn, her sleek Asian hair matted with pine needles. She ran into the street directly in front of Autumn Reiniger's BMW.

Autumn braked. "Oh, man."

The trader glanced at her but didn't break stride. With one arm she clutched a battered lockbox. The other arm she cradled to her chest, protecting what looked to Autumn like a broken wrist.

This was the place. Fun city.

The trader ran across the street to the driveway of Peter Reiniger's palatial home. She was the last to emerge from the eucalyptus grove at the edge of the Presidio. The others huddled on the driveway. Beside them, Reiniger sat on the tailgate of a Mercedes SUV.

Autumn got out of her car. She took a step, but Reiniger gestured for her to stay put.

The trader swayed to a stop. Nakamura, that was her name — Autumn recognized her from one of her father's glossy corporate brochures. Chest heaving, the woman dropped to her knees.

She set down the lockbox. After long seconds she raised her gaze to Reiniger.

Her silence made Autumn's skin tingle. Nakamura was controlling pain and raw emotion. And she was unintimidated — it was stirring. She knelt on the driveway, black hair falling across her face, and she held Peter Reiniger's gaze. With her good arm she fumbled open the lockbox. Inside, hundreds of multi-carat stones glittered like tears.

"I win," she said.

A hush pressed upon the street. Birdsong, wind through the trees, traffic down the hill along the San Francisco waterfront, all ebbed. Reiniger climbed off the tailgate.

"And?" he said.

She dug her hand into the stones and clutched a fistful. "Ransom my team."

The people huddled around the SUV cheered. Nakamura let the stones — cubic zirconia, playtime diamonds — cascade back into the box.

Reiniger pulled her to her feet. "You okay?"

She wobbled, but smiled. "You owe me a raise."

A medic jogged up. "Let's take a look at that arm."

Her colleagues thronged her. Autumn grinned and applauded. The woman was tough. From the roof of the Mercedes SUV, a cameraman panned the scene, catching their glee.

And . . . cut. Cue the music from *Chariots of Fire*. Autumn strolled toward her dad, hands in the back pockets of her jeans.

The game runner got to Reiniger first. "We'll edit the video and burn copies for everybody."

Reiniger nodded. "We'll stream it at our board meeting."

The game runner, a black guy with the hard fitness of a running back, poured antiseptic on a gauze pad and handed it to Reiniger. "Clean up."

Cleaning up was what Edge Adventures did. Absolutely. Reiniger pushed up the sleeve of his sweatshirt. Scrapes covered his elbow. This kidnap scenario looked to Autumn like it had been rowdier than most.

She took the gauze pad from him and dabbed at the scrapes. "Messy."

"Realistic," he said. "The screaming's all part of the game."

Only at team-building weekends run for Reiniger Capital.

"It's how I find out what my people are made of," he said.

Autumn had heard it from her dad before: Running a hedge fund could be risky and stressful, but Edge Adventures helped people find what was really inside. Toughness. Spirit. His staff now clustered around a cooler, beer bottles in hand, exhausted and proud. Two of them grabbed the lockbox and poured the fake diamonds over Nakamura's head, as if dumping a bucket of ice on the winning coach at a football game.

Edge Adventures didn't simply sell excitement. They showed clients the light.

Edge created urban reality games, role-playing scenarios that took clients into an imagined demimonde of crime and rescue. They threw people in the soup.

Edge offered kidnappings, manhunts by bounty hunters, and even a night locked in a morgue — all in all, the chance to face your demons and to act out fantasies of crime and danger. Today, Edge had grabbed Peter Reiniger's team off a street in downtown San Francisco for a simulated heist scenario.

Coates, the game runner, checked Reiniger's elbow. "It's fine."

"Don't worry, I'm not going to ask for a discount," he said.

Autumn saw a quick jab of anxiety on Coates's face, and thought: *And he's not going to sue you.*

"We're cool," Reiniger said. "This was what my daughter here calls sick fun."

Autumn rolled her eyes.

Coates slapped Reiniger on the back. "As always, we're happy to have your business."

"However, I do want to speak to you about our run-in with the police. See me inside in five minutes."

Frowning, Coates went to help the Edge staff load their gear into the SUV — ropes, emergency flares, and replica firearms that looked mean as all get-out.

Reiniger turned to Autumn. "You're half an hour late."

"My car isn't working right. There's a light on the dashboard."

"Which light?"

"The one that tells you it's time to buy a new car."

"You mean 'Service'?"

Laughing, she stretched and kissed his cheek. "Joking, Dad."

"Sure you are."

Autumn was a month shy of turning twenty-one. She bounced on her toes, knowing he would get the message. *Big birthday. Better think big gifts.*

She nodded at the scene on the driveway. "You wanted me to watch the grand finale *why*, exactly?"

"To see how things work."

"Work? You're playing *Ocean's Eleven*. And *Name That Phobia*." She raised an eyebrow. "Don't deny it."

"I don't."

"But you wanted me to sit on the sidelines. And what, cheer?" She crossed her arms. "Put Band-Aids on their boo-boos?"

He crooked his index finger and beckoned her to follow him. Inside, the house was gauzy with sunshine. The view through the living room to the terrace showed windswept Monterey pines and the blue waters of the bay.

Reiniger said, "Hold out your hand."

Lightness, anticipation, winged through her. *About time.* She raised her hand. And Reiniger slapped a heavy manila envelope into her palm. She eyed him uncertainly.

"Open it," he said.

Autumn tore open the envelope. Inside was a memo. It was stamped, in red, CLASSIFIED.

From: Edge Adventures
To: Autumn Reiniger
Re: Your assignment

"Welcome to adulthood," he said.

"You bought me a game?"

OUTLAW is an urban reality scenario that offers a variety of roles for you and your closest friends. Crime syndicate boss, bounty hunter, prison escapee. Edge employees will take other roles and run the scenario.

"A three-day weekend, for six of you." Reiniger smiled. "It's a designer crime spree."

Her confusion began to clear. *Ultra-deluxe. Outlaw. Prison break.*

"Oh my God. Do we get a speedboat?" she said.

"If you want one."

Helicopter rescue.

"Dad — is this for real?"

Hunt down the crime boss, or BE the boss and escape the long arm of the law.

"And this is totally plush, right? No team building. No 'get in touch with your inner hero.'" Her voice turned hard. "No 'fight your demons.' Just fun. And five star. Right?"

He pointed to the location of their syndicate headquarters: the Mandarin Oriental.

"Happy birthday," he said.

She threw her arms around his neck and kissed his cheek.

As Autumn hugged him, a Corvette revved into the driveway. Reiniger patted her on the back. "Go on."

It was her boyfriend. She ran outside, smiling like a cat that had just cornered a mouse.

Fight your demons.

She would know about phobias, Reiniger thought. Too bad hers didn't include fear of shopping.

His daughter was adorable: quick, clever, winning. And such a pretty girl, with the tumbling brown curls of a Victorian aristocrat. He'd never been able to deny her anything. She always wore him down. Her relentlessness was a quality he admired. So why did he get a nagging feeling of unease when he gave in?

Because he had acquiesced to assuage her heartbreak when he and her mother divorced. And to salve her grief when her mother died. He had lavished her with gifts. And what did that get him? Demands for more.

Autumn had the BMW. She had an apartment he'd bought her in the city. She had a spot at the University of San Francisco, a college to which he gave generous donations. And she regarded classes as a hindrance to her tanning schedule.

No team building. No "get in touch with your inner hero."

But heroism was precisely what he wanted her to discover.

Nothing compared to going out on the rim and facing your deepest fears. And Edge offered a red-in-tooth-and-claw experience, rarely found in twenty-first-century America, of feeling truly, deeply, alive. Its full-immersion adventures were the modern world's closest equivalent to primitive initiation rituals.

He paid through the nose, but it was worth it.

For years Autumn had asked to take part in an Edge scenario. And, abruptly, Reiniger didn't want to give her the thrill she coveted. He wanted to give her a wake-up call. She had peculiar fears. She wielded them as a weapon to manipulate him whenever her sense of entitlement was threatened. It was time to quash them.

Coates rapped on the open door. "You got a question about the SFPD?"

Reiniger waved him in. "Yeah. Why did they show up at exactly the wrong moment today?"

Coates was a former Oakland cop. He was Mr Law-and-Order and always alerted the authorities before a scenario was about to run. If a client was going to be grabbed off the street, Edge wanted the cops to know it was a party, not an abduction.

But the San Francisco police had nearly derailed today's scenario, right at the start. As Nakamura was being dragged toward the kidnap van, an SFPD patrol car had screeched up, lights flashing.

Coates shook his head. "Pure chance. No way to grab people off the street without being seen." He eyed Reiniger warily. "They left. I squared it."

"That cruiser arrived thirty seconds into the kidnap. Almost like they had a heads-up."

Coates stiffened. "From Edge? No way. We have zero motive to stall a scenario."

He glanced out the door at Reiniger's team.

"It wasn't one of them," Reiniger said. "They didn't know when the kidnap was going down."

"So it was nobody. Like I said — chance."

8

Reiniger wasn't convinced, but let it go. "I want to ask you something else." He checked that Autumn was out of earshot outside. "I want to add a layer to Autumn's birthday scenario. It needs to be more than a party."

"You want us to heighten the scenario's intensity?"

"It will do her good."

Coates considered it. "We can add a twist to the crime spree. Does she have an issue you want her to work on?"

Reiniger wanted Autumn to learn the value of teamwork. And with her stubborn streak, she would need to be scared into learning it.

"There is something," he said.

There was a big red button. Push it, and Edge would trigger a childhood loathing that had become a mulish dread.

"You know how some people hate clowns?"

"A not-uncommon childhood fear."

"Autumn hates cowboys."

"That's a new one on me," Coates said.

"It goes back to when she was little. This guy scared her at a party."

"Luckily, a cowboy phobia is unlikely to impinge on modern life."

"But it's silly, and she's let it grow out of all proportion. She calls him the Bad Cowboy."

Reiniger had barely seen him: a staff member at the party venue, corpulent and sweating in his boots and Stetson. He had stopped unruly kids from running in front of vehicles in the parking area.

That, apparently, was the origin of Autumn's loathing. The man had scolded her. Sharply — which shamed and spooked her. And for a dozen years since, she had complained about it, usually at awkward moments. The Bad Cowboy had *scared* her. Naughty children got punished, he said. Careless children got hit by cars and *killed*, he said. He was *creepy*. Why wouldn't Dad take it seriously?

Reiniger heard the subtext: *Pay attention to me, Daddy. Indulge me.*

"Guy was some ex-rodeo rider. Hefty kid with stitching on his shirt that said, 'Red Rattler'."

"And he dressed like he was still at the rodeo?"

"Fourth of July party. The staff wore Americana outfits," Reiniger said. "Here's my point. If Autumn could confront the Bad Cowboy during the weekend — and defeat him — it would be the icing on her birthday cake."

"Red Rattler — he was a pro rodeo rider? You got a name for this guy?"

"Doesn't matter whether you track him down. It's not the man; it's the bogeyman he's become in her imagination."

"It's what the Bad Cowboy represents," Coates said.

"You got it."

"Psychodrama."

Which Reiniger wanted to kill, dead. "Maybe you could have one of your game runners dress like him."

Autumn came into the living room, chattering to her boyfriend.

Coates nodded to Reiniger. "Leave it to me," he said, and headed outside.

Dustin Cameron, smooth and overeager, held out his hand. "Sir."

"Autumn's told you?" Reiniger said.

She looked giddy and calculating. "A crime spree weekend. And I'm going to play the queen of the underworld." She grabbed Dustin around the waist. "You be the DEA agent who's after me."

"I want a big gun," Dustin said.

Dustin lifted weights and tucked his expensive sunglasses in the open collar of his polo shirt. His aspirations were ill defined. But Dustin's father was a Washington lobbyist. The boy came from a family with power and swagger. He would do well.

And he could take Autumn places. Reiniger hoped she wouldn't tire of him. Dustin needed to emerge from the crime spree weekend a hero. He would ask Coates to ensure it.

Autumn squeezed the young man. "The game's going to be badass. Absolutely goddamned badass."

"Autumn," Reiniger said.

She laughed. "I'm getting into character. One you designed."

Reiniger's phone rang. He stepped away to take the call.

"Dad —"

He put up a hand to forestall her. "The Asian markets are opening soon."

He answered the call. After a moment Autumn pulled Dustin out the French doors onto the terrace.

She looked stung. Reiniger walked from the room and closed the door behind him.

In a copse of trees down the hill, Dane Haugen adjusted the focus on his Leica binoculars. The laser rangefinder gave the distance to Reiniger's terrace as 122 meters. Through the hazy sunlight, Autumn Reiniger looked as bright and unaware as a piece of glass.

"Photos," Haugen said.

Sabine Jurgens raised her Nikon and snapped a dozen shots of Autumn and the young man who was groping her.

"My, my," Sabine said. "Mr Cameron is testosterone personified."

"What are they saying?"

Beside Haugen, Von Nordlinger aimed a parabolic microphone at the terrace. He put a hand to his earphones. "They're talking about the game. She just got the invitation."

"Record the conversation," Haugen said.

Von pressed a button and listened, his slab of a face thick with concentration. The earphones stretched over his pumpkin-size head.

Haugen watched Autumn. "Does her description of the scenario match the specs Sabine pulled off the Edge database?"

Von nodded. "Prison break . . . speedboat . . . six in the party. Autumn's talking about who to invite."

Sabine snapped more photos. Her face was severe, her red hair cut boyishly short. Though she lacked any hint of softness, she moved with cold fluidity. Haugen found her stunning, in the way of an electric eel: smooth and cunning and purposeful.

Her intrusion into the Edge computer system had found *OUTLAW SCENARIO — Autumn Reiniger* booked for mid-October. But that hack was now twenty-four hours old.

"Get back into the Edge system tonight," Haugen said. "I want details — the scenario's starting point, the timing, the equipment Edge is bringing."

She lowered the Nikon. "Not all Coates's notes go on the computer system."

Von said, "I can search their office."

Haugen turned, removed his sunglasses, and stared at Von without blinking. Von scratched his nose and shrank back.

Haugen continued to glare. "We leave no footprints. We do nothing that could tip Edge to our existence."

Von looked at the ground. "Forget I mentioned it."

"Hardly," Haugen said.

But Sabine was correct: Terry Coates sometimes modified scenarios on the fly. That was why Haugen had shadowed the Edge team on today's kidnap scenario — to see whether they stuck to the script. And, crucially, to see whether the police stuck to the script when challenged.

Thanks to Sabine's hack, he had known where and when Edge would grab Reiniger's corporate team. When Terry Coates pulled up, precisely at noon, Haugen was watching from a coffee shop across the street. He had already phoned the police.

SFPD response time to a 9-1-1 call reporting an abduction at gunpoint: three minutes, forty-two seconds.

Time required for Coates to convince the SFPD it was a game: four minutes dead. Once the uniforms confirmed that Edge was running a team-building exercise, and that the department had been informed of this in advance, they drove away.

Excellent.

Haugen swept the binoculars and saw, on the driveway, Reiniger Capital's crew celebrating their escapade. He saw Terry Coates, buff and slick and unctuous. Peter Reiniger stepped outside and was swarmed by his acolytes. Accepting kudos, undoubtedly.

Haugen lowered the binoculars. "Do you understand who Peter Reiniger is?"

"Richer than God," Von said.

"He's a pivot point. He's the fulcrum that will provide the leverage we need. And, thanks to his daughter, he is going to be" — Haugen savored the word — "pliant."

"So we're going to grab her," Von said.

The air was sharp with salt, and with promise. Haugen raised the binoculars and took another look at Autumn. "Happy birthday, princess. Surprise, surprise."

CHAPTER
TWO

Wednesday, October 10

"Stop kidding. It costs how much?"

The guy in the attendant's booth didn't look up. "Twenty-four bucks for the first hour, twelve-fifty each hour after that."

Evan Delaney blinked. *For parking?* Maybe she should ram the exit barrier and escape the garage, instead of forking out. Then, because street parking in San Francisco meant a fight to the death, she could drive her Mustang straight downhill, launch it into the bay, and swim to her meeting.

The car in line behind her honked.

"Fine," she said. "You want me to open my wallet, or a vein?"

Talking to Jo Beckett had better be worth it.

The story Evan was investigating was big, strange, and wormy with holes. Trying to get the full picture was maddening — but that was typical of freelance journalism. That wasn't why she was going to talk to a forensic psychiatrist. No, Jo Beckett had called *her.* Because Beckett was also investigating the death of Phelps Wylie, attorney-at-law.

Phelps Wylie had collected antiques and bought his suits at Hugo Boss. He was short, bald, and toad-mouthed, with limpid eyes. Whenever Evan saw his photo, she heard "Froggy Went A' Courtin'."

He had been found dead in an abandoned gold mine in the Sierras.

Wylie had disappeared from San Francisco one Saturday morning the previous April. Months later and two hundred miles away, his remains were found pinned beneath rubble in the mine, so badly decomposed that no cause of death could be determined.

The local sheriff's department thought he got caught in a flash flood while hiking and was swept to his death. That, or he got drunk during a walkabout in the high country, stumbled on the mine, and fell into the shaft while exploring. Or he threw himself down the shaft deliberately. Basically, he took a midnight header to oblivion, and nobody knew how or why.

It was the biggest backcountry hiking death to hit the State Bar since the defense attorney's from the Manson Family murder trial, and Evan was writing a feature story about it for *California Lawyer* magazine.

But the story stubbornly refused to come together. She'd felt like she was poking roadkill with a stick, coaxing it to dance. Until, out of the blue, Jo Beckett, MD, phoned and asked to meet.

That was the reason Evan parked and hiked to a coffeehouse near Fisherman's Wharf.

Java Jones was steamy and felt lived in. The young barista had a silver nose ring, Tiggerish energy, and curls the color of the coffee she was brewing. Her name tag said TINA. *Bad Dogs and Bullets* was playing on the stereo.

Evan approached the counter. "This sounds like a honky-tonk requiem."

"You want something tall and strong to go with the song?"

"And hot. Make sure he can skin a bear, and looks good on a horse."

Tina smiled. "Americano, large?"

With a gust of wind the door opened and a woman came in: early thirties, *café Americano* curls, subdued athleticism beneath boho-chic clothes. She waved at the young barista and scanned the place.

She couldn't be called elfin — she was too sober. Her gaze seemed warm but guarded. Or maybe she was just analyzing the clientele.

Had to be the shrink.

"Jo?"

"Evan." The woman extended her hand. "Thanks for coming."

Evan nodded at the barista. "You're sisters?"

Jo smiled. "Yeah, but drink this coffee for a month and you'll look just like us."

She ordered an espresso containing so many shots that the mug vibrated. Evan glanced her over. So. This was the deadshrinker.

Jo looked the compleat Californian: Doc Martens and a Mickey Mouse watch, the hint of East Asian heritage a few generations back. She wore a Coptic cross on a chain around her neck. The light in her brown eyes looked both engaging and shrewd.

Evan bet that 90 percent of people who heard the words *forensic psychiatrist* got tongue-tied and skittish, worried that Jo was sizing them up for tics and compulsions. Because she was one of them.

Jo led her to a table by the windows. "I'm performing a psychological autopsy on Phelps Wylie. His law firm has asked me to investigate his mental state and try to determine the manner of his death."

"And how's that going?"

"It's frustrating." She sat down. "Wylie's life contradicts every assumption the sheriffs drew about his death. He didn't hike. Didn't like the mountains. He did like gold, but in the form of bullion traded by his corporate clients. And he liked booze, but when it was poured into champagne flutes at the opera house."

"Bear Grylls he wasn't," Evan said.

"Not by a New York mile. You know how a psychological autopsy works?"

"You examine a victim's psychological life to figure out how he died."

"Yes — when a death is equivocal. That is, when the police and medical examiner can't tell whether it was natural, accidental, suicide, or homicide. When they hit a dead end, they call me to evaluate the victim's mental state," she said. "I'm their last resort."

"And I'm yours."

Jo's expression turned piquant. "I'm aware of the irony."

18

Evan paused. Her skittishness was abating, because she saw on Jo's face the same drive and foreboding she felt herself.

"This investigation is getting to you, isn't it?" she said.

"It's under my skin like a tick. Tell me about Wylie. I need background, insight, some clue to Wylie's personality and motivations, any evidence that will help me build a timeline of his final twenty-four hours."

"Did he have a psych history?" Evan said.

"None."

"Think his death was from natural causes?"

"What, he dropped dead picking wildflowers, in a flood channel, and got washed into that mine by a convenient downpour?"

Jo's tone was caustic. Evan liked that. She batted down a smirk.

"Do you think Wylie was murdered?" she said.

"Possibly. Do you?"

"I'd lay money on it. He was a baby barracuda, angling to reach the top of the legal food chain. He made enemies. And his friends say that before his disappearance he seemed preoccupied and brooding. The word *edgy* has come up more than once."

Jo nodded. "And then there's the car."

Shortly after Wylie disappeared, his Mercedes turned up near the Mexican border, stripped, abandoned, and wiped clean of fingerprints.

"The gold mine is in a remote part of the Stanislaus National Forest. So maybe the car thief stumbled across the empty Merc on an isolated logging road and decided to take a five-hundred-mile joyride. But color me skeptical."

Evan nodded. "If you determine Wylie's state of mind, will that prove how he died?"

"Not necessarily. I don't have a Magic Eight Ball that says *murder* or *accident*. Clients who think I can dowse for death end up disappointed."

"Your psychological autopsy broke open the Tasia McFarland case."

Jo's gaze sharpened. "That case ended with the man I love shot and wounded, and the media crawling over me like scorpions. So be aware that I tread carefully when dealing with the press."

Evan's eyes widened. "Tread carefully? You fought a battle royale against the Creature from the Channel of the Blondes. And you took her down, live on national television. For which, by the way, I should throw confetti over you."

Jo laughed.

"And if you're so wary of the press, how come you called me?"

"You have a background as a lawyer yourself. You've been looking at the case from angles I probably haven't. And I'm told you're a straight shooter."

A shadow passed behind Jo's eyes. It seemed to say, *And I know how you got into trouble, Ms Delaney.* Did Jo know why this case pulled so hard on her? Her own father had gone missing. And though Evan had found him, in the aftermath the certainties in her life had boiled away in a cauldron of grief.

She went still. "Who gave you my name?"

"It's no secret you're doing this story," Jo said.

A tickle began at the base of her skull. "Still — who pointed you in my direction?"

"My sources are confidential. As are yours. Right?"

"As acid rain."

Jo looked at her calmly.

Cool down. Evan drummed her fingernails on the tabletop. "Very well."

They gauged each other for a moment longer. Then, simultaneously, they got out notepads, pens, and digital audio recorders.

Jo said, "Have you seen the police reports?"

"Tuolumne's. Not the SFPD's."

"Okay. The day before Wylie disappeared, he worked a full day. His e-mail and phone records show nothing out of the ordinary. His last call was to a client at 6p.m. He mentioned no plans to go hiking in the Sierras. Saturday morning, he pulled his Mercedes out of the driveway. He phoned his mother from the car and said he was headed to the office. That's the last anybody heard from him."

Something about the timing scratched at Evan, but she couldn't pin it down. "Have you spoken to his clients?"

Jo's expression became studiously neutral.

"That's confidential?" Evan said.

"Absolutely. However, Wylie's client list isn't. Nothing stops you from interviewing them."

"Got a copy?"

Jo handed her a file folder.

Evan smiled. "Okay, I'll trade."

From her backpack she took maps and photos of the rugged country near the abandoned gold mine. She handed Jo an eight-by-ten.

Jo looked surprised. "Satellite photos?"

"Orbital image taken two days before Wylie's disappearance."

"The resolution's amazing."

Evan handed her another. "Same patch of terrain, snapped from the same satellite, but this month."

Jo stilled. "How did you get these?"

"Relatives with the right passwords. See what I see?"

Jo pored over the photos. "The flood channel. It's much deeper on the recent image."

Evan unrolled a U.S. Geological Survey map. "Have you been up there?"

Jo's dispassion turned to disquiet. "I've carved out some time to drive up next week." She examined the map. "I know that part of the Sierras. The terrain's brutal. Look at the topo lines." She traced a series of closely convergent changes in elevation. "Forest, granite crags, sheer drop-offs, and when heavy rain falls, flash flooding is a real problem. *If* Wylie was hiking, he could plausibly have gotten caught in a washout. I mean, I know native Californians who think they're safe camping by the Russian River after a downpour."

"I'm from the Mojave Desert. I know people who thought they were safe driving across eighteen inches of rushing water on a highway," Evan said. "What are you thinking?"

"The sheriffs' photos didn't fully depict the severity of the terrain. Or . . ."

Evan raised an eyebrow. "The timing?"

Jo straightened. "I need to get up there ASAP. Because your satellite photos suggest that the flash flood occurred *after* Wylie disappeared."

"Precisely."

Noise swirled around them, the clatter of coffee cups and silverware. The intensity on Jo's face mirrored Evan's own feelings. She felt a weight, heard a deep-background snarl. It was menace, looming.

Jo said, "The question is, what drove Wylie to that mine? Or *who*?"

The scratchy feeling, Evan's sense that she'd missed something, intensified. "You said that the day before Wylie disappeared, his last phone call was from the office."

"Right."

"What about the dog walker?"

The evening before he disappeared, while checking his mail, Wylie had run into his next-door neighbor. The two spoke briefly.

Jo said, "I talked to him. He didn't mention a phone call with Wylie."

"No. He overheard Wylie take a call. When did you speak to him?"

"Two weeks ago."

Evan felt a frisson. "I spoke to him yesterday. He said they chatted for a minute before Wylie's phone rang. Wylie excused himself and answered it."

Jo looked consternated. "What time was that?"

"8p.m."

"Wylie got an incoming call on his cell phone."

"Yes," Evan said.

Jo's gaze sharpened. "Wylie's cell phone records show no calls after five thirty."

They both tensed.

"He had a second cell phone," Jo said.

"He damned well did."

"Whoa." Jo looked both irked and excited. "Did the neighbor overhear Wylie's conversation?"

"A few words. He said Wylie mentioned something about running, and a concert. A rock concert, he thought."

Jo sat straighter. Her eyes were alight. "Second cell phone. Was Wylie using it for sex or for bad business?"

"I'll check. But if this mystery phone didn't show up in Wylie's records, it's either pay-as-you-go or registered under somebody else's name. Unless we can unearth the number or the phone itself, we won't find out who called him."

Jo looked again at the photos. "What did the neighbor hear Wylie say? Exactly."

Evan checked her notes. "Wylie mentioned something about how they 'ran.' And 'rock.'"

Jo tapped one of the photos. It showed massive wedges of granite. "Maybe it's nothing. But maybe he was talking about the mountains." She stood. "I need to clear my schedule. I have to get up to the Sierras." She extended her hand. "Thanks for the information."

"We should compare notes again. Forty-eight hours from now?"

"You bet." Jo's smile was hardly neutral. It was hungry.

24

"Excellent. And who gave you my name?"

That smile became enigmatic. "I'll call you in forty-eight hours."

Jo headed for the door, blowing a kiss to her sister as she left. Evan took a breath, excited, and her stomach pinched.

Who had put Jo in contact with her?

The door opened and the wind whispered in, teasing her, hinting at his name.

But she hadn't told him about the feature story. She hadn't told him because she hadn't spoken to him — though he was the man who knew her better than anyone. He was the man she loved, and who had left her inconsolable, struggling through emotional wreckage after her father went missing. The man she didn't know how to face, the man she had promised to marry.

She slung her pack over her shoulder and walked out.

Jo jumped off the cable car near the top of Russian Hill. The tracks rang with the sound of gears and cables beneath the road, a bright noise that echoed the humming of her nerves. In the park across the street from her house, a basketball hit the backboard and sluiced through the net. Sophie Quintana grabbed the rebound, and saw her.

She hopped and waved. "Jo, you be on Dad's team."

Gabe stood beneath the basket, hands on his hips, catching his breath. "That was a quick meeting."

Jo jogged to the court. "Hurried back to be your point guard, Sergeant."

He looked good in the October sunlight. Ripped and smiling and welling with energy.

"What's that gleam in your eye?" he said.

Sophie turned and charged the lane, ten years old and confident that her agility would outgun the grown-ups. Her brown ponytail flicked in the breeze. Her cheeks were bright. Her smile, Jo was happy to see, looked unburdened.

She dodged around Jo and took the layup. The shot hit the rim.

Jo caught the rebound. "The campout with your cousins is this weekend, right?"

The little girl nodded. "Friday."

Gabe said, "What kind of plan are you hatching?"

Jo passed him the ball. "I'm going to the Sierras."

"And you want a pararescueman to ride shotgun?"

A whistle from the backcourt caught her attention. The man on the far side of the court raised his hands and called time-out.

"You no longer look like you want to take this day out back and shoot it," he called to her. "So I'm guessing your meeting went well."

She excused herself from the game and walked toward him. "You were right. Evan was the one I needed to talk to."

Jesse Blackburn smiled, short and sharp — a slice. "Glad to hear it."

His jeans had a hole in the knee. His T-shirt said FIND YOURSELF IN PARADISE and hung loose from his swimmer's shoulders. His eyes were blue and keen with questions.

26

Jo gave him the answers. "Yes, she wanted to know who gave me her name. And, no, I didn't tell her it was you."

He spun the wheelchair and coasted toward her. "Thank you."

"But, Jesse, she knows you crossed swords with Phelps Wylie in court. Of course she suspects. She can easily find out I was at UCLA with you. And that you're in San Francisco to argue a case before the Ninth Circuit."

An undertow seemed to pull at him. He and Evan had promised their futures to each other — and then they were assaulted by a cascade of Bad. He thought he had brought it down on them and couldn't see how to swim out from under. Now Jo had spent time with Evan, while he had not. The hurt showed on his face.

He lived with plenty of pain. He had survived more. And he would survive this. But merely surviving would be a waste. Evan was clearly his match. Together, Jo had no doubt, they sparked heat and light. For them to lose that connection would be heartbreaking.

She said, "If Evan asks me again, I still won't tell her. But you should."

He looked away, at the sun jumping off the blue waters of the bay. "Not yet."

"What will waiting accomplish?"

He pushed to the fence that bordered the park, hung his arms on top, and stared toward Alcatraz.

Jo leaned on the fence beside him. After a moment, she said, "I never thanked you for coming to Daniel's funeral."

He looked at her, surprised. "You don't need to thank me."

"You drove three hundred miles that day. I appreciate it."

"It was the least I could do." He paused. "Is that your way of reminding me that none of us has unlimited time?"

"You know what it's like to live a suddenly changed life. I appreciate that too."

Jo had become a young widow in the time it took to blow out a match. She knew all about being stared at. About being *That Girl. That Guy.* The one who lost . . . the ability to walk. A lover. The future that they'd never have. Jesse's friendship, the fact that he understood what she had gone through, meant a lot to her.

He stared at the water. "This cut is deep."

"When did wounds ever stop you? What did you tell me once?"

His smile was thin. "When you can't change a situation, and can't get out of it, you have to go forward. It's a fucking fact of life."

"I tattooed that statement on my rear end. Thanks for confirming I got the wording right."

His smile turned wry. "You and Evan are definitely going to hit it off." He laughed and shook his head.

Gabe called to them. "Guys, I need help on defense. Sophie's killing me here."

They headed back toward the basketball court. Sophie was dribbling the ball, bobbing and weaving in a circle around him. Her laugh sounded silvery.

28

Jo said, "I also remember the second half of that statement, Jesse."

"The important thing is not to be afraid. Even when you know what's coming."

She squeezed his shoulder. "Don't forget it."

CHAPTER
THREE

Friday, October 12

Limo didn't begin to cover it. They drove south down 101 in a sick beast of a vehicle: a stretch Hummer, black with honest-to-God flames painted on the sides. As if Autumn truly were the queen of a trashy, flashy drug cartel and this was her monster ride. She stretched on the plush bench seat and watched San Francisco rush by.

Dustin pulled a bottle of champagne from the Hummer's minifridge. "Time to toast the birthday girl."

Lark Sobieski shook her head. "Not a good idea. We need to stay sharp."

Lark's punkish black hair swooped over one eye, nearly covering her glasses. Her ouroburos tattoo rolled over the pudge of baby fat above the top of her jeans. The dragon swallowing its own tail was red and sumptuous against her brown skin.

Dustin unwrapped gold foil from around the cork. "Maybe you need to stay sharp. But this is how the *narcotraficantes* do it down in Juarez."

Grinning, he shook the bottle and popped the cork. It ricocheted off the driver's headrest.

30

Lark ducked. "Careful."

The driver glanced in the rear-view mirror. "Watch it, bucko."

Dustin laughed. "I don't own this ride. It wrecks, Edge Adventures pays."

He tilted the gushing bottle to his lips. Champagne poured across his chin. He wiped it off and made a face at the label: VEUVE CLICQUOT.

"Not half as good as the stuff my dad serves on his boat. But Edge *didn't stock Colt Forty-five*" — he raised his voice at the driver — "so it'll have to do."

He held out the bottle to his housemate. Noah Holloway put up his hands.

"I work for the G. No drinking on duty."

Noah had a sunny smile and laid-back manner. From across the limo, Lark admired his bed-head hair and uncomplicated surfer's calm. She seemed unaware that everybody could see her cheeks flush.

Peyton Mackie grabbed the bottle. "I'll drink on duty. Undercover agents have to practice holding their booze." She keeled back on the seat and coughed down a huge swallow.

Laughing, she wiped her lips with the back of her hand. "And speaking of law enforcement . . ." She raised her hand like a gun, two fingers for the barrel, thumb cocked. "Got you in my sights, Reiniger."

"Screw you, Fed," Autumn said.

Peyton's blond hair slid over her shoulder. She was wearing raspberry velour Juicy Couture track bottoms and a pink cami. She made a ridiculous federal agent.

Autumn snapped her fingers. "Sobieski. Take down Agent Pretty-in-Pink."

Lark sighted at Peyton down the length of her arm, as if it were a sniper rifle. "Pow. You've got no head, Fed."

Peyton wilted, eyes crossed, tongue hanging out. Lark blew on her fingers.

Autumn ran her hands across the crushed red velvet of the bench seat. The limo had been a surprise, a definite five-star stunner. When her doorbell rang, she'd found a man in sunglasses and a black Edge Adventures baseball cap on the porch.

"I'm the game runner. The clock is now ticking on your scenario," he said.

She paused, bemused. "We still have an hour to drive to the rendezvous point."

"Not anymore. Your father sent me."

Now her stomach fluttered. Her dad had told Edge to pick her up because he didn't trust her to arrive at the crime spree on time. The game runner, Kyle, was at the wheel of the limo, eyeing her and her friends in the mirror from behind his shades.

Peyton grabbed the champagne bottle and crawled along the bench seat to Cody Grier. She curled herself around him. "Share."

Grier's eyes widened in surprise. "The bottle? You trying to bribe me to turn against the syndicate?"

In honor of playing Autumn's *consigliere*, Grier had come dressed like a member of the Rat Pack. He adjusted his straw trilby and pulled Peyton against his side.

32

Lark continued to gaze at Noah, until she sensed Autumn watching. She turned to the window.

"Keeping an eye on the opposition," she said, and pushed her glasses up the bridge of her nose.

"Good. Tell me if anybody follows us." Outside, beyond the traffic, Autumn saw weeds and run-down wooden houses slumped against one another by the freeway. Her stomach tightened. "I'm serious about that."

Lark gave her a funny look. "What's wrong?"

Autumn gestured at rusting trash cans and busted cars parked on a crumbling hillside. "This is not five-star."

Get me to the Mandarin Oriental, she thought. Edge had reserved a cluster of rooms at the end of a hall, to emulate a summit being held by a crime syndicate. And all at once she didn't want to be stuck at the end of a hall. Cornered.

"Autumn?" Lark said.

"Over the past couple of weeks, have you had the feeling somebody's watching you?" she said.

"Like who?"

"Like somebody who moves away when I look out the window. Or steps behind trees on campus when I pass by." She waited for Lark to agree, but her friend stared with skepticism. "Never mind."

"Are you serious?"

"Maybe it's Edge, doing reconnaissance. They do, you know — they research all their clients."

"They spy on you?"

"They generate dossiers." She nodded at the driver, Kyle, and lowered her voice. "He probably knows all about us. Don't you get that feeling? That he's . . . *seen* us?"

Lark watched as Kyle changed lanes. "He looks like he's trying to get us there smack on the dot."

"Right."

Lark's mouth turned down. "Autumn, are you okay?"

"Never mind. Forget it."

Autumn folded her arms across her chest. Dustin and Peyton were swapping turns with the champagne bottle. Grier was texting — God, let it not be his dope dealer. They didn't need that complication this weekend. Noah was glancing at Lark from the corner of his eye.

Her father didn't believe any of them could drive across town on schedule. So he had rounded them up like sheep. The pellet in her gut grew hotter.

What, she wondered, had her father told Edge Adventures about her?

At the Emery Cove Marina, Terry Coates scanned the checklist. His brother and two other game runners were prepping the speedboat. Fuel. Life jackets. First-aid kit. *Check.* Phone call to the SFPD, alerting them that a scenario was about to run: *Check.*

"Looking good," Coates said.

The wind was stiff, the sun dazzling on the water. Across the bay, San Francisco spilled across the hills, white as chalk in the autumn light. Coates savored the view.

Running Edge Adventures was a sweet gig. It was Disneyland for the rich and adrenaline deprived. It was Self-Discovery a la carte and Phobias, Inc. rolled into one. And it was a whole lot more fun than driving a patrol car in downtown Oakland.

With his graying hair and the Edge Adventures polo shirt tucked into his jeans, Coates thought he looked exactly like a former cop. But he had a halfback's build, and people sometimes took him for a retired ballplayer. *Didn't you used to play for the Raiders?*

Maybe in another life he would have played pro ball. But in this life, he had found a niche — a profitable niche — helping others live out their sometimes-twisted fantasies. He had just one hard rule: In an Edge Adventures game, crime would never pay.

Anybody but him, that is.

He never let clients play a game in which criminals got away with murder. Scenarios designed around a sting were cool. An outlaw-with-a-code-of-honor thing was okay with him. Robin Hood. Butch and Sundance. But no scenarios where serial killers took victims or street gangs gunned down the cops. He wanted his games to end with exhilaration, and edification — *thus endeth the lesson* — that sent clients back to their boardrooms with some speck of insight into living a wholehearted life.

But today, he suspected, he would be playing ringmaster to a sorority food fight. Autumn Reiniger, according to her father, needed some severe excitement to wake her up to the realities of adulthood.

This scenario had a lot of unknowns. His research into the six kids who were going on the weekend had been cursory, because they had almost no history. Their answers on the Edge questionnaire told him only that they were green, protected college students. Autumn Reiniger and Dustin Cameron came from highly privileged backgrounds, which raised flags with him. The children of super-wealthy parents frequently thought that every crisis could be solved by having Daddy write a check.

The other kids — Peyton Mackie, Lark Sobieski, Noah Holloway, and Cody Grier — were question marks. They'd never been in trouble with the law. There were a couple of medical issues going on with —

"Terry?"

Coates turned. His brother stood at the controls of the speedboat.

"We're ready to rock."

"Outstanding," he said.

Coates prepared to cast off from the dock. As he united the boat's mooring lines, his phone beeped with an incoming text.

6 POB.

The message was from Kyle Ritter, driving the limo. Six passengers on board. They were headed to the assembly point.

Coates glanced again across the bay. At the southern tip of San Francisco, barely visible, was Hunters Point Naval Shipyard. Beyond it was the barren scrubland of Candlestick Point, where the speedboat would rendezvous with Autumn's party.

The boat fired up. The engine sounded like a throaty lion.

Coates hoped the twist he'd designed into Autumn's scenario wasn't too far out of bounds. Nothing was dangerous, simply — unpredictable.

Happy Birthday from Red Rattler. That little gift was going to light her up like a roman candle. Set her whole weekend on fire.

He tossed the mooring lines aboard the boat, and his phone rang. He glanced at the display and answered with deliberate, jaunty assurance.

"Mr Reiniger. Autumn's group is on the way. I just received confirmation."

"Good. Keep the rest of the weekend to schedule this tightly and I'll be pleased," Reiniger said.

Schedule? Reiniger kept changing it. Edge had scrambled to meet this morning's last-minute request to pick up the kids, and with a limo, no less. It was lucky they could spare a team member to drive.

"I'm boarding a flight," Reiniger said. "I'll be five hours en route, then I'm headed directly to a meeting. But phone me this evening. I want a status update."

"Will do."

Coates put a hand over his ear. It was windy, and people were approaching on the dock, laughing, swinging a picnic basket between them.

"Remember," Reiniger said, "Autumn may act assertive, but inside she's scared. If she tries to hide from her fears, make her hold her ground. Don't let her retreat."

"So she defeats the Bad Cowboy and crosses the Rubicon."

"And be sure her boyfriend comes off in a good light."

Reiniger ended the call. Coates stared at the phone, feeling vaguely uneasy. His brother said, "Terry?"

He looked up. The man and woman carrying the picnic basket had stopped beside the speedboat. They were wearing floppy hats and sunglasses. They had semiautomatic pistols in their hands.

Coates reached automatically to his hip for the Oakland PD service weapon he no longer carried.

"Don't." The man raised his pistol and centered it on Coates's chest. "Hands behind your head."

CHAPTER
FOUR

The limo pulled off the freeway into a sketchy industrial area of warehouses and machine shops. Autumn saw cracked asphalt, rusting cars, trash, men in dirty clothes. They passed a vast parking depot for empty big rigs: truck after truck after truck.

"*So* not five-star," she said.

Kyle glanced in the rear-view mirror. "This ain't the destination."

His voice twanged around the limo. It had an unpleasant echo. *I'm driving, and that's that.* Peyton took another swig of champagne. Grier turned up the stereo. Sinatra, "Come Fly with Me" — he was taking the Rat Pack theme to extremes.

Autumn knew the contours of the game. Terry Coates had outlined it and sent her forms to fill out, on everything from medical conditions to nut allergies. She'd had to sign on every dotted line. She hadn't been told that adulthood would involve so much paperwork. She didn't like it.

But she did like the crime spree scenario: She was the head of an international criminal enterprise that trafficked in pleasure. She was on the run after breaking out of prison. Running with her were Lark, her enforcer; Grier, her *consigliere*; and Dustin, her deputy and prime piece of beef. They would attempt to escape Peyton and Noah, the federal agents hunting her down.

And she wasn't just going to escape from federal custody. She was going to take down the enemies who had betrayed her and sent her to prison. She was going to destroy their centers of power, rob them blind, and collect booty. Loot, swag, pillage. Because it was her birthday.

She felt nervous and excited and — hungry. She couldn't wait to get going.

But she didn't know why the scenario had to start in such a dismal neighborhood. The Hummer sped by a huge parking lot, a sloping black prairie of asphalt, and she saw stadium lights. Candlestick Park came into view. It was a grimy concrete Frisbee plastered with billboards for the '49ers. An endless line of aqua blue Porta-Potties bordered the whole empty, sagging affair.

Then Autumn spotted golden fields dotted with stubby pines and caught the sparkle of sunlight off the bay. Kyle swung the Hummer through a gate. He gunned it through a long, empty parking lot and stopped sideways across four slots. The engine coughed and hacked until he shut it down.

He turned. "Okay, kiddies. We're here. Sack up."

Dustin squinted against the sunlight. "This is Candlestick Point?"

Kyle got out, opened the passenger door, and beckoned the group out. Noah held out his hand for Lark. She shook her head. "Opposite teams, Noah. I let

40

you grab my hand, next thing you're slapping a pair of cuffs on me."

"You take that risk." Smiling, he gripped her hand and got out.

Peyton followed, tugging Grier along. "Hey, I'm a U.S. Marshal. If anybody plays with handcuffs, it'll be me." She tucked a finger under Grier's belt. "And I'm talking to you."

Grier popped the collar of his shirt. "You won't get me. I pay people off. That's my job. If I can't, I run."

Kyle looked like he was trying to keep a straight face. "If you like shackling prisoners, Miss Mackie, shouldn't you be wearing a police uniform?"

She smiled, patently coy. "You like handcuffs?"

He smirked and poked up the brim of his cap. "Knots are more my style."

Autumn pushed Peyton forward and climbed out. "Move, Mackie." *Before you start doing a pole dance.*

Candlestick Point State Recreation Area was virtually deserted. The grass was unmown. The trees were gnarled by the wind. On the sand at the water's edge, a man was performing tai chi. In the distance an elderly couple ambled along, pushing a baby stroller that held their tiny white poodle.

Past the glittering water, on a spit of land that protruded into the bay, giant loading gantries and cranes stood idle at the abandoned Hunters Point Naval Shipyard. On the bay, a container ship steamed toward Oakland, its wake as white and frothy as cake icing. The wind battered Autumn's hair away from her face. She pulled on a Marine Corps utility cap and smoothed down her gold cashmere sweater.

She inhaled the strong sea air and shivered. All at once she felt great.

Dustin came up behind her and nuzzled her neck. "Last kiss before battle?"

She leaned her head back. "Last kiss till one of us takes the other as a prize."

On the asphalt next to the limo, Grier and Noah shadowboxed. Lark's phone rang, and she answered, "Reiniger Cartel World Headquarters, Sobieski the Assassin speaking. How may I direct your call?" Then, giggling, "Hi, Mom."

Kyle scanned the parking lot, one hand steepled over his brow. After a minute he reached inside the Hummer and took out a walkie-talkie.

"Ritter calling base."

Static.

"Ritter calling base, come in."

More static. He got his phone, made a call, and frowned. Autumn knew that look. It was the one she got when she called her father. *Voice mail.*

She tugged on Dustin's sleeve. "All that crap from my dad about getting here on time, and we have to stand around waiting for the game to start?"

Dustin shrugged. His smile was slippery, like it had been oiled. "They're going to spring things on us. It's cool."

"Ask the driver what's going on." She pinched him. "Dustin. This is boring."

42

Dustin raised his hands in submission and walked toward Kyle. "Hey, man, thought your team was supposed to be waiting for us here. What's going on?"

Kyle looked up, sheepish behind his sunglasses. "Coordinating with HQ." He frowned again at his phone. "It's just . . ." His lips, full and red, had constricted. He looked baffled.

Autumn crossed her arms. "Where are the other game runners?"

Ritter raised his hands, a mollifying gesture. "Guys, I'm as new to this as you. Let's just ride it and see what happens."

"New?" Autumn said.

He smiled, greasy and uncertain, trying to play it. "I'm Edge's most recent addition to the team."

"You're brand-new on the gig?" Dustin said.

"First time for everybody, man. It's no biggie. And I'm sure this delay is just a glitch." Kyle gave one more beseeching glance at his silent cell phone.

"Are you telling us we came to the wrong place?" Dustin looked around, weaving.

Autumn's voice rose. "This has been planned for months. And you came in at the last minute?"

The others stopped horsing around and walked over. Noah said, "What's going on?"

Autumn pointed at Kyle. "Did you screw up? Because if you did, my dad will have your ass on a skewer."

Kyle's expression dried, like a chunk of Sheetrock. "I did not screw up. We changed plans at the last second, thanks to a specific request *by* your father for Edge to

43

provide this limo. My boss called me at 7 a.m. We had to scramble to get this Hummer and pick you all up," he said. "So no offense, Miss Reiniger, but if there's a problem, it's your dad . . ."

Autumn stiffened, but Kyle caught himself.

"Let's all cool down." He forced a smile. "It's just a hiccup. I'm sure the rest of the team will be right along."

Peyton grabbed the champagne bottle from Dustin. She took Grier's hand and pulled him toward the Hummer.

"Knock on the window if anybody shows up," she said.

Autumn swallowed. The hot pellet in her stomach had returned. How could this turn bad, so quick? It was *her day*.

Lark looked around: at the empty, wind-bitten park, the flying saucer stadium, the bay. Then she stood straighter. "Oh. Look."

Dustin's gaze swerved around. "Whoa."

Lark jogged toward the bay. Noah ran after her. "All right."

Autumn blinked, fighting the sting in her eyes. On the water, arcing around the abandoned cranes at Hunters Point, was a white speedboat.

Kyle let out a breath, half laugh, half sigh. "There you go."

"That's them?"

He waved her forward. "Let's hit it." He banged on the window of the Hummer. "Peyton. Grier. Out. We got bogeys incoming."

Autumn's anger let go and a bright stripe of excitement painted the view. She grabbed Dustin's hand and pulled him toward the beach.

CHAPTER
FIVE

The speedboat razored through the chop past the cranes at Hunters Point and skipped across the bay toward Candlestick Point. Dane Haugen held the throttle wide open.

"Masks on," he said.

Von Nordlinger pulled a black ski mask over his face. Haugen did likewise. Over the mask he put on the wraparound sunglasses he had purchased that morning. His hands were already covered by black calfskin gloves.

He picked up his walkie-talkie and clicked Transmit. "This is Viking. We are three hundred meters from the beach and closing."

The boat bounced on the whitecapped water. Over the walkie-talkie, a woman's voice scratched at him.

"This is Ran. We are thirty seconds from the rec area parking lot."

Haugen smirked. *Ran*. How apropos of Sabine to employ a Norse goddess as a cover name, one that meant *theft*. "Masks on. Hold position."

"Roger," she said.

He had to wear the mask. He was fair, tall, well built, and so handsome that a Hollywood producer had once told him that he could have opened feature films. The word *chiseled*, he had decided, fit him best. And his presence was magnetic — almost bewitching to women. He saw himself as a classic figure, perhaps Spartan. Nobody who saw him could forget him. He was too striking.

He raised his binoculars from the strap that hung around his neck. At Candlestick Point, the trees bent beneath the wind. The park's sad picnic tables were empty. On the muddy beach, a group of young people jogged into sight.

"It's them."

Von slipped the pistol from the small of his back and chambered a round. Behind the ski mask, his watery blue eyes were eager.

"Clear the round," Haugen said.

Von glanced sharply at him.

"Do it now," Haugen said. "We will not damage the merchandise."

"But if they run —"

Haugen clipped him in the side of the head with the walkie-talkie. Von lurched and grabbed his ear. "Christ, you —"

"Clear the chamber, and safety your weapon. Now. Before I dump you overboard."

Struggling to hold himself steady against the chop, Von cleared the chamber and safetied the pistol. He wouldn't look at Haugen.

"*If* they run?" Haugen said. "Of course they're going to run. They're young and fit and pumped up, and they think this is a game. We *want* them to think it's a game. Our plan depends on them thinking so."

He shouted over the roar of the engine, enunciating each word carefully, as if lecturing a cognitively challenged janitor. Von stared at the prow of the boat. His lips were pressed white, his nostrils flaring beneath the ski mask, but he kept his mouth shut this time.

Haugen aimed the speedboat directly at the beach. The boat was a fine piece of machinery. And the drug runner's vehicle of choice. Credit Terry Coates — the ex-cop knew his stuff. Too bad for Edge Adventures that the boat had been so easy to steal.

Haugen breathed in the sharp salt air. So far, so perfect. His team had taken control of the Edge game runners without a fight. Coates had thought briefly about resisting, but the sight of Von's Glock had stopped him in his tracks. Coates didn't want to die over a bunch of spoiled college kids.

No, the Edge game runners had gone down on their knees with their hands behind their heads. Von and Sabine had needed mere seconds to cuff their hands with zip ties and march them to their SUV. Then Haugen and Von took the boat and headed for the rendezvous. Sabine and the other men on her team had driven away with the Edge game runners, transporting them to the leased big rig parked in the middle of the huge truck depot near Candlestick Park.

The fact that Sabine was now on scene, and in position at the recreation area, meant she and her team had stuffed the game runners inside the big rig — gagged and zip tied in a circle with their feet chained to

48

a ring in the center of the trailer. The game runners couldn't lie down, couldn't turn around, couldn't even kiss one another, much less scream for help or kick the walls to draw attention. And the walls of the trailer were draped with heavy padding, the kind used by moving companies to protect grand pianos in shipment. The padding would deaden any noise. Nobody was going to miss the game runners for at least forty-eight hours. Just like nobody was going to miss Autumn and her friends.

And that was all the time Haugen needed.

He finally glanced at Von. "Do you think there's the slightest chance I'll risk shooting Autumn Reiniger here, at a public park?"

Von stared at the beach. "Is that a rhetorical question?"

Haugen smiled thinly. "Is that wit? A bon mot?" Intellectual gymnastics from the man — Von had just earned back a point or two. "You're right. I was using a rhetorical device. We will not, I repeat, *not* risk damaging our investment by injuring Ms Reiniger."

"I think I got it now, boss." Von looked at the beach. "Just one question."

"Yes?"

"Six people in her party, right?"

"Correct."

"So why are there seven of them there on the sand?"

CHAPTER
SIX

Jo paused at the crest of the ridge. The sun was a gold needle in a deep blue sky. She leaned back against a boulder spackled red with lichen. A moment later, Gabe joined her.

She swept back curls that had escaped her ponytail. "Thirty seconds. Gotta catch my breath."

Gabe shrugged off his backpack and got out a canteen. He took a swig and handed it to her.

"Thanks." She drank and wiped her lips. "You have an altimeter?"

He shook his head. But the rise and fall of his chest told her they were at significant altitude.

Her truck was parked two miles back and probably a thousand feet below them on a narrow logging road. She and Gabe had been hiking for ninety minutes. According to her Stanislaus National Forest trail guide and the map Evan Delaney had given her, they were still a mile from the abandoned gold mine where Phelps Wylie had been found dead.

Gabe scanned the crown of the forest. All around, covering the mountainside, were lodgepole pine, white fir, and dogwoods turning crimson. He pointed at a soaring conifer whose dusty green boughs spread above them.

"That's Jeffrey pine. It only grows above six thousand feet." He smiled at her, a challenge. "Still way too low to worry about supplemental oxygen."

"Yeah, sure — you could have HALO jumped and beaten me here. No need to brag."

"Nah. The government gets annoyed when a PJ uses Air National Guard resources to meet his girlfriend for a date."

He set his Oakley sunglasses on top of his head. He looked like he was in fighting trim, and he was talking like it too, as a deflective mechanism. But he couldn't keep Jo from surreptitiously doing a visual sweep of his vital signs.

His skin tone was good: bronze, with a ruddy glow from the hike. Respirations were rapid, but that could be expected because of the altitude. His pulse was strong. She could see it beating in his neck, where it met the line of his jaw. His eyes were clear, dark, and focused. On her.

She slid her arms around him and kissed that beating pulse point. Wordlessly he pulled her tight against him and held her. She felt him breathing. He kissed the top of her head and then she tilted her face up and he kissed her right on the lips. Twice.

Then he smiled, patted her backside, and picked up his pack again. "Wasting daylight, campers."

Jo saluted. *Don't make a big deal out of it.*

But she couldn't stop herself from keeping an eye on him. *Tough cookie* didn't begin to describe Gabe, even on his worst day. And today was far from his worst.

He was strong and young and resilient. But he hadn't fully recuperated from being shot in the chest with a 9mm bullet.

He had only recently returned to work with the California Air National Guard, and to grad school at the University of San Francisco. He had not yet received medical clearance to return to active military duty. He hadn't put back on all the weight he'd lost in the hospital or recovered his stamina. A patch of sweat darkened his USF T-shirt between the shoulder blades. He still had a considerable amount of pain, which he refused to dampen with medication.

That, Jo knew, stemmed from pride and machismo and the determination to provide a clean and sober example to Sophie. And it stemmed from being a PJ, a pararescueman, with the Air National Guard's 129th Rescue Wing. Gabe worked search and rescue on land, sea, and air. And when on active duty, he performed CSAR, combat search and rescue, sometimes leaping into firefights from thirty thousand feet, using HALO parachute jumps — high altitude, low opening — designed to maximize stealth and speed and a PJ's chances of reaching the scene of the rescue alive.

Jo followed him along the crest of the ridge, through slices of sunlight in the cool air. The terrain was dry and spare and wild, beautiful and incredibly quiet. Looking up, past the green tops of the pines, she saw only sere blue. Her footfalls landed softly on dirt and pine needles. Beyond them she heard the rustle of the breeze through the boughs of the trees. The only signs of human encroachment were power lines strung from metal pylons that towered atop nearby ridges in the mountain range. The lines skimmed high above gorges and rivers, and for a moment Jo wished she could simply hang a zip line from one and slide directly toward the mine.

Gabe followed her gaze. "No way."

She laughed. Ahead, the trail switchbacked to the bottom of a ravine before crossing a rocky stream and climbing up the other side. But upstream, where the slope steepened and began its climb to the timberline and snowcapped crags of the high Sierra, power pylons stood on opposite ridges of the ravine, linked by an aluminum catwalk.

"It would cut three miles off our trip. Save us a couple of hours and hundreds of feet of climbing," she said.

Gabe leaned toward her. "*Bzz.*"

"Okay, there's high voltage, and the danger that the bridge would collapse."

"If it's thrills you want, let's get out of here and get a room. So come on and examine this mine, pronto."

"Right."

They had a reservation for the night at the Lodge at the Falls in Yosemite. That meant a couple of hours driving still to come, after the hike out. The wind sent a shiver through the trees. It sent a shiver through her as well.

Phelps Wylie would never have chosen this as an afternoon's recreation.

Maybe he had taken a joyride in his warm, luxurious Mercedes, listening to *Madame Butterfly* on his

German stereo system. But he never would have driven two hundred miles from home into a mountain range where, not much more than a century earlier, the Donner Party had become trapped for the winter and ended up eating each other.

Wylie's death was no accident.

"Wylie had a map. Or he had a guide. He had some reason for being up here."

Gabe glanced over his shoulder. "Not a good one."

"Got that right, Sergeant." A gust lifted her hair from her collar. "Okay, let's pick it up. This wind is only going to get stronger. And we're going to lose the sun."

Gabe nodded. "Weather's coming."

She felt a cold thread skim past her, like a hundred pinhead snakes. *Bad vibe* about covered it. "Let's move."

CHAPTER
SEVEN

Haugen eased off the throttle. As the speedboat settled lower in the water he counted the people on the shore ahead, running toward the beach.

Three women, four men. What was an extra man doing there?

"Maybe it's a random picnicker," Von said.

Haugen's jaw tightened. "Who runs *toward* a boat driven by men in ski masks?"

Von didn't reply.

The boat crept forward. The wind raised spray on the water. Haugen tented a hand over his forehead to cut the glare, then adjusted his sunglasses to get a clearer view of the extra man on the beach. With a start, he was reminded that these weren't his prescription pair. He had purchased these sunglasses this morning with cash, just as he had purchased his black work boots and gloves and pants with cash, all at separate stores, and had bought his black tactical gear online through a corporate account that couldn't be linked to him. Should anybody report his description to the police, nothing he wore could tie Viking, the kidnapper, to Dane Haugen.

But as a consequence, he couldn't get a crisp view of the people on the sand. He grimaced and covered. "We'll find out who it is in sixty seconds. We play it by the book, until we have to play it by ear. Follow my lead."

"No shooting," Von said. The black mask, stretched across his basketball of a head, rendered his expression unreadable. But complaint was in his voice.

Haugen turned his head toward the man. Haugen's dead-eyed glare was hidden, but Von still cringed, intimidated. *Good*.

Haugen got the walkie-talkie. "Ran, come in."

Sabine came back, staticky. "We're on site. Ready to egress. But our numbers are —"

"Extra man in the picture. Repeat, extra man in the picture. Possibly a bystander."

She paused. "Possibly not?"

"Don't know," Haugen said.

Another pause. "Understood."

He shoved the throttles to full power. The engine snarled. The stern of the boat dug into the bay, the bow rose, and they bounded across the whitecaps toward the beach. Haugen put the walkie-talkie to his lips again.

"Going in. Follow my lead."

Autumn ran behind Dustin toward the beach. The speedboat, white and sleek, knifed through the glinting water straight at them. Ahead, Lark and Noah jogged to a stop at the water's edge. Peyton was walking behind Grier, raspberry velour hips swaying, champagne bottle swinging in her hand. Up the sand in the distance, the tai chi practitioner stopped to watch.

Autumn caught up with her friends. The limo driver, Kyle, ran up behind her.

"All right, you all. Time to separate." He pointed at the boat. "They're coming to pick up Ms Reiniger and her muscle." He nudged Lark, Dustin, and Grier toward her. Then he pointed at Peyton and Noah. "You two federal agents — you best get lost, if you don't want to get taken down in a firefight."

The boat drew nearer.

"Or captured and interrogated," Kyle said.

Grier adjusted his straw hat. "Listen to the man — he knows the score. If you can't deny the charges or buy 'em off, you'd better split."

Peyton worried the charm bracelet on her wrist. Grier took off his smiling skull ring and handed it to her. "My marker, Marshal. You want to change teams, you call me."

Autumn rubbed her palms against her jeans. "The boat — they're picking me up after my prison break?"

"That's right. We are now on the clock."

Kyle reached beneath his Edge Adventures windbreaker and pulled out a handgun that looked like something Colonel Quaritch would fire at aliens in *Avatar*. Matte silver, with a huge telescopic sight atop the barrel.

He smiled, a cool leer. "And I, Ms Reiniger, am your nemesis. U.S. Marshal Kyle Ritter, tasked with apprehending you and preventing your crime spree. If I was you, I'd run before I got brought down like a deer."

Autumn blinked. Then she turned and sprinted toward the water.

Twenty meters from shore Haugen slewed the boat sideways and brought it to a halt. Von leapt over the side, gun out, and splashed through the shallow water toward the beach.

The Reiniger girl was running toward him. *Excellent.* Her friends seemed confused. In the distance, sprinting over the park's low hills, came the first members of Sabine's team.

Up the beach, a man in drawstring pants was doing tai chi. Haugen catalogued him. *Bystander.* Along the path, toward the fishing pier, an elderly couple ambled out from behind the trees. The woman was rotund. She was pushing a baby stroller that held a white poodle. Every few seconds she leaned over to pet and coo at it.

Bystanders. Their presence was not a problem. Haugen had planned on having to take Autumn Reiniger's group with people watching. That was the whole point of the way he had designed the operation.

They had waited to ambush the Edge Adventures crew until *after* the boss, Coates, had phoned the SFPD. So the cops now knew a scenario was running at Candlestick Point. They didn't have to like it. They just had to believe that, whatever happened from this point on, *it was all a game.*

Sabine sprinted into sight. A ski mask covered her face. A very real SIG Sauer was gripped in her right hand. She pulled herself to a stop. Walkie-talkie to her mouth.

"Seventh person in Autumn's group has a gun. Do we back off?"

Haugen raised his walkie-talkie and hesitated. Who was the man in the baseball cap, waving a toy science fiction cannon at Autumn Reiniger?

CHAPTER
EIGHT

Autumn saw the alien-killer gun in Ritter's hand, heard the *"let's play"* snicker in his voice, and ran. The non-smile lingered on Kyle's face. The speedboat bobbed in the cove, engine rumbling. A man in a ski mask was at the controls. Another was over the side and splashing through the water toward her. He was short and stout, with a huge round head covered by the mask. He too had some kind of gun in his hand, not as flashy as Kyle's, and was holding it high so as not to get it wet.

He waved. "Autumn. This way. I'll cover you."

She dashed for the water, her heart racing. She realized she was smiling. Grinning. She yelled, joyful.

The stout gunman pointed at Dustin. "You too." He reached shore and swung into a stance: arms straight, gun pointed at the other people on the sand.

Autumn heard Peyton shout. Noah cried, "Come on."

She looked over her shoulder. Three more masked people, swathed in black, had appeared behind them, armed, charging toward the beach.

The stout gunman beckoned to her. "Hurry."

She hesitated. Her boots were brand-new Stuart Weitzman black leather, buckled, gleaming, top-bitch riding boots. "I can't get these wet."

Peyton squealed. Autumn saw a masked attacker descend on her roomie, grab her around the waist, and sweep her off her feet. One of her little bow-covered ballet slippers flew off. Peyton threw her head back, squealing like a piglet.

Dustin splashed into the water.

"Wait — give me a piggyback," Autumn said.

Dustin slowed, unsure. The stout gunman charged past him to the beach, crying, "Get in the boat."

The man grabbed Autumn, hefted her into a fireman's carry, and began trudging back toward the boat. She heard the water sluice around his feet.

"Careful." She bounced up and down, her stomach thumping against his shoulder. "This is undignified. I'm the Queen of the Underworld."

She raised her head. On the beach, Peyton lay facedown on the sand, a raspberry velour prisoner with her hands laced behind her head. Nearby, an attacker marched Grier and Noah toward her, gun aimed at their backs.

Lark was farther down the beach. She was waving at the elderly couple with the poodle. The woman, chubby and black with a foam of white hair, had a cell phone in her hand. Lark was undoubtedly explaining to her that this was all a joke.

With a grunt the stout gunman heaved Autumn onto the speedboat. She clattered awkwardly over the side and Dustin pulled her in. The gunman clambered aboard. A tall man stood at the throttles, completely sheathed in black, from his ski mask to his wraparound shades to his tactical clothing to his gloves.

Using sign language, he told the stout gunman to take the helm. Then he leapt over the side of the boat into knee-deep water and forged toward the beach.

"Awesome," Dustin said. "Freakin' awesome, man."

The boat bobbed. Autumn grabbed the side of the hull to steady herself. "What are we waiting for? Let's go."

The man at the throttles turned and glared at her. "Come on . . ."

Why didn't he say anything?

Haugen splashed through the water to the beach. The situation on shore looked like kindling, ready to ignite. Sabine's team had three of the college students under control but the fourth, a crow-haired girl who had the earnestness of a librarian, was trying to soothe the old lady with the poodle. Lark Sobieski — Haugen recognized her from surveillance photos. Sabine was headed toward her.

The seventh man on the beach — the stranger — stood gripping a ludicrous toy gun in both hands. From seventy meters away his face was just a blur, but even so Haugen could see who the man was.

He was a damned Edge Adventures employee.

Haugen ran toward the tête-à-tête with the poodle couple.

". . . a role-playing game," Lark was saying. "Honest. It's a birthday party."

Sabine reached Lark. "Get in the speedboat, quickly. Your principal is unprotected."

Lark gestured to the poodle woman. "I'm explaining to them."

"My responsibility, not yours. And I have the business cards." Sabine put a calming hand on Lark's shoulder. "Get going."

With a final look at the elderly couple, Lark ran toward the boat. Young Ms Sobieski, Haugen thought, was going to be an irritant. She had an overdeveloped sense of responsibility.

But right then she wasn't the main problem.

The elderly couple glared at Sabine. From the baby stroller, their dog whimpered. Sabine lifted the mask from her face. Her expression was calm. With the blue contact lenses, dramatic make-up, and a blond wig, she was well-enough disguised. She handed the old woman a card.

"Sorry to alarm you. This is just a game," she said.

The woman pointed at Sabine's handgun. "Doesn't look like fun to me."

"Fake. It's from Toys 'R' Us. Listen, this was cleared with the parks department and the SFPD. The rangers should have posted signs. I'll speak with them about the oversight." She got out her phone. "Could I have your name, so I can tell them whom they've inconvenienced?"

She had it under control. Haugen stepped away and beckoned to Pat Stringer, one of Sabine's team. He was a black-clad little weasel of a man. Haugen drew him out of the others' earshot.

"We have a problem," Haugen said.

"Tell me about it." Stringer glanced up the beach at the Edge employee who was guarding Peyton and Noah with his toy gun. "Edge changed the scenario at the last second. They brought in an extra man. And I think I know why."

He nodded at the parking lot. Parked across four slots was the crassest, biggest Hummer Haugen had ever seen.

"Peter Reiniger asked Edge to pick up the kids," Stringer said.

Haugen eyed the Edge man from afar. Black baseball cap, sunglasses, Edge windbreaker, that absurd toy weapon. "Have you seen him before?"

"No. He's new. This is his first scenario."

Haugen's acid reflux flared. This should *not* have happened. This was not part of the plan. And it posed several difficulties.

His whole enterprise depended on keeping everybody in the dark — the public, the police, and of course the kids whose weekend was being hijacked. Perpetuating the illusion that the game was still in progress could not have been more vital.

He couldn't let this Edge newbie — "What's his name?"

"Ritter."

He couldn't let Ritter ruin his finely tuned scheme. But he couldn't leave him here. Nor could he beat the man unconscious and throw him in the back of the Hummer — the beach was crawling with witnesses. And he couldn't spare the time or the manpower to

64

subdue Ritter and deliver him to the big rig in the truck depot.

And he could not possibly leave the garish Hummer parked there for the weekend. The vehicle couldn't draw more attention if he put a giant ice cream cone on the top and played tinkling children's music. The dog-stroller granny would talk about it. The rangers would investigate.

And every second they lingered on the beach bent his exquisitely tuned timeline further out of shape.

Tick-tock.

"Has Ritter asked questions?" Haugen said.

"He asked why we were late."

Haugen turned slowly. "He thinks we're the real Edge team?"

"Like I said, he's brand new. He was hired by Terry Coates and hasn't met anybody else from the company." Stringer looked at the ground. "But Ritter's asking where Coates is — which brings up a third problem."

"What?"

With a jerk of his head, Stringer led Haugen to Sabine's Volvo SUV. He popped the tailgate.

The back of the Volvo contained their gear, including a six-foot army duffel bag with canvas tarps inside. One of the tarps had been removed and spread across a large lump in the back.

Haugen's jaw tightened. "Coates . . ."

"Fought back when we tried to load him in the big rig. He grabbed for Max's weapon and —"

"I warned you he was an ex-cop. I specifically told you —"

"That if anybody tried to attack it would be Coates. I know. It happened too fast."

Haugen lifted the edge of the tarp. The man's dead eyes stared through him.

It was not the first freshly killed body he had seen. But Haugen wanted to throttle Stringer, right there.

"You couldn't have loaded this in the big rig?"

"People were coming. We had no time. And it's too hot to leave him in the back of that truck. After three days . . ."

"Shut up."

Sabine ran over. "Got Ma and Pa mollified. But we have to get out of here or we're screwed."

Haugen kept his voice flat. "Why didn't you tell me about this?"

"I tried. You interrupted me."

He held still for a cold moment, staring at the corpse. Then he looked down the beach at Ritter and at the Hummer.

He took Sabine by the arm. "You're coming with me in the speedboat. We'll ride herd on Autumn." He pointed to Stringer. "You drive the Volvo to the dock. Von and Friedrich will take that Hummer, and Ritter, and follow you. We're going to turn this to our advantage."

"Extra man — Ritter's a loose wheel," Stringer said.

"We'll decide what to do with him later. Right now, we need to get all these people and that limo off this beach and get out of San Francisco."

66

Stringer slammed the tailgate and sprinted back to the beach, shouting, "Into the Hummer. Let's go, kiddies."

Noah Holloway, Peyton Mackie, and Ritter eagerly followed him back to the flame-riddled attention magnet.

Sabine faced Haugen, expressionless. She knew they were committed now. She pulled the mask back down.

Together they ran across the beach and splashed through the water to the speedboat. Von lugged them aboard. Autumn, Lark, Cody Grier, and a tipsy-looking Dustin Cameron turned toward Haugen eagerly.

"Ready to run?" he said.

"Finally. I have stealin' to do," Autumn said.

"Don't we all." Haugen slammed the throttles forward, spun the wheel, and sent the boat flying across the bay.

CHAPTER
NINE

The entrance to the abandoned mine gaped in the mountainside. Jo held back. The mine's wooden support beams were weathered and rotting. Inside was a void: gloom and mystery.

"It's all wrong," she said. "Everything about this."

The idea that Phelps Wylie had randomly hiked here, or that he had committed suicide by pitching himself down the mine shaft, struck her as absurd.

Gabe took a Maglite from his backpack and crouched in the entrance. The flashlight's hard white beam shone on rubble, animal droppings, an empty plastic water bottle. The mine tunnel looked like a throat.

"Do you want to go in?" he said.

She put a hand against one of the support beams. "Not without roping up."

She turned and examined the pine-stabbed mountainside. A fresh gash had been torn in the slope; a raw wound where the ravine had eroded violently under the force of fast-flowing, debris-strewn water.

"The flood channel certainly runs into the mine. I can understand why the sheriffs thought Wylie was swept to his death. Without having access to the satellite photos, it's a logical conclusion." She wiped her palms on her jeans. "I need to see the drop-off where his body was found."

She put on her climbing harness, tied the end of a rope to it, and handed the rope to Gabe. He slung it behind his hips and held on, ready to anchor her if the floor inside the mine gave way.

"Shout if you run into mummies," he said. "Or a mutant with a chain saw."

"Jackass."

"At your service, *chica*." He handed her the flashlight and secured his grip on the rope. He was smiling, which almost allayed her fears.

Cautiously, sweeping the beam of the flashlight ahead of her, Jo walked into the mine. Though the roof was several inches above her head, she ducked. A rivulet of cold warning ran down her back. Her throat constricted and the old, desperate dread threaded through her, hissing, *Small spaces collapse*. The wind moaned like a ghostly pipe organ.

Stop it. Calm down. She forced herself to breathe. The walls were cool rock. Thousands of chisel marks were hammered into them. She wondered if anybody, ever, had gotten rich out of this hole.

Or if Wylie had thought he might.

Fifty yards in, she found the drop-off. It was a vertical side shaft, about three feet in diameter, which plunged thirty feet to rocks and crags and mining debris.

Yes, Wylie could have been swept this far into the mine by a torrent and then over the lip of the drop-off. But what if he hadn't been?

She forced away the sensation that the walls were bulging, creaking, bearing down on her. Taking a breath, she continued along the tunnel. Soft dirt mounded beneath her boots, muffling her footsteps. Support beams were hammered into the tunnel's walls and across its ceiling. She rounded a bend, swept the flashlight ahead, and stopped. A pit was dug across the floor. It dropped at least fifteen feet. It was an emergency drain, in case of flood.

Directly above the pit, the old miners had inserted a crossbeam — a railroad tie. And above the crossbeam, dirt and rock had crumbled away. The wood was completely exposed. The sight didn't reassure her. She jumped across the pit and kept going. The tunnel continued to bend. The daylight behind her grew dim and dusty. The walls narrowed and the ceiling lowered. Then, when she thought it couldn't feel any more constricting, the tunnel branched. Tentatively she explored each offshot until she reached a final, dingy dead end. In the beam of the flashlight she saw only the occasional piece of trash. She turned and walked out.

"You all right?" Gabe said.

She nodded. She took off her harness, tilted her head back, and gulped fresh air. At the sight of the sky through the trees, her tension bled away.

"Somebody killed Wylie," she said. "I have nothing to back that up, except gut feeling. But I'd put real money on it. I'll drive up to Reno and lay odds."

She got out her camera. "The question is who, and why."

Gabe scanned the sky. Cumulus clouds were boiling in the west. "We're going to lose the light. And we're going to get rain."

"I'll hurry."

She spent ten minutes shooting photos of the mine and hillside. Then she stopped, gazing up the slope. The Tuolumne County Sheriff's Office had searched the mine and flood channel for evidence. But she now believed the flood channel to be irrelevant.

She looked at the trail.

Consciously slowing herself down, she walked up it. Creeping along, she scanned the ground, examining it foot by foot.

It took her twenty minutes, but high above the mine, she stopped. The sunlight kicked again — like a flash from a signaling mirror. Cautiously, keeping her eyes focused, she walked toward the source of the light.

Ten feet from the path, stuck between two rocks, she saw it.

"Gabe."

He climbed the trail to her side. "Is that what I think it is?"

Dusty and dinged, half covered with pine needles, it was a cell phone.

"Yeah. I need gloves."

She dashed down to her backpack, grabbed latex gloves and a Ziploc baggie, and ran back uphill.

"It didn't move," Gabe said. His tone was wry.

She took a clutch of photos showing the phone in situ. "The sheriffs were out here in summertime. The sun was higher in the sky. The phone's display wouldn't have reflected the light the way it does now."

"You coming up with a reason why they would have missed it?"

"Same when Evan came up last month — and besides, she wasn't looking for a cell phone, because a cell phone had already been found on Wylie's body and the cops didn't know he had a second one. Nobody did, until she and I compared notes."

She pried the phone from its cranny and held it, gingerly, by her fingertips.

Gabe said, "If it's Wylie's, it's been here five months, exposed to the elements. I wouldn't worry about fingerprints or DNA."

"You never know."

"And you don't want to march it triumphantly into the sheriff's station unless it actually belongs to the victim."

"Let's check."

She pressed the Power key. Nothing happened.

Gabe took his own phone from his pocket. It was the same, extremely popular brand.

"Got any more gloves?" he said.

She handed him a pair. He got his key chain — a carabiner on which hung a Swiss Army knife. From the knife he slid a straight pin. He used it to eject the SIM card from the dead phone. He swapped the SIM into his phone and turned it on. The phone lit up.

"Yes," Jo said.

The SIM was damaged. Only portions of the display showed up — if it had been a piece of paper, sections would have looked washed out from water damage. The entire display was weak and faded.

"It won't be stable," Gabe said.

Quickly she scrolled through the controls. She found the damaged SIM's phone number.

"Write this down." She rattled it off and Gabe scrawled it on his wrist. "The cops can get started with that."

With increasing excitement, she checked the call register. The damaged SIM displayed only partial phone numbers. And there was no identifying information on any of the callers. But the numbers were all in the Bay Area. That strongly suggested to her that it was Wylie's phone.

The screen flickered. "I'm going to lose it."

She got her own phone. As quickly as she could, she sent it data from the damaged unit. Then she looked again at outgoing calls. A series of three-digit phone numbers had been called in rapid sequence. 6-2-2. 9-4-4. 8-2-1.

She felt chilly. "I think somebody was trying to dial nine-one-one."

"Trying repeatedly to dial nine-one-one, and missing?"

The wind gusted around them. Gabe's expression sobered.

"Yeah," she said.

Somebody would miss if he was trying to dial 9-1-1 without looking at the display. If he was dialing for help surreptitiously — because the phone was in his pocket or behind his back. If he was in deep trouble.

The display faded briefly to white. It came back dimmer than before.

She needed to find everything she could before the SIM died. The sheriffs probably had tech experts who could revive it, but she couldn't take the chance. Hurriedly she scrolled through the phone's apps and found a dictation function.

She tapped Play.

She heard sounds. Noises. Scratching, muffled — the sound of the phone's microphone recording from inside in somebody's pocket.

She heard a man's voice. "*Where are we going?*"

She glanced at Gabe. His eyes were dark.

The man's voice again: "*Just tell me that much. How far should I plan to drive? Do I need to stop for gas?*"

Jo closed her eyes. Her heart was beating hard. "It's him. It's Wylie."

On the phone, a long pause. "*Well?*"

Finally, more distant, another voice answered. "*Drive.*"

"*Please, I just want —*"

"*Shut up.*"

The second voice was swaddled in ambient sound.

"Man or woman?" Jo said.

Gabe shook his head. "Can't tell."

They listened for another minute. They could hear Wylie breathing heavily.

"He's scared," Jo said.

Engine noise. Wylie spoke: "*Stay on Five-eighty? We're going to be at Altamont in a minute. How far —*"

A sound like a dull slap.

Jo clenched her jaw. "Wylie's driving someplace against his will. And he's trying to leave a trail, to tell people where he's headed."

Wylie's voice came through again, shaky now: "*Why are you doing this?*"

The other voice, distant, more muffled than before. Words too hard to make out. Jo held the phone closer to her ear.

"*You know what the score is,*" the voice said.

Who was in the car with Wylie? A man, or a woman with a deep voice . . . was it a jealous husband? A former lover? Because the voice sounded on the edge.

"*Shut up. Or*" — noise — "*punishment.*"

The recording cut out.

"Damn," she said.

Punishment.

"We have to get this to the sheriff's department."

She ejected the SIM from Gabe's phone and sealed it in the Zip-loc baggie. They hurriedly gathered their gear, and Gabe shouldered his pack.

"Hang on," she said.

They were too deep in the wilderness to get a signal strong enough for a phone call. But sending a text message required only a weak signal and only for a few seconds. She typed a message to Evan, headed: URGENT. She queued up all the data she'd pulled from the damaged SIM, and pressed Send.

Message failed.

She tried again. *Messages placed in queue. Will be sent as soon as possible.*

Jo hefted her backpack. The voice on the phone had unnerved her.

And she knew that Phelps Wylie had not been hiking the mountainside when the floods swept down. He had been dragged to the mine at the mercy of a human tormentor.

The speedboat tied up at a harbor on Treasure Island. The men in ski masks shut down the engine and leapt onto the dock. In the abrupt silence, the boat bobbed, water lapping against the hull.

Treasure Island: good omen.

Autumn climbed onto the dock. The ride had been thrilling. It had rattled her teeth. Lark climbed out behind her, followed by Grier and Dustin. A minute later the Hummer came tearing up, followed by a black Volvo SUV. At the sound of the engines a seagull took flight, squawking.

The tall man pointed at the Hummer. "Inside, on the double."

They ran along the dock and piled in. Inside were Peyton, Noah, and Autumn's "nemesis," U.S. Marshal Ritter, aka Kyle the Edge Adventures guy.

Autumn hesitated. "I thought we were broken into separate teams."

"There's been an adjustment to the itinerary," said the boat driver. "First, you get commando training. We're going to an assault course."

"I didn't sign up for training. I get a crime spree. Emphasis on *spree*."

76

The stout gunman climbed into the Hummer, grabbed their overnight bags and purses, and tossed them onto the dock. "Give me your phones. You're going to boot camp."

Reluctantly they handed their phones to him. He climbed out and slammed the door. Outside, more masked people scurried around. Somebody opened the baggage compartment at the back of the Hummer and began loading gear. A heavy object landed with a thud.

Haugen watched Stringer and Friedrich shove the heavy duffel bag into the luggage compartment of the Hummer. They slammed the hatch. Autumn leaned toward the window and stared out at him.

Von came over. "What if they figure it out before we get to the compound?"

"We've talked about this," Haugen said.

"They're not as stupid as I expected, and they're not drunk enough yet."

"You quiet them immediately. You do it in front of the group, *pour encourager les autres*. You film it, so Peter Reiniger will be convinced that we're serious."

"And then I get rid of the evidence."

"Yes. And make sure it's one of the disposables." Haugen paused, to be sure Von understood. "Not just the weapon — the one who becomes the lesson."

The stout gunman climbed into the driver's compartment on the passenger side. Another man, wispy and blond, pulled off his mask and got behind the wheel. He cranked the ignition, grinding it until the Hummer finally fired up. They got on the Bay Bridge and headed east, toward Oakland. Finally the stout gunman pulled off his ski mask. A head shaped like a pumpkin sat atop his chunky frame. He ran a hand over his hair.

"Greetings. I'm Von, your drill instructor."

Autumn leaned toward him. "I don't want an assault course. I want room service."

"Assault course and spa," Von said. "Honey, it's six-star. Don't worry."

Dustin raised his head. "As long as there's booze."

"There's always booze," Von said. "It's a party."

CHAPTER
TEN

Through the pines Jo saw, at last, the crest of the hill. They'd been hiking back toward her truck for two hours. She was thirsty, and an altitude headache was lurking. The sun darted in and out from between gathering clouds. The air had a nip.

She was itching to get Phelps Wylie's damaged cell phone to the Tuolumne County Sheriff's Office, down the twisting mountain road in Sonora. She took her phone from her jeans pocket. *No signal.* The messages to Evan Delaney remained in the queue to be sent.

"We're still probably forty miles from the nearest cell tower," Gabe said.

He slowed on the trail and took a careful breath. He looked golden in the sunlight. His eyes were warm and full of life. But breathing deeply could still cause him pain, because of scar tissue, gunshot damage, and surgical work. He was trying to get a lungful of oxygen without feeling as if a spear had ripped open his side.

She ran a hand down his arm and squeezed his hand. "Homestretch."

The final two hundred yards of the trail zigzagged around pines and October yellow cottonwoods and lichen green rocks, to a clearing beside the logging road. Through the trees she glimpsed sunlight bouncing off the windows of her Toyota Tacoma pick-up.

She heard music and voices. She and Gabe exchanged a look.

They walked into the clearing, and Jo slowed. Rock music was blaring from a car stereo, the Kings of Leon promising that your sex was on fire. A gargantuan black Hummer was parked by her truck. Red and yellow flames were painted on its sides. Its hood was up.

A motley group of young people loitered nearby. Young women with carelessly styled hair wearing tired jeans and expensive shoes. Fit young men trying to impress them. And failing — one guy sat on the dirt with his back against the Hummer, head hanging low. He was almost as green as the splotch of vomit a few feet away. A girl in pink velour lay on the backseat of the Hummer, feet sticking out the open door.

Gabe murmured, "Early in the day for so much hilarity."

Two men were bent over the Hummer's engine. One wore a baseball cap with EDGE ADVENTURES stitched on it. The other was dressed in black tactical gear. He was wiry and had a dark orange wisp of a mustache, like an overripe peach.

He straightened and said, "Von."

A third man walked out from behind Jo's truck.

Gabe didn't slow or say a word, but as they crossed the clearing he took his hands from his pockets and stepped a foot ahead of Jo. Her internal radar began to ping.

She said, "Engine trouble?"

The man called Von nodded. He too was dressed in tactical black. He was wiping grease from his hands with a rag.

"Hope it's just the battery, not the starter," he said.

Peach Fuzz added, "We're chauffeuring our young guests on their way to a weekend outing. One of them got car sick."

The young guest in question, the green-faced boy, was, at the moment, crawling alongside the Hummer toward a ditch.

Von nodded. He had a head like a basketball. "We stopped and then couldn't restart the engine. You got jumper cables?"

Jo's antennae continued to twitch. Was that why he was snooping around her truck? "Yeah. I can give you a jump."

She unlocked the truck and got the cables from the crew cab. Nearby one of the girls, a brunette wearing a gold sweater and jeans tucked into what looked like Prussian officer's riding boots, sulked against the side of the limo.

"*This* is six-star?" She crossed her arms. "Where — Appalachia?"

Von said, "Gonna get back on the road in two minutes, Autumn."

She ostentatiously checked her watch. "Two minutes max. Or you get me a helicopter and evacuate us to the Mandarin Oriental."

One of the young men from the Hummer, who was wearing a Dean Martin-style hat and a sweatshirt with GRIER printed on the back, wandered near the trees, unzipped his pants, and relieved himself.

"Weekend church retreat?" Jo said.

Von smiled. It looked robotic. "Twenty-first-birthday party. Daddy's picking up the tab."

Gabe took the jumper cables. His face was flat and his eyes alert. Jo got in the cab, fired up the engine, and maneuvered the truck grille to grille with the Hummer. Gabe raised the hood.

It took only a minute to get the Hummer started. The starter ground for a few seconds and then the big engine gunned to life, harsh and whiny in the mountain air.

The green-faced young man climbed to his feet. Swerving back across the clearing, he opened one of the Hummer's doors and grabbed a water bottle. He sauntered over to Autumn and nuzzled her neck.

She pushed him away. "God, Dustin. You smell like puke."

Gabe glanced inside the open door of the Hummer. Jo saw it too: a gleaming silver handgun with a telescopic sight.

Von said, "It's a replica."

The man in the Edge Adventures cap wiped his palm on his jeans and extended his hand. "Kyle Ritter. Don't worry none about the guns. They're for show."

Gabe smiled, as robotically as Von had. "Just wondering what sort of birthday party you're celebrating."

Von took a business card from his shirt pocket. "Edge Adventures. The ultimate in urban reality games."

Dustin walked over, water bottle hanging from his hand. "Yeah, we're federal agents, guarding our prisoner. See?"

He opened the front door of the Hummer. A rifle was propped on the seat. Jo recognized the curved ammunition clip and tall front sight on the stubby barrel. It was an AK-47.

The girl whose feet were protruding from the Hummer sat up. "Badass. We are badasses."

She pitched back on the seat again.

Jo checked the jumper leads. The Hummer's engine was gunning. "Think you're all set."

Gabe disconnected the cables from the pick-up's battery. Jo caught his eye. He was wearing The Look.

Not his laid-back *all-is-well* look. The other one. It set Jo's nerves on edge.

He slammed the hood of the pick-up. Casually, he said, "Let's roll."

Von stuffed the rag in his pocket, his eyes on Gabe. "The weapons are decommissioned." He gestured at Peach Fuzz. "Friedrich's an ex-cop, and we have former military on staff. Everything's cool."

"Great."

Gabe leaned into the crew cab and put the cables away. Under his breath he said, "Bullshit."

He glanced at Ritter. "His gun's patently a toy, something the guy picked up at a *Battlestar Galactica* convention. But the others are working firearms."

Behind him, one of the girls turned up the music and began dancing. Ritter slammed the hood of the Hummer. Von clapped his hands. "Everybody, let's go."

Gabe glanced at them edgeways. "I've been on one of these role-playing weekends. In Finland, with a bunch of think-tank guys. Executives playing Cold War. One side gets captured by a Russian tank, then out pop the 'Soviet' invaders — a bunch of Finnish lingerie models in Red Army hats. They had real Kalashnikovs, but it was obvious *at a glance* they'd been deactivated. The barrels were plugged. The firing pins had been removed. Colored tags were hanging from their muzzles to identify them as 'safe,'" he said. "Whatever this game is, it's a bad one."

"Let's go."

Jo was planning to drive straight down the mountain to the sheriff's station. When she got there she'd tell the deputies about this drunken rodeo.

Behind her, Dustin stood by the door of the Hummer. "Lark, where's Peyton?"

They looked around. The blonde in raspberry velour had wandered into the trees.

"Peyton," Lark called.

Dustin shouted, "Mackie, get back here. We got boot camp. And after that, you got escaped felons to hunt."

He reached into the Hummer and picked up the AK-47 from the front seat. "Peyton, come back before I come after you."

He slung the strap over one shoulder like he was Rambo. The muzzle began to come up.

Gabe jumped at him. "Don't." He got his hand on the barrel and pushed it down. "Aim the barrel downrange. *Never* aim it at anybody."

Dustin spun away. "What's your problem? The gun's fake. *Fake.*"

He ostentatiously swept the rifle in an arc, aimed it at the trees, and pulled the trigger.

The rifle fired. Four shots in a close burst, the sound cracking the air. Orange flame spit from the barrel, cartridge casings ejected, and the rounds hit the trunk of a pine. *One two three four*, splintering the wood in a rising progression.

The girls screamed. For the time it took to blink, Jo stood shocked. Then she yelled, "Get down," and dived to the ground behind the pick-up.

Gabe lunged at Dustin, twisted the rifle from Dustin's grip, and shoved Dustin away from him. "What the hell are you doing?"

Dustin stared at the rifle with horror. "Jesus, what — ? That thing . . ."

Peyton ran into the clearing. "What was that?"

Autumn clenched her fists in front of her mouth. Her eyes looked like silver dollars. Dustin gazed at her, baffled and terrified.

For a moment, the echo of gunfire stank around the clearing.

Ritter looked stunned but hyperalert, as if ready to jump — in what direction, Jo couldn't tell. Von, his face white, raised his hands calmingly.

"Sorry. It was supposed to be a surprise. My fault," he said.

Gabe spun on him. "Surprise?"

"Live-fire exercises when we get to the assault training course." He tried to smile. "That shouldn't a happened."

Autumn raised both hands and said, "That's it. I'm out."

She stalked toward the back of the Hummer. "This entire thing is *screwed*. Where's my phone? I'm calling my dad."

Von turned. "No."

She opened the luggage compartment. "Don't tell me what to do."

She froze. Then she screamed.

In the luggage compartment, a large green duffel bag had fallen partially open. A body was stuffed inside. A man's blood-soaked shirt was visible. Autumn lurched back. Friedrich charged, grabbed her by the hair, and twisted her to her knees.

Gabe took the rifle in both hands and brought it up and got his finger on the trigger. But behind him came the sound of a slide being racked on a semiautomatic pistol. Von and Friedrich both had guns in their hands, aimed at his head.

"Put it down," Von said.

Jo saw Gabe inhale. He was calculating. But the gunmen were too far apart to guarantee he could hit them both before they could get him. And there were too many people in the field of fire.

"On the ground," Von said.

Gabe put the rifle down and raised his hands.

For a moment the air seemed to tremble. Then the young man with GRIER on the back of his shirt turned and bolted for the trees.

Friedrich swung his gun and sighted it on the kid's back. The boy pounded toward the forest, arms flailing.

Autumn and Lark screamed, "*No.*"

"Friedrich," Von yelled.

Friedrich fired. The shot blew Grier off his feet.

CHAPTER
ELEVEN

Grier dropped to the dirt like a bag of sand. The shot echoed. Blood bloomed through his shirt. Autumn screamed, a loud, continuing wail.

Ritter shouted, "What are you doing?"

Jo lurched to her feet. And found a pistol pointed at her face.

"Don't move," Friedrich said.

A quicksilver fear rolled through her. Friedrich looked frantic. The gun was matte black. The bleak eye at the end of the barrel wandered across her face.

She struggled to keep her voice level. "I'm holding still. I'm unarmed."

Peyton applauded. "Bravo."

She wandered to the center of the clearing, offering a big, slow handclap. "Give Grier a hand." She whistled. "Grier, you can get up. Take a bow."

Autumn pressed a trembling hand to her mouth.

Peyton waved, broadly, at Jo and Gabe. "And welcome our newest escaped convicts." She laughed again. "Don't you get it? They're with Edge."

Dustin looked like he'd just pissed himself. Noah stood, hands raised, blinking like a strobe light. Gabe was sweeping the scene with his gaze, checking that nobody else with a weapon was behind him. He was looking for an out.

Von aimed his pistol at Ritter. "Get Grier out of sight. Into the trees."

Ritter cringed across the clearing. He picked up Grier's feet and began dragging him away. Von casually took out his phone and snapped a photo of the body.

Peyton watched, swaying. Grier's face dragged along the dirt, painting a trail with blood. Slowly, finally, understanding fired in her eyes. She gasped. Then she ran for the trees jaggedly, arms extended, hands like starfish.

Von picked up the rifle and tossed it to Friedrich. "Get them all in the Hummer."

He racked the slide on his pistol and charged after Peyton.

Autumn screamed, "No!"

Friedrich shoved her into the Hummer, then swung the gun toward Dustin. Hacking — "Don't shoot me" — Dustin stumbled in after her. Autumn clutched at him. Friedrich leveled the gun at Noah's knees.

"Chill, man. I'm going." Hands out, gesturing for calm, Noah climbed in as well. Lark was right behind.

Friedrich grabbed Jo by the biceps and beckoned Gabe. "You too. Right now."

Gabe's gaze was riveted on Friedrich. On Friedrich's momentum and direction and his jittering gun hand. Jo knew what he was thinking, what he was desperate to signal to her: *Don't get in the Hummer.*

If she climbed in that vehicle she was trapped. The quicksilver ran cold in her veins. She balked in Friedrich's grip.

He shoved the gun against her side and shouted at Gabe. "In, *now*. Or she gets a new orifice in her rib cage."

"Don't," Gabe said. "Lower the weapon. I'll get in."

In the trees beyond the clearing, Peyton's screams deteriorated into sobbing. Von reappeared, hauling the girl by her hair. She was barely keeping her feet beneath her.

Gabe climbed into the Hummer. Jo stood rigid on the dirt. Friedrich rose on his toes and put his orange mustache near her ear.

"This gun has fifteen in the magazine. If you're not in the vehicle in two seconds, I'll start with your boyfriend."

Jo couldn't breathe, couldn't swallow. She climbed into the Hummer.

Von shoved Peyton in behind her, sobbing. The girl fell to her knees on the thick carpet. Lark grabbed her and held her tightly.

Ritter finished dragging Grier's body to the trees and staggered back, tracked by the rifle under Friedrich's gaze. Ritter's eyes looked wild, spinning with shock.

"Hurry up," Friedrich said.

Von turned to make sure Ritter was cooperating. Jo looked at Gabe. Last chance — the door on the far side of the vehicle. She scrambled across the Hummer.

Friedrich fired the pistol into the backseat. The report was shockingly loud. Fabric flew and cordite

90

stank up the air. The screaming came from all directions.

"What the fuck?" Dustin yelled. His gaze rounded on Jo. "Hold still."

He grabbed her by the collar of her jacket and yanked her back. She fell on her butt on the floor.

Jo sank her fingernails into his wrist. Then Gabe grabbed Dustin's arm and twisted, quick and sharp.

Dustin let go. His eyes shone like cracked marbles. "What's wrong with you?"

Von shoved Ritter into the passenger compartment, climbed in after him, and slammed the door. Friedrich jumped behind the wheel and put the huge vehicle in gear.

The Hummer lurched forward, tires spinning, and slewed across the dirt in a brown swirl of dust. Von braced himself on the seat, pistol raised. Dustin's chest rose and fell. His gaze was frightened and resentful. Peyton cringed into a ball on the backseat, sobbing, fingers jammed in her mouth. Beside her, Kyle Ritter stared at Von, his face blank and hard.

Autumn sat rigid, blinking like an otter in the sunlight, fingers clenching the plush red seat. Lark and Noah had tumbled to the floor beside Jo. They looked like stunned fish.

Von held the gun steady. "Everybody lock your hands behind your head."

They cinched their fingers behind them. The narrow road rose up the mountainside. Friedrich accelerated. The Hummer had power, but in the altitude the engine labored. The trees whipped past. Von wiped his hand under his nose.

He gestured to Jo and Gabe. "Pockets. Empty 'em."

They threw their phones across the limo. Von scooped them up.

He nodded at Gabe. "Back pocket too, hombre."

Reluctantly Gabe took out his folded buck knife and slid it across the carpet to him.

"Nobody move. Not a muscle." Von climbed over the bench seat into the driver's compartment.

Peyton's sobs subsided to whimpers. Autumn was shaking. "Grier." She turned to Dustin, buried her face against his shoulder, and cried. He whispered in her ear, "Quiet."

In the driver's compartment, Friedrich shot Von a crazed look. "What do we do?"

"We keep driving. We get there, and then we deal with it."

"You know that Dane's gonna flip," Friedrich said.

"Shut up."

"And Sabine's gonna have your balls for breakfast."

Jo's stomach was cramping. *Von, Friedrich, Dane, Sabine.* They were being kidnapped by the damned Trapp Family Singers.

Ritter looked stunned. "My first scenario. I can't believe it."

Gabe said, "You work for Edge Adventures?"

"Started this week," Ritter said.

"You see this gang before today?"

"No. Just Mr Coates, the head guy. And I don't know where he is."

He's in the luggage compartment, Jo thought.

The asphalt ran out and the road became packed gravel. It kicked under the tires, loud and insistent. The Hummer bumped over a rut and everybody jostled against one another.

Von leaned toward Friedrich. Low and hard, he said, "We can't just dump them by the roadside."

Ritter whispered to Jo. "I thought something was wrong when these people showed up. They seemed surprised to see me."

They crossed a bridge. The tires droned on the concrete. Jo caught a glimpse of whitewater in the river below.

Dustin inhaled. "We gotta do something."

Noah, the quieter of the two college boys, murmured, "What?"

Von turned and stared at them. The gun loitered in his hand. "Keep quiet." He turned back to Friedrich. "This is a clusterfuck of major proportions. We got three people we never counted on and the kids know what's happening. We have to keep going. All we can do is get to the location and lock everybody down."

Friedrich shook his head. "We're screwed."

"We're screwed worse if we toss them out someplace."

Friedrich glanced in the mirror, and Jo's stomach gripped. She was afraid he was thinking, *Only if we toss them out alive.*

The Hummer boated over the gravel. The road was curving up a steep gorge. The tires ran along the road's edge, close to a drop-off.

"Just don't slow down," Von said. "Volvo's two hours behind us. We get there, we lock everybody down, we think it through."

Dustin gritted his teeth and hissed, "We should jump them."

Gabe gave him a slow, considered look. "What are you talking about?"

"We outnumber them. We can take them by surprise. Get control of the car."

Peyton shook her head, quick little movements. "No," she whispered. "Grier. No, no, no."

The road curved strongly, following the river in a hard continuous turn. Everybody slid toward the left side of the limo. The vehicle bumped over the uneven gravel surface. The trees grew thick on the right side of the road. The mountains rose behind. The gorge yawned on their left.

Jo scrambled onto a seat and buckled her seat belt. Autumn watched and did likewise.

Dustin lowered his voice to a sharp whisper. "We can swarm them."

Gabe didn't move. "Bad idea."

Dustin looked at Noah. "We can take them."

Von glanced at them, suspicious, but they were speaking too quietly to be overheard. He resumed his manic dialogue with Friedrich.

Dustin's breathing picked up. He whispered, "They're going to kill us all."

"This is not the place," Gabe said.

Dustin turned to him, pale, almost seasick. "And who are you, some guy who works at USF? Me and

Noah and Ritter here, we charge. Three on one. You can sit here with your girlfriend if you want, but we have at least three men who can do this."

Gabe's eyes flashed, briefly, and dimmed again. "Not yet. Not here."

His gaze slid toward the window. The Hummer was rocketing along the rutted gravel road, bouncing like a runaway covered wagon. To their left, an eroded gradient dropped into the depths of the gorge. There was no guardrail.

Jo whispered, "Dustin, look outside. Don't be rash."

They had no margin for error. The gorge was so deep that she couldn't see the bottom. The light swept across the interior of the limo as they continued to bowl around the long, sweeping bend.

Friedrich's hands jerked back and forth on the wheel like a cartoon character's. "We are screwed. *Royally*."

"Shut up."

Von got out a cell phone and punched numbers. As he did, a chime echoed from his pocket. Jo recognized the sound: It was her phone, sending a message. Von pulled her cell out.

Dustin's breathing accelerated. "He's distracted."

Dustin tensed. Gabe shot out an arm to grab him, but Dustin was beyond reach and in motion. Shouting like a wild man, he threw himself at the front seat.

Von heard the disturbance and turned, phone to his ear. Dustin lunged into the driver's compartment and tackled him.

Friedrich's head whipped around. "Shit —"

Gabe moved too, fast as a snake. Ritter was a beat behind him.

Jo saw Dustin's flailing legs and grunting face. He was fighting Von for control of the gun. Noah scrambled toward the melee. The pistol waved in Von's hand. Jo watched it swing. She couldn't possibly reach it. She couldn't get anywhere close to helping.

Friedrich gaped and lifted his foot off the gas.

"No," Von yelled. "Faster — don't let them jump out."

Friedrich slammed on the power again. The Hummer leapt forward.

With Dustin in the way, Gabe couldn't get close enough to grab Von's gun. Instead, he swept his right arm around the headrest, grabbed Von by the hair, and smashed his head against the door frame.

"Dustin, aim the gun away from us," Gabe said.

Von twisted and submarined and kicked like a trapped bull. Gabe slammed his head against the door frame again. With his left hand he gouged at Von's eyes. Von's knees came up and his feet kicked the dash and the gearshift and the windshield. Friedrich turned his head.

Von's boot connected with it. Hard.

Friedrich's head snapped sideways. He jerked the wheel.

Jo had a sick, falling sensation. *No, don't. Stay on the road.*

Friedrich hauled the wheel back and straightened out.

The gun in Von's hand fired.

Jo ducked. Peyton and Lark screamed. The windshield spidered and the Hummer swerved. Von kicked furiously. The pistol waved in the air. Dustin clawed at Von's hand, trying to grab the gun.

"No, turn the barrel away from us," Gabe repeated. "Pin his hand against the dash and aim the gun away."

Von's legs muscled wildly back and forth. Ritter dived for his knees. Gabe continued battering Von's head against the door frame. Von weakened. The Hummer veered left.

Jo yelled, "*Steer*. Hold the wheel and stop the car."

Lark threw herself onto a seat and grabbed a seat belt. She wrapped her arm through the shoulder strap and gripped it like a vine. The Hummer shuddered. The left front wheel caught the lip of the hill. Friedrich jerked the wheel, fighting, foot still to the floor. Jo saw Autumn's eyes gleaming with fright.

From the driver's compartment came grunts and shouts. The gun boomed again. Then again. Glass shattered and Friedrich's hands dropped from the wheel.

The Hummer straightened momentarily and tilted. The light turned in the sky, shadow overtaking the window.

"Oh my God," Autumn said.

Then everything went sideways, fast. Jo hit whoever was next to her. She cried out. She saw Gabe, arms around the headrest, gripping Von's head. He let go, grabbed a seat belt, and braced himself. He snapped the buckle and grabbed for Lark.

The front of the Hummer angled down, sliding, fast. Through the window Jo saw the slope, covered with trees and boulders.

They flipped.

The Hummer capsized, hard. The roof of the car hit the slope with a crunching sound. The windows shattered. People flew around the interior of the limo. Jo hung on to the shoulder strap of her seat belt like a commuter in a subway car that had just been kicked into a tumble cycle. The gorge steepened, and upside down, they slid forward down the slope. Jo saw light, shadow, felt the roof crushing. Dust blew through the shattered windows. She saw boulders and the silver glint of water at the bottom of the gorge. Her mind went firework white. They were going down, all the way.

CHAPTER
TWELVE

Evan Delaney paused at the foot of the marble staircase. She wanted to look meek and inconspicuous. Luckily, in the vaulted echo chamber of San Francisco City Hall, that wasn't hard. City Hall looked like the U.S. Capitol, but gaudier. It had a gilded dome. It flashed a little leg. She backed against the banister and watched the man in the pin-striped suit descend the stairs toward her.

The word *ambush* had a lovely ring to it. It was full of hope.

The man came down the stairs slowly, his white hair bouffanting like a televangelist's. He was surrounded by minions. He was a mortgage banker who had been testifying before the San Francisco Board of Supervisors. He had also been a client of the dead lawyer Phelps Wylie, and he was her last hope for an interview.

He drew near. She stepped out from the banister.

"Mr Higgins, I have some questions about Phelps Wylie," she said.

The minions rushed to block her, like a flannel wall. She persisted, batting them away as if they were Brooks Brothers moths.

"Mr Higgins, do you have any comment on your lawyer's death?"

He swept past her, down the stairs, into the cavernous foyer, and out the door.

She followed him to the street. Higgins climbed into a waiting car and zoomed away. The car disappeared into traffic, followed by the minion swarm.

Ambush? Strikeout. None of Wylie's clients wanted to speak to her. Only a few had even bothered to give her a no-comment. The rest had deflected her calls. Higgins had been her final shot.

Maybe it was time to go home. She turned and headed for the parking garage. She could already hear her credit card, shrieking in pain. And then her phone beeped.

It was a text message from Jo. She slowed. No — it was three messages. She opened the first, and stopped.

I found Wylie's 2nd cell. He was carjacked. Drove to Sierras under DURESS.

Evan's lips parted.

Wylie recorded conversation during drive. 2nd person in car. FORCED HIM.

"Oh my God."

More to come.

She opened the second message. It included Wylie's cell phone number and forwarded his call list. *Data corrupted*, Jo warned, and, indeed, Recent Calls turned up as incomplete phone numbers. But most had the first seven digits, including area codes.

Jo's third message included the log-in information for her voice-mail service.

> Sent Wylie's recording to my voice mail. Log in and listen. Must take cell to Tuolumne sheriffs in Sonora. Will call when get better signal.

She smiled at her phone. "Oh, Jo. I knew there was a reason I liked you."

Pulse racing, she tried to phone Jo back. She got a recording. *The number you are calling is out of range. Please try again later.*

A misty wind gusted. She found a seat on a nearby bench and, with trepidation, called Jo's voice mail and logged in.

She heard Wylie's voice. "*Where are we going?*"

A chill inched up her back. She closed her eyes, and listened to Wylie's desperate attempt to save himself and to leave a trail of evidence behind.

A new voice entered the conversation. "*Shut up.*"

It was a creepy reply from across Wylie's car, swaddled in engine noise. The hairs on her arms stood up.

"*— punishment.*"

She couldn't tell if the voice belonged to a man or a woman. But its tone, flat and imperative, frightened her.

The recording ended. She opened her eyes, stunned. Jo had sent her a message in a bottle — from a dead

101

man. Wylie had tried to tell people what was happening to him, even as he was being driven into the mountains to his death. He must have feared what lay up the road. But he kept talking.

She slung her backpack over her shoulder and headed to a Starbucks across from the Civic Center Plaza. On a legal pad she cross-referenced the corrupted data from Wylie's Recent Calls list. Different portions of each number had been lost, almost like a glass of milk had spilled across the screen. But she quickly saw that Wylie had called only a few numbers from the second cell phone. And he had received calls from only a handful of numbers. By cross-referencing, in most cases, she could assemble the entire number.

None of them belonged to Wylie's clients, friends, or family.

She went online, pulled up a crisscross directory, and tried to put names to the numbers she had pieced together. No luck.

Time to cold-call.

She got out her phone and dialed the first number on the list. The number rang three times, paused, and rang again with a new tone, as though the call were being forwarded. A woman picked up.

"Ragnarok Investments."

The voice was brusque, sharp. Impatient.

Evan paused. *Was Wylie using the second cell phone for sex or for bad business?* "I'm calling about the charity drive — for Our Lady of Perpetual Sorrow church."

The Ragnarok woman hung up.

Evan stared at the phone. Now, wasn't that interesting.

She turned to her computer and typed *Ragnarok*.

CHAPTER
THIRTEEN

The hissing sounded like a geyser, hot and wet. The light trickled through windows that had shattered white. Dust hung thick in the air, motes spinning.

Jo coughed. She was breathing.

The hissing continued. The radiator. Behind it she heard the sound of rushing water. She blinked. Her fingers and toes and skin were tingling, sending adrenaline distress signals: Hell was *this?*

The roof of the Hummer was beneath her back. She was lying on pellets of shattered safety glass. She turned her head and heard the glass crunch, like broken bottles in a Dumpster. Other sounds infiltrated her pounding head. A low drone, like a moaning animal.

Hot fear jumped through her. "Gabe?"

Oh God, the roof of the Hummer was hard beneath her back but the floor was close above her head. Too close. The Hummer had been smashed on its plunge down the side of the gorge, like a gargantuan jaw squeezing down. Her chest caught.

She put her hands up and pressed against the floor of the limo. It was crushing her. She stifled a cry. She had to get out. Where was Gabe?

"*Quintana.*"

Across the vehicle, behind the dust, someone moved.

"Jo."

"Gabe . . ." The rest of her words disappeared in relief and overwhelming fear.

They had to get out. The car would crush them. "Move."

The wire of panic heated her voice. She coughed back tears. Where were the others? Were they okay?

She was bruised and cut in a dozen places, her head was thundering, her muscles tighter than if she had tried to deadlift half a ton, cold. She had gripped the shoulder harness so hard that she had nearly sent her whole body into spasm. She fumbled for the buckle, punched it, got it to release.

She tried to turn over and banged her head on the roof — the floor — of the Hummer. Dust stung her eyes.

Behind her, the moan turned to hacking. Autumn was hanging from her seat belt, like a skydiver tangled in her harness. With the Hummer smashed, her knees scraped the roof below her. She was conscious, eyes wide. She hit the buckle release.

"Get out. Come on." Jo could barely keep from screaming.

She saw the other kids splayed around her. Lark had already unhooked her seat belt and was crawling toward Jo. Peyton was facedown across the vehicle, crying. Her lungs seemed to be working powerfully well. Her blond hair was streaked bloody red.

The air felt electrically charged. It prickled her skin like a million needles. Not from the dirt that had piled through the broken windows or the gray talcum-like dust from the airbag or the tiny motes of glass spinning through the vehicle, but from pure hellish energy. Jo turned onto her belly and looked for the door. It was four feet away, crushed shut. The sound that bled from her mouth was a whimper.

She began to shake. She heard a humming in her head. The light seemed yellow and cold. It smelled like cement dust, like the creaking of tons of roadway, pressing down on top of her father's car. The view spun, seemed to darken, to splinter.

She had to get out.

Get out before the top deck of the Cypress Viaduct collapsed completely and crushed her and her dad and brother and baby sister inside their old family car.

The view clouded, as if tons of pressure had obscured the sun. Gray, brown, dark. Smoke. The stench of gasoline and burning tires gagged her. She kicked and crawled and didn't care about the broken glass — she had to reach the door, before there was an aftershock and the whole double-decker section of freeway came down with them inside.

"We gotta move. Hurry."

"Jo, no."

"Now. *Move*."

A hand grabbed her shoulder. She yelped and shoved it away and scrambled for the darkened door. The hand swept over her shoulder and stopped her, pulled her tight.

"Jo. Hang on." Gabe held her hard. "Wait."

She was half a moment from hyperventilating. She buried her face against his chest and held her breath.

Jesus.

Her vision returned. She wasn't in her dad's car. She wasn't trapped on the Cypress Viaduct. The Loma Prieta quake had happened ages back, not now.

"Sorry." She held on to him. "God."

Her claustrophobia had jumped on her, rung her bell, chased her into a near-panic. Tears stung her eyes. "You all right?"

"Gonna be hellaciously sore tomorrow. But I can move."

His T-shirt was sharp with bits of glass. She didn't care. He was okay. "Sorry. I freaked. But we need to get out of the Hummer."

He held her back. "Not that door."

Jo wiped dust from her eyes. The crushed door in front of her would never move. The glass in the window had fallen out in a single, cracked sheet. It had landed outside, on top of Friedrich.

During the crash the driver's door had been flung open, and Friedrich had been thrown out. His body lay right outside. His face was crushed, his head deformed. In the blood and the mud, something else was trickling beneath him.

Gasoline. "The fuel line ruptured."

She couldn't keep the tremor from her voice. She would have been in more trouble if she'd climbed out and not just because she would have ended up face-to-face with the corpse.

Von. She whipped around to look at the topsy-turvy driver's compartment.

Empty. The passenger door was twisted open.

"Where's Von?" she said.

A voice from the back of the Hummer said, "Gone."

Kyle Ritter, the Edge Adventures employee, had propped himself up and was looking out the big stretch-limo-size side window.

"When we left the road he jumped ship," Kyle said.

Relief coursed through her. Both gunmen were gone. Then she understood what Kyle had just said. Von had jumped.

"So he may be coming down the slope after us," she said.

Gabe glanced around the Hummer. "Let's get these kids out of here."

Kyle moved. "Before he comes back. And brings his partners."

CHAPTER
FOURTEEN

Dane Haugen stared at the screen of his iPhone, downloading the latest market data. Outside, the road ran straight and gradually uphill. They had finally reached the eastern edge of the San Joaquin Valley and were beginning to climb into the foothills of the Sierras. By his calculation, their Volvo SUV was two hours behind the Hummer.

Everything else was bang on schedule.

The iPhone was valuable for gathering quick and dirty information online, but he had needed a solid hour on his secure laptop back in San Francisco. His laptop had heavy-duty encryption and connected through an anonymizer, so nobody could trace him online. The phone was nowhere so secure.

Everything was in place. In Dubai and Singapore and the intermediate accounts he had set up around the world. His prize today was going to be massive. And it would come home to him, where it belonged, where it should have been all along. But it would arrive only after taking a traipse around the globe, hopping from bank to bank, country to country, account to account.

At the wheel of the Volvo, Pat Stringer frowned at the highway. He looked like a songbird, so slight and flighty, but Haugen knew he could rely on the man to do what it took.

"Ease down. Save your mental energy for the hours ahead," Haugen said.

Stringer nodded curtly.

"We're on the winning side here," Haugen said. "These kids are cream puffs. They're Twinkies. This is not the yard at Lompoc."

The U.S. Penitentiary at Lompoc, California, was a medium-security facility, hardly Leavenworth or Marion. But it was a real prison, and Stringer had done real time there, for a real financial crime. Bank robbery.

Stringer was a real criminal and didn't apologize for it. He had gone after what he wanted, taken the risk for the chance at the reward. It hadn't worked out, and he had done his time. The problem, as Haugen saw it, was that Stringer wasn't cut out for management. He couldn't plan for contingencies and had failed to keep a back door open so that, when his plans went balls up, he had an escape route. So that when his getaway car got clamped while he was in the bank, he had a better way to elude the LAPD than running down Wilshire Boulevard.

But Stringer didn't complain. Not once. And Haugen had enlightened him, when he recruited him for this venture, as to what had gone wrong with his heist. Stringer had walked up to a teller in the middle of the day, with a note in his hand. That was a classic move, but not one that gave the best returns. No, to steal real money, you needed to get an investment banker to hand a piece of paper to a hedge fund

110

manager or derivatives trader. Do it with a smile and a stiletto in your voice. Do it big. Do it for hundreds of millions of dollars. Walk all over them. Do it that way, and you were one of the masters of the universe.

Like Haugen should have been.

Stringer kept his eyes on the road and said nothing. Outside, farmland was giving way to open countryside. Golden grass was cooked from a dry summer. Live oaks dotted the hills. In the distance, where the road rose, on and on, ponderosa pine began to take over. The sun was beating down, but the wind was stiff and banks of clouds piled up against the hills ahead.

Haugen glanced into the backseat, at Sabine. "We haven't heard from Von and Friedrich."

"Cell towers are scarce up there."

Haugen turned all the way around, slowly, and glared at her.

She sat up straighter, and dropped the languid pose. She had removed not only her ski mask but the blond wig, and her boyishly short red hair stood as straight on her head as a field of sorghum.

Haugen kept his voice low and flat. "Put the wig back on."

"The windows are tinted."

"We don't break cover. Do it."

Indolently, as though it were her own idea, she stretched and reached for the wig. She fit it on her head, smoothed it down with her fingertips slowly, and slid her gaze over him.

"That's more like it," he said. She looked like a woman now. The mannish power was subdued.

She wanted to seduce him, right then. They all did, women. They latched on to him, would do anything for him. Sabine was no different.

Except she was. She had a Wharton MBA, and years working for the Frankfurt Stock Exchange, and an eighteen-month stint working as a bond trader for one of the big financial players in the City of London. She was a magician. A cruel, vicious, greedy magician, with a lack of scruples he found completely fascinating. But she was loyal. Fanatically loyal to the idea of the money they were going to make. But her lust for him — and her desire not only to get inside his mind, but to burrow under his emotional skin and make *him* want *her* — were what truly kept her loyal to him. She might want to take the money for herself, but not yet. Not while she was in thrall to the idea that he could love her.

"I know cell towers are far between," he said. "And reception's spotty in the mountains. They should have found a landline and phoned ten minutes ago. They need to know I won't accept sloppy work. Phone them."

Sabine didn't sigh or pout. He gave her points for that. She took her sleek little phone and punched Friedrich's number with her French-manicured nail.

She put the phone to her ear and pinned her eyes on Haugen. She was wearing blue contacts, another part of her light disguise. With the blond wig, the startling aqua jumped out at him. *Ran.* Yes, with the disguise, she looked fully the Norse goddess. She could steal just about anything.

112

She could stand to lose fifteen pounds, but after this weekend, he would send her to a spa. Then she should be just about right.

After a moment she said, "Out of range."

The car bounced and took a turn hard. Stringer was pushing it.

"Stay under the speed limit," Haugen said. To Sabine: "Try again."

Sabine handed him the phone. "Hear for yourself."

As she stretched, her top gapped open and showed the tattoo.

Haugen felt the skin around his temples shrink. "Cover that up."

She continued to lean forward, phone extended. He could hear Von's number ring. She didn't shift or make the slightest move to cover the tattoo. As she inhaled, her breast swelled and so did the snake, a sea serpent, the World Serpent of Norse mythology, blue like the veins of her breast, flowing beneath the pale white skin, so rich and fearsome. The serpent's forked tongue protruded, flicking toward her unseen nipple. The sight repelled him.

He grabbed the phone from her. "Button your shirt or put on a jacket. Don't breach security, even in the vehicle."

She leaned back, taking her time, and glanced out the windows at the endless plains and empty farm fields and scrub pine. Then she smiled, as if she were humoring him, and buttoned her top.

Haugen put the phone to his ear. Von's number was ringing. But he wasn't picking up.

Sabine put her foot up on the center console. "We need to be within two miles to use the walkie-talkies."

"I know."

Why didn't Von pick up? Haugen slammed the phone shut. He nodded out the windshield and said to Stringer, "Step on it."

CHAPTER
FIFTEEN

In the sloppy rock and grit on the side of the gorge, the cell phone rang. Von could hear it clearly. But he couldn't find it.

It was Haugen, he knew. Haugen, calling because he had missed his check-in. Each ring sounded angrier than the last.

Huffing, he said to the mountain air, "I'm here, asshole."

He was stuck halfway down the side of the steep gorge, midway between the gravel logging road and the riverbed below. The Hummer had catapulted him free when it flipped. That had saved him. He couldn't believe he was alive, but he would take the luck.

Below him, dirt and vegetation were scraped away as though a crazed bulldozer had charged downhill at an angle. He hurt all over. He was covered with dust and scratched to bits and thought his arm might be busted. Maybe his eye socket too — things looked kind of crooked — and his head was screaming.

He glanced up. The hillside, this evil gorge, looked nearly vertical. He grabbed hold of a root that had been half pulled from the hillside by some protruding edge of the limo, and he leaned forward to look down.

He saw the Hummer.

It was — oh, man — it was probably four hundred feet below him, upside down on top of rocks at the edge of the river, tires pointed at the sky like a fat dead turtle.

He saw Friedrich.

Or the smashed shell that was left of Friedrich.

Royally screwed. No kidding. Friedrich, Friedrich — "Why'd you swerve?"

All he'd done was kick Friedrich accidentally, and the idiot lost control of the Hummer. That's what he'd tell Haugen. It was Friedrich's fault.

He heard voices. He heard a girl crying. So — they weren't all dead.

He wiped his nose. He had to salvage this. He couldn't let the kids get away.

His phone stopped ringing.

"Crap."

He needed the phone to ring so he could find it.

And he needed his gun to ring so he could find *it*.

He pulled himself to his knees. His head pounded like a frying pan was hitting it. He looked downhill. He should go down there. The weapons were down there. Friedrich wasn't using them. Nobody was guarding the hostages.

Then he took another look at the gorge. No way could he possibly climb down. The hillside was too steep and slick.

But he could climb up. He could scramble back to the logging road. And on the way, he could find his phone and his gun. And Haugen would be coming along. Haugen, and nobody else — this road was virtually deserted three hundred sixty days a year.

He would climb up to the road and flag down Haugen and Sabine and Stringer. The kids weren't going anywhere. It had been Friedrich's fault. Haugen would have to blame Friedrich.

His head was bleeding. He scrounged in his pocket for a handkerchief to stanch it and found the Glock.

The day might not be a total loss after all.

He could punish those numskulls in the Hummer, those college kids and the man in the USF T-shirt who had attacked him. They would pay.

He began to climb.

CHAPTER
SIXTEEN

"Once more."

On the count of three, Gabe and Kyle kicked at the long window along the side of the Hummer. This time, with a squeezing, crunching sound, the entire thing popped out of the frame and fell to the rocks on the riverbank.

Gabe checked outside. "It's safe to climb out."

Jo caught his eye. The unspoken message passed between them: *triage*. They needed to assess the group for injuries. Slowly, careful to avoid placing her hands in broken glass, she belly-crawled across the wrecked Hummer. Her heart was slowing. She blinked dust from her eyes.

She reached Autumn. "You okay?"

Autumn had unhooked herself from the seat belt and now huddled, in a fetal position, against the wall of the Hummer. Her eyes were vividly alert.

Jo put a hand on her shoulder. "Are you hurt?"

Autumn stared at her like a doe facing a wall of flame. Jo put her hands on either side of the girl's face. "Answer me."

"I'm okay," she said.

Jo nodded. "Good. We're going to get you out of here."

Autumn seemed all right: conscious, symmetrically mobile, oriented times three. Dustin's face was covered with dirt and debris and smeared with blood from abrasions to his scalp, but he was alert and had no obvious neurological deficits. Gabe had found a flashlight and was shining it in his eyes, checking his pupils for signs of head injury.

"You're all right." Gabe nodded at the window he and Kyle had kicked out. "Slide through there. Then stay put. I mean it."

Dustin nodded at the floor, avoiding Gabe's eye, and crawled toward the window.

Jo nudged Autumn after him. "You too."

Autumn didn't budge. Dustin held out a hand. "Come on."

Autumn gave him a coruscating glare. His expression wavered. Pale, he turned away and slithered out the window frame.

Peyton's moaning had become sporadic, though still loud. Gabe said, "Your collarbone's broken."

Lark lay on her stomach, looking around helplessly, patting the debris-strewn roof of the limo. "My glasses. I can't find them."

Autumn turned from the window and scurried toward her. "They have to be here."

Aside from the lost glasses, Lark looked all right for the moment. Jo turned to Noah.

He was propped against the back of the upside-down driver's compartment, covered in dust and glass, soaked with blood, mute.

She crab-crawled to his side. "You there?"

He didn't move, but a wave of pain seemed to roll through him. His gaze slid toward her. "Let's not take that ride again."

Jo tried to smile. She took his pulse. It was strong and going like a racehorse. "Where's the pain?"

"Everywhere. From the chest down."

"Chest pain?" she said.

He blinked, indicating *no*. "Shoulder hurts like a son of a bitch."

She saw a bloody hole in his T-shirt. He had been shot.

Triage divided casualties into four categories: green, minor injuries; yellow, non-life-threatening injuries; black, dead or near dead; and red, life-threatening injuries — those who could be saved but were at risk of death if they didn't get immediate transport for treatment.

Noah was a red tag.

Jo had experience in emergency medicine, but as a forensic psychiatrist she dealt primarily with history — with people whose lives were already over. Facing a crisis case, out of the blue, was always a moment when her chest caught.

She flicked her head, beckoning Gabe. He crawled over. He was filthy and bleeding and his gaze was black. But his voice was as soothing as a cool drink of water.

"Let's take a look at you," he said to Noah.

The young man was pale but alert. "You guys EMTs?"

"I'm a pararescueman, and Dr Beckett is an MD."

Noah's eyes widened. "My lucky day."

120

"You are definitely a glass-half-full guy."

Noah's hands were cold. Concerned about shock, Jo called to Autumn to find him some water to drink and looked around for something to put beneath his feet. She wanted to raise his legs to improve blood flow to his brain.

"Let's get a look," Gabe said.

Blood soaked Noah's shoulder and darkened the filthy surface beneath him. Gingerly Gabe tore open the young man's sopping shirt to see the wound.

The round had hit him at an oblique angle. Jo could see only a small entry wound. It looked garish, but it wasn't throbbing with blood. The bleeding was significant, but not arterial.

She heard a gasp. Lark knelt at the window, poised to crawl out onto the rocks, staring at Noah. She was frozen, her knuckles pale on the window frame.

Gabe palpated Noah's chest and bent low to see his side and back. "No exit wound. Bullet's still in there. Buddy, you're going to have a souvenir." He took Noah's right hand. "Squeeze."

Gritting his teeth, Noah gripped Gabe's hand. "Ow."

Appreciation flickered in Gabe's eyes. *Ow* was a major understatement.

"I think the bullet's lodged in the pectoral muscle, under the distal end of the clavicle. We can pack the wound and immobilize his arm and shoulder. Stopping the bleeding's our main priority."

"Got it," Jo said.

Lark crawled over to them. "Noah." Her voice broke. Then she gathered it back. "What can I do?"

Jo fought the impulse to tell her, *Nothing*. Autumn crawled up behind Lark and reached an arm around her shoulder. She handed Jo a water bottle. Their faces were stark.

"See if there's a first-aid kit," Jo said.

"Okay." Lark scuttled backward. She grabbed Autumn and said, "Come on."

Autumn, her voice low, said, "We'll find your glasses. They have to be here."

Jo needed a sterile dressing, but unless a first-aid kit turned up, she had zero hope she was going to get it. Her hands were grungy. She wiped them on her jeans.

She tore a strip off her own shirt, the bottom layer of her mountain-ready clothing, and right now the cleanest, least dusty and muddy and germ-ridden item she could find. She folded it and put pressure on the gunshot wound.

Gabe continued checking Noah for other injuries. When he touched the young man's lower right leg, Noah cried out. It was an animal yell, almost feral.

"Careful." Noah gasped. "Jesus, just — careful. Don't touch my leg."

"Gotcha." Gabe glanced at Jo. "We need to find my knife."

Jo could barely squeeze into the crushed driver's compartment. It was a mess, filled with dirt and debris, and the driver's headrest was dark red with blood. Jo blinked dust from her eyes and tucked her hands inside her cuffs and swept her arms through the wreckage.

The buck knife was jammed between the dash and the crumpled windshield. She dug it out.

"Here."

She handed the knife to Gabe and kept looking around. She found his carabiner key chain with the Swiss Army knife. She wriggled back into the passenger compartment.

Gabe unfolded the buck knife and sliced open Noah's jeans. Jo saw what was causing Noah such incredible pain.

Jo had a practiced, dispassionate "therapist" face. And she had a bedside manner — calm and focused and attentive. Right then, she fought to hold her blankest, most neutral expression. Fortunately, Gabe had far more experience at dealing with traumatic injury. He barely paused, and his voice remained laid-back and authoritative.

"Your leg's broken, buddy," he said. "But you'd probably guessed."

Noah lifted his head. Jo waited for him to scream, but he didn't say a word. He didn't pass out. But his eyes swam and he pressed his lips together.

He had an open fracture of both bones in the lower leg. His tibia and fibula had snapped and protruded through a tear in his skin.

He let his head fall back. "Who'd believe . . . getting shot isn't the worst thing that could happen to me today?"

His assessment wasn't far-off. Through pure luck, the gunshot wound looked like an injury they could stabilize. But the fracture could prove deadly.

Gabe and Jo stared silently at the wound. Then he glanced at her, a look that confirmed her fears: They couldn't count on transporting Noah to a hospital in the next couple of hours. They would need to reduce the fracture — to try to realign the bones. Leaving it open would be a nightmare of pain and an invitation to horrific infection. Moreover, bones aren't meant to be exposed. Left in the open air, they can dry out. They can die. Jo didn't want Noah to face undergoing bone grafts or, worse, losing the leg. They needed to set the fracture — and quickly — before muscle spasms set in and degraded their ability to manipulate the leg.

But setting the fracture was itself dangerous and tricky. They would need to be extremely careful. Raw, sharp bones, maneuvered even by trained professionals, could inadvertently slice into nerves or an artery.

And the wrecked, dirty interior of the flame-party-mobile was not a sterile environment.

Before Jo could speak, she heard shouting.

"Oh my God."

Peyton had crawled to the window. Halfway out, she had stopped, staring in shock at Friedrich's body.

"He's dead. Oh God."

Kyle Ritter dropped into view. "Be quiet."

"He's *dead*."

"And his partner's out there. You want him to draw a bead on us thanks to your slack-jawed shouting?"

Peyton squeezed her eyes shut. Kyle and Dustin maneuvered her through the window, watchful of her cracked clavicle. She sat down hard, pressed a fist to her mouth and cried quietly, rocking back and forth.

Kyle watched for a moment and, satisfied that she wouldn't start shouting again, walked toward the hood of the Hummer. He dropped to his hands and knees. Warily he edged forward, skirting Friedrich's body, and tried to peer underneath the vehicle.

"What are you doing?" Autumn said.

"He had a gun. We need it."

Kyle continued his search, rooting beneath rocks, scooping dirt from under the hood of the Hummer. "How about a little help? Anybody?"

Autumn didn't move. She stared at the corpse as if hypnotized.

"Autumn," Jo said. "Get something to cover him up with."

Autumn just stared at her. Jo's words barely seemed to register. Autumn wasn't in shock physically, but emotionally, she was numb.

"Go on," Jo said. "It's appropriate."

Autumn didn't acknowledge her, but grabbed a hoodie and crawled through the window. She dropped it across Friedrich's face.

"Lark, any sign of a first-aid kit?" Jo said.

From the back of the vehicle, Lark said, "Still looking."

Gabe made a hitchhiking thumb over his shoulder, asking to talk to Jo privately. Which was ridiculous in the confines of the Hummer, but they moved a few feet away and spoke in murmurs.

"We can reduce the fracture, but stabilizing him here is going to be a bitch," Gabe said.

"I'll try to prep as clean an environment as possible."

With Jo, Gabe dropped the affable *no-worries* façade. "His injuries are not the main issue. The situation is the main issue."

"I know."

She glanced out the window. The walls of the gorge rose above them in a V. They were eroded and bulging with rocks and overhangs and crags. The October sun had already dropped below the western lip of the gorge, brushing the pines along the ridgeline with orange light. At the bottom, near the granite-lined riverbank, they were in shadow. The temperature had dropped noticeably. And the sky above, while still blue, was crowded with cumulus clouds.

The only way to help Noah was to get him to a hospital. The only way to help the rest of the group was to get them back to civilization, under police protection.

Gabe's face was grave. "If we don't get out of here in the next few hours, none of these kids may survive."

CHAPTER
SEVENTEEN

Halfway up the slope, Von found the AK-47. He grabbed it like it was the best, coldest, life-giving bottle of whiskey in the world and hugged it to his chest. Every inch of him seemed to ache, a throbbing, nagging complaint that said, *Those little shits did this to you.*

He wouldn't let them get away with it.

He had to fix this before Haugen got there. If he didn't repair this disaster, Haugen might decide that he was disposable.

Like the body in the Hummer's luggage compartment. And that kid Grier.

He sat down on the crumbling dirt and caught his breath and gave the rifle a once-over. It had taken the same decision he had, when the Hummer began its dive: *I'm outta here.* It was his friend. And friends stuck together. Friends stuck up for each other.

He checked the action and made sure that dirt hadn't clogged any of the gun's mechanisms. Then he stood and leaned out to look down.

He needed to do the kids, right now. To keep them from getting away, from getting word out, from coming after him again like they had in the Hummer.

Haugen would understand — if everything was already taken care of by the time he arrived. Von would explain that he had been backed into a corner by circumstances. He didn't have a choice. It was — what would Haugen call it, some Francey foreign phrase? — *fate accompli.*

He knew which ones he should keep alive, for now. Miss Autumn *Ka-ching* Reiniger. And that vixen in the Juicy pink tank top — Peyton. As an example, the *encourager.* One plaything, to keep Autumn in line. The rest could go.

And they needed to go, right now. Starting with the Edge Adventures douche, Mr Kyle with-the-toy-gun Ritter. Then the two hikers who had hitched along. Up here, nobody would hear the echo of rifle fire, and nobody would miss those two.

He kept climbing, slowly, inch by inch — which made him all the more furious.

The wind cascaded through the pines. Distantly, running water flowed over rocks. From below him, bouncing off the sides of the gorge, came voices. Shrill, stressed-out rich kid voices. Probably wondering why their Mocha Frappuccinos and platinum credit cards couldn't get them out of there.

Carefully, Von leaned forward to see what the disposables were doing down at the bottom of the gorge.

He couldn't see a thing.

The slope of the gorge was too shallow at this point. It kept him from seeing all the way to the bottom. He couldn't get them.

He sat down again. "Little shits."

He slung the AK over his shoulder. He needed a better vantage point. He turned and climbed toward the road, crawling yard by yard, up the crumbling slope, with the hot-stove sizzle of rage growing louder in his head.

A minute later, he found his cell phone.

"Stay still and hang tough," Gabe told Noah. "We'll be right back to set your leg."

Noah nodded grimly. He was as pale as a fish belly, with pain spinning in his eyes. Lark hovered near him, outwardly calm but humming like a pipe under pressure.

Jo crawled behind Gabe across the roof-cum-floor of the wrecked Hummer. He slid through the empty window frame as smooth and lithe as an eel. She followed, stiff and bruised, and dropped to the dirt.

The air smelled of gasoline and rubber, and wet moss. She crouched for a moment, inhaling the sense of space around her. It was huge. It was freedom.

Carefully, feeling every ding and laceration, she straightened. And she got her first full look at the wreck. Her throat went tight.

The Hummer had slid down the eastern slope of the gorge. Halfway down, it had scraped against a line of boulders. Slowed by its impact with a sluice gate of granite, it had veered into soft soil and plowed down to the riverbank at an oblique angle. That had prevented it from dropping like a bomb off a ledge about eighty feet above them.

The ledge was heavily eroded. It had roots protruding from it, and rocks and crumbling dirt clods. Going over would have killed them all. Instead, the Hummer had come to rest upside down about a dozen feet from the edge of the rock-strewn river.

She walked to the river's edge over clacking pebbles and mossy rocks. Upstream, the river rushed around boulders. The water sounded like reassurance. But farther out, it looked strangely turbulent.

They'd been lucky. She didn't want to comprehend how lucky.

She was still shaky, but her pulse was no longer pounding in her ears. She didn't have the odd sensation of tasting cement dust or smelling oily black smoke. But her mouth was dry, her legs wobbly. She turned.

And saw everybody staring at her.

They were loitering in a semicircle near the vehicle. Not exactly shivering, not crying. But scared and shocked and lost. And looking to her.

"What are we going to do?" Peyton said.

Jo took a long breath. She tried to adopt her bedside manner. *Calm down. You need your shit together.* Peyton was eyeing her like she had on a cape.

"We're going to figure out how to get help and get out of here," Jo said.

"How we gonna do that?" said Kyle. "Who are you?"

"I'm a physician," Jo said.

Dustin pointed at Gabe. "So who's he?"

Gabe kept his expression low-key. "I'm a pararescueman with the California Air National Guard."

130

"Huh? Para-what? Thunderbirds are go?" Dustin spread his hands. *So?* "What's that mean?"

"Search and rescue. Combat rescue and battlefield surgery."

"Combat? Where were you when I needed your backup in the Hummer?"

Jo bristled. *Oh no, you did not just say that.*

Dustin stepped toward Gabe. "I was trying to save us, and you just let me . . ."

The rest of the sentence hung in the air: . . . *let me make an ass of myself and crash the limo.*

Dustin wiped grit from his face with the back of his hand. He looked equally ready to spit and cry. "I could have used more help, man. Maybe we'd still be on the road. Maybe *we'd* be at the wheel of the Hummer now, calling Delta Force or whatever brigade you belong to."

Jo clamped her jaw tight. *Keep quiet, Beckett. Just shut up.*

Gabe simply took his hands from his jeans pockets and let them hang loose at his sides. "Maybe. Or maybe if you had waited, we wouldn't have crashed."

Dustin turned to his friends, shaking his head. "You believe this weekend warrior?"

Kyle tipped back his baseball cap with an index finger. "I know who he is."

Everybody looked around at him.

"He's the guy who probably kept you from getting shot," he said. "He cracked Von's head against the door frame until the man nearly passed out. Got him to lower his gun hand instead of continuing to fire."

"What?" Dustin said.

Kyle sauntered toward them. "Von was firing like a frightened schoolmarm." He nodded at Friedrich's covered corpse. "Von shot the driver."

Autumn gaped. "You're serious?"

"Why do you think the limo went off the road? Dustin was wrestling the guy with the gun, and the guy with the gun started firing, trying to hit all you little sons of bitches. The only things he did hit were your friend Noah and his *compadre* at the wheel."

Dustin paled.

Kyle nodded at Gabe. "He's the guy who disabled Von. If he hadn't, you'd probably all be dead." He paused, then walked toward Gabe. "I know who you are. You're the guy who took a bullet for Robert McFarland."

Everybody went silent, and Peyton actually stepped back, as though she'd been shoved. Autumn's eyes went as round as saucers. Dustin looked confused.

"You took one for the president. You preserved the constitutional order and saved the commander in chief." Kyle stopped in front of Gabe. "Partner, that makes you the man."

The river burbled. In the distance, thunder rolled. Kyle's gaze was intense and demanding.

"So, you tell me," he said. "What's the plan?"

Gabe eyed Kyle slowly and then the rest of them.

"The plan," he said, "is to survive. And here's how we need to do it."

132

CHAPTER
EIGHTEEN

Evan hitched her backpack over her shoulder and trooped out of Starbucks, feeling energized and full of suspicion.

Though the October sun was warm, the shadows were a cool whisper. The sky was deep blue, gold streaked, headed toward evening. People crowded past her on the sidewalk. She stopped at the corner for a red light, wondering about Ragnarok Investments.

It didn't exist.

It was a phantom. The number on Phelps Wylie's second cell phone — the number Wylie had repeatedly received calls from in the days before he died — belonged to a business that was a hollow shell.

Ragnarok's presence in the world was limited to a listing in the California Department of Corporations database. No Web site. No news, not even a press release. No information about the owners or its business. No official phone number. Ragnarok was a front. It was a curt woman answering a cell phone.

Who was she to Wylie? A subterranean business partner? A lover?

The carjacker?

If she could piece together the other partial numbers from Wylie's damaged phone, perhaps she could find out. She stopped at a hole-in-the-wall restaurant, grabbed Hunan chicken and a cold Tsing-tao, and took them to the tourist motel where she was staying. In her room, the fading sun cast red light across the Formica table. The television weather report predicted storms in the Sierras.

She got out her laptop and the list of partial phone numbers. But before she started cold calling, she phoned Santa Barbara.

Her neighbor and friend, Nikki Vincent, answered on the seventh ring. "Don't make a pregnant woman run like that."

"But it's my favorite game," Evan said. "How're things?"

"Jiffy."

She smiled. Nikki was a tightly sprung African American artist who wore her hair in dreadlocks. Hearing her say *jiffy* was as incongruous as hearing Nancy Reagan sing lead for Metallica.

"Georgie's fine. I'll put her on," Nikki said.

Georgie — Georgia Delaney — was Evan's eleven-year-old half sister. Evan had recently assumed her guardianship, under difficult circumstances. Georgie was struggling to make sense of life in California with the big sister she had only just met, the new surrogate mom who might or might not continue in that role for — a month? a year? forever?

And now Evan was out of town for a couple of days. She felt a pang.

134

On the end of the line, the phone rattled. A little girl's voice came on. "Hiya."

"How's your day going, sugar?"

"We played football after school, and now Nikki's cooking paella."

By football, Georgie meant soccer. Her English accent was strong. They talked for a few minutes, and Georgie said, "See you Sunday?"

"That's the plan. Be good, little sug'. I love you."

Evan ended the call, holding the phone in the quiet of the motel room. The pang lingered. *I'm doing this job for you*, she thought. *For both of us. To prove to the world that I'm still here, that I care, that I'm on the side of right.*

And to prove that Phelps Wylie mattered. His death should not be left unexplained or picked over by gossips. He deserved an accounting.

She laid out the list of partial phone numbers from Wylie's call register and set out to systematically phone every possible combination of numbers that could complete them. It took her ninety minutes to work through the list and cross off numbers that were out of service or obviously had no connection to Wylie.

The last number she dialed rang endlessly before a robotic machine answered. "*The person you are trying to reach*" — there was a pause, and a different voice came on — "Ruby Ratner" — back to the robot — "*is not available. Please leave a message for*" — "Ruby Ratner" — "*after the tone.*"

Evan left a message asking Ratner to phone her back. *Ruby Ratner.*

It was an androgynous voice. A high tenor or a low alto. Asked to bet whether it was male or female, Evan would have hedged.

Could it have been the woman who answered the phone for Ragnarok? Could it have been the carjacker?

Searching online for *Ruby Ratner* brought up nine results, most from the U.S. Census, offering to search for the prevalence of the name. But one result was a public-records search from a site that listed half a dozen Ruby Ratners in the western United States. Two in the Bay Area. One in San Francisco.

And the phone number in Wylie's call register was a San Francisco number. She checked the phone book. Ratner's street address was listed.

The public-records site promised juicy details — credit histories and records of criminal convictions — if she paid a premium subscription. Which she could, just by entering her credit card number.

The blinking cursor, enticing her to fork out, wasn't exactly a growl. But it was a whisper, suggesting that something rough and toothy might lie behind the pay wall.

She wasn't about to chuck $59.99 into that hole. However, one of her rules, honored occasionally, was *Don't stumble blind into thickets where you hear things growling.*

She didn't have many favors she could call in. Not at the moment, not with the law enforcement community. This called for finesse. Charm. Distraction. She phoned a contact at the Santa Barbara Sheriff's Department, Detective Lilia Rodriguez.

Rodriguez was off duty, so she left a message. "I'm writing an investigative piece on Phelps Wylie, and I've unearthed a lead. Lily, it's big. It'll mean gold stars to the detective who brings it home." She left the name Ruby Ratner and asked Lily to phone her back.

She grabbed her things.

Ruby Ratner's house was a dreary yellow box in a dispirited neighborhood near an elevated section of 1-280. The yard was paved with concrete and decorated with plastic windmills, bright as a box of crayons, stuck by the dozen in a chain-link fence. When Evan pushed open the creaking gate, a dog inside the house cut loose with yippy barking.

She was halfway up the weed-bearded walk when the door cracked open. A barking orb of noise appeared, parked between the sturdy legs of a woman with a gray perm. The woman's face was framed by the darkness behind her.

"You the party planner?" she said.

Her mouth was pinched, like she was sucking on a pebble. Her cat's-eye glasses may have been fashionable when Harper Lee sat down to write *To Kill a Mockingbird*. Maybe. In trailer parks that got the older editions of the Sears catalogue.

Evan smiled. "Ruby Ratner?"

"You a process server?"

"No, ma'am." Not today.

The little dog bared its teeth and barked like it was about to have a seizure. The woman nudged it aside with her ankle. It bounced back as if magnetized and lunged for the crack in the doorway. The woman squinted at Evan.

"Mrs Ratner? About the party?" Evan said.

The woman appeared to think about things for a moment. The dog began to hump her ankle.

She shook it off. "Pepito, go get your squeaky toy."

The dog turned and ticked away. The woman scowled at Evan for a moment longer. Without a word she stepped back and opened the door.

"He's not here, but we can talk about the party," she said.

She invited Evan in. To the OK Corral.

CHAPTER
NINETEEN

Dane Haugen peered at his screen. A Peterbilt tractor-trailer, loaded with timber, lumbered past the parked Volvo SUV. They were at a truck stop in the Sierra foothills, with the sun hidden behind storm clouds. The coffee shop had wireless, for the benefit of truckers and tourists and hikers looking to get jacked up on java and the news before rock climbing or screwing or driving a semi over the mountains.

Haugen checked his Bermuda account online. He glanced at Sabine. "Flight radar on Reiniger's plane?"

She swiped her screen. Accessing real-time flight radar data, she spotted the tiny yellow image of the jet carrying Peter Reiniger to New York City.

"It's over eastern Ohio. On schedule."

Haugen grunted an acknowledgment. He was also editing his film reel, the teaser material that he would show Reiniger in a few hours. It was the trailer for his new disaster film, so to speak.

Photos, video, sound — the trailer showed him with Autumn and her friends, showed the Edge Adventures game runners in custody, and showed, vividly, the consequences of noncompliance with his demands. Reiniger would see this as the most compelling prospectus of his financial career. He would invest. He would strip himself to the bone and sell his own marrow to grab this opportunity.

The deal was on, even though Reiniger hadn't heard about it yet. And getting him the new film trailer, *Autumn! Part I!* was the first phase of the plan.

Haugen paused the video to admire an elegant shot: Autumn, smiling, with Von behind her, hooded, gloved, pointing an AK-47 at her back. Exquisite.

His phone rang. He checked the display and answered, "About time."

Von said, "We got a problem."

The air had taken on a low, chilly note. Gabe faced the group.

"We have to protect ourselves," he said. "This is survival one-oh-one."

It was, Jo thought, a crash course for newbies who never thought they'd need it.

"We stay together. Nobody — and I mean nobody — go off on your own," he said.

Dustin said, "Not even to take a piss? We need the buddy system?"

"Yes."

Dustin didn't reply. Autumn was hugging herself. Peyton seemed to be gradually sobering up, and it meant that the pain of her broken clavicle was growing more intense. She cradled her right arm against her chest. Her left hand played with a silver charm bracelet compulsively, as if it were a rosary. Bit by bit, it was hitting them: *This is for real.*

"We need help. We're not going to get it here," Gabe said. "We're going to have to contact somebody."

Autumn said, "Our phones aren't here. They took them back in San Francisco."

Kyle said, "I got mine. They had no excuse to take it."

"Great," Jo said.

"Don't got a signal, but it's in my pocket."

"My phone and Gabe's might still be in the Hummer."

Autumn opened her mouth to speak, and Jo put up a calming hand. "It would be a huge help if you'd start looking. Because the first thing Gabe and I need to do is stabilize Noah's condition."

Autumn took a breath. "Okay."

Gabe said, "We need to plan for short-term wilderness survival. Start pulling together a survival kit."

"Short term?" Autumn said.

Jo said, "We're talking about overnight. Maybe up to four days. We need to be as prepared as we can."

Gabe said, "One of you get back in the Hummer and grab this stuff if you can find it. A lighter. The flashlight. All the water bottles you have."

"What about beer?" Dustin said.

"We're not going to drink alcohol, but grab all of it. Plus anything we can use as an instant body shelter. A tarp, sleeping bag, tube tent, plastic trash bag. Rope. Then signaling devices. Whistles, signal mirrors, strobe lights —"

"Like that's going to be in the Hummer?" Dustin said.

Gabe turned on him. "This was supposed to be a game, right? Did you bring stuff to play with?"

Kyle nodded. "I'll look."

"I have two knives. See if you can find any others," Gabe said. "Maps. A compass — did you bring that? And GPS — the Hummer had a self-contained unit on the dashboard. See if by any chance it didn't get smashed."

Gradually, the group roused itself.

"First items — shelter and hydration. We need shelter from wind, cold, wet. Any two can kill you. Wish we could start a fire, but that would draw attention from Von and his gang."

"What about food?" Peyton said.

"Gather it up. I hope we won't be out here long enough to need to forage," he said.

"Forage, like for nuts and berries? I'm allergic to *everything*."

"Noted." He panned the group. "And post a lookout. Von's out there. Presume he can show up at any moment, with reinforcements. We'll rotate. Kyle, will you take the first watch?"

Ritter nodded. "I can do that."

"Safety is our number one concern," Gabe said.

Kyle nodded, staring at Gabe with an intensity that almost sizzled.

Gabe paused. "Above all, we stay strong. We stick together. We pay attention, we hang in there. We're

142

going to get out of here. All of us." He looked around at them. "Got it?"

Peyton didn't move. Dustin nodded. Autumn said, "Got it."

Gabe stepped into the center of the circle and held his hands out. "*Got it?*"

Stronger, they said: "Got it."

Gabe turned to Jo. She said, "Let's do it."

They clambered over rocks to the riverbank. Jo shook dust from her clothes and hair, then crouched down and plunged her hands into the water. The cold sent an ache up her arms. She washed up and rinsed the dust and grit off her face. Gabe did too. Then they crawled back inside the Hummer. Jo took off her jacket, turned it inside out, and moved to Noah's side. He was anxious, his eyes glossy with pain.

"This gonna hurt?" he said.

"Definitely."

He let out a non-laugh. "I thought you'd at least lie to me."

"It'll be painful, but we won't do anything that causes more damage. And reducing the fracture will be safer for you." She put a hand on his uninjured shoulder. "It won't take long. Then we'll splint the leg. Can you deal with that?"

"Have to."

"That's the spirit."

From the driver's compartment, Lark called, "I found the first-aid kit."

She scrambled through to the passenger compartment. Her face was drawn. She brushed dusty black hair back from her eyes and opened a red lunch-box-size kit.

"Band-Aids and gauze pads, iodine, athletic tape. An EpiPen for bee stings. Tylenol."

Tylenol would do little for Noah, but Jo gave Lark a thumbs-up.

"Gloves?" she said. "Antibiotics?"

Lark squinted at the contents of the first-aid kit, tilting her head, concentrating hard. All at once, Jo wondered how poor Lark's vision actually was.

There were no antibiotics, but the girl found latex gloves. Jo and Gabe put them on. Jo gave Noah two Tylenol. Then she packed his gunshot wound with gauze and immobilized his shoulder.

Noah's jeans and gym sock had, thankfully, kept his leg from becoming impregnated with dirt and debris. The wound site was mercifully clean. Still, Jo opened a plastic water bottle.

She leaned over Noah. "Need to irrigate and disinfect the wound. Hold Lark's hand."

Noah reached up and grabbed Lark's hand. Jo positioned herself at his knee and poured the water and then the iodine on his leg. He moaned and squirmed. She held his knee firmly and emptied the bottle.

"Done," she said. "Now I need to put my jacket underneath your leg to keep the site clean."

There was a huge risk of infection but this was the best they could do.

Gabe positioned himself at the boy's feet. "Going to lift your leg so Jo can slide the jacket underneath it."

144

When he put his hands underneath Noah's calf and lifted, the young man writhed. Jo slid the jacket into place.

"Doing good. That was step one," Gabe said. He took a distal pulse at Noah's ankle to check for circulation. He nodded — it was good. "Now take a deep breath."

"She already told me it's going to hurt," Noah said.

"Like a son of a bitch, but it'll be over soon."

Jo held the proximal end of his tibia — just below the knee. Gabe took hold of Noah's ankle and foot. The grotesquely broken bones of his leg protruded through the skin.

Firmly, carefully, Gabe pulled on Noah's lower leg. The young man went rigid. He kicked his uninjured leg, hard. Jo could hear him trying not to scream. Gabe pulled firmly and hesitated, testing, feeling his way. Then he pulled harder, and the exposed bones slid back beneath the torn skin and muscles.

"Almost there."

Noah panted. He kicked the floor of the Hummer with his good heel. Gabe cautiously kept going until the bones seemed to realign.

"Done," he said.

Jo looked at Noah. He was as pale as flour, and tears were leaking from his eyes. He was breathing like a fish on a dock.

"Let's not do that again," he said.

She touched his arm. "You did great."

Gabe checked his distal pulse again. They splinted his leg from above the knee to below the ankle with the cardboard packaging from two cases of Heineken and a roll of athletic tape. Then they elevated the limb to reduce swelling.

Gabe said, "You're doing good, man."

He and Jo climbed back out the Hummer's window. The shadows were deeper, and the wind was gusting higher. Gabe wiped his brow with the back of his hand. The back of his T-shirt was stippled with sweat, and blood.

Dustin, Autumn, and Peyton gravitated toward them, but Gabe said, "Just a minute," and walked to the riverbank, crouched down, and washed his face.

Jo followed. Nonchalantly, she sat on a rock beside him. "That was good work."

He nodded but didn't look up. "We have to get these kids out of here. If Noah doesn't get to a hospital, he's not going to last. He needs surgery."

And antibiotics, a blood transfusion, a warm bed, and more, Jo thought.

"You all right?" she said.

He nodded again. "Think I tore a shoulder muscle. And I sliced up my side."

"About time you told me."

"No point in worrying the others."

You dumbass, she thought. *You brave, stoic dumbass.*

"Sit down, right now, and don't get up." She got the first-aid kit and came back. "Shirt. Off."

With difficulty he pulled it over his head. A piece of metal, or broken glass, had cut a long slice up the back of his ribs. It was ragged, but not deep. Just incredibly painful.

She cleaned it, closed the wound with butterfly bandages, wrapped his ribs with gauze and strapped them with athletic tape, good and tight. Then she handed back his shirt.

"Don't do any dancing tonight, Sergeant," she said.

He didn't laugh.

She gently put a hand against his heart. For a moment, emotion threatened to overwhelm her. Though she tried to stem it, he saw and wrapped his arms around her.

"Thank God you're okay," she said.

He held on to her. "We're going to get out of here."

She nodded, tightly. *Hold it together.* "Absolutely." She blinked away tears and swallowed the tremor in her voice. "I love you."

"I love you too."

He stepped back and she wiped her eyes with the heels of her hands. She exhaled. Then, lowering her voice, she said, "This situation is freakish."

"That doesn't begin to cover it. Was this an actual kidnapping for ransom?"

"You have to be psychotic or a hard-core felon to risk kidnapping for ransom in America."

After the Lindbergh kidnapping, the FBI had essentially shut down abductions for financial gain in the U.S.A. The crime was virtually obsolete.

Gabe said, "Still, the simplest explanation is most likely to be the right one."

"Agreed. I just don't want to discount the possibility that something less straightforward is going on." She brushed her hair back from her face. "And I can't let these kids get on my nerves."

He put his hands on her shoulders. "Stay cool. They're young and scared. And they're not aliens. Autumn even looks like Tina."

Jo glanced at Autumn: the jaunty Marine Corps utility cap, the gold cashmere sweater, the leather boots. Despite the straits they were in, she had an unassailable, alpha-girl air — like she was the Queen of All Prom Queens.

"Autumn is nothing like Tina."

"But hang on to that idea. It'll keep you from biting their heads off."

In the distance, Kyle was watching them. "What's the plan, Chief?"

Gabe gingerly pulled his shirt back on. "We get out of here. But first, we figure out what's going on."

He put an arm around Jo and walked over to the group. "How did you end up here, without even knowing your birthday party had been hijacked?"

Jo had another question. *Why?*

CHAPTER
TWENTY

Ruby Ratner shuffled into the dim interior of the house, carrying the little dog under her arm. Evan followed.

The television was turned to a talk show. On a TV tray, Mrs Ratner had a jigsaw puzzle in progress. The carpet smelled like Pepito.

The house was decorated floor to ceiling as if Mrs Ratner had just stepped off a wagon train. On the mantel a collection of plates from the Franklin Mint memorialized *Gunsmoke* and *Have Gun-Will Travel*. Porcelain dolls were lined up on shelves around the room, like a firing squad: Paladin, Annie Oakley, Doc Holliday, the Earp brothers, the Dalton Gang. Above the mantel hung a paint-by-numbers portrait of Chuck Connors, decked out as the Rifleman. A dinner bell hung in the kitchen. Even her muumuu was gingham.

She sank onto the sofa, the dress softly pillowing, like a jellyfish. "Tell me what the fee is."

"For the party?"

"Course, the party. Nothing's free."

Evan sat on a creaking Naugahyde chair. She was beginning to think she'd come on a wild goose chase. Either that or Mrs Ratner was part of some super-kinky underground scene Phelps Wylie had secretly belonged to: Old West Swingers.

Pepito snuggled against Mrs Ratner's side, button-eyed and snarling.

"Hush, baby. Mama's talking." She peered at Evan through her cat's-eye glasses. "Before I sign any contract, we nail down the details. Are we talking about the whole act, or just the puppet show?"

Evan didn't know whether she was supposed to be buying or selling here. Much less what the product was. She hoped it didn't involve sock puppets that fit over anybody's private parts.

"What options were you considering?" she said.

"Two hours means the gunfight, the trial, and the hanging. Half a day means the entire jail setup as well as the rope tricks and the puppet show."

"Mrs Ratner, I have a confession."

"Save it for the party. That's what the gallows are for."

What the *hell* kind of party? "Okay. But . . ."

"I know you just want somebody to handle odd jobs and clean-up at the venue, but you ought to seriously consider my entertainment package."

Evan couldn't help herself. "Does *anybody*?"

The woman stood up, rocking forward a few times to gain the momentum to hoist herself off the sofa. "I'll get the flyers."

If she came back with pictures of herself lap dancing with a pony, Evan was going to dive through the window. She'd throw the growling dog through first, to break the glass, then jump out after it.

150

Her phone buzzed. Checking the display, she saw it was her contact at the Santa Barbara Sheriff's Department, Detective Lilia Rodriguez. She answered quietly, one eye on the hallway where Mrs Ratner had disappeared.

"Evan, what have you gotten yourself into?" Lily said.

"Nothing but investigative journalism. Why?"

"Ruby Ratner. There's a long jacket on this one."

Evan's stomach dropped. "Tell me."

"Assault, armed robbery, grand theft auto," Lily said. "By the time we get to the conviction for mayhem, we're talking about real prison time."

"*Mayhem?*" It was a common-law felony, generally involving physical mutilation or torture. "We're talking about Mrs Ruby Ratner of San Francisco. Lady's about sixty, walks like she's got arthritis."

"No. We're talking about Ruby Junior."

"Who's that?" Evan glanced at the dog. Pepito stared at her like an attack mop.

Lily said, "Mrs Ratner Senior is the mother of the guy I'm talking about."

"Guy?"

"Yeah. Ruben. Nicknamed Ruby Ratner, Junior." Lily rattled off the phone number Evan had given her, along with the address. It was the same one.

"I'm at the house," Evan said. "Quick, tell me about the son."

"Ruben Ratner, age thirty-three, white, five foot eight, one-forty. Ex-con. He's on parole for his last prison stint."

"Parole since when?"

Mrs Ratner shuffled back with some cheap flyers. "Who are you talking to?"

Evan tried to smile. She reached for the flyers. Mrs Ratner held on to them.

Evan tugged harder. "Thanks." She pulled them from Mrs Ratner's hand. "Sorry, got a call from a friend."

"What did I hear you say about parole?"

Evan kept the phone line open. "It was nothing."

The woman adjusted her cat's-eye glasses. She lifted her nose to get a better look at Evan. "Who are you?"

"Mrs Ratner, I think you're under a mistaken impression."

"You a cop?"

"No."

"You got a warrant?"

"I'm not a cop."

"Then get out of my house."

"Yes, ma'am."

She was already moving toward the door. Her skin goose-bumped. She looked back, and saw Mrs Ratner reach into a gingham pocket. She came out with a pearl-handled revolver. It didn't look like a prop from *Hang 'Em High*.

"Off my property now." Mrs Ratner whistled. "Pepito, Mama needs help."

Evan slammed open the screen door and was down the front steps and out the gate, past the insanely spinning plastic windmills, before Pepito could launch his stubby legs off the sofa. She ran to her Mustang, got in, stabbed the keys at the ignition a few times before she got it started, and over-revved it down the street. In the mirror she saw the little dog rush after her, yapping.

She didn't stop until she was a mile down the road. She pulled over and picked up her phone again.

"Lily?"

"Not involved in anything?" Rodriguez said. "What just happened?"

"I think I'm on to something."

"Yeah, Ruben Ratner. He's seriously bad news."

Evan looked at the flyers crumpled in her hand. "So where is he?"

CHAPTER
TWENTY-ONE

Peyton bit her thumbnail. "Everything seemed normal, until the shooting started."

Autumn crossed her arms. "Not exactly. The plan was changed a couple of hours before the game began." She glanced at Kyle. "Right?"

"That's right," Kyle said. "I was supposed to show up at Candlestick Point with the rest of the game runners. Instead I got the call to pick you up."

"Why you?" Jo said.

He considered it. "Because Coates had to get the speedboat. And because I have a commercial driver's license."

Jo looked at Autumn. "Who are you guys? Why are these hijackers after you? What's their goal? Because it sounds like they planned this very thoroughly."

Kyle kicked pebbles with the toe of his boot. "Her daddy's got megabucks."

Autumn glared at him, and her eyes seemed to brighten with pain and alarm.

Gabe said, "Anybody else here have deep pockets kidnappers can empty?"

Autumn said, "My dad's a hedge fund manager. Dustin's dad is a lobbyist in Washington."

"Excuse me for being intrusive, but how rich? How powerful?" Gabe said.

Autumn's shoulders rose.

"I've served in countries where kidnapping is the equivalent of grabbing cash from an ATM without having to wait in line. But in America, generally you need at least eight digits in your bank account before a kidnapper will think it's worth risking the federal prison time. So?"

"My dad arranged this weekend. He's done Edge Adventures scenarios himself. Everybody knows he loves this stuff. It's because of him."

She looked around at her friends. Her eyes were shimmering. Then she turned away and hid her face, staring at the river.

"So what's the kidnappers' plan?" Gabe said. "Grab you, stash you in a barn up in the back of beyond until your dad ponies up the cash?"

Peyton hugged herself. "Who cares? Somebody has to climb back up to the road and flag down a car."

Jo looked up the side of the gorge. "Not that way."

"Why not?"

"Retracing the fall line's too steep and slippery. And, like Kyle said, Von's up there and his partners are coming," Jo said. "We do need to contact help. But we have to do it safely."

Peyton wiped her nose. "But somebody's going to be looking for us, right?"

Gabe turned, a tight expression on his face. "The wrong people."

Peyton made a *no, stupid* face. "The police. Forest rangers."

Dustin said, "How come you think that?"

"The guys who picked us up from the beach in San Francisco weren't the real Edge Adventures guys." She looked at Kyle. "Right?"

"I never seen them before," he said.

"So the real Edge guys, they'll be looking for us."

The river whispered in the background. She looked wired and hopeful.

"No," Autumn said.

"Why not?" Peyton said.

"Because the hijackers got rid of the team from Edge." Autumn looked at Kyle. "Back at Candlestick Point you kept calling, and they didn't answer."

Kyle stared at her. He had an intense gaze, his eyes a hard brown with an almost golden ring around the edge of his irises. His gaze wasn't a thousand-yard stare, but it was depthless.

"She's right. They're toast," he said.

Peyton shrank into herself and worried her bracelet again. Autumn's eyes seemed haunted. A weighted silence pressed on them.

"But we didn't show up at the hotel," Peyton said.

Autumn said, "We aren't scheduled to check in yet. Nobody's looking for us."

"But . . ."

"Peyton, why would anybody search for us in the Sierras? The game's supposed to be in the city."

Jo said, "How long will it be before somebody in San Francisco knows something's wrong?"

156

Autumn looked stricken. "None of our families expect us to call until the end of the weekend."

"You mentioned a hotel."

"The Mandarin Oriental. But if we don't show up, they'll just cancel the reservation."

Lark said, "They wouldn't call the police. That's for sure."

Peyton looked helpless. "Won't somebody?"

Autumn turned. Her face was angry, and she looked fed up. "We've been abducted. Don't you get it? They figured a way to grab us so nobody would notice."

Peyton said, "You mean nobody knows where we are?"

Jo shook her head.

Gabe raised a hand. "Help me understand what happened earlier. You went to the beach at Candlestick Point."

Kyle picked up a stick. "Yeah. Then this new gang showed up, wearing ski masks."

"They hijacked the Edge Adventures team and then hijacked your group."

"That looks about the size of it," Kyle said. "I thought the trip up here was another twist in an evolving scenario. Coates kept switching things up at the last minute — I figured this was just another curve ball."

Gabe held out his hand. "Give me that stick and get yourself a bigger one. Get seven bigger ones."

He took out his buck knife.

"What's that for, Chief?"

"We're not going to sit here unarmed. We'll carve spears."

"Sounds like a plan." Kyle ambled toward the trees.

Jo said, "They ambushed you at Candlestick Point. Why not grab you on your way to class at USF? Why grab everybody on your birthday party weekend?"

The wind swirled through the gorge. It was beginning to feel chilly. Jo was beginning to feel chilled emotionally again. *Why take the whole party?*

Autumn's hair haloed in the breeze. "Because the police were informed it was a game. They wouldn't interfere."

Gabe and Jo both gaped. Simultaneously they said, "What?"

"That's how Edge runs mock abductions. They call the cops beforehand, so nobody tries to make an arrest."

"You gotta be kidding me," Jo said.

Autumn hunched into herself. "It made perfect sense at the time."

And it had horrific implications. Jo glanced at Gabe and could tell that he was thinking the same thing.

She saw why the hijackers had grabbed the whole group to begin with. But with Autumn under their control, why hang on to the extra captives?

There was no reason to keep all of them around. They had been taking them into the wilderness to get rid of them.

The kids were out of the frying pan, for the moment. But they were skirting the edge of the fire. She didn't want to state things so baldly, not yet. But she needed to convey her sense of urgency.

"Nobody knows where we are except us and Von. And if Von climbs the hillside up to the logging road, he'll flag down his buddies or contact them by phone."

Autumn's shoulders rose and dropped. "What do we do?"

"We have to contact the authorities." Jo looked at Gabe. "Somebody has to go for help."

Gabe stepped forward. "We're in a survival situation. So listen up. I'm going to tell you about SERE."

"What's that?" Dustin said.

"Survive, Evade, Resist, Escape. It's the military's survival training. And you're about to get a crash course."

"Out," Haugen said. "I'm driving."

Unhappily, Stringer climbed from behind the wheel of the Volvo SUV. Haugen stalked to the driver's side, clenching and unclenching his fists.

"Get in the back," he said. "Sabine, you ride shotgun. Log on from my phone. Hook up the laptop."

He jumped in and accelerated away from the truck stop, tires squealing.

This should not be happening.

The Hummer had wrecked. Friedrich was dead. Von had escaped but didn't have control over Autumn's group. They were stranded at the bottom of the gorge, but not fenced in.

He pushed his foot to the floor and raced up the highway, accelerating past eighty, eighty-five, ninety. Sabine reached over and flipped on the headlights.

"We're still on schedule," she said. "Reiniger's plane won't land for another hour. We have the initial video and the photos of the Edge game runners. Nothing has changed."

"And when Reiniger demands proof of life?" Haugen said.

"He won't. Not yet. He'll be in shock."

He slammed his palm against the steering wheel. "This should not have happened." He glanced in the rear-view mirror at Stringer. "Why did nobody predict that these college boys might mount an attack?"

From the sour look in Stringer's eyes, Haugen knew he was reading the implication accurately: Why didn't you predict it?

Sabine tried to stay calm. "Von is maneuvering into position. All he needs to do is get close enough to see them. He can pin them down. One shot, they'll hear the echo and dash back inside the limo. They'll cower."

Haugen glanced at her. "Get Von on the phone again."

"Why?" she said.

He shot a hand out and grabbed her around the throat. "Now."

Quickly, silently, she grabbed his forearm and dug her nails into his flesh. Hard.

He let go of her.

"Both hands on the wheel, Dane," she gasped. The look she gave him was filthy.

He put his hands at two and ten. His vision was flashing red. He reached back across the SUV to stroke her cheek, and like a cobra she slapped his hand away.

160

"I will tell you why we need to phone Von," he said. "Because he needs to understand the rules of play. They've changed."

Stringer leaned forward. "How?"

"One gunshot, fired into the rocks or the river, will scare these kids back into the Hummer. One gunshot fired into somebody's head will convince them the risks of escaping are worth it." He wrung his hands on the wheel. "He needs to save his gunfire for when it counts."

He looked again at Sabine. "He needs to wait to kill them until I'm on the scene."

"Unless they try to escape," Sabine said.

"Unless. Then all bets are off."

Gabe stood at the center of the semicircle, all eyes on him. "We survived the wreck, but that's not even half the battle. To evade capture and escape, we need to know who our opposition is."

Jo said, "How many people were in the group that took you?"

"Five," Kyle said. "And one was a woman. The two clowns who drove us into this gorge, they wasn't in charge. Another man was giving them orders."

Autumn said, "The tall man who drove the speedboat."

Kyle appeared to think about it. He nodded.

Gabe said, "So we should count on at least four hostiles coming for us, heavily armed and determined to recapture the group."

Everybody looked at Autumn. Thinking: or recapture her and kill the rest of them.

"The quickest way to get help is to contact the local sheriffs. And we still have to find Jo's and my cell phones," Gabe said.

"On it," Jo said, and headed for the Hummer.

"We can't just sit here," Dustin said.

"I'm not suggesting it. Somebody's got to climb out of here. But we can't all go."

"Then what are you saying, man?"

"Noah shouldn't be moved unless it's absolutely necessary. Peyton, you're going to have difficulty hiking severe terrain. Ideally, we'd move to a defensible position and get under cover. But for now we stay here and protect ourselves."

Peyton looked tired and shaky. "How?"

"Night's coming. The temperature is going to drop, maybe below freezing. And there's a storm blowing in."

"You gotta be shitting me," Dustin said.

"We can't build a fire because it would pinpoint our location in the dark. If you brought warm clothes, get them. Put them on, keep them zipped up. Stay dry."

Jo circled to the wrecked driver's compartment of the limo, avoiding Friedrich's crushed body. The door was open, twisted like a bird's broken wing. She squirmed inside. The interior of the vehicle had deepened into gray shadow.

She rooted around. She heard voices in the passenger compartment. Lark and Autumn had crawled inside.

"You okay, Noah?" Autumn said.

162

He rocked his hand side to side: *so-so*, "Had better days."

Lark pressed her lips tightly closed. For a second she looked like she might cry.

Jo said, "You all right back there?"

Lark shook her head. "Hardly." Then she got hold of herself. "But we will be. Right?"

"That's the plan."

Jo crabbed through the wrecked driver's compartment, flinching away from broken glass and twisted shards of metal. She sifted through trash and debris until, at the bottom of it, she found her cell phone.

"Got it," she said.

The phone was powered up and didn't look damaged. She dusted it off.

No signal. They were too deep in the gorge. She kept looking for Gabe's cell, but had no luck.

Autumn was looking around the interior of the Hummer. "None of our stuff is here. They took it."

"What about the luggage compartment?"

A freighted pause. "But . . ."

Autumn glanced at Jo. Her expression practically begged, *Don't make me.*

"I'll go with you," Jo said.

She climbed back through the twisted door into the cooling evening, and trudged with Autumn to the rear of the Hummer. Autumn opened the latch on the luggage compartment. It creaked open about two feet. Autumn moaned and shook her hands, the universal sign for *grossed out.*

The army duffel bag was visible. In the crash, the body had been dislodged and slid halfway out. Jo recognized the outfit the corpse was wearing: the tactical black of the hijackers. She didn't recognize the corpse. His skin was pale white. A gunshot wound pocked his temple.

"Just got to grit our teeth and grab any gear that's back there," Jo said.

She knew that what she was asking Autumn to do was tough. But they had not one single second to wallow in self-pity. They had to get on with it. Tough was what they had to be. Some of them were going to have to climb out of the gorge past Von — while it was still light, and he might target them through his gunsight. They had to. Traveling in the dark was a recipe for death.

Whimpering, Autumn reached into the luggage compartment and pulled out a black sports bag. She stumbled back from the Hummer, shuddering. Dropping the bag, she unzipped it and began rustling through it.

"What . . . ," she said, her voice shaky. "What is . . . ?"

Her chest heaved. "What is this doing here?" She straightened. She looked ready to bite somebody. "Who did this?"

"Did what?" Jo said.

Autumn pulled a cowboy hat and a lasso from the bag. "The Bad Cowboy. This is his stuff. What is it doing here?"

CHAPTER
TWENTY-TWO

For the tenth time, Evan tried calling Jo. And for the tenth time she heard, *The number you are calling is out of range*.

She paced across the motel room. She had sent Jo texts and a photo from Ruby Ratner's flyer. She had received no reply. She should have.

Save yourself the work — hire a cowboy!

Ruben Ratner was a handyman and jack-of-all-trades. The flyer offered his services to haul trash to the dump, set up parties, and teach horseback-riding lessons at knock-down prices. But he had no business license and, from what Evan could determine, no record of ever teaching buckaroos to ride the range. That, she thought, was his mother's pipe dream, a gleam in her prairie-clouded eye.

She looked at the other flyer: Mrs Ratner, dressed in singing-cowgirl garb, with an Indian Chief hand puppet. Evan didn't know whether she had been hired to perform at a single party. The term *buyer beware* had never seemed so pertinent.

It was getting dark. Jo shouldn't still be out of range.

Maybe it meant nothing. Maybe Jo was sitting by a roaring fireplace in Yosemite, phone turned off, making out with her boyfriend.

Except that Jo had said she would check in. Evan pulled up the text messages Jo had sent from the abandoned gold mine. *Must take cell to Tuolumne sheriffs in Sonora.*

She phoned the Tuolumne County Sheriff's Office.

"Afraid I don't have any idea what you're talking about," the desk officer said.

"Could I speak to the senior officer on duty?"

"That's me, and I've been here since 8a.m., ma'am. Believe me, if anybody showed up with evidence that Phelps Wylie was murdered, I would remember it. And if I didn't, there would be a record in our log and a cell phone in our evidence locker. There's nothing."

"Dr Beckett —"

"I've spoken to Dr Beckett before. She hasn't been here."

Evan hung up, worried. She tried Jo one more time. No luck.

Grabbing the flyer, she drove to the coffeehouse near Fisherman's Wharf. The sun was going down. She hoped the place would still be open.

As she jogged toward the door she saw chairs stacked upside down on tables, and a man mopping the floor. Damn. She rapped on the door.

The man called, "We're closed."

She cupped her hands against the glass. "I'm looking for one of your baristas — Tina. It's important."

The man leaned on his mop. He looked tired and in no mood to help. Then he turned toward a back hallway.

"Tina," he said.

A moment later, the young woman who looked so much like Jo came out wiping her hands on her black Java Jones apron. When she unlocked the door, her face was perplexed.

"I need to get in touch with Jo. It's urgent," Evan said.

"Do you need her phone number?"

"I've been calling her for hours."

Concern sparked in Tina's eyes. Then it cooled. "She's at the Lodge in Yosemite."

"Excellent."

But even so, Evan began to feel more anxious. If Jo was at the lodge, she presumably had access to a landline. She got the number from directory assistance and phoned.

The receptionist said, "Ms Beckett hasn't checked in."

"She hasn't?" Evan said.

Tina's eyes turned wide and shiny. "Maybe they registered under Gabe's name. Quintana."

"Try Quintana," Evan said.

"No reservation under that name," said the receptionist.

"Thanks." Evan hung up. "She's not there."

Tina stood worriedly for a moment. "Let's go to her house. Maybe she left some information there."

Autumn held up the cowboy hat and lariat as though they were venomous snakes. "What the hell is this?"

"What's wrong?" Jo said.

Dustin walked over and tossed clothes out of the black sports bag. Onto the rocks he threw a gaudy Western-style shirt with red roses stitched across the front. Then a pair of crocodile-skin cowboy boots, dyed sky blue. And a pair of chaps.

"This is wack," he said.

Autumn spun in a circle. "It's not funny."

The others approached. Kyle peered into the luggage compartment at the body. The man's face was bluish white. Peyton caught sight of it and flinched.

Autumn shook the cowboy hat in her fist. "This stuff belongs to the Bad Cowboy. It's a sick joke."

"The Bad Cowboy?" Gabe said.

"Red Rattler. The asshole . . . I hate him. Everybody knows that."

Dustin nodded. Peyton said, "We do."

Autumn looked pale and fierce in the dusk, her long brown curls swirling in the gusty wind. "Who did this?"

Kyle turned from the luggage compartment. "Edge Adventures did it."

"What are you talking about?"

"Those clothes, they're a costume. Edge Adventures supplied them. To me."

"Why?"

"I was supposed to play the role during the weekend. You were supposed to get to confront this character, this Bad Cowboy" — air quotes — "and defeat him."

"Are you serious?" she said.

"Terry Coates, he told me it was a customized element of your reality scenario. You pay to play, so you get whatever toys mean the most to you."

168

Autumn gaped at Ritter and at the cowboy hat in her hands and the lariat. She dropped them like they stank. "How did Edge know about the Bad Cowboy?"

Dustin said, "Autumn . . ."

Her face flushed. "Why would he? Why would my dad tell Edge?"

Peyton rolled her eyes. "Because it's supposed to be a game. A stupid game, Autumn. Not a phobia. Look at you."

Autumn began to blink, rapidly. "This is sick."

Jo said, "Can somebody explain?"

Peyton said, "When Autumn was little she went to a party where this Red Rattler guy was parking cars. He screamed at her when she got too close. He spooked her. He just blew her fuses."

Autumn shook her head, fiercely. "That's not it. Not at all."

She grabbed the Western shirt and chaps, picked up the sports bag, and marched toward the river. "This crap can float downstream."

Jo ran after her. "Don't. We need the clothing. It's going to drop toward freezing in a couple of hours." She grabbed the bag. "Don't."

For a moment Autumn held on, like a toddler clinging to a toy. Then she relented and tossed the bag and clothes to the ground. She clawed her hands into her hair and lowered her voice.

"It's not funny — it's *sick*. He's not a cartoon character. He's a freak." She gestured ferociously to her eyes. "He had this white circle around the blue of one eye. Bright white. He said it was a snake eye. He said it would be *watching* me. It would know if I told anybody about him, and had the power to *hurt* me."

She stood with her feet planted, challenging Jo to doubt her. When Jo didn't, she stalked off, kicking the bag as she went, and gave Kyle a dirty stare.

He raised his hands. "Hey, missy, not my fault." He shook his head and turned to Dustin. "What was that about?"

"You tell me," Dustin said. "What did Edge Adventures want you to do?"

"They said the birthday girl had a particular dislike for an ex-rodeo rider she met as a kid. Halfway through the weekend, I was supposed to slip away, put on those clothes, and then burst in on her. See how she reacted."

"That's the stupidest thing I've ever heard," Dustin said.

"Not my script. Edge cooked it up based on information Autumn's father gave them. If it's wack, it's her daddy's idea."

Dustin shook his head. "Man. Her dad's a piece of work."

"What does her dad have to do with it?" Jo said.

"She complained to her dad about this guy. The guy gave her nightmares. But her dad pokes fun at it. Autumn hates that."

Jo turned to Kyle. "And Edge simply asked you to take on the role?"

"I'm the new hire. The rest of the outfit, they all have assigned roles, because of their background and training."

"What's your background and training?" Gabe said.

"Needing a job, man. Willing to work hard."

"You're not this Red Rattler?"

"I never even been on a horse," Kyle said. "And now can we stop fussing over Missy Reiniger's hurt feelings, and get this rescue organized?"

Jo didn't like the buzz that was vibrating through the air. But she didn't have time to hash it out. They needed to move.

"Yes. We need to send two people out of here to get help."

"I'm one of them," Kyle said. "I ain't about to hang around and listen to Autumn tell whiny stories around the campfire."

"I'm the second," Dustin said.

Gabe stirred, about to speak, but Dustin shook his head firmly.

"Let me do this. I'll get help." He turned to Kyle. "We'll go together. We can make good headway before dark."

Kyle took a pack of cigarettes from the pocket of his windbreaker. He started to tap one out, but Gabe shook his head. Kyle thought about it, and put them away. Then he said, "We get back to the road, we can follow it downhill. There was some side roads — driveways, looked like. There's ranches up here. Few and far between, but we'll find somebody. Or at least keep going until we get phone reception."

Dustin waited for Gabe to knock him back. But Gabe said, "Good."

Jo scouted the path they should take. It was going to be tough.

She was an experienced rock climber who had no trouble with 5.10 climbs. The hillside the Hummer had plowed down wasn't rock, wasn't even anything that would be rated by climbers. But it took her ten minutes to climb forty yards back up the slope, around an outcropping of boulders, to a place where she had a comprehensive view of the terrain.

The ground was crumbling and slippery with pine needles. And when she stopped and balanced on the slope, she saw more of the damage the limo had wrought on its sleigh ride to the bottom of the gorge. The Hummer had sideswiped a pine tree halfway down, hard enough to score a bite from the bark. A pale and splintered gash stood out in the waning light.

She looked down at the riverbank. On a rock near the gliding water, Gabe sat whittling inch-thick branches into spears. The buck knife flashed. Close by, Kyle and Dustin peered up at her.

Downstream, the riverbank was nothing but boulders and brush. There was no path on their side.

She half slid back down the hill and shook her head. "You can't go downstream on this bank. You have to cross the river and climb up the other slope."

They examined the slope on the far bank. It was dense with ponderosa pine and yellow cottonwoods. The trees lining the ridgeline high above just caught the red embers of sunset, beneath a boil of dark clouds.

"Keep trying your phone all the way up, Kyle," she said.

He nodded. "We better hit the trail."

Dustin took a breath. Gabe stood up and handed him the spear.

"Take this."

Dustin gripped it firmly but awkwardly. He might as well have been handed a lightsaber.

Gabe looked grave. "Before the crash, I heard Von say that the others were a couple of hours behind. Figure you have one hour to get a signal and call nine-one-one."

Kyle nodded.

"If you get a signal, call the cops first, then text Jo. We need to know if you've raised the alarm."

Jo said, "In twenty minutes I'll cross the river and head up the slope to try to get a signal myself. Text me your status. I want to know if you've reached the sheriffs, if you're coming back to the Hummer, or if you see signs of civilization."

"Got it," Kyle said.

Gabe's voice was solemn. "If we don't hear from you in ninety minutes, we'll have to figure the opposition is closing in. We'll have to move out on our own."

Gabe handed Dustin the flashlight, a map, and the compass. Dustin stuck them in his various pockets. Then he walked over to Autumn and put his arms around her.

"I'll be back. With help, baby."

She nodded tightly. "Be careful."

Dustin eyed Gabe. The boy looked on the verge of saying something. Jo hoped it was an apology.

Dustin stuck out his hand. "Take care of Noah, man."

Gabe shook. "We will."

Kyle had dug his backpack out of the luggage compartment. He slung it across his shoulders. "We'll be back with the cavalry."

They trudged into the river, wading across against the pull of the current. Jo felt time sliding away. Ninety minutes, counting down.

Autumn stood nearby. She clenched her hands into fists and pressed them against her mouth.

"I should go, not Dustin."

Jo was surprised. "Why?"

"This is my fault."

"No, it's not."

She was pale, but her cheeks were flushed. "The hijackers grabbed everybody just so they could get me."

"Autumn, this is the fault of the people who hijacked us. You're the victim."

She looked on the verge of tears. "I invited Grier. I asked him to come."

At the mention of Grier's name, Jo's throat caught. She spoke quietly. "You're not responsible for what these criminals do."

Autumn watched the water flowing in the river. It was slate gray and silky in the dusk. "My dad's on a flight to New York. When he lands, they'll phone him. He'll pay a ransom. I know he will. And he'll want to talk to me. They'll have to let him talk to me."

God, the girl felt completely alone. Jo stepped toward her, intending to put an arm around her shoulder.

Autumn virtually swatted her away. "I'm fine."

Jo told herself to keep calm. She was the adult here. Autumn was only *supposed* to be reaching adulthood this weekend. And she was wound up like a piece of tangled string.

Everybody has to hold it together. Mental attitude can make the difference between survival and death.

"Think positively," Jo said. "Let's hope you're the first one who calls your dad — to tell him you've gotten out of here and we're all okay."

Across the river, Dustin and Kyle clambered slowly up the steep side of the gorge.

Autumn said, "Please let them find help."

Jo hoped she'd see them again.

CHAPTER
TWENTY-THREE

Peter Reiniger was first off the plane at JFK. The flight attendants thanked him for flying their ever-more-depressing airline. The captain stood in the cockpit doorway, wanting, what, a tip? Reiniger walked past, head tilted down at his BlackBerry.

No calls from Autumn. Good. That meant Edge Adventures had stuck to their guns and confiscated her phone. And Autumn had not been able to pout or charm her way into wrangling it back.

The terminal was bustling. Outside the plate-glass windows, a jumbo jet taxied across the runway. He scrolled through his phone book for Terry Coates's number.

He hated flying commercial, but in the current economic climate it was lamentable but necessary. Because the second he signed up for NetJets or stepped off a G5 somewhere, some idiot would snap him on an iPhone and upload it to Twitter and call him the devil incarnate. Financial evil, Satan on wheels. This new century was an era of approbation. The age was off its hinges. But he could not afford to draw the spotlight. Not until people's acute sense of outrage over their financial losses had faded to manageable tones.

Reiniger phoned Coates as he maneuvered around hordes of slow-moving people who looked lost in the terminal, probably wondering which way Times Square was. His driver was waiting with a card saying P. REINIGER.

Coates's phone rang.

He and his driver stepped out the doors into a crisp fall night. Clear skies, a cool breeze. Shouting skycaps, touts trying to scam him into accepting an expensive limousine ride. The driver led him to a waiting Town Car and opened the rear door for him.

Coates's phone continued to ring.

Terry Coates's cell phone lit up and began to sing.

Sabine picked it up. "Dane. Showtime."

Haugen pulled to the shoulder of the darkening highway and killed the engine. He took the phone from her. It was playing the theme from *Shaft*.

"Cliché, no? Black ex-cop, playing action movie games," he said. "But apropos. The shaft is what he got."

Sabine's expression was meant to be flat, emotionless, but her eyes were guarded. "Don't be so sure. Back at the truck depot, Coates managed to grab Max's gun and kill him. Or don't you recall us stuffing Max's body into the luggage compartment of the Hummer?"

"Max also managed to wound Coates. Coates will bleed to death in the big rig before the weekend is out."

The phone continued to ring.

"Answer it," Sabine said.

Haugen plugged the voice modulator into the phone. He took a centering breath and slid a steel door into place over his emotions.

Keep it chilly. They were down two men but still had hours to rectify the mess up the road. Only one thing mattered: preventing Autumn Reiniger from getting away and contacting the authorities. But she was trapped in the bottom of a gorge forty miles from nowhere, and he was closing in on her. Right now, what counted was sticking to the script and keeping Peter Reiniger on schedule.

Haugen answered the phone. "I thought you'd never call."

In the enveloping quiet of the Town Car, Reiniger held the phone to his ear. The driver pulled into traffic. The voice on the line sounded distorted — a deep basso, stretched beyond normal human range, and twisted like taffy.

"Coates?" he said.

"This is your new reality," the voice said. "This is your moment of crystalline present tense."

Reiniger checked the display. He'd dialed correctly. "Who is this?"

"And if you want a future, you'll listen quietly and do exactly as I say."

"What's going on?"

"Let me clarify. If you want a future that includes your daughter, you'll close your mouth and follow instructions."

178

The Town Car accelerated into the New York night. Reiniger watched the road slip by.

Haugen placed Coates's cell phone on the center console of the Volvo SUV and put it on speaker. Outside, lightning flashed. Wind buffeted the car, but the snaking, forested road was deserted and the voice modulator distorted all sounds, ensuring that Reiniger could not decipher their location from background noise. And he had no means to triangulate their position. Tracing the call would be virtually impossible. Haugen had insured that Reiniger could not pinpoint his geographical position and make a grab to rescue Autumn.

"I take your silence as assent," he said.

Reiniger said nothing.

"You know this drill. You've seen it a thousand times on television," Haugen said. "You will not contact the police. You will certainly not contact the FBI. Do you understand? If so, say yes."

"Is this a joke?" Reiniger said.

"Wrong answer," Haugen said. "I repeat, *you know this drill*. I am positive you know it from corporate security training. Your firm has kidnap insurance. You have had abduction protection training. It's impossible that you have not."

"Where's Autumn?"

"Shut up."

Reiniger shut up.

Submission. Haugen glanced at Sabine. In the dashboard lights, her face was eerily lit. She was clicking her tongue against her teeth. He flicked his hand at her, telling her to knock it off. In the backseat, Stringer hunched in the darkness. He knew not even to breathe.

"You have had the training," Haugen said. "Your corporate muscle told you to phone them in the event anybody is abducted. They told you they would handle any ransom, and the recovery, and that the police need not be involved. This is, after all, nominally a capitalist country. The free market reigns, am I correct?"

"What do you want?"

"I want you to stay in the moment, Peter. Focus your energies on the present. You will not alert your corporate security. No bodyguards, no insurance company flacks, no claims adjusters, or proof-of-life mercenaries. This is not about a simple ransom."

"Then what is it about?"

Haugen listened to the stress in Reiniger's voice. It was sharp and being suppressed. Either Reiniger was having a mental breakdown, or he was not alone. Otherwise, Haugen felt sure, he would be shouting and throwing things. Haugen had made a study of Peter Reiniger.

"First, I need to impress upon you the consequences of ignoring my directives," Haugen said. "If you contact anybody — *anybody*, aside from those I tell you to — people will die. Do you understand? Say yes."

"Who?"

"Are you asking about Autumn? Or about her friends? Because it's all related." He picked up his phone and scrolled to its stored photos. "Starting point. You need proof that I'm serious."

180

He selected a photo and sent it to Reiniger. "Take a look."

In the back of the Town Car, Peter Reiniger felt like he'd taken a two-by-four to the chest. His hands were cold. There was a keening sound in his ears.

He called to the driver. "Privacy barrier."

The driver eyed him in the mirror, and the glass partition slid up. Reiniger tried to swallow and found his throat too dry. He kept his face blank. Blank and strong. He was good at doing that. It's how he made his money, at poker and in finance. But his heart was beating too hard, skipping around.

His phone beeped. A photo had been sent. He opened it and stopped breathing.

It was a picture of Autumn. She was on the beach at Candlestick Point. The photo had been taken from the deck of a boat. Autumn was dashing toward the water, accompanied by Dustin. She was laughing. She looked exhilarated.

But behind her were three figures clad in black, wearing balaclavas. Carrying automatic weapons.

Reiniger — as the voice on the phone alleged — had indeed been through security training. Anti-kidnapping preparation. He had worked with close-protection bodyguards when traveling overseas. He recognized the weapons the people in the photo were holding.

They were working firearms. Not the decommissioned toys that Terry Coates and Edge Adventures pointed at people.

Real guns. They were aimed at Autumn's head.

And she didn't even know it. She thought it was a party. The party he had planned for her. The party he had sent her to.

The party that Edge Adventures had phoned in to the SFPD.

The twisted robot voice warbled from the phone. "Pretty girl. So oblivious."

"What have you done? Who is this? Where's Coates?"

The phone pinged again. A new photo arrived. Reiniger opened it and his vision grayed at the edges.

It was a photo of Terry Coates. The Edge Adventures owner was lying on the floor of — what — a tractor-trailer? His hands were bound and he was gagged. And he was covered in blood.

Reiniger tried to focus. "Is this a hoax?"

Ping. New photo.

It was Cody Grier, splayed on the dirt.

Reiniger gripped the phone and tried to convince himself this was a prank, a trick, a massive ruse designed to swindle him. He couldn't manage it. He dry heaved.

The voice returned. "Threats, I've learned, are insufficient. Action is required. Isn't it?"

"Don't hurt her."

"I'm glad you understand."

The voice, deep and ghostly, so mechanical, seemed to mock him. Seemed to be *enjoying* this. Reiniger felt nausea and a disintegrative rage, a sense that his center wasn't holding. He was in a limousine driving down the Long Island Expressway toward Manhattan, his suit pressed, his Rolex gleaming in the streetlights. And death was whispering at him through the phone.

"Give her back to me. I'll do whatever you want. Just don't hurt her."

Haugen tightened his hands into fists. Reiniger was breaking. It was a breathtaking sensation. His heart, dry and knotted, beat faster.

"Step one — acceptance. I'm proud of you, Peter."

Sabine frowned at him. *Don't toy with Reiniger*, the look said. He ignored her. This was the culmination of years of planning. It was a moment to be savored. Sabine could fret about the problems up the road. He deserved this moment.

"Now. Step two. You won't call the cops, or your kidnap insurers and their security Neanderthals, because if you do, the rest of Autumn's companions will die."

"You can't kill them."

"Do not interrupt me. Autumn's companions will die *first*."

He paused to let the statement sink in. "I don't believe that you have a moment's concern for Autumn's friends. You wouldn't care if Lark Sobieski or Noah Holloway died in a private rescue attempt, as long as Autumn came home."

He slowed his speech. Modulate, he told himself. No vocal inflections, no clues. Just the plain facts.

Sabine tapped her watch. *Cut it short*. He couldn't risk the chance that Reiniger had, despite his orders, alerted his corporate security team to find Coates's

183

phone. He needed to get off the line. And then to toy with Reiniger some more.

"But if I spot the FBI's hostage rescue team preparing to deploy or even some steroid-juiced bodyguard getting ready to storm in and rescue your daughter, I will execute the rest of Autumn's companions one by one. She'll watch. And I'll tell her it's your fault."

Reiniger didn't respond.

"And if Autumn comes home after being liberated, it won't be for long. My operatives will find her. They'll kill her. And they'll do it while *you* watch."

He let Reiniger think about it.

"Still considering?" Haugen said. "I don't think you want the SEC to start digging around in your business doings, either."

"Bastard."

Superb.

"What do you want?" Reiniger said.

"I'll phone back in half an hour." He allowed himself the smallest of smiles. "When I do, be sure you have a pen."

CHAPTER
TWENTY-FOUR

Jo walked to the back end of the wrecked Hummer, where Autumn and Peyton were piling up survival supplies.

Two lighters. Half a dozen plastic water bottles. A case of Budweiser.

It was a start.

The wind gusted up the gorge, rushing through the darkened pines and shirring the dark steel surface of the river. Peyton sat down on a rock. Hunched over, in pain, she looked bedraggled and small. It made her look younger, emphasized her nerves and fright.

"When it gets dark, predators'll come out," she said. "Maybe cougars."

Jo had wilderness experience, thanks to years of rock climbing and backpacking trips in the Sierras and Cascades. Though it was nowhere close to Gabe's training, she knew the basics. She knew that things could go wrong at the snap of a finger and that nothing should be taken for granted. Life and death were only fragile, irrevocable breaths apart.

And she knew that there were real, and tough, psychological aspects to survival in a wilderness emergency. Gabe knew it too: He'd been trained to recognize it in himself and his men and women. But he was busy taking care of perimeter defense. Jo kept an eye on the roiling emotions around her. Pain. Thirst. Cold. Fatigue. Isolation. Fear.

Hopelessness.

"Cougars are highly unlikely to attack a group of people," she said. "They —"

"Scorpions. Snakes. They crawl into empty shoes and sleeping bags. *Don't* say it's unlikely — when I was little I almost got poisoned by a rattler on a family camping trip."

"We're going to stick together and keep our eyes open. We'll protect each other," she said.

Gabe came up behind her. "Worrying about everything?"

"Of course. And, yes, I have read the U.S. Air Force survival manual."

Autumn said, "Anything we *don't* have to worry about?"

"Shark attack," Jo said. "We lucked out there."

Peyton pulled on a lock of her blond hair and wound it compulsively around her finger. The movement hurt her fractured clavicle, and she grimaced. "I can't believe this is happening to us."

"You were expecting an extreme reality experience, right?" Jo said.

Autumn glanced at Jo and actually laughed. "And now we're getting it."

"Yes. Though you should ask for your money back."

"But you weren't expecting any of this," Autumn said.

"No." Jo nodded toward the limo. "Bundle up and get inside the Hummer."

Peyton just sat on the rock. Her eyes were glossy. "We're going to die."

"No. We're going to get out of here if it's the last thing I do," Jo said.

"Like you guys are the X-Men? Give me a break."

"Hey, Peyton?" Autumn said. "Shut the hell up and get in the Hummer."

Peyton didn't cringe, but she frowned, intensely. *Good*, Jo thought. Get her mad. That was better than caving in.

"I'm the queen of the weekend," Autumn said. "Your ruler and your bad boss. So move your pretty pink ass."

Peyton stood and headed for the limo, picking at her charm bracelet. Jo looked at Autumn and thought she seemed taller than she'd first imagined.

When Peyton neared the Hummer she turned her head to avoid looking at Friedrich's corpse. Jo girded herself. They had an unpleasant task to take care of.

"We should move the bodies," she said.

Gabe nodded. Autumn and Lark looked nauseated. But the idea of huddling in the Hummer, surrounded by brutalized corpses, was too gruesome to contemplate.

The four of them dragged Friedrich, and then the man in the luggage compartment, away from the vehicle — far enough that getting back inside the Hummer no longer felt disgusting or ghoulish.

"Thanks," Jo said.

The girls didn't reply. They clattered across rocks and sand to the river, crouched down, and scrubbed their hands, arms, faces, furiously. Jo and Gabe were right behind them. The cold bite of the water felt more than cleansing. It felt emotionally necessary.

Jo dried her hands on her jeans and checked the time. It had been twenty minutes since Dustin and Kyle struck out across the river.

"Time to cross the river and try to get a signal on my phone. Don't know how much elevation I'll need. Wish me luck."

Gabe looked unhappy. "Be careful."

She found a spot upriver where the water streamed over the granite like glass, only an inch deep. She crossed to the western bank and darted into thick brush. The last embers of daylight painted highlights and shadows on the steep slopes of the gorge. She scanned it, looking for movement, for color, for flashes of metal. If Von was out there, he was concealed.

She glanced back across the river. Gabe waved.

Beneath the trees, she climbed in shadow up the hillside. *Keep going.* As long as she kept moving she could suppress her fears.

She climbed a hundred meters and crouched behind a gray boulder. The sky was indigo with the last brush of daylight. But thunderheads were stacking ever nearer, and dusk had drawn a gray veil over the gorge. She pulled out her phone, cupped her hand over the display to hide its light, and pushed a button. The display popped on, hot blue in the twilight. *Searching.* The wind buffeted the side of her head.

You weren't planning any of this.

How had she and Gabe ended up here, on this mountainside, in such straits?

Life was riddled with accidents. Chance was a fearsome force in the cosmos. She believed in free will and relished her own patch of accountability, her ability to grab the throttle and adjust course, even in a quantum universe. However, this accident didn't feel entirely random. This felt like a collision of loaded dice on a craps table. But she couldn't see who had thrown them.

One bar on the phone. She had a signal. "Yes."

She held the phone gingerly, as though it were a tiny bird's egg with a fragile shell. She didn't want to adjust the angle of the antenna and lose the little symbols on the display. She dialed 9-1-1.

Call failed.

"Dammit."

She had to get a stronger signal. Tucking the phone in her back pocket, she scurried up the slope, around worn rocks and the rough bark of tree trunks. Pinecones crunched beneath her hiking boots. The thin, cold air caught her as she climbed.

Halfway up the slope she ducked behind another boulder. She crouched with her back against the stone. It was cold, rough, solid. Birdsong had died and all she could hear was the water rushing in the river below.

She took out her phone. Heard it *ping*.

She had a message.

Gabe stood on the riverbank, scanning the far side of the gorge. He could no longer see Jo.

Autumn, spear in hand, walked over. "Something wrong?"

"Can you spot Jo?"

Autumn walked upstream. After a minute, she pointed. "Behind that rock."

Gabe relaxed, but not by much.

Autumn peered up the hill. "Should I keep her company? Buddy up?"

He turned to her in surprise. "Good idea. As long as you stick together."

Autumn found the inch-deep granite pan and splashed into the river.

She had a message. No — messages. That meant she had a signal. Delicately she tried, again, to call 9-1-1.

Call failed.

The signal had vanished. She moved the phone around. Nothing. She leaned her head back against the rock.

If there was any chance of getting a stable signal, it would be at the crest of the gorge. She would have to keep climbing.

She opened the messages. The first was from Kyle Ritter:

Made the ridge, got signal, but sketchy. So far only texts going, no voice calls. Will continue. See lights downhill to west.

She wrote back:

Halfway up slope, will follow.

She tried to send, failed, and left it in the queue.
The next message was from Evan Delaney.
Evan.
Jo hadn't checked in with her after forty-eight hours.
Maybe, please — maybe Evan was pissed off and trying
to reach her.

Found owner of Recent Call number from
Wylie's phone. BAD NEWS. Ex-con, violent.
Name Ruby Ratner. DANGEROUS. CALL ME.

Her heart pounded. A lead. They had a lead in the
murder of Phelps Wylie. But that didn't matter to her at
the moment. She tried to redial Evan's number.
Call failed.
She stood and kept climbing. Was her phone
damaged after all — could it receive calls, but not make
them? It pinged again with one more message from
Evan. She ducked low and stared at the display. And
stopped.
She tried to calm herself, told herself she was seeing
things in the dusk, that the shock of the day's events
was causing her to misunderstand.
She began to run up the slope. She wasn't mistaken.
This was too much of a coincidence, and she didn't
believe in coincidence. Just nasty, colliding chance.
Past rocks and trees she ran. Her lungs burned. The
wind kicked against her, and the first drops of rain

pattered through the pines and hit her face. Two hundred yards above her, the hillside peaked.

No signal.

The message Evan had sent her was a photo. Taken from Evan's own phone, it was an image of Ruby Ratner. It had been taken from some kind of cheesy flyer.

Red Rattler! Horseback riding/roping lessons. Former Pro Rodeo Circuit cowboy.

Sucking air, she reached the crest of the hill. She aimed west, in the direction Dustin had gone, at a run.

Evan had sent her the photo of a man in a cowboy hat. He had a white circle around the blue iris of his left eye. It looked like a white snake. He was grinning like the Reaper.

It was the Bad Cowboy. It was Kyle Ritter.

CHAPTER
TWENTY-FIVE

Dustin trudged behind Kyle, hands stuffed into the pockets of his sweatshirt. The wind had turned cold. His entire body felt bruised from the crash, and his hangover was pounding.

"I'm sure I saw the light over there. To the west," he said.

The shadows were gone, flattened by the dusk and the lowering clouds. Rain speckled his face.

They were headed southwest, on the downslope about a mile past the crest of the gorge. The pines were thinning out. As the first fat drops of rain pinged to earth, the smell of dust sharpened in the air.

Dustin began to jog. "Yeah, I'm sure that's it. That's west, right?"

Kyle kept walking, eyes on the horizon. He took off his baseball cap. "That's where the sun went down. So, yes."

Dustin gained speed on the downslope. He broke out of the trees into an open meadow. Ahead he saw something better. A barbed-wire fence.

He ran toward it. "Private property. Somebody lives here."

Kyle called out from behind him. "Slow down. This could be the Ponderosa. We might still be ten miles from somebody's house."

"What-a-rosa?"

"*Bonanza*, for God's sake."

Reaching the fence, Dustin ducked and climbed through. A barb caught and tore his sweatshirt, but he didn't care. He ran across the meadow. He knew he'd seen a light someplace on the far side, farther down the hill.

Halfway to a copse of yellow cottonwood trees, he heard the cows. Mooing.

"Hey," he called, though he knew hollering at cows was stupid. Cows wouldn't help him. Behind him Kyle laughed, like he was a dope.

But cows didn't stay out all night, did they? Didn't they have to go back in the barn? And they didn't have cattle GPS. Somebody had to . . . to . . . round them up.

"Hey," he repeated.

Behind him, Kyle whistled, like he'd put two fingers to his teeth. Dustin glanced back. Kyle was pointing south.

A man on a horse was riding across the meadow.

Dustin's heart kicked. "Over here." He waved wildly and sprinted toward the stranger.

The man on the horse wore a tan cowboy hat and black down vest over a denim shirt. He came toward Dustin at a trot. When Dustin got within a hundred yards, he saw that the man had on rawhide gloves and a scowl. And that he had a shotgun slung next to his saddle.

Dustin raised his hands. "Man, we need your help."

The horseman pulled back on the reins and turned his mount sideways to Dustin. "Is that right?"

"We've been in an accident."

The man hauled out the shotgun. "First, tell me what you're doing on my land."

Jo was blowing hard when she reached the top of the ridge. Through the pines, the wind gusted and rain spit cold against her face.

She looked downhill for any sign of Dustin and Kyle. The forest was too thick. She looked at her phone. Still no signal.

Her skin was creeping. Kyle Ritter was without doubt Ruby Ratner. Ratner was the Bad Cowboy. Kyle had lied about his identity.

Evan's text warned that he was a dangerous ex-con. Jo could read between the lines: He had been involved in the death of Phelps Wylie. His phone number — there on Jo's display, with his text message to her — matched the number in Phelps Wylie's Recent Calls list.

Stop, Jo. Think. Why had Kyle texted her? Did he want to draw her away from the safety of the group? Maybe. But Dustin was in imminent danger. She had to find him and get him away from Kyle.

And she had to warn the rest of the group and get them to safety too.

But without a phone signal, all she could do was queue up text messages, and hope she would pass through a zone where a cell tower might pick up her signal and shoot them off.

Hands shaking, she punched the buttons on the phone.

To Gabe:

DANGER Kyle IS bad cowboy, LINK TO WYLIE. Must move group ESCAPE.

Though she hadn't found his phone, maybe he had in the time since she'd left.

She had no mobile phone contacts for the Tuolumne County Sheriff's Office, and she couldn't text 9-1-1 for local emergency response. She frantically texted the best cop she knew.

HELP. Hijacked off state logging road near mile 92, E of turnout for mine trail. Crashed, in gorge. Hostiles armed, coming. TRIANGULATE.

She addressed it to Lt. Amy Tang of the SFPD.

Message failed. She told the phone to keep trying. Send the damned thing. Take wing, whenever, soon.

She put the phone in her pocket and ran down the slope, toward a thinning in the line of trees.

Dustin stopped in the field, chest heaving, hands raised. The man on the horse sat in the saddle, one hand on the reins, trying to keep his horse from wheeling. He continued to aim his shotgun at Dustin.

"What are you doing on my property?"

What was this, a scene out of some old Western? "We were in a crash, a couple miles from here, into this river. People are hurt. We need the cops and an ambulance."

"How'd you get here? Didn't you see the fence?"

"Man, that's exactly *why* we're here, because we saw your fence. It's civilization. Sorry I'm tromping on your cow pasture, but my friend's been shot."

The rancher's horse sidestepped and tossed its head. "Shot?"

Kyle stepped forward. "Sir, I apologize for Dustin here. He's been through a real trauma." He pointed at the Edge Adventures logo on his hat. "I work for an outfit that takes people on adventure outings in the backcountry. Bunch of college kids with me today, and basically we got carjacked. The vehicle's wrecked in a gorge over those hills to the east, and people are hurt. We need law enforcement in significant strength and rescue evac."

Kyle's eyes were bright and intense. With his hands in the air, he looked like a supplicant. Dustin nodded in agreement with him.

"So frog march us to your property line if you want. Have your horse there kick our asses halfway back to San Francisco. Hell, invoice Edge Adventures for your time tonight. But once you do all that, phone for help, 'cause otherwise a bunch of folks is gonna die."

The rancher looked suspicious but concerned. He was in his late fifties, with a tanned, round face and a solid belly that spoke of a love of good steak. He stared from Kyle to Dustin and back again.

He lowered the shotgun. "My house is beyond that stand of trees at the bottom of the pasture. We can phone the sheriff and County Search and Rescue from there."

He returned the shotgun to its scabbard beside the saddle. Then he wheeled the horse and spurred it toward the trees at the far edge of the pasture.

Dustin ran after him. He felt Kyle close at his heels.

CHAPTER
TWENTY-SIX

"Double park," Tina said.

Evan pulled her Mustang to the side of the road. They were on Russian Hill, in a quiet neighborhood of apartment buildings with bay windows and Easter-egg-colored Victorian homes. Monterey pines were a vivid green in the sunset. A cable car passed by at the corner, heading downhill toward Fisherman's Wharf. In a small park, a group of young men were playing basketball, scrapping and shouting to one another.

Tina jumped out, dodged between parked cars, and ran up the front steps at a small house with brick red trim. Evan put on her flashers and followed.

The porch light was on. Tina's key jangled as she unlocked the front door. "Jo?"

In the front hall she kicked a pile of mail that had fallen through the slot. She rushed down the front hall, glanced in the living room, turned into the kitchen. "Jo."

The house was small but exquisite. Evan liked small but exquisite living spaces, tucked away from the road, where you could observe the world without it scrutinizing you back.

The compact living room had a sense of spaciousness. Modern furniture, a Persian rug on sanded hardwood, Japanese wood-block prints on the walls. Gold orchids, throw pillows in red and orange and white, a spread of color like the furnace of a forge.

A table lamp was on in the hall. The place looked exactly like a house that had been locked up while its owner went away for the weekend.

Tina ran out of the kitchen and up the stairs. Thirty seconds later she ran back down. "She isn't here."

"She didn't go alone," Evan said. "Would her boyfriend —"

"Gabe."

"And he . . ."

"He can take care of himself. He's a PJ with the Air National Guard, for God's sakes. And Jo can take care of *herself*. But they went to an abandoned mine, and you said you found a connection to this ex-con . . ."

Evan jammed her hands in her back pockets. "Anybody else she might have contacted?"

"Maybe the guy next door." Tina locked up and they hurried down the steps. "Ferd keeps an eye on the street. Mainly because he has a major crush on Jo and he's always hoping to run into her." She made a face. "Or to get her to diagnose his latest ailment. He's a bit of a hypochondriac."

Evan said, "Was that Gabe's photo in Jo's office — looked like they were camping in Yosemite?"

Tina led her along the sidewalk. "That's Daniel. Jo's husband."

Evan glanced at her sharply.

"He died three years ago."

"I didn't know. I'm sorry."

"Medevac helicopter crash. He was an ER doctor. Jo escaped just before it went down." Tina glanced at her. "She is one lucky cat. But even cats get only so many lives."

Next door, a redbrick mansion loomed over the street. The plants that lined the walk were sculpted as if by an exacting Brazilian waxer. Statues of Roman gods adorned the balcony, fat cupids and leering goat men. Tina pounded on the door.

The man who answered looked both eager and nervous. "Tina?"

"Ferd, have you heard from Jo today?"

He wore a Compurama T-shirt and had enough gel in his hair to lubricate defibrillator paddles. When Tina mentioned Jo, he stood taller and flushed a deep red.

"No. What's wrong?"

"She drove to the Sierras to do some work for a case and was supposed to go to Yosemite this afternoon. She hasn't checked into the hotel."

He actually clasped his hands and began wringing them. "I don't know anything about it. But you look so worried. Come in, come in."

Evan followed Tina inside. The hardwood floor and heavy maroon drapes gave the house a nineteenth-century feel. The staircase was grand, in a *Phantom of the Opera* way. Gamers' magazines and a textbook on simian behavior sat on the hall table.

Ferd scratched his chest as though he were breaking out in a rash. "I saw her truck pull away this morning about ten. You can't reach her at all?"

Evan said, "I think it's time to take this to another level. We should get somebody looking for Jo."

Tina nodded, fretful. "I know who to call. She's an SFPD homicide detective. Her name's Amy Tang."

CHAPTER
TWENTY-SEVEN

The wind whistled through the pines. Lightning flashed, illuminating tree trunks in stark black and white. Downhill a few hundred yards, Jo saw that the forest opened into a clearing.

The thunder rolled. Dustin and Kyle had headed west, downhill, this way. She slowed. She didn't want to come upon Kyle unaware. She needed to get Dustin away from him — but if she couldn't find him soon, she would have to give up and get back to the Hummer.

She reached the edge of the trees. In the stormy sunset, she faced a broad meadow. About two hundred yards from the tree line, a barbed-wire fence ran across the ground.

A fence meant private property. It meant somebody owned this land and might be around. Her spirits leapt.

Far across the pasture she heard cattle lowing. A herd of shorthorns was huddled on the distant edge of the pasture, where the forest resumed.

She ran to the fence. Just outside it she saw a crumpled cigarette pack. It was the brand Kyle had pulled from his pocket earlier.

She eked her way through the barbed wire and took off across the meadow.

* ★ *

Dustin and Kyle ran alongside the loping horse. The rancher peppered them with questions.

How many people were trapped? What were their injuries?

"How did you get carjacked?"

"Long story," Dustin hacked. He could barely keep up.

"We have another few hundred yards to go before we reach the phone. I have time to hear it."

Kyle was wheezing, going at a hard run in the altitude. "Man, we need your help. The guys who did it have friends out there. They'll be back."

"What are you saying?" the rancher said.

"You got more guns at home? Ammo, a rifle, something we can use to protect ourselves? 'Cause these hombres ain't playing around."

Dustin understood what Kyle was saying. He wondered why the rancher didn't just ride ahead and call the cops.

"We're not going to break into your house and steal your stuff," he said.

Kyle shot him a pinched look. He rubbed a hand over his chest.

"What?" Dustin said. "I'm too tired to beat around the bush. Mister, we're in bad trouble. Just gallop on ahead and phone the sheriff."

The rancher glanced down from beneath his cowboy hat. He seemed to be sizing Dustin up.

"Where exactly is this wrecked Hummer?" he said.

Dustin wanted to kiss him. "In the gorge, off the logging, where it turns to gravel. It's —"

"*Oh my Lord.*"

With a hard thud, Kyle fell to the ground.

Dustin turned. "You okay?"

Kyle rolled and grabbed his chest. His face contorted. "I can't . . ."

The rancher wheeled his horse around. "You all right?"

"Can't breathe."

Dustin dropped to one knee at his side. "What's wrong?"

"Chest. Tight." He gulped a breath.

The rancher slung a leg over the saddle, climbed down, and knelt next to Kyle at Dustin's side.

Dustin looked up at the rancher. "I think he's having a heart attack."

The man took off his hat. Gravely, he said, "Where's the pain?"

"Left arm, my chest. Oh God." Kyle squeezed his eyes shut.

The rancher eyed him for several long, hard seconds. "We'd better call an ambulance."

He put his hands on his knee and made to stand. Kyle gripped his sleeve. "Don't leave me here."

Dustin said, "Get him on your horse."

"I have to ride back to the house to call an ambulance."

"We may not have time for an ambulance to get here. You have a car at your house? A truck? I'll drive him to the hospital."

The rancher paused, hesitant, but looking at Dustin's face, he finally softened.

"Son, on this side of the gorge we're twenty miles from access to the logging road. You're right, we need to drive him. Help me lift him into the saddle."

Dustin slung Kyle's arm around his shoulder. "We're going to take care of you, dude. You're going to be okay."

The rancher tossed Kyle's other arm over his shoulder and they carefully lifted him to his feet. The rancher said, "What are your names?"

"I'm Dustin, and this is Kyle."

"I'm John Yarrow. Let's get him in the saddle."

They walked toward the horse. Kyle's feet twisted and dragged. He gasped for breath. "Hurry."

"Almost there," Dustin said.

Kyle glanced up at the horse. He was virtually hanging in the other men's grasp. Yarrow grabbed him tighter. "I'll lift you."

Kyle groaned and pitched forward in pain, his arm slipping from Yarrow's shoulder. He lurched forward out of Dustin's grasp.

He took two fast steps ahead of them and reached the horse. He pulled the shotgun from its scabbard on the saddle.

Dustin said, "Kyle?"

Kyle said nothing. He swept the barrel around.

Yarrow leapt for the gun.

CHAPTER
TWENTY-EIGHT

Haugen pulled the Volvo off the road on a curve with an unobstructed line of sight to the sky south of him. He dialed the satellite phone.

After a few seconds' delay, it rang. The voice modulator was attached. And this phone connected through an exchange in the UK, so that geo-location would be impossible. Nobody could track him.

Peter Reiniger answered curtly. "You're not going to get what you want. I don't deal with extortionists."

"But you are dealing with me. You're having this conversation. You answered, you haven't hung up, and you aren't going to," Haugen said. "Keep this up, and your daughter will walk away without a scratch."

"You won't let me phone my lawyer or the company's emergency action team, so how —"

"They don't need to be involved. Perhaps you were too shocked the first time to understand me."

"Then explain," Reiniger said.

"It's about maximizing returns. It's about value for money."

"Put it on the table."

"If you want your daughter back, you're going to pay me twenty million dollars. You're going to transfer it to an account number I will give you."

The connection crackled. "Twenty million? Are you crazy? I can't get that money."

"Stop complaining. You sound like a whiny schoolboy."

Haugen curbed himself. He had to slow his words, make sure his voice and vocabulary couldn't tip Reiniger off. He didn't want anybody to suspect his identity. But this was such a delicious moment that it was nearly impossible to control his . . . venom.

Reiniger loved games. Haugen had discovered this about him. Reiniger liked to test his subordinates, put them through the wringer under the guise of self-enlightenment. But now it was Haugen's turn to put Reiniger to the test.

"I did not ask if you could get the money. I said if you want to see you daughter alive, you will pay me. You have until 6a.m. The clock starts now."

"Wait — no, you can't —"

"I can. I am. Do it."

Reiniger certainly could do it. Haugen knew *exactly* how he could arrange the payment. He had only one way to secure the funds, and that realization had to be hitting him between the eyes. He knew how to add. He knew where his marbles were.

And Reiniger undoubtedly knew what would happen when he paid. His partners in Reiniger Capital would be unhappy. Their backers would be livid. Peter Reiniger would pay a heavy price for ransoming

Autumn. He might lose his company. He might be taken to court, or worse.

Perfect.

"You're operating in a mental battle space that's incorrectly configured," Haugen said. "You still think this is about making sensible business decisions. You think it's about maintaining your reputation as a hedge fund great white shark."

"You bastard, that's not what it's about."

"The game board has been upended. When we finish this call, you will phone your partners in Singapore. They're always ready to make a provision for seamless financial transactions."

Reiniger was quiet for a long moment. "When do I get my daughter back?"

"When I say."

"That's insane."

"It's no more insane than you staying at the helm of Reiniger Capital when others in your employ take the fall for you."

He shouldn't have said that — he realized it as soon as the words slipped from his mouth. But Reiniger *should* feel worried. He should be concerned about Haugen's rationality. Let him worry that a madman had his baby girl.

"I'll make the call," Reiniger said.

"Good. Besides, why are you worrying? Reiniger Capital insures against kidnap, does it not? Senior executives, spouses, and children."

Haugen had analyzed this too. Reiniger Capital insured its senior management against kidnapping in the amount of ten million dollars. There was only one problem for Peter Reiniger, capitalist reptile, iguana-in-Armani.

Haugen stared at the sky. The clouds boiled overhead, gray and threatening. The strangled silence on Reiniger's end, the purity of its helplessness, was sweet.

Reiniger's voice rose, stress bleeding through. "Just give me my daughter back, you bastard."

Haugen smiled. It was all so neat. And Reiniger was going to help him tie the bow.

"Now, for part two. The jet."

The Town Car raced back toward the airport. Peter Reiniger clutched the phone. His chest felt like a band had been placed around it. *Kidnap insurance.*

This cocksucker on the other end of the line had done his research. Reiniger Capital did insure senior executives and their families against ransom demands.

But children were insured for two million dollars. This bastard wanted twenty.

Reiniger could barely breathe. The animal would kill Autumn's friends, one by one, and then he would kill Autumn. He had to get the money.

There was only one way to do it: by raiding Reiniger Capital's cash reserves.

Reiniger Capital had just over a billion dollars in gross assets under management. That money was invested on behalf of the fund's select group of private clients. It was invested in stocks and bond funds and credit default swaps and collateralized debt obligations. It was 98 percent invested.

But the business kept 2 percent of assets in liquid form — cash — as a reserve. Twenty million.

Reiniger could get it. He could access it instantaneously, day or night.

He would use it to buy Autumn's freedom.

His chest squeezed. This would cost him dearly. Because raiding the reserve account would have drastic consequences for his fund and investors. It would trigger immediate demands for collateral to secure the depleted balance. He would have to call in payment from his biggest investors to cover the withdrawal.

Painful didn't cover it. Catastrophic did. His fund was highly leveraged, as were his partners' investments. They'd have to scramble to meet their obligations to him.

But that was down the line. Right now, what counted was that *he could do this*. He had the means, at his fingertips, to save his daughter.

"Tell me where to send the money," he said.

"That's better," the voice said. "That's a good first step."

The man gave him an account number. Reiniger scribbled it down.

"What about the jet?" he said.

"A Gulfstream G-Five," the voice said. "I want it on the runway at Reno airport at 6a.m., fully fueled and with a fresh crew, ready to fly."

"All right."

"Not any jet — your jet. And I want you there to greet me."

Jo ran across the field. The grass was beaten down, the earth rocky. In the west, lightning flashed. Cold rain spattered her face and shoulders.

The thunder rolled. At the far side of the pasture, a gate led to a path that headed deep into the trees. She climbed over and kept going.

A deeper thunder cracked the air. She jumped.

The second blast came moments later.

In the pasture, the cattle lowed. Crows cawed overhead and took flight in the stormy dusk. She ducked into the trees, chest pounding.

The gunshots echoed and faded. She forced herself to be still and listen. All she heard was the wind and the nervous shuffling of the cattle in the field.

Two shots. She was sure. From a big gun. She couldn't tell how far away.

She ducked deeper into the trees and then, slowly, warily, began to parallel the trail. She felt as spooked as a cat. The rain pattered harder. Lightning in the clouds bleached the scene ahead. She stopped.

Though she was still deep in the trees, she could see it. Barely. The wind slapped her in the face. Heart drumming, she edged her way toward the trail. Another flash of lightning etched the view. Just for a moment — white, blue scale, dark.

Two people lay on the trail.

One lay face-up, arms thrown wide — a big man in a down vest and cowboy boots. The second lay a few feet

212

beyond him, face-down, as if he'd been flung to the ground with violent force. Jo recognized his USF sweatshirt. It was Dustin.

The thunder fell across the hillside like rocks in an oil barrel.

Jo stood frozen, looking at the men. Looking around the trail, the trees, trying to see where Kyle was.

The rain came. Full on, cold, whipped by the wind. She could see nobody, no movement. None at all.

She bolted from the trees toward the two men.

The wind blew cold rain into her face. In the distance, the cattle lowed. She reached the big man in cowboy boots. His face was ruddy and weathered. His eyes were open and unseeing. A blast to the chest had cored him.

She closed his eyes, her hands shaking, and ran to Dustin's side.

"No," she moaned.

He had a massive blast wound in the center of his back. His sweatshirt was shredded by buckshot and sopping with dark blood. She pressed her fingers to his neck, searching for a carotid pulse.

He was gone. Death, she knew, had probably been immediate. But the moment of fear beforehand would have been horrific. The blast had torn through him, narrow spread, blown apart his spine and probably most of his lungs and his heart. Shotgun, large bore. Close range. In the back.

She swallowed the urge to retch, to scream, to cry, to try to help the poor kid.

She looked around. Where was Kyle?

She had to presume the shotgun belonged to the dead man. Kyle had gotten it and killed the rancher and Dustin. Where had he gone?

The rain peppered her back. It chilled her hands and face. Lightning flashed again.

The rancher's pockets had been turned inside out. Had Kyle taken his keys? Lying by the man's hip was his wallet. It was open and had been emptied of cash. A snapshot flicked in the wind. A woman with two young kids.

More lightning flashed. And in the stark shadows it supplied, she saw tracks: boots and hooves.

They followed clearly along beaten tire tracks.

Kyle was headed for the rancher's home. Maybe for his family. She stood up and ran after him.

Kyle kicked open the door at John Yarrow's knotted-pine ranch house. The lights were off. The house was cold.

He stormed through the place room by room, shotgun raised. He threw open closet doors and peered under beds. Anybody who thought he could stay alive by hiding had another thing coming. But if Yarrow had a wife or kids, they were long gone. There was only one plate in the kitchen sink. One glass drying on the drain board.

He found a plate of chicken in the fridge and tore into it with his bare hands. He drank a quart of milk and tossed the carton on the floor. He went to Yarrow's bedroom and found a T-shirt and heavy flannel shirt. They would have fit him when he was young and fat.

214

But they would be warm. In the front closet he found a brown duster. Tonight was going to be a bitch, weather-wise.

He dumped the Edge Adventures polo shirt. He said good riddance to Kyle Ritter too. Who cared anymore if he was using the alias? Ruben Kyle Ratner, Kyle Ritter, Red Rattler — all the same to him. His driver's license had worked good enough to pass Edge Adventures' background check, but then the license he'd given them didn't match the name on his records in the California prison system.

Finally, he popped out the colored contact lenses. He checked his eyes in the bathroom mirror. The white ring that circled the blue iris of his left eye was, medically speaking, a defect. *Arcus juvenilis*. It didn't mess up his vision, but it had a powerful effect on the weak willed and superstitious. White fire snaked around his blue eye. It intimidated.

Outside, lightning smeared the clouds and thunder rumbled. Rain chittered against the windows. He rifled through drawers and closets, looking for more weapons, but the shotgun was apparently the only firearm Yarrow owned. In a kitchen drawer he did find a box of shells. He emptied them into the pockets of the duster.

Then he went looking for the phone.

His own cell phone still had no signal. So he couldn't tell if Jo Beckett had taken the hint in his text — to follow him out of the gorge. He hoped she had. *Here, kitty, kitty. Come this way, all alone.* He scrolled through his phone book and found the number he wanted.

He picked up Yarrow's landline and dialed.

A woman answered. "Yes?"

"I got Autumn Reiniger and her friends in my sights. You want the money? You deal with me."

CHAPTER
TWENTY-NINE

Sabine lowered the phone. "Dane, you need to hear this."

The Volvo droned up the two-lane highway in the lowering dusk, climbing through the pine forest into the mountains. The wipers squelched across the windshield. Haugen flicked a glance at her from behind the wheel.

Sabine's face was sober under the dashboard lights. She put the phone on speaker. "Say that again."

A staticky voice came through. "I'm in the driver's seat now."

Haugen turned sharply. "Ratner?"

"Surprise, surprise."

"Why are you calling?" With a queasy burst of suspicion, Haugen added, "Where are you?"

"I'm way ahead of you, is where. I'm ready to dig Autumn Reiniger and her buddies a grave you'll never find. So whatever it is you're pulling, you're now pulling in a new direction. Mine."

A blast of rain obscured the view. Haugen said, "What are you talking about?"

"You didn't know, did you? I was along on Miss Reiniger's birthday outing. Seems she has a phobia, so her daddy asked Edge Adventures to add it to the scenario. And Edge outdid theirselves. They tracked down the guy who, what's the word . . . *instigated* the phobia. They found the actual Red Rattler for their role-playing shindig."

Haugen frowned at Sabine. She shrugged and mouthed, *No idea. Never heard anything about that.*

Ratner's voice took on a nasal whine. "Never thought to include me in your plans, did you? I had to find out about this the hard way. Get carjacked, in a damned limousine, by your gang of candy-ass stooges."

"What do you want?" Haugen said.

"You can guess," Ratner said.

In the kitchen at the rancher's ransacked house, Kyle Ratner — *that's Mr Ruby Kyle Ratner to you, partner* — broke open the breech of the shotgun and began loading shells.

"This is what it's all been for, ain't it?" he said.

"You have no idea what you're messing with here," Haugen said.

"No, I got a good idea. And it's getting clearer every minute. This carjacking, scooping Autumn off the street, was the whole point of everything from the beginning, wasn't it? It's what's gonna get you your money and your mojo and that round-rumped redhead, am I right?"

He smiled in the dim light from the open fridge.

Haugen said, "I don't know what you think you're doing, but you need to put down the phone, back away from this, and disappear from the scene."

Kyle barked a laugh. "Disappear? You made a mistake when your stooges pointed their weapons at me. I am the best operative you had. And you blew it. Now we're gonna deal. Or the only thing that disappears is all that money you're planning to take from Peter Reiniger."

Over the line, Kyle could hear noise in the background. Sounded like Haugen and Sabine were in a car, headed someplace fast. Headed this way.

"I want in," Kyle said. "You're planning a big score. Well, guess what, partner?"

"I'm not your partner. I'm your boss."

"No. You *were* my boss. But you *fired* me," he said. "I rode that Hummer down to the bottom of a ravine with a bunch of screaming brats. I'd say that constituted a field promotion. So this score now involves both of us."

Haugen paused. "I don't need to talk to you any longer."

Kyle's smile deepened. He knew all about Dane Haugen. "Yes, you do. You don't know where the birthday gang is. You don't know how quick I can kill them off. You don't even know how quick I can expose you as the person behind this — behind this and so much more. Ain't that right?"

"You're in way over your head," Haugen said.

"That's rich. Who threw me in the deep end? Why, I think you did. But now that I'm face-down in the muck, I see everything. I see how much money you didn't want to tell me about. So what do you say? Fifty-fifty split. That's fair."

"You're out of your mind."

"Right. Sixty-forty for me."

"Shut up, Ratner. This is way beyond you. Get involved and you're going to screw it up for everybody. You'll get nothing."

"Then neither will you." Kyle's smile stretched his lips. "I suggest you reconsider your position. We'll talk again when you find the crash site. I'll have been there and gone."

"Don't —"

Kyle hung up. Then he ripped the phone from the wall.

Haugen would reconsider. He would reconsider while he was driving like a maniac and sweating through his Prada turtleneck and calfskin gloves.

Treating Ruby Kyle Ratner like an errand boy. Thinking he was stupid. He closed and latched the shotgun's breech.

In the rancher's garage he found a gasoline can. He poured a stinking trail from the front door to the pile of greasy rags he heaped on the kitchen floor. He dragged the propane tank for the barbecue into the house for good measure.

He'd kept hold of his lighter, back when Mr Gabe Search-and-Rescue asked everybody to donate survival supplies. Zippo. Clean and reliable, it caught the gasoline with a bright happy flame.

He was running for the rancher's truck by the time the inside of the house lit with laughing fire.

CHAPTER
THIRTY

Under the scarlet glow of the dashboard lights, Haugen stared at his phone in astonishment. Ratner. His ulcer burned. The gall.

The storm outside the Volvo had turned vicious. He seemed to see it through a pulsing, bile-yellow scrim. *Ratner* was the Edge Adventures employee who had been on the beach at Candlestick Point — the newbie, whom he hadn't been able to see clearly. Ratner. The unmitigated *gall*.

Sabine and Stringer sat like crash-test dummies, dumfounded and unsure of how they should react.

Haugen shoved the phone at Sabine. "Call Von. Tell him we have a freelance thief attempting to commandeer the mission."

She punched the number. "Ratner's got a head start on us."

"Tell Von to eliminate him at the first opportunity." He put the vehicle in gear and floored it up the highway. "And tell Von to eliminate everybody besides Autumn. Don't wait for us to arrive. See one, shoot one. He needs to do whatever it takes to get Autumn *now*."

She put the phone to her ear. Haugen pushed the Volvo faster.

Jo jogged raggedly along the track. It was nearly full dark now. The wind channeled through the pines and the rain came in hard bursts.

Why had Kyle killed Dustin and the rancher? Again she seemed to hear the eerie voice on the cell phone of the dead lawyer, Wylie, promising *punishment.*

She had to presume Kyle had killed Wylie and dumped his body in the abandoned mine. How had Edge Adventures managed to get mixed up with Kyle, beyond hiring him to replay Autumn's childhood encounter with the Bad Cowboy?

Who the hell was he?

And if he was headed to the rancher's house, what did he want — money, a phone, a vehicle? Kyle had shot the rancher and Dustin without mercy. She thought of the snapshot in the rancher's wallet: the woman, the smiling children. The image drove her to keep up her pace.

The rain scoured down on a gust of wind and caught her flat across the face.

Ahead, an orange glow flickered to life. It rose and pulsed and backlit the trunks of the pines. It was a fire, a big one.

Behind the wind and spatter of the rain, she heard an engine. She ducked into the trees. The engine sounded loud and heavy — a pick-up truck. Headlights picket-fenced through the forest ahead. The truck was coming this way, jangling over the rutted cow path.

222

Jo dodged deeper into the trees and flattened herself against the ground. The headlights drew nearer. The crooked lights of an old Chevy truck veered into sight. It was ancient and rusty and its suspension groaned as it ached its way over ruts in the trail. It swerved past her and kept going.

The orange glow blossomed vividly and the ground shuddered. A moment later the explosion boomed, flat and hard.

She got up. Sticking to the trees, she ran toward the fire. Soon she saw a ranch house fully engulfed in flames, a jet-black shell screaming orange and red from within, black smoke boiling from the roof.

Her hopes of finding people and a phone and help were futile. She ran around the burning structure, calling out, hoping that nobody was trapped inside. She got no answer.

The burning garage was empty. No car, no motorcycle, no bike. And the dirt driveway, it became apparent, meandered deeper into the forest — the house was nowhere near the highway. She was still cut off from civilization.

She made a full circle of the house and stopped, shoulders heaving, on the verge of tears. The heat became a radiant wall against her body. It felt like life and death all at once. The crackle grew to a roar that overcame all else.

Until she heard a frightened whinny.

She found the rancher's horse in its corral, shying away from the flames, too skittish to run toward the open gate.

★ ★ ★

The wind whipped rain against the sides of the Hummer. Lark ran back from the riverbank and shimmied through the smashed-out window to get out of the storm. Gabe walked down to the water's edge. The river was rushing over the rocks. It looked purple, almost black, in the strange, deepening light.

He checked his diver's watch. He looked up the gorge, wondering where Jo had gone.

It had been fifteen years since Jo had climbed on a horse. In the hierarchy of dangerous rides, she figured they ranked as less powerful than motorcycles but ten times as unpredictable. But Kyle had the rancher's truck and a head start. The horse might be surefooted, fast, and able to climb through terrain the rancher's truck couldn't.

She put up her hands. "Easy, boy. Easy."

The horse tossed its head and danced away from her. It was saddled and had on its bridle. The reins hung free, draped in the dirt. She approached slowly, keeping her voice low.

"Whoa, boy. Whoa."

The horse stopped and lowered its head. In the reflected firelight, its eyes were liquid. She walked toward it, her hand trembling.

"That's it. Whoa." It was the only thing she could think to say, and apparently it actually, really worked with horses.

"Whoa, boy. It's okay." She stroked the horse's flank, felt its muscles twitch. It smelled of sweat and dust and leather of the saddle. She took the reins.

"Make you a deal. Let me up, and I'll get you out of here."

Carefully she put a foot in the stirrup. She grabbed the saddle horn, pulled herself up, swung her leg over, and settled into the creaking saddle.

She checked her balance. The stirrups were too long for her; she could barely keep her feet in them. But she had no time to figure it out. She jammed her hiking boots as far in the stirrups as she could get them.

She saw the empty scabbard. She didn't need to be told that it was designed to hold a long gun.

Gripping the reins and twisting her fingers into the horse's mane, she said, "Okay, let's go."

She kicked the horse in the ribs. It took off like a stone thrown from a slingshot and raced out of the corral.

"Dammit."

She gripped its mane, pitching crazily backward, as it galloped through firelight up the trail. She pulled herself forward. The animal bunched and rolled beneath her. In the gusting rain, she could barely see.

She had to get back to the Hummer. If Kyle got there first, God knows what he would do. And nobody knew he was coming.

Two minutes later, she approached the wide spot where the bodies of Dustin and the rancher lay on the path. The horse was going at a hard canter, and she was squeezing the reins and its mane, the saddle horn, everything she could. She had barely gotten into the rhythm of its gait, beginning to feel that she wasn't going to fly off, when it veered away from the track.

"Whoa," she called.

The horse dug its back legs into the dirt and stopped sharply. Jo's inertia carried her forward. She slid up the horse's neck like it was a Slip 'N Slide. She tackled it, held on, bumped back down half out of the saddle.

The horse tossed its head. It sidestepped and tried to wheel. Jo pulled on the reins.

"Whoa, boy. Whoa."

It didn't want to approach the bodies in the path. She pulled on the reins and kicked her heels into its sides and managed to get it to dance half sideways toward the site. As she did, lightning scored the clouds. Her skin wriggled. The rancher's body lay in a different position than she'd seen earlier.

Kyle had driven straight over him. The force of the blow had flipped him over. He lay side-on to poor Dustin, hand draped over his back.

It looked as though the rancher had tried to pat Dustin on the shoulder, to say, *Ain't this a low blow*. Thunder warbled, hard and close. Behind it, above the wind, another sound twisted in the air. It was a keening, broken sobbing.

Jo blinked, her skin prickling, and tried to hold the horse still. The night had gone dark again, the bodies indistinguishable from the ground, even with the clouds blowing past, the moonlight cutting through the rain in piebald patches.

The horse threw its head up and down and whinnied.

The keening increased. And a swatch of moonlight passed over the bodies. Out of the trees, hands gripping her head, staggered Autumn.

CHAPTER
THIRTY-ONE

The cop who showed up at Jo's house was an Asian American detective with vivid eyes and a hard glare, dressed in black from head to toe. She greeted Tina and shook Evan's hand.

"Amy Tang, Homicide Detail."

Tang was the size of a mongoose and looked as likely to stand her ground against cobras and all other threats. She knew her way to Jo's kitchen.

"Still no word," Evan said. "Her number is out of service, she hasn't checked in at the Lodge in Yosemite, and she never made it to the sheriff's office in Sonora."

"What time did you last hear from her?"

"Got the text message just before 4p.m. She was on the trail returning from the abandoned mine."

Evan rolled out her USGS topographical map on Jo's kitchen table. "The mine is here. Jo's message indicated she was approximately here" — she tapped a spot — "and even if Jo's a slow hiker, she should have made it back to her truck in an hour, max."

Tang stared at the map. "She's absurdly fit. She'd think this hike was playtime. Was she by herself?"

"Gabe went with her," Tina said. She balled her hands into fists. "You think something happened?"

"I do. But don't panic. She could have gotten a flat tire. Quintana's with her. That alone should reassure you."

Tina nodded tightly, looking the opposite of reassured, as though thinking: If something had happened to Jo *even though she was with Gabriel Quintana*, things had to be bad.

Evan put a hand on the young woman's shoulder. "Think we could rustle up some coffee?"

She didn't want to be presumptuous, but if Tina didn't do something, she was going to pop like a jack-in-the-box.

Tina nodded briskly. "Good idea." She rounded the kitchen counter and began preparing a pot.

Evan turned to Tang. "What do you know about Ruby Kyle Ratner?"

"What do *you* know? Run me through it."

Evan explained how Jo had found Wylie's cell phone, discovered he'd been carjacked, and heard the carjacker's muffled threats. She described how she herself had pieced together partial phone numbers and uncovered Ragnarok Investments. And how she'd met Mrs Ruby Ratner, the pistol-packing muumuu.

From her jacket she got the flyer Mrs Ratner had given her. "I know Ruben Kyle Ratner's an ex-con with a violent record. You could use his photo to terrorize inmates at Gitmo."

On the flyer, Ratner looked lean and leathery. The white ring around his eye gave the appearance of crazed light leaking from within. His gaze was beyond intense.

In it, Evan read both cunning and a challenge. *What you looking at?*

Tang took the flyer. "This is off the record. Background only."

"What can you tell me?"

Tang didn't carry a purse. She wasn't even wearing a badge. Clearly she'd been off duty. She took her phone from her jacket and pulled up the camera roll. On it she had uploaded a series of photos of Ruben Kyle Ratner.

"Here's an early mug shot."

He was softer physically. Much heavier. He was in his early twenties, and he weighed perhaps seventy-five pounds more than he did now.

"Prison takes the weight off and turns it into muscle, doesn't it?" Evan said.

"And into poison," Tang said.

The early-edition Ruby had smooth, round cheeks, like an egg, and a bushy Pancho Villa mustache. A long ponytail hung down his back.

Tang said, "When that lawyer disappeared, the department had its eyes on this guy. You've just brought him back onto our radar."

"Tell me about it."

"Caveat — Phelps Wylie's disappearance was not my case. None of this stuff has officially crossed my desk."

Tina looked up from the burbling coffeemaker. "Didn't Jo get in touch with you?"

"Of course she did. She tried to sweet-talk me into giving her information about the case. But we had no leads strong enough to be considered probable cause."

"What kind of leads did you have?" Evan said.

"Most of them turned out to be dead ends."

"Whose ass are you hanging a big fat towel over? What information did the SFPD have?"

"It was deemed of interest but not dispositive. Until tonight."

"You knew about Ratner?"

"I didn't. But —"

"He's dangerous?" Tina said, rounding the counter and approaching Tang. "And you knew it and didn't tell Jo?"

Tang put her hands in her jacket pockets. She looked smooth and implacable. "The department had a lead on a possible — I emphasize, *possible*, as in tentative, speculative, uncertain — connection between Wylie's car and Ratner."

"The Mercedes?" Evan said. "What connection?"

When Wylie's car turned up abandoned in a Calexico strip mall, everybody had gone wild, thinking he might have crossed the Mexican border and fled the country.

"It's a five-hundred-mile drive from San Francisco to Calexico. Farther than a Mercedes can go on a single tank of gas," Tang said.

She pulled up a new photo. "9p.m. the day Wylie disappeared. Truck stop on I-Five in Bakersfield."

It was a still, grabbed from a CCTV surveillance video at a gas station. Center of the frame, license plate fully visible, was Wylie's black Mercedes.

Nobody was in the car. But walking toward the minimart was a man in a hooded parka. He was white, wearing sunglasses. That was all Evan could discern.

"We think it's Ratner," Tang said.

"He paid with a credit card?"

"Cash."

"Why do you think it's him?" Evan said.

Tang flipped to another photo: inside the minimart, the man with the parka at the counter. Paying for gas and cigarettes and a package of Hostess Ho Hos.

"He withdrew money from the ATM in the minimart," Tang said. "With an ATM card belonging to Mrs Ruby Ratner."

Tina brought the coffeepot. "You've positively ID'ed him?"

"No. These photos are not any kind of proof. But they raised our suspicions. Especially because Ratner is on parole and it's a violation for him to leave San Francisco without informing his parole officer."

"So why didn't you arrest him?" Tina said.

"Mrs Ratner reported her ATM card stolen that morning. And she alibied him. For what that's worth."

"But you knew this felon was the car thief and you did nothing, and now he's done something to Jo?"

Tang raised a hand. "Tina, I knew none of this until forty-five minutes ago. After you phoned me, I checked it out. What I can say now, with much greater assurance, is that because of the evidence Jo and Evan have uncovered, it looks like Ruby Ratner was involved in Wylie's disappearance."

"Involved? He caused it," Tina said. "And he's out there. You have to find Jo."

"We have no evidence that Ratner is within a hundred miles of Jo."

Evan said, "But you're worried, or you wouldn't have brought up his name."

Tang's face was tense. "If he's involved in Wylie's disappearance, it's very bad news. He is not somebody I want Jo to come in contact with, outside of custodial interrogation. In which Ratner is cuffed and shackled to the floor."

Evan's stomach tightened. "You'd better tell us."

"You want me to start with the bank siege or with the mutilations?"

CHAPTER
THIRTY-TWO

Tina sat down at the kitchen table and rubbed her temples. Evan poured coffee for all of them.

"Ruben Kyle Ratner dropped out of high school and struck out for the rodeo circuit," Tang said. "Tried to make it riding saddle broncs. Didn't get far. Made ends meet by petty thievery. Eventually he switched to rodeo clowning, which proved frightening."

"He didn't draw the bulls away from riders who got thrown?" Evan said.

"He did, but somehow always managed to circle back toward the cowboy. And if anybody got trampled or gored, he found it amusing."

"Fun guy."

"He was fired from a number of rodeos. When he left, they'd find tires slashed, other vandalism. Eventually they found horses injured."

"Oh no," Tina said.

"Ratner is a first-class psychopath."

Tina stood, one hand pressed to her lips, and walked to the French doors. The rising moon cast white stripes across her face through the shutters.

Evan said, "You mentioned mutilation. The horses?"

"He knew how to hobble them. Some had to be put down."

Tina's hand trembled. "Oh my God."

"And the bank siege?" Evan said.

"When he was a juvenile. He was the driver, who got tired of hanging around on the street while his buddies grabbed the cash inside."

"He left the getaway car and went into the bank?" Evan said. "Impulsivity is an issue, I'm guessing. And impatience."

Some people said the same about her. She declined to consider the comparison.

Tang nodded. "He ambled in just before the police arrived. His buddies barricaded the front entrance. He ran out the back and ratted on them, like that." She snapped her fingers.

"Not a team player, then."

"He got leniency from the court, because of his age."

"So he's moved on, in terms of his criminal ambitions. Substantially."

"Unfortunately."

Tina turned from the doors. "And this guy now advertises his services as a handyman? So somebody's grandma may hire him to paint her kitchen?"

"Not everybody runs a criminal background check on casual laborers."

Evan said, "I'd venture that almost nobody does."

"And you'd be correct."

"Especially not when said handyman has his mother booking jobs for him." She eyed Tang. "What finally sent him to prison?"

"He put a rattlesnake in a guy's mailbox."

Evan squirmed. "I'm guessing that's the mayhem conviction."

The lieutenant's expression was taut. "The victim spent a month in the ICU and lost his hand."

They were silent for a moment.

Evan said, "What's Ratner's connection with Phelps Wylie? Because he did not randomly target him. On the recording from Wylie's cell phone, the abductor says, 'You know the score here.'"

"I don't know what the connection is. But I know what I'm going to do."

Tang phoned the SFPD and asked for an address check and information on any vehicles Ruben Kyle Ratner owned.

Tina said, "Are you putting out a warrant on him?"

"I don't have probable cause to arrest him yet. I need more evidence. But I want to bring him in so we can interview him as a material witness."

"That's not good enough, not if he's out there with Jo," Tina said.

"I know." Almost delicately, Tang set a hand on Tina's shoulder. "I'm calling the Tuolumne County Sheriff's Office." She nodded at the USGS map. "Show me again which road Jo would have driven to get to the abandoned mine."

Tina looked at her watch. Evan could practically hear the second hand ticking, ticking around.

Jo held tight to the horse's reins and peered up the braided trail at the clearing where the bodies lay. In the moon-shattered light, Autumn stood over Dustin's body. The girl threw her arms wide, dropped to her knees, and wailed.

Grabbing the saddle horn, Jo awkwardly dismounted and led the horse toward her. The horse danced in a circle. Gripping the reins, Jo knelt at Autumn's side. "I'm sorry."

Autumn's shoulders heaved. Her breathing came in choked bursts. Her hands, outstretched above Dustin's body, trembled in the moonlight. She let out another garbled cry, an aching, scathing shout.

"Autumn." Jo put a hand on her shoulder. "Hush."

Autumn grabbed Dustin's sweatshirt. She dug her fingers into the fabric. The wail spiraled into the wind and up into the night. Jo pulled Autumn against her shoulder to muffle her cries.

"No." Autumn pulled away. She grabbed Dustin's body and shook him. A long string of drool slid from her lips and stretched and fell on Dustin's back.

Jo held on to her. "You have to be quiet. The shooter is out there."

Autumn jerked and caught herself mid-cry. Lightning flashed again. Her face was streaked with something beyond fear, beyond nightmare. It was the phosphor shock of death's finality.

Jo's heart went out to her.

Autumn gritted her teeth and tried to suffocate her cries. Her hands gripped Dustin's sweatshirt like she could shake him awake. Jo's eyes welled.

She'd been there. She'd been in the exact same position as the girl, holding on with both hands,

237

looking into the face of the man she'd loved, seeing him gone. And she'd had to be dragged away, screaming and fighting.

"We have to go," Jo whispered. "Now."

Autumn was as tense as electrical wire. "I can't leave him."

"We'll come back. We'll take care of him. But we have to stay alive."

Autumn touched Dustin's hair. "I'm sorry. So sorry."

In the distance, beyond the meadow in the trees, white lights spiked the night. Headlights. They swept across the landscape as the rancher's pick-up turned in a radius around a curve.

Kyle was coming back.

"Come on." Jo pulled Autumn to her feet. "Get on the horse."

She threw the reins over the horse's head, grabbed the saddle horn, and mounted. The headlights swept across them and kept turning, like a lighthouse beam.

Then they stopped. The wind swirled, and Jo heard the pick-up's engine. She heard it change gears.

The lights reversed direction and swept back toward the clearing.

"Up," she said. "Hurry."

Autumn struggled to pull herself into the saddle. The horse stamped its feet and tried to spin. Jo held tight to the reins. Autumn swung a leg over the horse's back and grabbed Jo around the waist and struggled onto the horse's rump behind the saddle.

"Who killed them?"

"Kyle."

Autumn went rigid. "Kyle? *Kyle?* He's one of them?"

"And he's in that truck. He tried to drive up the track all the way to the gorge, but obviously couldn't. He's come back, looking for another way to get there."

The headlights swept across the trees, strobing like an old-time movie reel. They caught Jo and Autumn, and stopped. Spotlight.

"Hang on," Jo said.

She kicked the horse, whipped it with the end of the reins, and held her breath. They took off east toward the forest.

CHAPTER
THIRTY-THREE

The horse clattered over the rough ground, gaining speed, working hard with two riders on its back. Jo urged it forward with her hands. Behind her Autumn bumped around, squeezing tight to her waist. From behind them, the headlights illuminated their path. That was incredibly helpful and very bad. Through the wind Jo heard the round growl of an old, big internal-combustion engine.

"He's coming," Autumn shouted.

Jo squeezed the horse's flanks and fought to keep the toes of her hiking boots in the stirrups. "Hang on."

She bent against the horse's neck, flicked the reins, and shouted at it — "*Hah*. Go, boy. Go."

The horse accelerated. They galloped across the pasture toward the trees. The rain was cold and stinging in the wind. She kept low, bending to the horse's neck, keeping her weight over its shoulders. She might make it. She started to believe. She could get up the hill, get to the ridge and down the other side, all the way on horseback if she had to. In the truck, Kyle would not be able to do that.

It was four hundred yards farther on, in the near dark, that she saw what she had forgotten. The barbed-wire fence.

In the garish light from the pick-up's headlamps, the wire was a dull glint. Jo wouldn't have seen it if not for the rain. They were headed straight for it.

"Oh God."

She pulled on the reins, turned the horse right, and spurred it parallel to the fence. Ahead the cows were bunched, heads in, growing unsettled by the noise of the approaching hooves and the truck.

"I'm slipping," Autumn said.

Jo felt the girl jerk up and down behind her. "Hang on."

"I can't."

Behind them the truck broke from the trees and jounced across the field toward them, lights jinking crazily over the rough ground. The engine gunned. Lightning flashed, and the horse spooked.

It bucked and took off across the field, kicking its hind legs. Autumn cried out, lost her grip on Jo's waist, and thwacked to the ground.

Jo hauled back on the reins. "Whoa. Whoa."

"Help," Autumn shouted.

Jo tugged and groaned and got the horse to slow down and turn. It was frightened, and she knew her own fear was transmitting to it. She kicked its ribs and nudged it forward. The truck was coming.

"I'm caught," Autumn shouted.

Jo saw her in the zigzagging lights of the pick-up. She had been thrown into the barbed-wire fence. She had flown through the gap between two strings of wire — and caught her shoulders on the upper wire, her legs on the bottom. She was tangled like Raggedy Ann, her butt on the ground on the far side of the fence, her clothes and hair snagged on the barbs, pinned.

Jo swung down from the horse's back. Holding on to the reins, she ran to Autumn's side.

"Hurry," Autumn said.

The lights of the pick-up grew brighter. The cattle lowed and milled behind them. Jo picked at Autumn's sleeves. The barbs had gone through and twisted inside the fabric of her sweatshirt.

"I have to pull the sweatshirt off," she said. "Wriggle your arms out."

Autumn panted and twisted and her hands disappeared up the sleeves of the sweatshirt. Jo pulled the sweatshirt over the girl's head. Blood streaked the girl's arms, but Autumn didn't react. Jo picked her jeans free of the barbs. Autumn's gleaming leather riding boots didn't catch on the fence.

"Clear," Jo shouted.

Autumn rolled away, breathing hard, and clambered to her feet on the far side of the fence.

"Run," Jo said.

She took off across the barren ground, aiming for the hills and the tree line two hundred yards away.

The truck was nearly upon Jo. For a second, she thought about crawling through the fence and making a

242

dash for it behind Autumn. But she didn't have the time or the speed. Only the horse did.

She grabbed the saddle horn, jammed her left foot in the stirrup, and shouted crazily at the animal. The cattle scattered in all directions behind her as the truck pounded through the pasture.

The truck's headlights swelled. The horse broke into full flight, with Jo hanging off its left side, one foot dragging on the ground. The horse was powerful, bunching and stretching, racing across the field. If she lost her grip on the saddle horn, she'd fall with her foot caught in the stirrup, and she'd be dragged. Her arms ached. Her hands were wet from the rain. The truck roared across the field.

She smelled leather and the strong, dusty scent of the horse and ozone from the lightning. With a shout, she hauled herself up and threw her upper body across the saddle. She thumped up and down. The horse was running, simply running from the truck alongside the barbed-wire fence.

The truck had not chased Autumn. It was coming after her.

It scattered the cattle and plowed across the field, bucking almost worse than the horse. The horse's head bobbed as it galloped across the pasture. Jo jammed her foot securely in the stirrup and held on to the saddle horn and, teeth gritted, grabbed its mane. For a moment she bounced, out of synch. Then she found the rhythm. She got her balance in the stirrup and swung her right leg over the saddle.

She pressed her knees into the saddle and against the horse's flanks. Behind her the headlights dipped and rose, like a boat on a crazy sea. The truck's suspension crunched.

Fence posts raced along to her left. The night ahead swallowed the view. The headlights caught her, swung up, down, centered again.

Straight ahead, the fence made a ninety-degree turn to the right. It turned in a neat rectangular corner, like the land grant plot it probably had been back in Gold Rush days. Adrenaline flooded her system, scalp to fingers to toes. The horse was blowing. She bent to make herself as tight against it as she could. They raced across the ground, the horse's mane hitting her in the face.

The headlights threw the horse's shadow ahead of Jo, stretching toward the barbed wire, the wire now gleaming and rain slick in the lights.

Then the truck slowed and the lights veered away, to the right, sweeping an arc across the pasture and the night. Jo let out a cry.

The driver had seen the fence. He was anticipating that she would turn. And he was going to cut her off by turning first.

By turning inside her, he would put the driver's window side-on to her. And by doing that, he would give himself a big, unobstructed field of fire. He had the rancher's shotgun. And as an old hunter once told her, the best thing about a big shotgun was the margin of error.

She kicked the horse. She whipped it with the reins and screamed out loud, and she aimed straight at the fence.

244

CHAPTER
THIRTY-FOUR

Under the amber lights in Jo's kitchen, Tang punched numbers on her phone. She said, "I need you to connect me to the Tuolumne County Sheriff's Office."

Tina paced like a frantic cat. Evan couldn't get the young woman to slow down. She took up pacing with her.

Tang squinted out the French windows as, apparently, the call was connected. "This is Lieutenant Amy Tang of the San Francisco Police Department. I need to speak to the watch commander. It's urgent."

A moment later, she said, "Sergeant, I need you to check on a possible missing person."

She laid out the basics quickly and aggressively. Evan could barely hear the Tuolumne County sergeant asking questions. From Tang's face, he seemed to be asking the right questions.

"Dr Beckett is investigating a murder. She hasn't been seen since reporting from her foray on foot to the abandoned mine." She gave him Jo's last-known coordinates. "Thank you. I'll be on this number."

She hung up. "He's on it."

Tina finally stopped pacing. "What's he going to do?"

"Send a deputy to the spot where Jo most likely parked."

Tina tipped her head back. "Why couldn't Jo have a quiet psychotherapy practice, like a normal shrink? Why does she have to put herself on the line?"

Tang said, "We're doing everything we can."

Tina nodded and caught her breath and put her hands to her eyes. "Okay."

Tang glanced at Evan and nodded her into the living room. The cop moved with sharp economy. In black, with the elbows and spiky hair, she reminded Evan of a stealth fighter. Swift, quiet, giving nothing away.

She crossed her arms and faced the bay window. "Finding Jo is mission critical. But it's not my only concern."

"The issue isn't only where Jo is. It's where Ruby Kyle Ratner is," Evan said.

"Right." Tang stared out the window. In the low light, her reflection was a dark wisp, backlit in gold. "We need to presume he's a factor in the death of Phelps Wylie. An active factor."

"He killed him, you mean."

"And he may be a continuing source of momentum and entropy."

Evan eyed her. "You think there's some game going on, and he's an active player."

"That's my fear."

"Mine too," Evan said. "'Punishment.' That's the term the car-jacker used. And it didn't sound like a spur-of-the-moment thing."

"Think Wylie was murdered because of something he had going with Ratner? Personal? Business?"

"Maybe. Or because of something Wylie had going as part of . . . call it a larger concern."

"Because there's no record of Ratner being a client of Wylie's."

"None," Evan said. "Wylie's firm handles corporations, financial entities, venture capital and hedge fund clients, and high-net-worth individuals. That doesn't fit Ratner, unless his mother's cowboy figurines are rare collectibles."

Tang thought for a moment. "We need to find out where he is."

She gave Evan a tart look.

"Yeah, I figured as much," Evan said. "We're going back to Ma Ratner's hoedown, aren't we?"

"The operative word being *we*."

"You'll be armed. But you want me to ring the doorbell."

Tina walked in. "Open the trunk."

She pointed at the steamer trunk that served as a coffee table. Evan removed a stack of books and magazines and opened the lid. She nearly laughed in surprise.

"Thanks, but I think I'll rely on my ability to jump into the bushes while Lt. Tang holds Ma Ratner at bay with her service weapon."

"Think about it," Tina said.

Inside the trunk, resting on a blue silk cloth, was a Japanese samurai sword. It was sheathed in a black lacquered scabbard that looked exceptionally old.

Tina walked over. "Tokugawa era. Our grandmother bequeathed it to Jo."

"I have no doubt it would do the trick," Evan said.

Evan wanted to say, *Who is she?* Who was Jo Beckett, who kept books on psychoanalytic diagnosis on her coffee table, beside her *Outside* magazines. Who had a *katana* within quick reach. And she decided that Tina's words had a double meaning: *Think about it.* Think about Jo. Think about honor and about fighting all the way to the end.

On the mantel were framed family photos. One pictured Jo and Tina with a young man who had to be their brother. Another pictured a couple in their late fifties she took to be their parents. They had California tans and wore flip-flops and aloha shirts. The mom looked slightly more Asian than her kids. The dad looked slightly more Mediterranean. In another photo, Jo sat on a picnic bench, looking relaxed and sun splashed. Sitting beside her was a man in his early thirties, with strong looks and a grin that seemed both loving and watchful. He looked — Evan stared for a long, solid chunk of seconds — supremely fit. Deceptively relaxed. Cut from some sleek and polished brand of stone. He didn't look proprietorial toward Jo, but there was no doubt they were together. Swimmer's shoulders. That confidence. And something beneath the affable, "*it's cool, bro*" smile.

"Is that Jo's partner? The guy she's with today?"

"Gabe Quintana," Tina said.

Tang's smoked-glass, mirrored gaze, which let her see out without letting others peer in, slipped for a moment. Her face registered a strong burst of emotion.

She said, "He's a PJ with the One-twenty-ninth Rescue Wing of the Air National Guard. Nobody knows more about wilderness survival."

Tina's expression thinned. "That's the situation you think they're in?"

Tang's mask came back down. "If they are, Jo couldn't be in better company."

Evan held her counsel. The strength of feeling in the room could have registered on a Geiger counter.

Evan had her little sister, Georgie. And she had her brother, Brian, a naval aviator. She adored them. She would do anything for her family.

Tina's fear was naked on her face. So was her sense of helplessness. The *not knowing* was unbearable. Evan understood that sensation too.

She closed the lid of the steamer trunk. "Anybody who cares for a sword so lovingly has my vote. Tina, you keep it close. The lieutenant and I will try to find out more information."

Out the door, she and Tang jogged down the steps.

"You really think Gabe and Jo are all right?" Evan said.

"If they're not, I'll personally gut Ruby Kyle Ratner like a rotten fish."

Evan gave her a look.

"Long story. But I owe them. Owe him. It's complicated."

"No, it's not," Evan said. "It's friendship. That's enough."

She hoped it wasn't life and death.

CHAPTER
THIRTY-FIVE

The horse pounded across the pasture at a hard gallop, a half-ton of muscle racing straight at the barbed-wire fence.

The headlights of the pick-up truck spotlighted Jo's path. Behind her the engine revved and dropped and the truck's suspension squealed as it chased her. Cattle ran in all directions. A flickering white trail of light, of hope, of nightmare, stretched ahead of her. The fence loomed.

She'd jumped horses a couple times as a kid — over fallen logs. It was about balance. Staying centered over the horse. She could do this. Because, if she fell, she'd be roadkill. The truck would have no trouble crashing through the fence and running over her.

She urged the horse forward with her hands against its neck. "*Go*," she shouted.

The horse bunched and launched itself into the air without breaking stride. Jo felt a huge shift in momentum, smooth and powerful and shocking, as the animal leapt, fearful and intent, into the air.

Don't hit the barbs. Don't fall. She saw the wire fly by beneath her.

250

She leaned back. The horse came down, its head stretching forward. She heard the truck shift gears, the engine lift. It was slowing.

The horse landed. It landed hard, its head dropping low.

Jo was gripping the reins tight. Too tight. As the horse's head swung down, her hands jerked down with it.

Slingshot. She catapulted forward. The horse regained its balance and gathered itself to keep running. Jo hit its neck and lost her grip. Her feet came out of the stirrups.

The horse continued running and Jo felt herself slide sideways, catastrophically.

She told herself to hang on to the reins. If the horse got away she was toast. *Adios*.

"Ow —"

She pounded into the damp earth with a thud. The breath crashed out of her. She saw sparks.

But she held on to the reins. She slid along the ground over pinecones and rocks, shouting, "Whoa."

The horse pulled up.

Back in the meadow, on the far side of the fence, the truck braked.

Jo slid to a stop at the edge of a ditch. It was an eroded gully where roots of fifty-foot pines had been washed out during a storm, and turned into an eight-foot-deep trench by rocks and runoff. The horse spun, uncontrollably spooked now.

If she hadn't fallen, they would have run full speed into the gully.

The headlights veered, barely catching her now. She realized the driver had turned the truck at an angle to her.

And there was only one reason he would do that. He wanted an unobstructed view. Down the barrel of a shotgun.

She scrambled to her feet. Holding the reins, she got up to run. She was limping. She was muddy and bruised.

She looked back. It was a mistake. She saw the barrel of a long gun work its way out the window of the truck. And she and the horse made a huge target. The veritable side of a barn.

Her first impulse was to let go of the reins and slap the horse on the rump. The second, which shamed her, was to duck to the horse's far side and use it as a shield.

That's what she did and ran toward the trees.

The driver fired.

The roar of a shotgun is terrifying. It sends a shock through you, down to your bones, that says, *Get the hell out of the way*. Up close, it's the blare of death.

He missed her, and the horse, but hit the trees. Wood flew; chips of bark. The horse whinnied, frantic. It tossed its head. The bridle clinked. She ran deeper into the trees, keeping the animal between her and the pick-up. She heard the truck's transmission grind. Heard the engine whine slowly. The headlights danced and their cones of light diminished. It was backing up.

Because the driver wanted to take a good, long run at the fence, to get up some speed before he bashed through it.

She pulled the horse to a stop, tried to get it to quit wheeling. She grabbed the stirrup and stuck her foot into it. She could barely get her leg up. Finally she pulled herself back into the saddle.

She paused, just for a second, pinned by the headlights. *Yeah. Right here. Get a good, long look.*

The truck revved.

She turned the horse, hands trembling. "Don't dump me, boy."

She kicked it toward the hills.

The truck roared and crashed through the fence. She heard the barbed wire twang as it tore, heard the fence posts rip from the ground and barbs scrape over the hood of the truck. The engine blared. It came straight at her.

She kicked the horse uphill and yelled, "Come *on*."

The horse lunged up the hill, digging into the soft earth. The truck's engine spun up. Its lights veered from side to side as its suspension rebounded from crashing through the fence. *Come on.* Ratner poured on the speed.

And ran straight into the gully.

The truck's headlights dropped as if they'd been slapped down. Its grille smashed hard into the far side of the trench. Its back end lifted into the air, carried by momentum, and smacked back down again. The engine continued roaring.

The horse kept lunging up the hill. Jo held on. Branches swept across her face and shoulders, cold, glistening with raindrops. They scratched her neck and left the sharp smell of pine resin in her hair.

She urged the horse onward, waiting for the roar of the shotgun. One more glance behind. Down the hill, the truck's headlights were dimmed brown by swirling dust and steam from the busted radiator.

The door of the truck creaked open.

After that, she didn't look back.

CHAPTER
THIRTY-SIX

The horse was blowing hard, and lathered like soap. Jo crested the ridge where, an hour earlier, she had climbed out of the gorge. She heard, beneath the wind and downpour, the rushing of the river at the bottom. She nudged the horse through the trees, staying low against its neck. She knew she'd outpaced Kyle, knew she was out of range of the shotgun — but only for the moment. He was coming.

Thunder banged from the night sky, and the rain finally let loose. It poured down, rattling through the trees, soaking her. Her hair flattened and stuck to her head in strings. The hill steepened. She nudged the horse.

Despite its fatigue, it faithfully responded. She patted its neck. After all this, she couldn't keep calling it *Horse*.

"Faithful," she said. "That's you."

The rock came out of the darkness. It just appeared in midair, flung hard, and hit her in the forehead.

Pyrotechnics flashed in her field of vision, electric red and yellow against the night. The pain echoed through her head, dull but shocking.

She was barely aware that somebody had jumped out on the trail ahead of her. A shrill voice cried, "Stop. Stop, horse."

The horse dug its feet into the soft ground and hauled up. Jo grabbed for the horse's mane even as her butt headed sideways and south.

She hit the dirt and heard a girl's voice. "Crap."

Jo looked up, her eyesight pulsing with light, and saw Autumn's sleek riding boots gleaming in the rain. The girl was trying to mount the circling horse. It was an awkward jittery dance, Autumn hopping on one foot as the horse pivoted away from her.

Jo couldn't believe it. "You're horse-jacking me?"

"No. I goofed." Autumn got one foot in the stirrup and held on to the saddle horn. The horse kept circling. "Get on."

Head throbbing, Jo bumbled to her feet. "Don't you dare leave me."

Steadying herself, Jo cautiously, reassuringly, raised her hands to the horse and said, "Whoa."

Like magic, the animal stopped spinning. It tossed its head and blew out its nostrils and stood still.

Jo grabbed the reins. She couldn't keep the outrage from her voice. "Why did you throw a rock at me?"

"I thought you were *him*." Autumn grunted and pulled herself awkwardly into the saddle. "Hurry."

Jo pushed Autumn's foot from the stirrup, painfully lifted her own boot in, and struggled her way into the saddle behind the girl.

"I'm not him. And you're lucky." Squashed behind Autumn, she swung both arms around the girl. "He's coming. We have to get back to the Hummer and get everybody out of there."

Autumn was breathing heavily. The altitude and the run through the forest were taking a toll. Jo clucked Faithful into a walk.

"If I'd known it was you I wouldn't have thrown the rock," Autumn said.

Jo's head throbbed. "Okay."

"I thought it was me or him. Better safe than sorry."

Autumn's voice had a thread-line crack in it. She twisted and looked behind them. Nothing was visible in the darkness.

"Where is he?" she said.

"Coming."

Jo nudged the horse in the ribs. Faithful broke into a trot.

"I seriously didn't mean to hit you with the rock. It's . . . I was taught . . ."

"Taught what?"

"Never to hesitate. To protect myself."

"By attacking?"

"Look out for number one. Cruel world, all that. My dad drummed it into me. You know, how you should never swerve on the road to avoid an animal? Because you might crash and kill yourself?"

"My dad told me the same thing when I learned to drive. But that's a long way from *brain people with a rock*."

Autumn seemed as tight as a cloth caught in a wringer. "My dad was serious. Full on. Like, the world is a road where everything's trying to make you swerve.

It not only doesn't care if you live, it will actively hoard life to itself. You have to take your chances where you can get them, without regret or remorse."

Jo let the words blow away in the rush of the wind. "Hard attitude."

"It was ingrained in me. Protect myself. And sometimes, protecting myself requires proactive steps."

Jo already, in general, hated the word *proactive*. Now she had an additional reason. "Preemptive war. See something, take it. Hell of a world-view."

"Seize the day. Without hesitation or fear." Autumn quieted. "Okay, I was mistaken."

Jo ducked as a branch swayed down in the wind. "Is this an apology?"

"My dad also said never apologize. It's a sign of weakness."

"I hate apologizing too. Having to say *sorry* sucks," Jo said. Her tone left room for Autumn to hear, *but* . . .

"I panicked. I won't again," Autumn said. "Are you okay?"

Apology, then. As close as it came. She'd take it.

"I'm okay," Jo said. "So are you. Even if you're a king-size pain in the ass."

"I feel like my nerves are on fire." Autumn's voice thickened. "My dad's plane has landed by now. Think he knows what's happened?"

"Maybe."

They rode. Jo thought about how to broach the subject she needed to talk about — without panicking Autumn. The girl was one spark away from an explosion.

258

"Tell me about the Bad Cowboy."

Autumn stiffened. "Why do you care about it?"

It, not him.

"This weekend was planned as a way for you to defeat him. Edge and your dad set it up so you'd have the tools to do that."

She spoke in the past tense to distance the conversation. She didn't want to scare Autumn by bringing him into the present moment. Not yet.

She added, "It was built into the fabric of the reality scenario. It could be important."

Autumn's shoulders rose. Her shoulder blades protruded from the back of her sweater, bird-like. Jo sensed her fighting competing urges — to cry, to scream, and to keep it suppressed. Not the top layer of the story. The grit. The garbage she'd buried in the basement, years back.

"My dad never believed me that the guy was bad," Autumn said.

"Did your dad ever see this man?"

"He says he doesn't remember him. But I'm sure he did."

Jo kept her arms snug around Autumn's ribs, holding her steady as Faithful trotted through the trees. "This was at a birthday party?"

"No, somebody's huge open-house thing. Fourth of July weekend. Cocktails and croquet on this enormous lawn, and pony rides for the kids. Keith Urban played a private set for the adults."

Autumn's Fourth of July parties definitely outdid Jo's. When she was a kid, her family would drive to the beach at Bodega Bay and sneak a few sparklers along. Jo and Tina and her brother, Rafe, would run barefoot along the sand, racing the waves, waving their white-hot sparklers in the sunset. Then there would be hot dogs.

"This guy Red Rattler was on the staff?" she said.

"Valet parking the guests' cars. All the staff wore costumes. He wore a cowboy hat and a shirt like the one in the sports bag. God, I want to gag. I can *smell* it."

"What happened?"

"Some of us kids were playing hide-and-seek. I thought I'd outsmart everybody. I crawled through a hedge and ran to this field where the cars were parked, and I hid in my dad's car," she said. "So I was kind of scrunched down in the backseat, peeping out the window. And I saw him."

"Red Rattler."

"Going car to car, searching through them."

"Stealing?"

Her birdlike shoulders tightened another degree. "Maybe. Probably. He was systematically going through each car. I didn't know what to do. And he kept coming closer, and I got scared, so I hunkered down. I knew something wasn't right, but I was frozen. I thought if I got out, he'd see me." She stopped. "And then he came to Dad's car."

"Oh, Autumn."

"I ducked down on the floor of the backseat but he opened the door, and he was *whistling*. He found me right away. The way he looked at me. It . . ." She paused a long moment. "It was like, *burning*. Like his

260

eyes were on fire, and he wanted to drill a hole through my head."

"How terrifying. What did he look like?"

"Those clothes. Except much bigger. He was fat."

"How fat?"

"He was a whale. He wheezed when he talked, and he sweated. And he had long hair, like the hippies, or Indians —"

"A braid?"

"Exactly. He was early twenties, maybe. He had a mustache, Pancho Villa style. But that wasn't the thing about him," she said. "It was that weird eye with the white ring around it. And he said, 'What do you think you're doing?' He seemed so angry. Then he grabbed me and . . ."

She went quiet.

Breathed. "He pulled me up, staring at me. Like staring would put me under his power. He said, 'You was spying on me, wasn't you?' Then he said, 'Spying's a nasty habit.'"

Jo felt a chill.

"He was smiling, but not with his eyes. His eyes were probing me, like somebody pushing against you with a stick. Or with . . . eager fingers."

"Did he touch you anywhere else?"

"No. He just stared, and talked. 'You know who spies? Dirty worms. Crawling through the dirt so nobody can see them.' Then he said, 'You know what we call worms who spy on other people and then tattle? We call them snitches.'"

"Autumn, that sounds awful. Were there no adults around?"

She shook her head. "He said, 'Bad things happen to snitches.' Then he pushed his face right up next to mine. He pointed at that freaky eye, and said, 'This is the white snake. It sees everything. If you snitch, it'll see. And it'll send other snakes to get you.'"

"Dear God." Jo felt a hot lump in her chest — empathy with the confusion and fear Autumn had felt. "But you didn't keep silent. You told your dad about him."

"Not at the party. Later." Autumn's voice sounded thick. "It took days to work up the courage. I felt — dizzy. Scared to tell him."

"Why?"

"Embarrassed. Frightened of the Bad Cowboy. He made me feel so . . . *ashamed* for some reason. And I was scared my dad would explode. He can be overpowering. Like a black tornado. But he . . ." She took a beat. "He thought I was blowing everything out of proportion."

"This is your dad who tells you to watch out for number one? To strike first because the world is out to get you?"

"I know," Autumn said.

But Jo didn't. "What is it?"

"It was right after my parents divorced. I was seen as having adjustment issues."

"Your father thought you fabricated the incident?"

"Embellished. Exaggerated. Misconstrued it. Got hysterical."

262

"How confusing for you . . . to be told your experience wasn't real by someone you trusted."

The girl's shoulders drew even tighter. She said, "Huh." She seemed to fight for breath.

"Autumn, you were a child. Red Rattler was an adult. And he terrorized you. He was —"

"Mind-fucking me."

"Yes."

"And my dad didn't believe me. He thought I was trying to manipulate him. To *get* something from him by complaining."

Jo wondered what was coming next.

"Screw my dad. For not believing me."

Her shoulders shook and she began to cry again. "Dustin . . ."

Jo wrapped her arms tighter around Autumn's waist.

She thought of other things Autumn might come to realize: that the power of the Bad Cowboy probably arose not only from the fear she experienced when he threatened her but from the rage she felt toward her father for not believing her — which left her not only terrified but *alone* with her terror. This was probably one reason the Bad Cowboy had invaded her unconscious life to such a degree. He represented her deepest fears of being powerless and unprotected in what her father had led her to believe was a terrifying world. She even used the word "worm" repeatedly — she felt invaded. The Bad Cowboy *and* her sense of not being heard, seen, felt, had wormed their way under her skin. And so it developed into a canker sore. Which she

263

picked at, trying to make her father see what she needed from him.

And instead of listening to Autumn, instead of recognizing her terror, her father saw her as having developed a phobia. But the Bad Cowboy was not an illusion. Not a clown to be deflated. Emotionally, he was a continuing slap in the face.

Unfortunately, in real life he was something much worse.

Jo heard a noise behind her.

Autumn turned in the saddle. "What was that?"

Down the slope, through tree trunks that stood like toothpicks, Jo saw — what? Possibly a form, flowing in the darkness. Possibly nothing but her own fears.

"Let's go," she said, and kicked the horse in the ribs.

Faithful broke into a canter. Autumn tried to see behind them.

"I'm scared," she said.

Who isn't? "We're going to get back to the Hummer and get everybody out of there. Hold on."

They hit the crest of the ridge a minute later. Jo hauled back on the reins. Faithful tossed his head.

"You ever gone down a hill on horseback before?" she said.

"Yeah. If we slip, or you start to fall . . . jump."

She nudged Faithful forward. He edged down the hill, digging his feet into the slope. The pitch of the wind changed. The trees overhead caught it and sent it whispering back at Jo, a fearful hush.

Below, the clouds parted for a moment, and she saw the white-water frothing over rocks. The rain was

264

thundering down, and the river was higher than when she'd left.

"Here we go," she said.

They got halfway down the slope before the soil on the hillside slipped, and the horse lost his purchase.

CHAPTER
THIRTY-SEVEN

Von crouched behind the trunk of the pine tree just below the gravel logging road, sheltered from the wind. The bark was cracked and sticky with sap. The rain had momentarily stopped. The clouds were split, moonlight crackling down on the scene. But the temperature had dropped, like he'd opened a freezer door. He stuck his hands into his armpits and fought the shivering.

He still had no vantage point on the wrecked limo. He didn't have the night vision goggles. Those were with Haugen and Sabine and Stringer in the Volvo SUV with its seat warmers and climate control and cup holders.

No, he was shuddering here in the bitch-cold mountain air. The last Mohican, holding the fort against those little shits from the birthday party who had caused this train wreck. So to speak.

And he hurt. He was so sore he could barely move. He needed a damned drink. Even a swig of Wild Turkey from his flask would heat him through. Oh yeah. But the flask had gone to the bottom of the gorge with the Hummer.

He peered around the trunk of the tree. Though moonlight shone between tumbling, hairy clouds, all he could see were the contours of the gorge. Trees bearded its flanks. He heard the river at the bottom, roaring. He couldn't see the party brats. Down there, staying warm in the Hummer, no doubt.

Rain pattered through the trees and needled his face again. "Unbelievable."

The sound didn't jump out from the rest of the noisy night, but it caught his ear, because it seemed — *sideways* to the wind and rain. Like it cut through the air and was circling him. He turned. The gravel road was empty.

He flattened himself against the tree trunk and peered down the slash of the gorge. Rocks and dark and endless trees.

That sound again. He swiveled and drew his gun, arm extended. What *was* that noise?

It came as a whistle, a slap through the air, at the same moment his gun hand jerked. His wrist stung.

Something had hold of him. Something had — like it had bitten him, but it was smooth, a snake, or a trap, or —

His arm jerked straight upward. The something was pulling on him, hard. He heard a rasping noise.

"Hey —"

Then his shoulder jerked and he was lifted off the ground. His hand was caught in a noose. The rope was slung over a branch in the pine tree and was hauling him up like a window shade.

"Shit."

The rope was hemp, thin and rough and ferociously tight. Von's shoulder stretched in its socket.

The rope hummed like a saw over the branch above. Von wheeled in the air. His toes kicked, a few inches off the ground.

He swiped at the rope with his left hand. He was hanging at an angle, shoulders uneven, right side yanked so high and so hard he couldn't reach the rope with his left.

But he managed to hold on to the gun with his right hand. Perhaps he could shoot the rope. He grimaced and tried to squeeze the trigger. He couldn't. The noose squeezed the tendons in his wrist so hard that he could barely move his fingers.

He dangled, spinning. Someone had suckered him.

With a fucking lasso.

"Swinging like a fox, with its paw caught in the cookie jar. Ain't that a sight."

Von kicked and swiveled, looking frantically for the source of the voice.

"You picked a fine tree to cower behind."

"Let me down," Von said.

He kicked for the tree trunk. If he could stretch with his toes, maybe push off from the trunk, swing out, then back in — maybe he could grab the trunk with his free arm, shimmy up, take the pressure off.

And get the gun.

"Know why that tree is such a fine place for you to swing from?" the voice said.

It was a familiar voice. He'd heard it recently. A high tenor, no accent. It was the rhythm — the hard emphasis and drawn-out vowels. Like he wanted to

268

hold you in his thrall while he tarried his way through his long, slow words. Playing with you.

"It's the perfect tree because it's old and big, and even branches twenty feet off the ground are strong enough to hold a grown man's weight, six feet out from the trunk, where that rope's hanging."

"Let me down."

"Go on, kick. The rope's wet. This rain already soaked it good. The more you fight it, the more the rope's gonna dig in and tighten up."

Boots squelched on the gravel. The man sauntered out of the shadows.

"Kyle?" Von said.

The Edge Adventures newbie nodded. Only he no longer looked like an Edge Adventures tool. His preppie windbreaker had been replaced with an oilskin duster and a battered cowboy hat. Kyle touched the brim.

"Let me down," Von said. "My arm's killing me."

"I let you down, you'll shoot me," Kyle said.

"No, I won't."

Kyle laughed. The brim of the cowboy hat hid his eyes. But Von saw his mouth, teeth showing in the moonlight.

Then Kyle lifted his chin. His eyes did catch the white sheen of the moon, before a cloud blew across it again. More rain tapped against Von's cheeks. He didn't like the look in Kyle's eyes. Not at all. One eye seemed to glow white.

"Where's Dane?" Kyle said.

Von felt the rain as hot dots against his skin. *Screw* Friedrich for mentioning Haugen's name in the limo. "Who?"

"Huh." Kyle looked at the ground and shook his head, as though gravely disappointed.

"Let me down and I won't hurt you," Von said.

"You won't hurt me right where you are. Grub worm like you, hanging there squirming — no, you won't hurt me."

The AK-47 was resting against the tree trunk. Kyle threw it down the slope into the dark.

Despite the chill of the rain, Von felt himself steaming. "My arm's killing me."

Caught in the hideously tight knot of the wet lasso, Von's right hand throbbed. It felt like a cartoon hand, swollen and thumping. He swung his left arm, trying to reach the pistol. He tried to bend his right elbow and lift himself with a one-armed pull-up, but couldn't.

"Don't bother," Kyle said. "All you'll get is more pain."

"Fuck you, bastard."

Kyle spit on the ground. "Now, see . . . ," he said slowly, like he was talking through molasses, "that kind of talk will get you hurt."

"Cut me down or I'll shoot you."

"Right." Kyle stuck out a finger and pushed Von in the stomach.

Von kicked at him violently, and the rope tightened around his throbbing wrist.

Kyle put all his fingers against Von's belly, and pushed. Harder. Von began to swing.

"Where's Haugen?" Kyle said.

"I don't know. Let me down."

"Who's with him?" Kyle said.

"Nobody. I don't know. An army of assholes who are going to bounce your head off this tree if you don't cut me down right this goddamned second." His arm was about to rip loose. "I'm going to kill you."

What the hell did Kyle want? Was he angry because of the crash? "You should be after those little shits from the birthday party," Von said. "They're the ones who caused this mess."

Kyle pushed him again, making sure not to let him swing toward the trunk of the tree, but only parallel to it. The branch creaked overhead.

Then Von figured out what this guy wanted. "I'll pay you. Let me down, I'll give you a cut."

"Ninety percent," Kyle said.

"What? No."

Kyle pushed him again. The rope swung in a bigger arc. "Ninety-five, then."

"Are you an idiot?"

Von held on to the gun even though his cartoon hand had to be throbbing like a police light, red and huge. He was going to shoot this son of a bitch.

"When is Haugen getting here?" Kyle said. "Who's with him, besides Sabine?"

"I'll give you twenty-five percent of my cut," Von said. "Come on, man."

"We're still at ninety-five. Haugen, Sabine, you, Friedrich — who, sadly, is lying beside the Hummer like a squashed sandwich — that's not enough people

271

to corral six college students. Who else is with Haugen?"

"Nobody — come on, man." Von swung, feeling the centrifugal force, his feet flying out. "Fine, thirty-five percent."

"Enough nonsense," Kyle said.

He caught Von around the waist and stopped him cold.

"Know how much pressure it takes to dislocate a human shoulder? To pull the joint clean out of the socket?"

"What are you —"

"Less than you'd think."

Von kicked and punched with his left hand. But Kyle just took it, wrapped his arms around Von's shoulders like a movie starlet leaning in for a kiss with the leading man, and lifted his feet from the ground. His smile gleamed in the moonlight, a grimace like a jack-o'-lantern's.

Inside the Hummer, huddled together to share body heat, Gabe stilled. Lark and Peyton were murmuring, low. Noah was breathing shallowly.

"Shh," Gabe said.

The girls looked up. "What?" Peyton said.

Gabe heard it. Far away, uncertain, caught by the wind. But he recognized the sound, and his skin tightened.

"Someone's screaming," he said.

CHAPTER
THIRTY-EIGHT

The horse lunged down the slope, gaining speed. Jo submarined forward in the saddle. Autumn slid up its lathered neck.

"I'm slipping," Autumn cried.

They heard the river rushing, louder. The horse picked up his forelegs to avoid a fallen log.

Jo lost her balance. "Oh no. Jump."

The horse kicked his rear legs to avoid the log, and Jo and Autumn peeled off.

She had hated falling the first time, and hated it even more now. *Tuck and roll*, she thought.

Wet pine needles and soft dirt saved her. She crashed into the slope and didn't bounce, didn't flip, just slid down the grade with the wind knocked out of her as if she'd been hit with a door.

She heard Autumn thump along in the dark, nearby. She turned face down and clawed her fingers into the earth as if they were ice axes, trying to arrest her fall.

She bumped backward into a tree trunk and jolted to a stop. She heard Autumn thud into something.

In the dark, Autumn shouted, "Crap."

"You all right?"

After a moment, Autumn clambered to her feet. "You call that horse Faithful?"

"Not if he gets away." She pushed herself up onto one knee. "Damn."

She was filthy and shaking. And if she'd wanted to slide downhill over and over, she'd do it on a snowboard. She stumbled forward, climbed over the log, and saw the horse ten feet away, head down, drinking from an eddy in the river. Its tail swished lazily.

Jo limped over and grabbed the reins. Chill needles of rain hit her face. She heard the sound of feet splashing through the river and brought her head up sharply.

Moonlight split the clouds. On the slab of rock upriver, Gabe was running straight at her. He had a length of metal pipe in his hand, held low, like a *katana*.

He saw her and his lips parted. His eyes were bright.

Jo hobbled toward him. "We have to get everybody out of here. We've got trouble."

He ran onto the riverbank. "Where's Autumn?" His voice had a hot note, like an electric coil.

"Here." Autumn came out of the trees, her hair blowing around her face.

Jo grabbed Gabe's arms. "Dustin's dead. Kyle killed him."

"Holy mother."

"He's armed with a shotgun. We need to roll. Now."

He put his arm firmly around her shoulder. The wind was whipping the river. She held the reins and urged Autumn back into the saddle, then hauled herself

274

up. A sharp pain in her hamstring told her she'd strained something, deep, when she'd been thrown. She swung her leg over and settled in. She saw what Gabe had in his hand: not a piece of pipe but a Club steering-wheel lock. Not bad.

He slapped the horse on the rump. "Go. I'll cross on foot, where it's shallow."

Jo clucked and nudged the horse with her heels, and they splashed into the water. The wet air around her felt saturated with cold. She felt the riverbed slope and kept the horse at a slow, steady pace, rocking from side to side as it carefully progressed forward. Big, even steps, haunches rolling. The sound of the water grew louder.

"Pick your feet up, Autumn. Keep them dry," she said.

Autumn scrunched her knees up against Faithful's neck.

"When we get back to the Hummer, tell Peyton and Lark that they need to gather up all their survival supplies. And look for something we can use to carry Noah to a safer location. A coat, a sheet of plastic, anything."

Maybe they could construct a travois. "Otherwise, we have to get him on the horse."

The water swirled around the horse's belly. Jo lifted her feet from the stirrups. The horse's hooves clacked against stones on the bottom. She gingered it forward, and the bottom sloped upward and they came out on the rocky bank.

Jo jumped down. Her entire body ached, sore and cold.

Autumn's voice sounded like fractured ice. "He's the Bad Cowboy, isn't he?"

"Yes."

Gabe splashed across the granite pan upstream and caught up with them. His dark hair was plastered with rain. His mouth was a sharp line against his skin.

He pointed to a fallen log with broken branches protruding. "Tie the horse up. Half hitch."

"I won't let the horse wander off untethered," Jo said.

He was walking away. He stopped. "You're cold. You're wet. You're . . ." He paused, as if biting off the words. "I don't know what you might forget."

She drew up, stung. "What did I do?"

He shook his head, raised a hand, and headed for the limo. "Forget it. We need to move."

A gust of wind swirled rain into her eyes. Perplexed, sensing his anger, she swallowed her questions and tied the horse's reins to the log. Then she ran after Gabe.

Or tried to. Her hamstring, her entire right side all the way up her back, grabbed like cold iron. She hissed, limped to the car, and slithered through the window after Gabe. Her back pinged, as if a needle had been jammed in it.

The interior of the Hummer was dark but dry. It was beginning to smell of sweat and nerves. Jo heard hard crying, muffled. Autumn was curled next to Lark, shaking.

Peyton, huddled in a corner, hands hugging her knees, was nothing but a silhouette, edged by moonlight. Blond hair and round, glimmering eyes.

"I don't want to go out there," she said.

Autumn looked up. "We have to."

"Don't make me," Peyton said.

Gabe crawled to Noah's side, examined the dressing on his gunshot wound, and checked his broken leg.

"Jo? Explain the situation," Gabe said.

There was a measure of command in his voice. It surprised her. Not because he was ever hesitant — he could be maddeningly reticent, but never tentative. It was because it sounded like he was giving her an order.

She battened down her emotions and kept it curt. "Dustin and a local man have been shot to death."

Autumn's shoulders heaved. She buried her face in Lark's shoulder to stifle her sobs.

"Kyle killed them both. He's armed with a shotgun," Jo said.

Peyton shrank. "Kyle? That makes no sense."

Autumn looked up, fierce. "He's the Bad Cowboy. He shot them and stole a shotgun and a truck, and he's coming back to get us."

"How do you know? Wouldn't he try to get out of here?"

It was a good question.

Jo postponed thinking about it. "He chased me in a pick-up truck. When he crashed, he got out. We have to presume he's on his way."

"No, we don't." Peyton looked out the window. "Any fool would get back to the highway and get out of here."

"Peyton, he's not any fool. And we don't have the luxury of time to debate this. He knows where we are.

He killed Dustin and an innocent bystander. If he did that simply to steal the rancher's truck, he wouldn't have chased me. We need to leave."

Lark cleared her throat. "You said it's dangerous to leave your location after a wilderness accident."

"Unless staying put becomes more dangerous. Which it now is."

Gabe said gravely, "We need to evacuate. Kyle's out there and he's not playing games. I heard somebody screaming."

The silence in the car felt heavy. Outside, the rain nailed the Hummer, angled on the wind.

Jo's skin felt, all at once, fuzzy. Charged. The air had a strange energy.

Everybody else felt it too. They looked around, perplexed. Then Jo saw Peyton's dry blond hair lift from her shoulders and rise, like a dandelion.

Static electricity.

"Lightning," Gabe said.

"Everybody down," Jo cried.

She balled up and heard the rest do likewise. With a huge crack, the interior of the Hummer flashed blue-white. She heard wood splinter as if it had been hit with a cannonball. She turned her head. Ten feet from the Hummer a pine had been struck. It had exploded and stood smoking in the rain.

The downpour increased. The rain came down so hard that it drummed on the Hummer like ball bearings. The view outside turned indistinct. The noise was unbelievable. More lightning sliced the air.

Jo looked at Gabe. They weren't going anywhere.

278

CHAPTER
THIRTY-NINE

On the logging road in the Stanislaus National Forest, Deputy D. V. Gilbert slowed for a curve. The weather had turned vicious. Outside his Tuolumne County sheriff's cruiser, rain nailed the road so hard it bounced and buzzed through the headlights. The lodgepole pines that crowded the shoulders of the road were barely visible through the downpour. The cruiser handled solidly in weather, but his windshield wipers were useless.

His radio squawked. The desk officer from the station checked in and asked for an update. Gilbert had been on the road forty minutes, since taking the phone call from the San Francisco PD.

An SFPD consultant and a PJ from the 129th Rescue Wing were missing after investigating the death of that lawyer from the city. They'd been out of communication for — he checked his watch — eight hours now. Not outrageous, certainly not for a PJ. But in this storm, it was troubling.

Gilbert took the radio transmitter from its cradle below the dash. "I'm at mile ninety-two," he said, noting the marker as he drove past. "No traffic for the past fifteen miles. Nobody's out. It's raining like the end of the world."

"Inform when you reach the turnout," the dispatcher said.

"Roger that." Gilbert smiled. Of course he would radio. The worrywart dispatcher knew he would.

He set the radio back in its cradle and focused on the deluge outside. Gilbert's first name was Ron, but nobody called him that, not even his mother. They called him D. V. because his deep, rattling voice reminded them of Darth Vader.

In his rear-view mirror, far down the mountain behind him, he thought he saw headlights. Just a blur of white, flashing bright against the rain-smeared rear window. If so, it was the only other vehicle within twenty miles.

Then he came around the curve and realized he was wrong. He saw the clearing and the dark blue Toyota Tacoma pick-up.

He pulled off the asphalt, stopped, and hit his spotlight.

Uh-oh.

He knew that wasn't a deputy-like thought, but it was always what sprang to mind, never more than now.

He double-checked the Tacoma's tags. They matched those of the missing doctor's truck. He picked up the radio transmitter.

"I'm at the clearing. The Tacoma's parked here."

"Copy that," the dispatcher said. "Any sign of the two persons the SFPD is looking for?"

"Negative. And there's a situation."

The truck was blowing exhaust from its tailpipe. Its lights were off. The driver's door was open. Nobody was in sight.

"The truck's parked here. Running. I can't see anybody inside." He stared at the pick-up, the exhaust swirling around its back tires like a billowing white skirt. "I'm going to investigate."

He got his Maglite. He unsnapped his holster. He looked at the shotgun locked upright beside the cruiser's center console, but had no visible cause to break it out. Just a bright, buzzy feeling that this scene held the leftovers of chaos.

Zipping his winter jacket to the top, cinching his hat down on his forehead, he climbed out. The rain hit him like an icy shower.

He approached the truck cautiously. Though his headlights starkly illuminated it, he held the Maglite at his shoulder and ran the beam over the truck's tires, its door, its interior. He lowered the beam and swept it across the ground.

The downpour was pummeling the dirt in the clearing. Rivulets of water were already turning into streams and running toward the road. Still, he could see multiple tire tracks in the turnout and lots of footprints. They wouldn't last.

Maybe that meant nothing. Maybe they belonged to hikers who had passed through over the last week. But he doubted it.

He approached the Tacoma's open driver's door. Shining the flashlight into the truck's interior, he held his breath. It was a bad habit, one his football coach and the sheriff had been trying to make him aware of. He exhaled.

Nobody inside. But a backpack was on the passenger seat.

He circled the truck. He saw tire tracks from another vehicle, a long parallel sliding curve, like a double smile. Or like a vehicle that had peeled out of the gravelly dirt clearing at high speed and slid the back tires around.

He swept the beam across the dirt on the far side of the pick-up and toward the looming trees and hillside. Through the stinging rain his breath frosted the night air.

Down the highway, once again, he caught the diamond shine of headlights coming up the road. Then he heard an engine.

In this weather, it wasn't campers. At this time of year, it wasn't gamblers headed to Reno — the road over the summit was already closed for the season. This time of night, it was likely to be one of the few ranchers who lived back here. Might even mean they had started out earlier in the day, driven down to Modesto or Sonora for supplies and dinner, and were headed home. Might mean they had passed this spot already today. And if they had, they might have seen something meaningful.

He walked to the edge of the asphalt.

The headlights swung around the curve and lit the trees in a white arc. The engine sounded smooth and solid. And big. Gilbert stood at the edge of the road, waved the Maglite, and flagged them down.

A black Volvo SUV, glittering in the rain, pulled into the clearing behind his cruiser.

CHAPTER
FORTY

Haugen braked the Volvo SUV cleanly to a halt. In his headlights, the young sheriff's deputy leaned into his patrol car, grabbed his radio, spoke briefly, then shielded his eyes and tramped toward him through the downpour.

Sabine had not tensed so much as coiled herself. "What does he want?"

"Information, I presume. That pick-up truck possibly belongs to the hikers who entangled themselves in our operation today."

From the backseat, Stringer said, "I bet you anything you're right. Why else would it still be running?"

He shouldn't have said that. And Haugen thought, not for the first time, that preventing Stringer from blurting information at the wrong moment was a tricky task. The man was brave and bold, but stupid.

He looked in the mirror at Stringer. "Keep your mouth shut. You're Sabine's brother. We're on our way to a weekend at a cabin in the Sierras. I'll do the talking."

Amy Tang pulled her car — a girl-racer Honda Civic with low-profile tires and chrome rims, obviously her personal vehicle — to the curb in front of Ma Ratner's house. For a moment, Tang looked like she didn't want to leave the vehicle unguarded. She turned off the stereo. Beyoncé went silent.

She and Evan stared at the house — the chain-link fence with the ratty plastic windmills; the cracked sidewalk, and listing concrete steps up to the front door; the dingy porch light.

"You can stay here," she said.

"To keep Mrs Ratner's dog from pissing on your shiny hubcaps? I think not," Evan said.

They got out into a cutting wind. This was weather, and a neighborhood, that San Francisco hid when designing its tourist brochures.

The windmills sputtered at them. The gate cringed open. Through half-drawn drapes, Evan saw the reflected blue light of the television. Tang rang the doorbell and barking erupted inside.

"Pavlov's rat," Evan said.

Tang had her badge wallet in her hand. It was the first thing Mrs Ratner saw when she opened the door.

Her eyes, behind the cat's-eye glasses, were the color of cloudy marbles, and as cold. "And here I was hoping you was something less toxic, like sewer gas."

The dog, Pepito, bounced and yipped behind her. It was wearing a teensy bandanna and a Western-style vest with a little sheriff's hat and star. Mrs Ratner's gingham presence filled the doorway. She frowned at Evan.

"Where's your badge, Starsky?"

284

"I'm a citizen. But Lt. Tang is cop enough for both of us."

Tang put away her badge. "We'd like to speak to your son, Ruben."

"He ain't here."

Pepito continued to bounce around Ma Ratner's feet. Higher, and more agitated.

"Can you tell us where he is?" Tang said.

"Nope."

"May we come in?"

"When horses piss champagne."

From the living room came an eerie sound, otherworldly singing. Wavery, high-pitched. It was cowboy yodeling, an old Slim Whitman record. The sound made Evan's skin contract. Pepito barked, *yip yip yip*, and pogoed on clicky little dog toes, straight up into the netherworld inside the parachute folds of Ma Ratner's dress. The barking stopped and the dog dropped to the floor. Cringing, it trotted down the hall, tail between its legs. Ma Ratner continued to glare at Evan.

"You lied before, about wanting to hire Ruby Junior for a party. Go on. Get."

"I came here earlier because I need to get in touch with Ruby Junior. We have a mutual acquaintance." Or close enough. "But you chased me away with a forty-five. And now Lt. Tang has a few questions."

Tang was half Ma Ratner's size but showed not the slightest sign of feeling intimidated. "The flyer says he's available not just to haul trash but to tend bar and organize parties. What kind of events — children's birthday parties? Does his parole officer know this?"

"Get off my property."

"And I take it you're his business manager. Have you been forthcoming with prospective clients? Because I have to believe that Mr and Mrs Suburban might ask, every once and again, if the dude in the snap-button shirt is a violent felon."

Ma Ratner muttered something, low and quick.

"What was that?" Tang said.

Evan said, "An Old West endearment. At least, I *think* 'skanky dykes' is meant to be endearing."

"Oh." Tang tilted her head, just slightly, like the flick of a knife. "I can call Ruben's parole officer. He'd be interested in all of this. Especially in the possibility that Ruben may have left San Francisco without informing him."

"I never said that. Don't twist my words." Mrs Ratner shifted in the doorway. It was almost tectonic. "He ain't working a children's party. And it's perfectly legal. Don't you dare make trouble for him with the parole people."

"Where's he working, Mrs Ratner?"

"It's a twenty-first-birthday party. And he's on the payroll for a corporate outfit."

"What outfit?" Tang said.

"Edge Adventures."

Tang wrote it down. "What kind of outfit is that?"

"They take rich folks on scare-you-silly weekends. To make 'em feel alive."

"Have a phone number for Edge Adventures?"

"No. But you're a smart fortune cookie, you'll figure it out."

286

Tang scribbled in the notebook and underlined something, hard. "Gotcha."

Evan heard clicking on the broken cement walkway behind her. Like Pepito's little claws, but heavier. And breathing. No, snorting. And the clink of a chain.

She and Tang turned in unison.

On the sidewalk behind them in the dark was a dog. Maybe a dog. It came up to Tang's shoulder.

"This is Calamity," Mrs Ratner said. "You'll be going, now."

"Call it off."

"I didn't summon her. She's got a mind of her own."

"Quite the bitch, then," Evan said.

"You'd know, I expect," Mrs Ratner said.

Its teeth showed under the porch light. It looked like a cross between a Rhodesian ridgeback and a razorback hog.

It growled. Evan didn't think it was a dog.

She turned to Tang. "Shall we retire to your salon?"

"Where we'll consider warrants, and perhaps call Animal Control. Depending on what happens in the next ten seconds." She looked pointedly at Ma Ratner.

Mrs Ratner scratched under her pendulous bosom. Then clapped. "Sit."

Calamity parked its rear on the cement and sat panting and drooling. Evan and Tang inched down the steps and across the concrete lawn, giving it a generous berth.

Tang opened the creaking gate. Mrs Ratner called, "You leave my boy alone. You come back here, you'll need more than a warrant to get in."

"Thanks," Evan said. "It's been a blast."

The sound of the whining gate worked like a starter's pistol. From the house, Pepito bolted out the door, straight at them.

"Damn." Tang rushed to the car and hopped in.

Evan jumped in a second behind and slammed her door. She stared back at Calamity. "What *is* that thing? A *bear?*"

Outside her window Pepito appeared, in pogo mode, leaping up and barking at her. *Yip yip*. Down. Up. *Yip*.

Tang started the engine. "Edge Adventures."

"Already on it."

Evan got the number and dialed. Tang put the car in gear. Pepito ran into the street and popped up in front of the grille. *Yip*.

Tang braked. Evan gritted her teeth. If they hit the dog, Ma Ratner would wail loud enough to summon folks from her prairie misanthropes reenactment society, wielding pitchforks and branding irons.

On the phone, the call was answered breathlessly by a voice that was young and female. "Terry?"

"Is this Edge Adventures?" Evan said.

"Kind of . . . who's this?"

Kind of? "My name is Evan Delaney. I'm with Lt. Tang of the SFPD. I need to speak to someone in authority from Edge."

Silence, abrupt and shocked. "Police?"

"Miss? Can you connect me to somebody from Edge?"

The brakes shuddered. Pepito landed on the hood of Tang's car. From the doorway of her house, Ma Ratner gave an anguished cry.

"Pepito. You rammed Pepito."

She charged down the steps, dress floating.

Tang gaped at the hood. "Get that thing off my car."

"I'm not getting out," Evan said.

Pepito yapped at the glass. Then, with its tiny snarling mouth, it sank its teeth into the windshield wiper.

"You have got to be kidding me," Tang said.

"Go," Evan said. "Ma Ratner's coming."

"Tell her to get the dog off my car."

Evan leaned across to Tang's side and hit the windshield wiper switch. The wipers started up. Pepito twisted and flew off the car with a high-pitched yelp.

Tang floored it.

Evan glanced out the back window. Pepito lay on the curb, feet pawing the air, sheriff's hat cocked askew.

Friday night in the city. Who needed Disneyland?

She returned to the phone call. "Miss — I'm sorry. Are you still there?"

Nerves fizzed in the young woman's voice. "Is it Terry? Is he okay?"

"I'm putting you on speaker." Evan hit a key. "Who's Terry, miss?"

"Terry Coates, my boyfriend. He owns Edge. Is he okay?"

"Why do you ask?"

"Because he drove a speedboat out of the marina this morning, and disappeared."

CHAPTER
FORTY-ONE

Haugen kept his hands in sight on the steering wheel. The young sheriff's deputy walked toward the Volvo, a hand tented over his eyes. Haugen sensed Sabine's tension, and said, "Happy citizens all are we."

He put the window down. "Officer?"

The deputy hunched into his heavy winter jacket. His face was round and ruddy. He looked like any of a hundred thousand small-town boys who played on the high school football team and then, to maintain his position of authority, put on a badge. Eager and easily buffaloed.

Sabine was coiled in the passenger seat. Haugen felt her cool energy, husbanded, ready to lash out.

The deputy approached. "Evening, sir."

"What's going on?"

"Wondering if you're on your way up the hill for the first time today, or whether you might have passed by this spot on your way down earlier."

"We drove up from Los Angeles. Been on the road since this morning. Is there a problem?"

"Couple of people reported missing. That's their truck."

Haugen, Sabine, and Stringer dutifully looked at the blue Toyota pick-up. Haugen adopted a look of surprised concern.

"What happened?" he said.

"Don't know. I was hoping you might be able to offer some information."

"Sorry, it's a mystery to me."

"Where are you headed?" the deputy said.

"Up the road a ways."

"I ask because it's possible these folks were hiking and got disoriented in the forest. They could have headed in the wrong direction. There's a trail that meets the road about seven miles uphill. The trailhead's clearly marked."

"Understood. We'll watch for them."

"I appreciate it."

The deputy was deliberately avoiding shining his big Maglite in the window — that being a provocative act, indicative of suspicion — but his country-boy eyes were running over Haugen's face. This rube was sizing him up. He had to play the encounter at the correct pitch. Not disinterested, and definitely not antsy to leave.

Haugen nodded at the hard-driven Toyota pick-up. "Who are they?"

"A doctor and an Air National Guardsman from San Francisco."

Sabine turned at that. "What were they doing up here?"

The deputy paused. He eyed Sabine, which Haugen didn't like.

"She's a police consultant. She's working on an investigation. They probably hiked up that trail there."

He aimed the flashlight across the clearing. The beam swung toward the trees and illuminated the gleaming rainfall, bright and white. And something else.

The deputy stared. Raised a hand. "Hold on a minute, would you, sir?"

He walked across the clearing, past the blue pick-up, focusing the flashlight on a spot on the ground. He stopped.

"I don't like this," Sabine said.

"Nor do I," Haugen said. What was the deputy looking at?

"Go," Sabine said.

"No."

"Turn off the headlights and floor it. Get out of here before he gets more suspicious."

"You idiot, he already has our plate number."

"He didn't write it down."

"But he radioed the station. And look at his dashboard. He's got us on video."

Sabine saw the cruiser's miniature camera, its lens aimed at the Volvo. "This is bad."

The deputy crouched down and picked up something from the dirt. It was only a couple of inches long. It was brassy colored. He shined the flashlight on it.

It was the casing from a rifle cartridge.

Evan put the phone on speaker. "You can't reach Mr Coates?"

292

"He's not answering, or replying to, my messages. Neither is his brother," said the young woman. "I'm at his place. Calls to Edge's office phone get forwarded here. That's why I answered."

Tang leaned toward the phone. Under the wash of streetlights, her face was grave. "This is Lt. Amy Tang of the SFPD."

"Oh," the young woman said. "I'm really worried about him."

"Is it unusual for him to be out of contact while he's — what did you say — running a scenario?"

"It's not the first time, but I can't get either him or his brother. That's weird."

"What can you tell me about his plans today? Who's his client?"

"I don't know. But it's a twenty-first-birthday party."

"Can you find out?"

"Can you find Terry?"

Evan said, "What's his cell phone number?"

Tang handed over her little notebook, and Evan wrote the number down.

Tang said, "You check out his client. We'll be back in touch."

"Please, be quick," the young woman said.

Evan ended the call and dialed Coates's number. Tang raced up an on-ramp onto 280 and headed downtown.

Coates's phone rang.

Tang made her own call. She identified herself and gave her badge number. "I need location services on a cell phone." Reciting Coates's number, she said, "Let me know ASAP."

She changed lanes, not even looking. "If the battery in Coates's phone is working, we'll pinpoint its location."

In Evan's ear, Coates's number rang.

Sabine sat forward in the Volvo and peered at the deputy through the gleam of the headlights. The downpour scattered like BBs from the deputy's hat and jacket.

"He's got the brass from Von's AK-Forty-seven."

The deputy stared at the cartridge casing for a long second. His head jerked up. He swept the beam of the flashlight across the dirt.

A glinting collection of cartridge casings littered the ground.

"We gotta haul, boss," Stringer said. "This scene's gonna get ugly, real fast. That kid'll call in the cavalry."

Haugen put his hand on the gearshift. Sabine turned her head. Her gaze was fierce.

The deputy stepped around the clearing, eyes on the cartridge casings. Then he aimed the flashlight at the trees.

Sabine said, "Dane."

"I see it," Haugen said.

He couldn't let the deputy call this in. He put the Volvo in drive and jammed his foot on the gas.

The deputy looked up. He had only a moment to flinch before the Volvo hit him square in the midsection, like a wrecking ball.

294

The man buckled, his head hit the hood, and he stuck there.

Haugen continued accelerating. Sabine hissed and leaned back against the seat, bracing herself.

Haugen held the wheel and sped across the clearing. At the last second he braked. But still, the heavy SUV was going at noticeable speed when he drove straight into the nearest pine tree.

The brakes kept the airbag from deploying, but still they jerked to a stop.

The deputy made no sound. He hung pinned between the tree and the grille of the Volvo. By the time Haugen put it in reverse, Sabine had jumped out.

He backed up. The deputy slumped off the hood and slid to the ground, out of sight in front of the vehicle. Sabine ran to the spot. Haugen stopped. She bent and came up with the deputy's service weapon. Swiftly she aimed it at the spot below the hood where the deputy had sprawled.

She fired twice in rapid succession.

Haugen said, "Stringer, put him in the trunk of the patrol car. Then get the other one out of the trees and put him in there too. And clean up the brass."

Stringer looked at him like, *huh?*

"The deputy called in this stop. When the station can't raise him, they'll send another deputy to investigate. We have to dispose of the evidence that something happened here."

He wasn't worried about the blood. The rain was already washing it away.

Stringer got out. The wind swirled through the Volvo, wet and stinging.

Haugen should have been in the cabin already, tracking market movements and funds transfers. He needed to get up there, quick.

Stringer hunched against the downpour and ran to Sabine's side. They dragged the deputy's body toward the patrol car. Halfway there, Sabine stopped. She looked at Haugen, reached into her pocket, and took out her phone.

Correction. A phone.

"It's Coates's again," she called to him.

He shook his head. *Don't answer.*

When they had loaded the bodies, Sabine looked pointedly at the deputy's car, and at the idling blue Tacoma pick-up. Haugen rolled down his window.

"I'll drive the cruiser. Sabine, you take the Volvo. Stringer, take the pick-up."

"We should dump it," Stringer said.

"Later. We don't want to discard a useful vehicle." Especially since Von and Friedrich had wrecked one already today.

Stringer hopped in the pick-up and put it in gear. The lights came on. Haugen got out of the SUV and headed for the cruiser.

Sabine said, "Once the sheriff sends another car to investigate, it will take maybe an hour to get up here. If we're lucky, it will take longer. If we're not lucky, they'll declare their man missing and begin a search."

"But we'll be so far gone and so deep in the gorge, in the dark, that they'll never find us. Come on."

Sabine climbed into the Volvo. Haugen put a hand on the door. "Who was calling Coates — Peter Reiniger?"

"No. It wasn't a four-one-five number. I'll check to see who it was once we get away from here."

Haugen got in the deputy's cruiser. There was a shotgun locked beside the center console. The key for it was hanging on the ring in the ignition. Excellent.

He pulled out and headed up the logging road higher into the mountains. The rain came down in sheets, thrown against the windows by the wind. It drummed so hard he could barely see the tail-lights of the Volvo twenty meters ahead. They crept toward the gorge at five miles an hour.

The cruiser's radio squawked. A man said, "D.V.?"

The dispatcher sounded worried.

"D.V., you there? Deputy Gilbert?"

Haugen eyed the radio. Perhaps they didn't have as much time as he'd hoped.

Then they reached the gorge, and Haugen saw a sight that thrilled and terrified him. The river was battering at the footings of the bridge.

CHAPTER
FORTY-TWO

The storm continued for hours. Inside the Hummer, everybody huddled together for warmth. Jo pressed herself to Gabe's side. She had taken off her soaking outer shirt and left on her thin but dry thermal fleece. Nobody spoke. The rain needled into the undercarriage of the Hummer above their heads, driven by the wind.

Gabe kept his eyes on the windows and his buck knife in his hand. He was stiff, and Jo didn't think it was simply from nerves and pain. Though he kept his arm over her shoulder, he seemed distant. She tried to draw him into whispered conversation, but he muttered brief replies.

About 4a.m., chilled and thirsty and aching, Jo popped awake, unaware she'd even fallen asleep.

Gabe was no longer by her side. She pried her eyes open. Something had surprised her into wakefulness.

Noise. It had changed.

The rain had eased and the wind had dropped. She no longer heard the near constant, tumbling crack of thunder. But she heard something else.

Gabe was crouched by the window of the Hummer, scanning the terrain outside. Moonlight fell across his face, white and cold.

He was staring at the river.

The sound, the new, raw sound, was water roaring through the gorge. But that wasn't what frightened her. What frightened her was the sound of the river lapping at the crushed frame of the Hummer.

Gabe moved. "We gotta go. Now."

He slid across the cramped interior of the limo. In the white moonlight, Jo saw the scene outside.

The lightning had ended. They could safely evacuate. And the rain had stopped. The clouds had blown away, and their opposition now had a clearer, easier chance to come after them. But that wasn't what scared her.

She saw the river thrashing through the gorge.

"Everybody up," Gabe said. "Hurry. It's an emergency."

Flash flood.

The Hummer had slid to rest a dozen feet from the riverbank, perhaps a meter above the level of the water. But the torrential mountain downpour had created flood conditions.

They were in a granite-lined gorge, where the water couldn't soak into the ground. It could only run off. Jo saw it — wild waves, turbulent, dangerous, and rising quickly. The spot upriver she had hiked across earlier, the inch-deep rock slab, was deeply submerged. Muddy torrents lapped at the side of the car.

"Quick," she said. "Gather up all the supplies. Help us get Noah out."

Nearby, the horse nickered and stamped its feet. Autumn and Lark crawled out the window of the

Hummer. They laid a thick coat across the windowsill. Jo and Gabe knelt on either side of Noah.

"Ready?" Gabe said.

Noah nodded halfheartedly. "Surfin' USA. Let's go."

"On three."

They slid him across the Hummer, grating against dust and chunks of shattered safety glass, to the window. Jo crawled out. She gestured for Autumn to help. They reached back inside and grabbed Noah's shoulders.

"This is going to hurt," Jo said.

"Do it."

She eyed Gabe. Then she and Autumn pulled. Gabe lifted Noah's legs. Noah's face looked vampire pale, but he didn't cry out. With a hard tug, Jo and Autumn hauled him through the window onto the rocky sand outside.

"Shit," he muttered.

"We're going to get you on the horse," Gabe said. "Then we're going to walk out of here."

Peyton continued to huddle in the far corner of the Hummer. Over the roar of the river, she said, "Don't make me. They're out there."

"And they're coming. We have to leave." Jo gestured to the river. "Look."

"Where can we even go?" Peyton said.

Jo turned, hopeless, to the river. Even in the time it had taken them to get out of the Hummer, the water had become more turbulent. There was no chance they could possibly cross it now, no chance at all to climb out of the gorge and somehow make their way back to the dead rancher's burned-out home, where a driveway led toward a way out. They were trapped on this riverbank. The gorge, already lined with stone and pines, was becoming a sluice gate of waves and debris and whitewater. Past them flowed branches and mud. The river was nothing but hard force, grinding wave action, the certainty of drowning.

And it was rising faster. It now slurped against the ruined headlights of the limo.

"Higher ground," Jo said. "Quick."

A thought rattled around her exhausted head, about the geography of the gorge, the direction of the logging road above them, and this portion of the national forest, but she couldn't fit it all together. Not right then, with the roar of the river growing ever louder.

But she had a gut feeling, a snap of certainty, that oriented her.

"Upriver," she said. "We need to go up the gorge and gain height."

Lark shook her head. "Farther into the forest? No — that's the way they were taking us. We need to get back to civilization, and it's downriver."

"Downriver is the direction the bad guys are coming *from*. We want to get farther away from them. Trust me." The nebulous thought was pulling at her, but still wouldn't come into focus. "Come on."

Legs trembling with fatigue, fingers stinging with cold, she untied the horse. Autumn and Lark linked arms to form a human armchair.

Gabe turned to Noah. "Can you do this, man?"

"Let's go," Noah said.

"Whatever you do, don't scream."

Jo and Gabe lifted Noah onto the girls' linked arms. The young women groaned and stood up. Wobbling, they carried Noah to Faithful's side. Noah wheezed through his teeth, trying to keep from shouting in pain. In the dark, with only the moonlight flaring through the clouds, his face was ghostly.

Gabe put Noah's good leg in the stirrup. Jo boosted him up. Groaning, Noah straightened and nearly fell across the saddle. Jo swung his broken leg across. He gripped the saddle horn, about to pass out.

He settled in the saddle. "Got it."

He hadn't, he was close to fainting, but he was holding on.

Gabe looked at Autumn and Lark. "One of you get on behind him and hang on."

Lark said, "I've never been on a horse."

Autumn put a hand on Lark's arm. A restraining hand. "You ride. I'll lead Faithful."

Lark didn't resist. She mounted awkwardly and settled behind the saddle on the horse's rump. Autumn held the reins.

"Where are we going?"

Jo felt all eyes on her in the thin white moonlight. "We're going upriver until we can find a safe spot to climb the hill to the logging road. We'll get out of the gorge, cross the road into the forest, and work our way back down from there."

Gabe had stuffed their emergency supplies into Kyle's black sports bag and slung it across his shoulders like a backpack, gingerly, protecting his sliced-up ribs. He held on to his buck knife and the steering-wheel club. Each of the others took up one of the carved spears. They started up the sandy bank, following the sound of rushing water.

Jo leaned into Autumn's ear. "How bad is Lark's eyesight?"

"Bad. She has juvenile macular degeneration."

Jo's chest squeezed. That was awful news. "Does she have any central vision?"

"Fuzzy. And her night vision is crap." Autumn looked out from under her Marine Corps utility cap. Quietly she added, "Don't mention it. She doesn't want any help. And definitely not any sympathy."

Jo nodded. "You're a good friend."

Autumn looked at her weirdly. She seemed baffled.

"You okay?" Jo said.

"It's . . . you think so?"

Gabe scanned the river and hillside. Without a word, he waved them upriver. Slipping across wet rocks and muddy ground, they began to climb.

The log scraped and scoured the roadbed, slowly, grating against the wet gravel. Headlights off, brake lights shining, the Toyota pick-up dug in and struggled to clear the fallen pine from the logging road. The ropes tied to the pick-up's trailer hitch stretched and groaned.

On the opposite side of the tree, Haugen nudged the Tuolumne sheriff's cruiser against the heavy trunk. The cruiser's push bumper connected with the wood. Painfully, inch by inch, the tree rasped across the road.

Haugen waved Stringer forward. "Keep going. You're getting it."

Finally, creaking and snapping, the tree slid out of the way. Haugen gave the all-clear sign and jumped out of the cruiser.

The rain had finally stopped. The night, however, was unrelenting. He heard the river tearing through the unseen gorge below. The downpour had turned into a flash flood. The river was a maelstrom.

He ran to the pick-up and helped Stringer untie the ropes from the pick-up's trailer hitch.

The logging road was nearly impassable. Under the force of the rain, rocks had cascaded down the hillside. Waterfalls of mud had poured down onto the road. Visibility became nonexistent. He, Sabine, and Stringer had been forced to stop and huddle until the downpour eased. Then they had wasted hours clearing debris and inching past washed-out sections of the road. The toppled pine was the third tree they had dragged from the road. But now at last they could make progress toward the spot where the Hummer had plunged into the gorge.

The bad news was that Von was no longer answering his cell phone.

But it wasn't all bad news. The bridge was gone. Haugen had watched debris-laden water sweep over the railings and tear the bridge in half.

His cold fingers fumbled with the knots in the rope. Sabine jogged over.

"Dane. How do you plan to get out of this hellhole with the bridge out?"

He couldn't get the knots. Stringer took out a switchblade and bent to cut them. Haugen turned to Sabine.

"The bridge washing out is good news," he said.

"How do you figure that?"

He heard a snapping noise and a thin form snaked around his calf. He shouted and danced back, kicking his foot to get rid of the thing.

"Where is it? Where?" he said.

Stringer picked up the rope he had just cut. "Sorry."

Haugen's ulcer flared. He could barely see for his rage. "Never do that. It could have been a lyre snake or a rattler. I might have shot it. And you."

Sabine crossed her arms. "Dane? The good news?"

Haugen smoothed down his hair and headed for the cruiser, blood pounding in his temples. "Law enforcement won't be able to drive up here this morning. We have complete run of the wilderness."

With the bridge out, nobody could get up the road. Not a sheriff's posse, not the highway patrol, nobody who might attempt to rescue Autumn Reiniger. Haugen had free rein. He got in the cruiser and led his three-vehicle convoy up the gorge.

CHAPTER
FORTY-THREE

Jo stepped gingerly along the sloping hillside. The river below sounded deafening, but she could still hear Peyton whimper. Autumn led the horse at a rolling walk. Lark and Noah rocked in the saddle. Jo strained to follow in Gabe's footsteps up the trail.

There was no trail.

Just rocks, pines, and dogwoods, and the sting of frigid wind on her skin. The clouds had cleared. Stars sprayed the sky, white ice.

Behind them, in the deep of the night, the screams had stopped. But they lingered in the air like static electricity, like djinns hovering over her shoulder, ready to swoop. Something was out there. She couldn't help feeling it closing on them.

"Gabe, I think we should risk the flashlight," she said.

"Not yet."

His voice, even at a whisper, was tight. "The trees aren't thick enough here to provide cover against the light. Wait till we find heavier foliage. Then I can run ahead to recon a path."

His silhouette was all she could see. He continued walking cautiously over the uneven slope. She glanced back. They'd traveled perhaps a quarter of a mile upstream from the Hummer.

"Lark?" she said. "Noah? How you doing?"

"Still here," Lark said.

Noah gave a weak thumbs-up. In the starlight, his eyes shone with pain.

His gunshot wound had stopped bleeding, and his vital signs were surprisingly good. His broken leg had to be agony, but he sucked it up. The kid was hanging on through youth, fitness, and the raw tenacity of life itself. Still, no matter how much grit he had, his tank would eventually run dry.

Peyton murmured, "It's so cold."

Autumn said, "Deal with it."

Peyton began to rub her wrist again.

Jo slowed to let Autumn catch up with her. "Tell me something. What was the idea behind the mock crime spree?"

"Adventure. My dad thinks these weekends take you places no other experience can." She glanced around at the forest. "He was right."

"Why not Outward Bound? Why a crime spree?"

"Dad designed it for me. He thought I'd get into it."

Jo managed to swallow the *wow*. "And you chose to play the cartel queen?"

"It's my party."

Jo raised an eyebrow. "So the crime boss seemed the natural choice to you?"

Autumn seemed to slow. Her gaze lengthened. "You mean, why didn't I decide to play a U.S. Marshal?"

"Do you feel like an outlaw?"

"No way. I . . ."

She frowned, struggling to put words to it. Maybe, Jo thought, struggling to put feelings to it.

"I'm the 'perfect daughter,' you know? I'm the ballerina twirling in the music box." She paused. "The one with *spoiled* written on the back."

"What were you supposed to do during the weekend?"

"Break out of prison and try to get away."

The horse tossed its head and took a hard step, lurching before it found its footing amid rocks on the hillside. Autumn soothed her hand along its nose and kept walking. Jo didn't think the girl realized what she had just said.

"What was going to happen at the end?" Jo said.

"I got it all. I ended up in custody, but bribed the marshals to join my team. We partied." She looked at the ground. "Dumb, huh?"

Jo couldn't even begin to catalogue the issues Autumn must have with boundaries. She could only imagine the girl's need to be held tight and given bright guidelines, before she could break free. And she thought the person Autumn really wanted on her team was her dad.

The horse hesitated on the slope and flicked his tail. Jo checked to make sure Peyton wasn't close to his hind legs. All she saw was trees and darkness.

"Where's Peyton?"

Autumn glanced back. Lark turned in the saddle.

"She was right here," Autumn said.

Lark stage-whispered, "Peyton?"

No reply.

Jo tried to see shapes in the fulminating darkness. Nothing. Autumn held on to the horse's bridle. Lark tilted her head up and listened to the night wind — alert, Jo thought, for errant noises.

Autumn's voice went flat. "She went back to the Hummer."

Lark nodded. "Yeah."

Jo's shoulders dropped. "Dammit."

They listened to the river thrash. "I'll go back," Jo said.

Gabe turned. "We both will."

His voice was hard. He waved to Autumn. "Lead the horse over here."

They continued along the riverbank for another fifty yards, until they could shelter behind a boulder. Autumn was shivering, Lark and Noah less so — the big animal was the warmest thing in the forest.

"Stay here," Gabe said. "Stay quiet. We'll be back."

He and Jo took off down the slope, watching each step in the dark. Jo's hands ached with cold. Gabe stepped carefully, agile in the night, semi-sidestepping so he wouldn't fall facedown if a root or rock tripped him.

"She can't be that far ahead," Jo said.

"Not far," Gabe said. "But this isn't good."

Peyton hugged herself. Her hair flew around her head in the wind. She staggered back the way they had come, eyes on the ground. It had to be here.

She had lost the bracelet. It was gone. It had fallen off her wrist sometime after they left the Hummer. She balled her freezing hands into fists. She had to find it.

Moonlight spilled on the ground through the trees. The silver bracelet would catch the light. She could find it. She had to.

She checked that nobody was coming after her. None of them would understand. They would have stopped her. They already thought she was silly and stupid, and they didn't know. She fought down a sob. They didn't understand.

She had to find it. Her grandmother had given it to her. Grier's smiling skull ring was looped around it. It was all she had left. It was everything and she had to retrieve it.

She scanned the ground, stumbling, her hair tangling in the wind. The river roared. She would find the bracelet and then she would run back and catch up with the group. They wouldn't even know she'd been gone.

But she had to find the bracelet before she started crying again and her eyes got too full of tears to see it. She stumbled through the brush and rocks, hoping.

Gabe and Jo ducked and bobbed, avoiding pine boughs, placing their feet carefully among the rocks and roots in the dark. Worry chewed at Jo. Peyton could have fallen. She could have tumbled into the river. With the water thundering, they would never hear a splash.

"I don't like this," she said.

"No kidding."

His tone, even at a whisper, was stinging. She felt fed up. "Why are you angry at me?"

He shook his head and continued working his way along the slope beneath the pines.

"Hey," she whispered. "Give me something. Anything. We're in a situation here. What's out of whack?"

He bent low and raised a hand. Jo stopped. She had heard it too.

A moment later, a spectral form flew past them. Wings cut the air. Her skin prickled and she ducked, gasping.

"Owl," Gabe said.

Jo held still, her whole body cramped. Gabe paused. He watched and listened, judging the scene as the night poured down on them. *High-level situational awareness.*

She stared at him until he looked at her.

He said, "You chased after Dustin and Kyle without telling anyone."

"There was no time. And I couldn't phone you."

"You disappeared. Never do that in a wilderness survival situation. You know that, Jo."

Despite the snapping cold wind, she felt hot. "It was an emergency." Her whisper felt choked. "I had to try to reach him."

"You put yourself in additional danger."

You left me worried sick, he meant.

Moonlight whitewashed his face. "It was an impulsive decision. You didn't stop to think about the risk to your own life."

Her head felt hot. She wanted to grab him and argue. But the irony was hitting her — of defending her actions while searching for Peyton. Hitting her, painfully. She swallowed her pride and kept silent.

His voice sounded strained. "You tried to save him. That's amazing. But you could have ended up —"

"Don't."

He held her with his gaze. She couldn't bear the vehemence in his eyes, or the fear.

"Next time I'll think it through," she said.

For a moment he said nothing. Then he gripped her shoulders, leaned in, and put his lips next to her ear. "I don't ever want to be the one who has to tell your family. Telling you was as awful as it gets."

Jo couldn't move. She wanted to slug him and run away and burst into tears and bury her face against him, all at once.

Gabe had been the PJ on scene the day her husband, Daniel, suffered fatal injuries in the medevac chopper crash. He had broken the news to her.

She nodded. "I get it."

He clasped her tight. "Be sure you do."

He turned and sped down the hill. She followed, chased by the wind.

CHAPTER
FORTY-FOUR

The forest closed in on both sides of the logging road, black and shaggy in the headlights of the Tuolumne County sheriff's car. Haugen rolled along at 5mph. The engine thrummed and the heater blasted. Overhead, the clouds had sped away, and the temperature continued to drop. The wind battered the car and scattered gravel across the road. Mile after mile, it was nothing but bitter emptiness. California was America's most populous state, yet so much of it was unbelievably isolated.

Then the road curved. On the left the hill dropped away into the river gorge where the Hummer had crashed.

He slowed further, looking again for Von. And, absent Von, looking for skid marks in the gravel, indicating where the limo had plunged off the road.

He stopped.

The cruiser's radio squawked. "D. V., come in. Ron — are you there?"

Haugen didn't answer. Didn't look anywhere but straight ahead, at the looming ponderosa pine at the edge of the road.

The tree was huge. It stood well over one hundred feet. Maybe one-fifty. Its trunk was fat, its bark tough and split with age. He was amazed no logging company had hacked it down.

Von was hanging from it.

Behind the patrol car, Sabine pulled up in the Volvo. Stringer edged around it in the blue Tacoma pick-up. When he flashed the high beams, the light caught Von's broad back, round head, and black jacket, glistening with rainwater.

He hadn't been hanged, not by the neck. That, to Haugen, was the most surprising thing. He was swinging from one dislocated arm, his hand cinched in a noose that swung from a high branch in the pine. The skin of his hand had the bluish tinge of frozen fish.

On the passenger seat, Haugen's walkie-talkie crackled.

"Howdy, partner," said Ruby Kyle Ratner.

Von twisted from the rope, his coat rippling in the wind. Haugen reached for the walkie-talkie.

Ratner continued, singsong. "You know your fractions, don't you? The smaller the denominator, the bigger each piece of the pie. And I love pie. My, yes, I do."

"Work with me, and we'll share," Haugen said.

Ratner laughed. It was a *squee*-like giggle, a whinny. "You are a card. You know that? An absolute card." He stopped laughing. "A joker."

Haugen put down the cruiser's window and waved urgently to the vehicles behind him. *Get over here.*

314

Stringer and Sabine climbed out and jogged up, hunched into their jackets. Haugen lifted his thumb from the walkie-talkie's Transmit button, so Ratner couldn't hear their conversation.

He pointed at the ponderosa pine. "Ratner did this. He has Von's walkie-talkie, so presume he has Von's gun as well."

Stringer squinted against the wind. "And?"

"Get him."

Stringer simply stood there, eyes on Von. "Should we cut him down?"

Haugen's anger rose. "I said, get Ratner."

"But —"

"If Autumn and her friends reach the road, this sight will terrify them and weaken their will. Listen to me. Ratner knows what the game is. He figured it out. If he gets us, he'll contact Reiniger directly. We have to take him out." He snapped his fingers. "Go."

Sabine leaned close to Stringer's ear. She was six inches taller than he was. "Don't be a pussy."

Stringer drew his weapon from inside his coat. He racked the slide on the pistol and jogged up the road, into the cone of the headlights. When he passed Von, he reflexively shied away.

Haugen didn't look at Sabine. "Your insult was ostentatious."

"Stringer doesn't respond to subtlety. He needs the loving lash of correction."

"Ratner is playing with us. This nonsense about the lasso. His stupid cowboy patois. He's a fool."

Despite the cold, she took a long, cool moment to appraise him. "No, he's not. He's a psychopath."

"He's a stupid man."

"Because he didn't go into high finance, like you? He's not stupid; he's calculating. He has the upper hand. He's out there and we don't know where."

"He's a thug."

"A loose cannon. A sick, unhinged loose cannon. You already had proof of that. Now you've got more. Don't underestimate him." She began walking back to the Volvo. "I'm going to drive up the road. You and I need to put distance between our vehicles. That way, if anybody climbs out of the gorge, we can pinch off their escape." She looked back. "And we need to drive this situation. Do something, Dane. You're in a damned police car. Use it."

She hopped in and gunned the SUV up the road, spewing gravel from beneath the tires.

Peyton scanned the ground for the bracelet, but the ground was stupidly covered with pinecones and rocks and roots. Her teeth were chattering. The cold made her furious. Her head was pounding and her mouth was dry. Stupid altitude. Stupid Dustin, opening the champagne and handing it to her in the limo.

Her chest heaved. She let out a breath, full of tears.

Dustin was gone. Grier was gone. Noah was hurt. That pararescue guy, Gabe Quintana, was a hard case. He would not have understood about the bracelet. If she had asked him about it he would have told her no. She had no choice but to go back, on her own, quickly.

The light in the sky flashed so briefly that she thought at first it was more lightning. But the thunder didn't come. The light flashed again. Blue, white, red, it swept across the mountainside. She let out a sharp breath and changed direction and pummelled up the slope toward it.

It was a police car. Her heart pounded. Her mouth was so dry she couldn't even swallow anymore. The cops were there. The nightmare could end, right now, if she could just claw her way up the slope to the road. Her feet slipped on a slick patch of moss and she dropped to her knees. She got up, staggered, wiped her hands on her shirt.

"Help," she said.

The police car was really there, straight above her. The lights were strobing between tree trunks, like angel wings.

"Help me."

Her voice didn't carry. Panting, she wobbled up the slope. The lights grew brighter. She thought she heard static from a police radio.

"Hey. *Help*."

She cut through a break in the trees. For a moment the view up the slope was unobstructed, all the way to the road far above her. Parked at the edge of the drop-off, angel lights spinning, was a black-and-white police cruiser.

"Help me."

Wings beat the air, and a bird swooped past. She cringed. "Shit."

Ducking, she turned and saw an owl glide through the trees along the slope.

She ran a hand over her hair, making sure that the filthy thing hadn't crapped on her head. Her fingers stung with cold. Her hair was damp and clumpy from the rain. Her nose was running. She wiped it and turned back around.

A man stood in front of her.

He was a small man, in black, wearing an Edge Adventures windbreaker. His face was obscured by the night.

A moan ran from her throat. He slapped her. *Smack*, her face stung and her head jerked sideways. He grabbed her sweatshirt, pushed a gun under her chin, and pulled her up against him.

"Cry like a bitch and I'll shoot you."

The gun felt cold against her skin. The man's face was right in front of hers. His eyes were narrow and he smelled of sweat. He'd been at Candlestick Point. He was one of the hijackers.

He raised a walkie-talkie. Static squawked from it, and she realized that was the sound she'd heard a minute earlier, the sound she had taken for a police radio.

He pressed a button. "Got one."

A moment later came the reply. "Who?"

"Peyton Mackie."

From the walkie-talkie: "Where are the others?"

She recognized the voice. Smooth and chilly. It belonged to the tall man in the ski mask, the one who had driven the speedboat. The boss.

The gunman leaned close to her and whispered, "Where are the others?"

She whimpered.

"You're not valuable on your own," he said. "You're only valuable for the information you can provide me. And with every second you don't provide it, that value shrinks toward zero."

She took a breath of the cold air and blinked stinging tears from her eyes and tried to keep from peeing her pants.

Through her teeth she said, "They crossed the river and climbed out of the gorge. Headed west. There's a ranch over there."

"How far?"

"I don't know."

"See, there goes your value, headed downhill again."

"Maybe a mile." She pointed, straight across the river, ninety degrees from the way they had actually gone. "And they're going slow. You can catch them."

Damn, why did she say that? Why did she make him think he could track the group down on his own? She should have . . . "I'll take you."

His smile was sudden. "You don't know anything about negotiation, do you? You just know about giving in. Too late, stupid."

Her legs sagged. "No. Please. Don't —"

The gunshot didn't sound loud. Just close and shocking. The blow felt surprisingly muffled. Peyton went down, hitting the cold dirt beneath the little man. The blood felt warm. And there was so much of it.

The pain in her collarbone was terrible. She was on her back. He was lying on top of her. His breath came in one long, sick exhalation. Oh God.

He was bleeding all over her.

She slapped at him and kicked and shoved him off her. He slid to the dirt, and his black Edge Adventures windbreaker looked shiny with blood and there was a smell in the air, acrid and sharp.

She wasn't shot. He was. She kicked at the man's body. She shoved him away with her feet and crabbed backward on the dirt.

She looked around frantically. "Who's there?"

Another man stepped from the shadows. He held a pistol in his hand. It shone in the moonlight.

"Get up," Kyle said.

Peyton gaped. "You shot him."

"You bet I did. He was gonna kill you."

"Don't hurt me."

He looked at her with those crazy eyes, bright and fluid under the moonlight. "Why would I hurt you?"

"Please, don't. I'll give you anything you want."

He didn't blink, even in the brisk wind. Something seemed different about his eyes. Slowly, deliberately, he put the gun in his pocket.

"You don't have to give me anything. Just tell me why you're so scared."

She looked at the dead man. Revolted, she shut her eyes. *Kyle had saved her.* "Where have you been?"

"Looking for a way out of here. Where's Dustin? Did he come back?"

She went still. "What do you mean?"

"We got separated. He took off when he thought he saw lights through the forest." He held out a hand. "Come on, let me help you up. We best get moving."

"Kyle, Dustin's dead."

"What?"

"Jo said Dustin was shot."

"Oh Lord." He put a hand to his temple. "Sweet Lord, no. Did Von get him?"

She hesitated. She didn't know what to believe. She glanced at the body again.

Warily, she took Kyle's hand.

He pulled her to her feet. "You're shivering."

"Jo thought you . . ."

"What?" His voice sounded gentle.

"She said you shot him."

He recoiled. "Me?"

Peyton nodded. Her breath steamed the air.

Kyle raised his hands. "That's plain crazy. Dustin? Me, shoot Dustin? Why on earth?"

"That's what she said."

He put both hands to his temples this time, as if he couldn't process the news. "Jo said she saw me shoot him?"

"No, she said . . ." What had Jo said? "She found his body. Him and a rancher."

"So you only have her word that any of this happened. None of you saw it. Dustin may still be out there, hurt. Or trying to escape."

"Why would Jo . . ."

It made no sense. She was cold and confused and very frightened.

But Kyle was calm. "What do you actually know about Jo?"

"She's a doctor."

"So she says. You seen any proof?"

"She . . ." Peyton tried to think. "She set Noah's leg."

"Did she?"

Peyton felt a new chill. "Actually, Gabe did."

Kyle looked around watchfully. He took her elbow and led her deeper into the trees, out of the moonlight. "How do you know she is who she says she is?"

"Who else would she be?"

"She showed up at the clearing where the gang pulled the Hummer off the road. Came strolling out of the woods as cool as all get out. What are the chances of that?"

"Are you saying there's another reason she was there?"

"There ain't no such thing as coincidence. You think anybody would drive up that logging road if they didn't have a special reason to be here? No way."

"Wait — you think Jo was *lurking* there?"

"What did she say was the reason she drove all the way out to the back of beyond?"

Peyton's stomach was tangling in a knot. "She didn't."

"Exactly." He looked worried. "This ain't good."

"What do you think?"

He rubbed his neck. "You tell me if we're on the same wavelength."

"You think Jo's working with the people who hijacked us?" she said.

"What possible other reason could there be for two groups to end up at that spot?"

Her stomach, her entire body, felt twisted. "Oh my God."

"Where's Autumn and the rest?" He smiled. "I mean, where'd they go, for real."

She felt her face flush. "You heard me tell that hijacker they crossed the river?"

"Crafty girl." The smile spread. "You were quick on the draw back there, to bullshit him. And brave."

That smile of his was mega-bright. It bucked Peyton up. She gave him a smile of her own.

"They headed up the river, on this side. They've got a horse, and they're planning to find a way up to the road. You know, get in cell phone range and call the cops."

"That's what Jo wanted you to think."

"Oh God. What should we do?"

"We have to warn your friends. Come on."

He ushered her past the dead body. They ran along the hillside through the trees, parallel to the raging river below. All at once she felt warm.

"Thank you for what you did back there," she said.

"Nothing any man wouldn't do." He flashed the smile. "For a beautiful lady."

"That guy — the dead guy — what was he after?"

"Good question. I know Autumn comes from money, but what about the rest of you?"

"Dustin's family, you bet."

He glanced at her. "What about you, pretty lady?"

"My dad's a stockbroker."

"Megabucks?"

"Hardly."

She stumbled. She was deeply out of breath. Kyle caught her wrist and steadied her. His eyes lingered on her face. She'd seen that look before. He was captivated by her.

"How far upriver are the others?" he said.

"We walked — I don't know — twenty minutes?"

Below them the water rushed by, choppy with whitecaps. A branch hung low in front of them. Kyle swept it aside with his right hand. The gun glinted in the moonlight.

And she thought: How lucky that he had that gun. Where did he find it?

CHAPTER
FORTY-FIVE

Gabe and Jo crept along the riverbank. Jo's breath frosted the air. The sky was crisp and close, the stars overpowering, a white fire fall. But in the clear air the temperature continued to drop. The wind cut through her.

Gabe raised a hand. *Stop*.

She brought herself up. Ahead, on the bank above the churning torrent that had become the river, she saw what had drawn Gabe's attention.

Gabe crouched down. He held the buck knife low by his side. Jo nudged up behind him. She took a long look at the lump on the hillside. It was a man's body.

Gabe held still for a slow, deliberative half minute. He and Jo could see the man's shirt, shining with something dark and wet. They didn't hear or see anything else. Finally Gabe stood and ran up the path. He knelt and put two fingers to the man's neck.

"Dead. He's been shot," he said.

Jo took a closer look. The wound in the man's back was an entry wound. No exit wound on his body. A single hole. "Not killed with a twelve-gauge shotgun, that's for sure. This was done with a handgun."

Gabe looked across the river, and up the hill. "Kyle."

"Where'd he get the weapon?" she said. "And who is this?"

As soon as the words left her lips, she knew. Her skin seemed to ripple. "They're here."

They scanned the hillside.

"How much farther to the Hummer?" she said.

"Couple hundred yards." He peered up the path as though trying to force X-ray vision. "Peyton ran across this guy."

She thought about it for a moment and realized he was right. There was no other explanation or reasonable likelihood.

"I bet he was armed. But I doubt she disarmed him," Jo said.

Their eyes met. Gabe said, "I think we're in the middle of a battle."

"Between the kidnappers and the Bad Cowboy?"

"I didn't say it made sense."

Jo looked around. Where was Peyton?

The dirt crumbled beneath Peyton's feet. "Wait."

She was so out of breath. These mountains had no air in them. Kyle, jogging beside her through the thick trees up the hillside, turned with a sharp look on his face.

"What's the problem?" he said.

"I'm so tired. My shoulder's killing me. I have to stop."

He looked, for a second, absolutely baffled. Then he eyed her, up and down, as if trying to fit her into some particular slot. His face, those bright intense eyes, softened.

"Okay. We can rest a minute. Have a seat."

He gestured to a rock. She sat down. The stone was cold and wet. This sucked.

Kyle put a hand on her shoulder. "Catch your breath. Just sit tight."

She nodded and tucked a damp, ropy lock of hair behind her ear. Her breath turned white in the air. Kyle stepped away.

A moment later, he took a walkie-talkie from his pocket. He pressed a button.

"It's Howdy Doody time," he said.

He released the button and static scratched from the walkie-talkie.

Peyton said, "What's that?"

A moment later, a man's voice crackled from the walkie-talkie. "Don't bother using up the battery. I have nothing to say to you."

Kyle pressed the button again. "You're awful quick on the presumption there, Dane."

Peyton stood up. "Who are you talking to?"

Kyle motioned her closer. Put a finger to his lips, conspiratorially. She leaned in and whispered, "What's going on?"

Kyle slid an arm around her waist. She wasn't surprised. She'd been expecting it. She knew exactly how to handle guys like this. And, to tell the truth, he wasn't the worst thing she could have come across on this disaster of a trip.

He put the walkie-talkie to his lips. "You think I've been bluffing. You are sorely mistaken."

Well, except for Kyle's peculiar cornpone way of talking.

"You want the birthday party gang. But you don't know where they are."

The walkie-talkie crackled. "Babble all you want. You're alone in the night in the wilderness. You should be thinking about getting out of there before you freeze. Or get eaten by a bear."

"Oh, I ain't worried about bears. There's other wildlife that's on my mind." He squeezed Peyton to him. The flirt.

"You know, I could listen to your drivel all night long, if I had insomnia. But I don't have the time. So I'll be signing off now."

"Not yet," Kyle said.

He let go of the Transmit button. To Peyton, he said, "Unzip my backpack, will you?"

He turned and slid it off his shoulders. She whipped the zipper around.

"Hand me that sack," he said.

"Which sack?"

The backpack was heavy and crammed with ropes and water bottles and a burlap sack and what looked like nice felt drawstring bags — the kind that expensive whiskey came in, like Royal Crown. Or the kind that expensive shoes came in.

"The big one," Kyle said.

Leather boot size, Peyton thought. She pulled it out. It was surprisingly heavy. And lumpy. Something shapeless filled the bottom.

Kyle crouched down and untied a knot in the end of the sack. He picked up the walkie-talkie again.

"Dane?" he said. "You find Von yet?"

Peyton looked at him.

"I'm gonna take your silence as a yes," Kyle said.

She grabbed his sleeve. "Von? That asshole who was in the Hummer?"

Kyle pulled his arm free and shushed her. She grabbed him again.

"Did you see Von?" she said.

"Don't get scared. Von can't hurt you."

Her mouth opened. "Did you get him too?"

"I tried to get him to tell me what's up with Jo Beckett. He didn't want to."

That explained it. "Is that where you got the gun?"

He blinked, and his eyes looked unsettled for a moment. "Yeah. From Von."

"What happened to him?" she said.

Kyle eyed her, heat in his gaze. He put the walkie-talkie to his face and pressed the button. "Did you take a close look at him?"

There was no reply, but Kyle smiled. Peyton felt a wriggle of worry. What was Kyle talking about?

He hefted the felt drawstring sack. In the dark, with shadows flickering across the hillside, it was impossible to see it clearly. But Peyton thought she saw it sway.

Then she saw the movement again. And it wasn't an optical illusion. It wasn't the shadows that were moving. It was the sack. Her stomach clenched.

"*Crotalus scutulatus,*" Kyle said.

Static clicked over the walkie-talkie. But the man on the other end didn't say anything. And Peyton thought about that man's voice. It was familiar.

She thought it was the man who had been in the speedboat earlier. It was the head honcho of the ambush gang. And Kyle was giving the guy an earful.

She just couldn't shake the feeling that something was *off*.

"Can you translate that?" Kyle said. "No? Mister big-brain, always the inte-goddamned-lectual, has no idea, does he?"

Peyton whispered, "Don't make this guy mad, Kyle."

His head whipped around. "I know what I'm doing."

Back to the walkie-talkie. "Y'all know me as the Red Rattler. But I got something here that's a little bit fresher." He looked at the sack. His eyes seemed eager. "I got me a green. *Crotalus scutulatus*, a Mojave green."

What was he talking about?

"You think I'm just blowing smoke?" Kyle said. "I want you to listen closely."

He set down the walkie-talkie. Then, holding the sack close to his chest, rubbing it, he told Peyton, "This is gonna blow your mind."

She pulled her hands in. "I don't think so."

She felt an urge to move back. She stood up and took a step.

Kyle shot out an arm, quicker than a whip, and grabbed her ankle. Before she could react, he yanked. She lost her balance. On the steep hillside she threw her arms out and fell backward.

She thumped down on rocks, hitting her head. Her broken collarbone shot through with pain. She tried to breathe but the agony was too sharp. She saw stars, flying stars, mingling with the others in the sky.

Kyle jumped on top of her, straddled her, and before she knew it, pinned her hands beneath his thighs. He pressed a hand to her mouth. Her eyes went wide.

With his free hand, he gently tugged open the top of the drawstring sack. Still grasping it, he held it out and set it on Peyton's chest.

Oh God. It was heavy. It was like a three-foot-long muscle placed on top of her. A coiling, *purposeful* muscle.

There was a snake in the sack.

She kicked her legs, dug her heels into the soft dirt and pine needles on the hillside, trying to push herself out from under Kyle. He was lithe and light, but stronger than steel cable. He squeezed her thighs and pressed his hand down harder on her mouth. His eyes were pinned on her. She tried to scream, but the sound was muffled by his hot palm.

The snake nudged its nose through the opening in the sack. Slowly, steadily, its head appeared. It was big. It was gray under the ashen moonlight. Its tongue flicked out.

She rocked, trying to escape. The chill of the earth, her broken collarbone, everything zeroed into fear.

"Can't tell what color it is right now," Kyle said. "But it's a Mojave green. That's a rattlesnake."

Peyton thrashed and shrieked behind his hand. She tried to buck him off. Her sweater caught on a pinecone beneath her and pulled off her shoulders.

"You're just making him mad," Kyle said.

The snake gradually slithered out of the sack six inches, then a foot. Its tongue flicked again. Kyle adeptly pinched its neck, just behind its head.

"Can't hear the rattle for all this wind," he said. "Shame."

The snake flicked, trying to get away.

"Ooh, he's riled up now." He smiled at the snake, shook it, made a hissing sound himself. Then he dropped it on Peyton's face.

The snake coiled and spun and slithered around. The bite came quicker than a bolt of electricity. The snake lunged and sank its fangs into her arm.

She felt the shock, a new pain. Kyle pulled his hand from her mouth, grabbed the snake, and wrestled it back into the sack. Then he picked up the walkie-talkie. He pushed Talk.

He didn't say a word. He held the walkie-talkie while her screams filled the air.

CHAPTER
FORTY-SIX

The screams came from the trees, uphill in the dark. Jo turned toward the sound. Gabe stepped in front of her. He had the club in his left hand. In his right he held the buck knife.

"Peyton," Jo said.

The sound was uncontrolled, unconcerned about drawing attention. It was beyond desperate.

And it was moving.

"She's running," Jo said.

The screams vectored in the direction where Jo and Gabe had left Autumn and the others.

"Come on," Gabe said.

He turned and ran back up the trail. Jo paused, looked at the dead man, and saw the walkie-talkie peeking from the pocket of his jacket. She grabbed it. Then she chased after Gabe, following the sound of screaming, hoping to intersect it. She was thinking the same thing Gabe had to be: If Peyton was that loud, everybody on the mountain would be coming.

And there weren't any rescuers on the mountain.

Autumn heard the screaming and wheeled, brandishing her whittled spear.

The horse raised its head in the moonlight. Its bridle clicked. The screaming intensified.

"It's Peyton," Noah said.

They heard panting, wheezing, hands shoving branches aside.

She burst from the trees and staggered into Autumn's arms. "Help me."

Her eyes were frantic. She threw her head back and collapsed. Autumn dropped to her side.

"What's wrong?" Autumn said.

Kyle stepped from the trees. "What isn't?"

Jo pushed her pace up the hill. "We have to hurry."

Gabe ran, but he didn't outdistance her. With a bright zing of worry, she realized that his breathing sounded ragged.

They pushed through the brush and arrived at the clearing above the riverbank where they had left the group. Jo didn't see Autumn, the horse, or Lark and Noah. But she saw a figure in dirty raspberry velour. Peyton knelt in the center of the clearing like a communicant. The screaming was unhinged and mixed with sobbing.

She raised her head. "Help me."

They ran to her side. Gabe tossed the club to Jo and flipped on the flashlight. Peyton's chest was heaving. Her eyes were insane. Her sweater had been torn off. Blood was running down her right arm from two puncture wounds to the biceps.

Jo tried to hold her still. "Don't move."

"It bit me," she shrieked.

"Snake? A rattlesnake?"

Peyton nodded.

"Sit down," Gabe said. "And be quiet."

"Help me," Peyton said. "I don't want to die."

"None of us do. So keep quiet and hold still."

Jo squeezed her shoulders. "Look at me, Peyton."

"It bit me." Peyton shut her eyes, leaned back, and screamed at the sky.

Jo shook her. "Stop it. Right this second."

Peyton kept sobbing. Gabe's face knotted with frustration. Jo pulled Peyton tight against her shoulder, pressed the girl's head to her chest and spoke firmly into her ear.

"The more you scream, the harder your heart pumps, the worse the effects of the venom. Be quiet."

It worked like a slap in the face. Peyton's head jerked up.

Gabe pointed at the ground. "Sit down. Come on. Quick."

Peyton shakily sat down. "He . . ." She huffed, fighting another sob. "He held me down. He let it out of a sack."

"Kyle did this?" Jo said.

Gabe glanced at Jo. His eyes told her: *Too late.* Peyton's screams had alerted the bad guys. She was both a message and a beacon.

"They're going to be coming," he said. "Soon."

"No," Peyton said. "They're already gone. Kyle took the others."

On the slope, several hundred feet uphill from the ragged panic in the blond slattern's screams, Kyle crouched on top of a boulder, waiting.

The sack was tied securely. The snake was back inside it. He had slipped it inside his coat, to keep the snake warm. He liked the feeling of such power coiled against his body.

Down the slope through the forest below him, the blonde continued sobbing and screaming. The wind rushed through the pines. It carried the girl's wails up the slope. He glanced toward the logging road.

Haugen would hear her. He'd pinpoint the noise. He'd come.

Kyle smiled. He had three kids and a horse — and a twelve-gauge shotgun, aimed straight at them. They wouldn't run. They wouldn't utter a peep. Noah couldn't. Lark wouldn't run because she knew if she tried, he'd shoot Noah. Love — what a neat little knot it tied in people's lives.

And Autumn, his prize-above-all-prizes — she was too damned loyal to her friends. She just couldn't stand what would happen to them if she ran.

Sucker.

He gave her the stare. The good old evil eye. She shrank from him, but she couldn't look away. The white snake didn't have to touch people to poison them.

He waited while Peyton quieted down. Either she was passed out, or the helpful doctor and her beau had found her. Either way, they'd be tied up for a bit.

"Let's go." He nudged the group forward with the barrel of the shotgun.

He would have loved to linger and watch Peyton die. But he heard more sounds in the forest nearby. Haugen and his band of merry men. He got a move on.

He had the walkie-talkie. He had hostages. Haugen would come to him.

Peyton thrashed. "It hurts. Oh God, it burns."

Jo held the girl's arm to keep her from raising it. "You need to keep the site of the bite below the level of your heart. That helps limit the venom from pumping through your body."

It was standard advice, but probably too late. Peyton had run across the mountainside, her heart thundering. She was likely to be well envenomated.

Her eyes were still wild. "Suck the venom out. Cut an X on my arm and suck the venom out."

Gabe shook his head. "That's the wrong advice."

"You've got that knife." She grabbed his shirt. "Come on, do it."

He took her hands. "They used to do that. Not anymore."

"You scared you'll swallow the venom? Give me the knife. I'll do it."

How he maintained his composure, Jo didn't know. He held tight to her hands. "Sucking the venom *doesn't work*. Staying calm does."

But it would only work for the time being. Peyton needed to get to an ER and be evaluated to see if she needed antivenom.

"First-aid kit?" Jo said.

Gabe shrugged the sports bag off his shoulders. Jo rummaged inside for the kit and got out gauze and antiseptic. Cleaning the bite might be little more than a calming gesture, but calm was what Peyton needed.

Tears welled in the girl's eyes. "What about a tourniquet?"

Gabe spoke in measured tones. "No. That could cause more harm than good. What will help is to stay calm. Because there's good news. Most rattlesnake bites are not fatal."

Tears spilled down Peyton's face. Her eyes were puffy. "He said it was a green."

Jo felt a jolt, a trace of electricity down her arms. "The snake?"

Gabe said, "A Mojave green?"

Peyton nodded. "He talked on the walkie-talkie. Said I had no chance."

"Peyton," Jo said, "listen to me. He's a liar. A psychopath."

"What did the snake look like?" Gabe said.

"Like a goddamned rattlesnake. With fangs. He said it was a Mojave green."

Jo and Gabe exchanged a glance. Jo's heart sank.

Haugen put down the window of the deputy's car. He heard the wind, a cold moan. The girl's screaming had finally stopped. The walkie-talkie had gone silent.

He flashed the lights at Sabine, up the road in the Volvo. She flashed back. She'd heard Ruby Kyle Ratner's little broadcast too.

He opened the door. He had to move on Ratner before the psycho killed Autumn. But as he did, the police radio crackled to life.

"Unit Four, come in, over."

He paused. This car — he knew from the dispatcher's pathetic attempts to raise the dead deputy, D. V. Gilbert — was Unit Two. The dispatcher was now calling somebody else.

Backup.

The dispatcher: "The state logging road north of mile marker ninety-two."

A distant, staticky voice replied: "Roger. I am on my way. I'm forty miles from there. Where's the CHP?"

"The nearest highway patrol unit is in Oakdale, but proceeding to the location."

"Should we set up a roadblock?" said Unit Four.

Haugen held still. A roadblock would be fatal to his plans. A roadblock would catch him with his playthings, here in the wilderness. There was no other way out of this desolate forest besides downhill on this road.

He smashed his palm into the steering wheel. *Dammit*. This *should not* be happening.

But the Tuolumne County deputies were forty miles away. The highway patrol was even more distant. He had time.

And if he didn't?

The walkie-talkie cackled. "Dane. Oh, Dane . . ."

Whispery, singsong, Ratner continued taunting him. "You best hurry, partner. My piece of the pie can only get bigger."

Ratner giggled again. It was a high, slippery sound. It made Haugen's throat contract. He climbed out of the car.

"I suggest you get on the highway and start walking," Haugen said. "Because you're getting nothing. And if you stick around, you'll die."

"That's an awful rude thing to say to me."

"You can't extort me on this."

"Course I can. I'm an expert at it."

You're an imbecile, Haugen thought. "No, you simply have no limits."

"Bingo." Ratner laughed again.

Haugen walked up the road. Ruben Kyle Ratner was nothing but an impediment. He could not be allowed to derail this finely calibrated plan.

"Okay," Haugen said. "I'll deal."

"Just like that?"

"Just like that. I know when it's best to divide up the market. But I'm doing this in the expectation that there will be reciprocity down the line."

"I was in the Hummer when your morons drove it into a ravine. Reciprocity starts with you paying me for pain and suffering. Ouch. Think I have a touch of whiplash." That whinnying laugh again.

Haugen paced along, gravel squelching beneath his boots. He listened. The wind was gusting, but he knew Ratner was close. He had to be — otherwise these short-range walkie-talkies wouldn't be working. He slowed and listened for Ratner's voice to emanate from his hiding place.

340

He approached the tree from which hung Von's body. The wind moaned and beat against Von's flapping coat. Haugen held quiet. The moan changed pitch.

Haugen turned sharply and stared at Von.

Von stared back. "Boss. Help."

Jo stroked Peyton's back, trying to calm her.

"I don't want to die," the girl rasped.

"You're not going to. Got that? You're going to survive — like almost everybody else. The most important thing to do is to lower your heart rate."

But hearing that the snake was a Mojave green had alarmed Jo. Mojave greens were more aggressive than any other rattlesnake. Their venom was a neurotoxin. A high-enough dose could stop a person's breathing. They had a fearsome — and justified — reputation as the deadliest variety of rattlesnake.

"Do *something*," Peyton said. "Ice it — pour cold water on it."

Gabe said, "Afraid not. Cold keeps the venom concentrated at the site of the bite."

"That's not a good thing?" she wheezed.

"No. The concentration can cause extreme tissue damage."

Necrosis. Tissue death. Muscle and bone could literally dissolve. Jo had seen it in the ER. And Peyton's condition was already perilous. The bite wound was bruised red and blue and was swelling markedly. And her breathing sounded forced.

"It burns so bad," she said thickly. She scratched at her stomach and legs. "And itches all over."

She gulped for air. Under the glare of the flashlight, Jo saw that she was flushed.

"Got to . . ." Her voice was a bare whisper. ". . . Stand up."

Her eyes widened. She opened her mouth and gasped for breath. All Jo heard was a rasp. And that instant was all the time it took. She clawed at her throat. Her eyes rolled back and she slumped to the ground.

"She's not breathing," Jo said.

"Lay her flat," Gabe said. "Airway."

They straightened her out on the ground, and he lifted her chin and tilted her head back and put his face near her lips to check for breath. Jo felt an overwhelming rush of panic. This shouldn't be happening.

She had told Peyton she was going to survive. Almost everybody does. But Peyton lay motionless on the dirt, limp, sightless, her chest still.

It shouldn't be happening, but it was. Peyton was gone.

CHAPTER
FORTY-SEVEN

Tang swung her Hot Wheels racer into the parking garage at the Hall of Justice. Evan followed in the Mustang. The hulking building took up an entire city block. It was the size of a beached ocean liner. It looked flour white in the early morning air.

The homicide detail was deserted, a skeleton staff on duty overnight. Fluorescent lights gave the office a cold sheen. Tang picked up her desk phone and dialed the Tuolumne County Sheriff's Office.

Through the speaker, the sheriff sounded strained. "Lieutenant, yes, we sent a deputy to investigate. He found the pick-up truck."

Evan moved closer to the desk.

Tang said, "And Dr Beckett? Mr Quintana?"

"No sign of them."

Tang's face tightened. She stared at the phone and straight on through. After a moment, she gathered herself. "Can you connect me to Deputy Gilbert?"

The sheriff hesitated. "He's not responding on the radio. I can't raise him."

Tang sat down. "You've lost contact?"

"Another patrol unit is on its way to Ron's last-known location, but they're forty miles away and the weather's deteriorated."

Tang absorbed it. "How did Deputy Gilbert describe the scene where he found the pick-up?"

"Truck was parked in the clearing at the trailhead leading to the mine. Driver's door open, engine running."

Evan rubbed her forehead. Nothing good could possibly be spun from the news.

She leaned in. "Evan Delaney here. I'm the one who contacted Deputy Gilbert with information about that location. Did he explore the scene? Did he go up the trail?"

Tang's cell phone rang. She stepped away from the desk and answered it.

The sheriff said, "If Ron went up the trail he didn't tell me. And I don't think he had time."

Evan felt another prickle of worry. "Time?"

"A vehicle came up the logging road. He flagged it down to find out if the driver had seen anything. He radioed that it was a late-model Volvo SUV."

Tang ended her call and immediately her phone rang again. She answered, spoke briefly, hung up. When she spoke again to the sheriff, her voice took on a new urgency. "Did your deputy get the Volvo's tag number?"

"His dashboard camera captured it and sent it through." The sheriff read it off. "It came back registered to a corporation. Ragnarok."

Evan wanted to grab the phone and pull the sheriff through the line onto Tang's desk and kiss him.

344

Tang leaned over. "Listen. I just got off the phone with our Bayview station. They got a call this afternoon from a citizen who was out for a walk at Candlestick Point. She wanted to report 'shady business' on the beach."

Evan turned. "Meaning?"

"She described it as *Beverly Hills, 90210* meets *Miami Vice*. Bunch of shiny-looking young people pull up in a limousine, drinking champagne. A few minutes later, a speedboat drives up and gunmen in ski masks chase them down."

The sheriff said, "What?"

"However, one of the kids told the citizen it was all make-believe. It was a party. And one of the supposed gunmen — a woman — gave her a business card."

"Let me guess," Evan said. "Edge Adventures."

Tang pointed a finger at her, like a pistol. "Bull's-eye."

"So what gives?"

"The female 'gunman' didn't completely mollify the citizen. After the kids splashed away in the speedboat, the citizen took down the license numbers of two vehicles — the limousine and a black Volvo SUV. She phoned the police to report the incident. She said something didn't smell right."

The sheriff said, "Was it the same Volvo SUV?"

"Yes."

"Damn."

Evan held her counsel. Tang looked both energized and pale with worry.

"Here's the thing," Tang said. "The Bayview station reassured the caller that everything was fine. Edge Adventures phoned two days ago to inform them they'd be running an 'urban reality game' at Candlestick Point today."

Evan said, "Are you saying that everything's copacetic? The SUV, the scenario — it's all aboveboard?"

"No. Edge Adventures doesn't own an SUV." She paused a beat. "And the second call I just got was from Terry Coates's girlfriend. She gave me the list of game runners for this weekend's reality scenario. Not one of them is a woman."

All wrong blared in Evan's head. Way, far wrong. "There's something else, Sheriff. Ragnarok — the company that owns the Volvo SUV — its number was in the cell phone Jo found near the abandoned mine."

The sheriff broke the humming silence. "We need to track down that vehicle."

Tang said, "You need to set up a roadblock."

"My thinking exactly, Lieutenant."

"Keep me informed."

Evan opened her mouth to speak, and paused. "I hope Deputy Gilbert turns up safely."

Tang said, "Ditto that. Good luck."

She hung up. After a heavy pause, she said, "Coates's girlfriend had another piece of information. Edge Adventures' client this weekend is a young woman named Autumn Reiniger."

"The twenty-first-birthday girl?" Evan felt a buzz. "Excellent. That's great."

346

Tang made another phone call, to a detective on duty. She told him to find out everything he could about Autumn Reiniger. When she finished, she shut her eyes and pinched the bridge of her nose.

"You should be more excited," Evan said. "What is it?"

"The Tuolumne deputy. It's bad news. There's not going to be a happy ending."

"Don't be so sure."

"Deputy Gilbert found Jo's truck abandoned with the driver's door open and the engine running. Now he goes missing, immediately after this mysterious Volvo SUV appears on the scene. I'm not about to shake the pom-poms."

"You encouraged the sheriff. Encourage yourself too," Evan said.

Tang's eyebrows rose. "Are you kidding? Do you know who that was? Sheriff Walt Gilbert. He's Deputy Ron Gilbert's father."

CHAPTER
FORTY-EIGHT

Peyton lay stretched out on the chilly dirt. Her eyes were half open. Her face was slack. Her chest was still. Gabe knelt beside her. Emotion burst across his face, flaring like a match. He swiped the back of his hand across his forehead. Jo's own chest was tight with anger and disbelief.

Losing a patient hurt. Losing a young patient could be crushing. Doctors, paramedics, firefighters, PJs, all barricaded their emotions against the impact. And when it happened, it didn't feel like a blow. It felt like a drain had opened, swallowing everything and leaving a vacuum in its wake.

Jo could hear the river. It was turbulent, braiding around rocks, pouring cold down the mountain. Again, she thought: None of this should have been happening. Rattlesnake bites didn't kill people this fast. Not even a bite from a Mojave green.

She leaned over Peyton and flicked the beam of the flashlight at her eyes. Her pupils constricted.

She was still there.

"CPR," Gabe said.

He leaned down and began blowing air into Peyton's lungs. Her chest didn't move. Still no respirations. No sound, no evidence that Peyton was getting oxygen. She remained limp.

"Airway's completely blocked. Her throat's swollen shut," he said.

The sinking, dizzy feeling ran through Jo and settled hard. Peyton was falling toward the far side, maybe already there. Jo seemed to hear echoes in her head. *We have to go. He's dead. I'm sorry.*

No. She focused.

She looked at Gabe. "We are *not* going to have to tell her parents."

He stared at Peyton. "Absolutely not."

The vehemence in his voice, even *sotto voce*, felt like pressure in Jo's chest.

"Trach?" he said.

It was a desperate idea, giving Peyton an emergency tracheotomy, but the situation was critical. He drew his buck knife and palpated Peyton's neck.

"Perimeter. Watch for people coming," he said.

Jo scanned the darkened slope. She could see nothing but shifting shadows in the moonlight. She grabbed Peyton's wrist and checked for a pulse. It was there, solid. *What was causing this?*

"Maybe an especially powerful load of venom?" she said.

Wrong, wrong, this was so wrong — but real, and right there. Peyton's words . . . "*When I was little I . . .*"

Jo stilled. *Oh my God.* "Anaphylaxis?"

The venom of a Mojave green could paralyze its prey and stop its breathing. But it should not cause a victim's throat to swell shut.

But a severe allergic reaction might. Anaphylactic shock.

Gabe looked surprised and doubtful. "Allergic reaction to a snakebite?"

Anaphylactic shock was a rare complication in snakebite. It could only happen if the victim had been previously exposed to venom.

"Peyton said, 'When I was little I almost got poisoned by a rattler,'" Jo said. "I thought she meant a snake got into the campsite. But —"

"Maybe the rattler actually struck her?"

Jo grabbed the first-aid kit. She foraged through it and grabbed the EpiPen.

Gabe sliced a hole in Peyton's velour track bottoms and ripped the fabric to expose her thigh. Jo popped the cap from the back end of the EpiPen and jabbed the pen into Peyton's quadriceps, injecting epinephrine directly into the muscle.

She pressed, counting slowly to ten. It seemed to take forever. She pulled out the needle and massaged the injection site.

They waited, aching. Jo monitored Peyton's pulse. The buck knife hovered in Gabe's hand, gleaming in the beam of the flashlight.

Peyton breathed.

She wheezed. Her chest rose.

Jo whispered, "Come on. Come on, honey."

Gabe held the knife poised above her throat. She gasped. She was getting air.

"Recovery position," he said.

They rolled her onto her side. Her lungs were working. Her airway was open. Her mouth opened. Her eyes opened.

"That's it," Jo said. "Peyton. Hang in there."

Gabe sank back on his heels. Despite the chill, he was sweating.

Peyton looked at Jo. Whispered, "What happened?"

"Allergic reaction. We gave you an injection of epinephrine."

She shut her eyes. "Thank you."

Tentatively Jo reached out and with the tips of her fingers brushed tangled, wet strings of hair from the girl's face. "When you were little, did the rattler bite you?"

"Dry bite."

Jo frowned.

"Jerked my leg free before its fangs sank in. But this time . . ."

Jo and Gabe exchanged a glance. The childhood bite must have contained some venom.

Eyes still shut, Peyton said, "I'm sorry." Her lips quivered. "My bracelet. Grandmother gave — I just . . . sorry."

"Save the apologies for when we're home. You can buy me a beer."

"Buy you a case." She took a breath. "When I turn twenty-one."

Jo tucked Peyton's hair behind her ear. "Deal."

They kept Peyton in the recovery position for fifteen minutes. Her breathing eased. The flushing and itching subsided. Her face, though still drawn with pain, no longer looked puffy. Her pulse remained strong and her respirations became regular.

Gabe stood up and beckoned Jo out of the girl's earshot. "We have a decision to make."

Peyton rolled over. "I don't want to stay here."

"You just rest. We'll figure it out."

"No. Don't make me stay here." She struggled to a sitting position. "I can walk."

They looked at her, patently doubtful.

"Really." She held out her left hand. "Help me up."

Jo thought, *First, do no harm.* Hiking out with a rattlesnake bite was far from ideal. Doing it in the aftermath of anaphylaxis was even more uncertain. But even more important than keeping Peyton still was getting her to an ER. Anything that reduced the time it took to get her to a hospital would improve her chances of survival and recovery. And staying here, where Kyle could find them, was the most dangerous option of all.

Peyton pushed to her feet. "I can walk. Please. We need to stay together. I'll do whatever you want, whatever you say. I promise."

Keeping Peyton in one place until she could be evacuated would be ideal, but she couldn't be left alone. Jo could stay with her, but Gabe's expression said in no uncertain terms that he would not let that happen. Either they all stayed, or they all went. And none of them was going to stay.

Gabe looked up the slope, into the forest. Jo felt certainty hover in the air between them. They were going to find the others.

"Let's go," she said.

CHAPTER
FORTY-NINE

Evan felt a finger poke her shoulder and smelled scorched coffee. She jerked upright in the plastic chair beside Tang's desk. The windows reflected the humming fluorescent lights. Outside, the sky was black. Tang handed her a cup of coffee.

She took a harsh swallow. "Styrofoamy. Thanks."

Tang had to be tired, but it showed only around her eyes. She had put on glasses with black frames. She looked like Buddy Holly. She handed Evan an eight-by-ten photo: a grainy shot taken by the dashboard camera in Deputy Gilbert's cruiser. The camera had been aimed backward, through the wire mesh screen and out the rear window. It was adjusted for night vision, and the lighting was green and eerie. The Blair Witch Cop Car.

Parked behind the cruiser, headlights a screechy white, was the Volvo SUV.

Evan came wider awake. "Two people inside it. No, three — somebody's in the backseat."

The driver was a white man. A white woman sat in the front passenger seat.

Despite her fatigue, Tang looked pumped up. "Ragnarok Investments is a Potemkin corporation that hides a rat's nest of businesses-on-paper behind it."

"And you found something," Evan said.

Tang handed her a printout. "Sabine Jurgens. She's listed as the minority owner of a company four layers removed from Ragnarok."

"Who is she? The woman I spoke to on the phone this afternoon?" Evan held up the dashboard camera photo. "Her?"

Tang sat down at her desk and typed on her keyboard, quick and fluid. She brought up Sabine Jurgens's California driver's license. Jurgens had pixie-short red hair and a gaze that could strip things bare — assets, a machine gun, men — and leave them burning.

"She's got dual U.S.-German citizenship. Looks clean, but there's a strange flag on her file, waving deep in the background. I haven't been able to crack it yet. It's got an Interpol tag on it."

"That sounds bad."

Evan compared Jurgens's driver's license photo with the grainy green figure in the dashboard camera photo. She couldn't tell whether it was the same woman.

Tang brought up new pages. "I also got the name of the company's majority shareholder." She hit a key, and a photo appeared on the screen.

He was in his early forties, handsome in a movie-star way. In the way of a man who plays the Nordic villain in a Bond film. Hooded eyes, thin lips, a patrician glare. His hair was Gordon Gekko after a romp in the sack, with all the Old Spice Guy's arrogance and none of his charm or surreal sense of humor. The Iceman Cometh.

"Thinks a lot of himself, doesn't he?" Evan said.

Tang tilted her head. "I bet he plays Wagner on the stereo at the office."

Evan held up the dashboard photo. "It's him. Who is he?"

Tang started to speak but gave her a sidelong glance from behind her Rockin' Robin eyeglasses. "I don't want that remark about Wagner to go in your story."

"Fine. Tell me about him. Please, Lieutenant."

"It's Amy."

The phone on the desk rang. Evan jumped. They were the only people in a room of empty desks, and the sound jarred her.

Tang picked up. "Yes?" Her expression turned perplexed. She hung up and headed for the front desk, gesturing Evan to come along. "Ferd Bismuth's here."

When they arrived, the desk sergeant was giving Jo's neighbor a visitor's badge.

Evan said, "He looks like his puppy just fell down a well."

Ferd had on a '49ers cap and a distraught expression. And he had a capuchin monkey tucked in a Baby Björn sling on his chest. It looked like a tiny alien pilot, in the driver's seat and perhaps controlling him.

Ferd scooted around the desk. "Tina's at Jo's place. I couldn't rest. I'm so worried." He held out a box of cupcakes. "For you two."

"Appreciate it." Tang took the box and pointed him at a sofa in the break room. "Hang out there for a minute."

Evan took a cupcake. Tang reached for one but looked at the monkey. It had sprinkles stuck to its face.

She withdrew her hand. Evan kept eating. She was too tired and hungry to care. The monkey peered at her and made a garish face, like a shaman gripped by a prophetic vision foretelling of *her doom*.

Ferd rocked from foot to foot, unwilling to leave. Tang made a spinning gesture with her finger. "I'll be right there. Go on."

He trudged to the break room. Tang and Evan returned to the computer and the photo of the man who was driving the Volvo SUV.

"Who is he?" Evan said.

"Dane Haugen."

"And who is he?"

"He's a financier. He has a degree in mathematics and a gift for sliding in and out of financial industries that are largely unregulated. Mortgage bonds. Derivatives. His modus operandi has been to position himself in the middle of a speculative bubble, selling investments he knows to be garbage. He slurps up money from investors — often average Joes, through their retirement funds — and creams off fees for himself. Millions."

"Are we talking securities fraud, or plain old Wall Street slick dealing?"

"Sleight of hand. Financial three-card monte. Move the money so fast nobody can keep track, churn investments and rake off fees, bet against his own clients in the market — anything to line his pockets."

Evan stared at the photo. "He's a crook."

"And he's cold. Know how my source remembered him? From one of those Himalayan expeditions that hauls neophytes up peaks for a price. He paid megabucks to attempt Annapurna. Where he walked past two dying climbers without a second thought or a kind word. Later he gave an interview to the BBC. 'They knew the risks and the consequences. Expecting my team to abandon a summit bid to save people from their own miscalculations is unconscionable.'"

"Great guy," Evan said.

"And he's pulling the strings here. He's taken the Edge Adventures team off the board."

"And he took those kids from the twenty-first-birthday party off the beach? Why? And what does Ragnarok have to do with it?"

"That," Tang said, "is a very good question."

"I sense that you have the answer."

Ferd appeared in the doorway of the break room. "Lieutenant?"

Tang turned. "Hold on a minute."

"I heard you mention Ragnarok."

Tang's shoulders tightened. "Did you?"

"What's the connection between Jo's disappearance and Norse mythology?"

"I haven't found any link with Norse mythology."

Evan said, "What do you mean, Ferd?"

"Ragnarok. It's the end of the gods. Fate, disaster. Like Gotter-dammerung."

"You know this how?"

"Online gaming. Mythological themes are big."

Evan exchanged a glance with Tang. "Think these jokers might have a sense of irony — or destiny?"

Ferd said, "I'm going to check out a few things."

"Let us know what you find," Evan said.

He returned to the break room. Tang said, "If anything happened to Jo, I think he'd kill the people responsible in a Klingon murder-suicide ritual."

Evan gestured at the onscreen photo of Dane Haugen. "What's the rest?"

Tang crossed her arms and lowered her voice. "Haugen worked for a hedge fund in the city. Made a bazillion bucks for himself. But he was fired in disgrace. It was kept hush-hush because the fund is private. But rumor has it he had to wriggle out of lawsuits and possibly prosecution."

"Did that cost him his bazillion bucks?"

"Haugen was forced to liquidate his positions with the firm — all the investments he was managing for his own account. Gave up his partnership, equity position, and profit sharing. He had to sell everything he owned. His house, his other house, his third house, his horses, his boats, his mistresses. Eventually he declared bankruptcy. In an industry where there's no such thing as disgrace, Haugen came close."

"And then?"

"He went off the radar. Maybe to lick his wounds. Maybe to work at the drive-through window at In-N-Out."

Tang was fizzing with energy. Evan felt it.

"What's the punch line?" she said.

"The hedge fund Haugen worked for is Reiniger Capital."

The room seemed to brighten. Evan's skin tingled.

She said, "This is not a straight kidnapping for ransom."

"No," Tang said.

Evan turned to her laptop. The search took her five minutes.

"Peter Reiniger. Founder and Chairman of Reiniger Capital. And satisfied customer of Edge Adventures."

Edge's Web site listed its corporate clients and included a promotional video: action footage from Edge Adventure games. Between footage of lawyers and stockbrokers racing around San Francisco hanging out of sports cars, tired executives smiled at the camera and said, "It was awesome. Thanks, Edge."

One man in particular, craggy and imposing, said, "I'm Peter Reiniger. I always count on Edge to hone my employees' sense of the sharpness of life."

"Quite the recommendation." Tang was already dialing her own phone. To a detective on the other end, she said, "I need numbers. Cell, home, office, personal assistant, dog if you got it. Name is Peter Reiniger."

"What is Haugen's game?" Evan said.

She couldn't see a former multimillionaire financier simply kidnapping his ex-boss's daughter for ransom. Why commit one of the lowest percentage crimes in the United States, when he could be back in the slop, playing the game of Money — the easiest scam in the western world? No. It made no sense.

"What is going on?" Evan said.

"Revenge."

"And more. This guy has not switched to committing violent felonies on a whim. He's up to something big."

CHAPTER
FIFTY

Haugen crept to the edge of a protruding rock. The whisper of twilight in the east afforded him a view of the gorge and the cascading river below. He lay prone and raised the binoculars.

Sabine slid into place next to him. "Any sign of them?"

"Not yet, but they have no other way to escape from the gorge. Keep watching."

He panned the forested hillside. He would find them. They were exhausted, frightened, and lacking in wilderness training. The group would be as visible, and audible, as bison blundering through the trees.

"How's Von?" he said.

"Ready to kill the first one of those 'little shits' he sees."

Fifty yards behind them, the Volvo was parked off the road under the pines. In the gray twilight Von hunched in the front seat, cupping a mug of coffee.

"Will his shoulder injury allow him to hold a weapon?" Haugen said.

"He can shoot with his left hand."

"Why did Ratner ramble to me over the walkie-talkie about a rattlesnake? Could he —"

"He was taunting you. Dane, the guy *is* a rattlesnake."

Haugen's skin quivered. Snakes. They meant nothing good. They led only to downfall.

He lowered the binoculars, rolled onto his back, and took a Ruger from his shoulder holster. He flipped open the cylinder, checked that it was fully loaded, and snapped it closed again with a solid click.

"Once it gets light, we're going to get a lot more company," she said.

"Danger is also opportunity."

She sat up. The wind had chapped her face. Her short red hair was tucked beneath her ski mask, which she had rolled up like a watch cap.

Her expression was scathing. "The authorities will block the road. If we don't capture Autumn before then, how will we get out of this gorge?"

His first impulse, to tell her they would go farther into the mountains and hunker down until the yokels in uniform gave up, quickly abated. His second impulse, to strike Sabine for questioning him, also abated. She was armed.

His original plan had given him sixty hours to bleed twenty million dollars from Peter Reiniger. The idiot children in Autumn's crime spree party would not be missed until late Sunday night, when they failed to return to San Francisco. He had intended to stash them in a cabin thirty miles farther up the logging road. But that plan was blown. It had blown when Von and Friedrich shot up the clearing, and when Deputy D. V.

Gilbert noticed the brass littering the ground like birdseed.

"Dane?" Sabine's voice was a stiletto. "If the weather stays clear, they'll send search and rescue helicopters."

"They don't know the kids are out here."

"They'll send them to look for the *deputy*."

He rolled onto his stomach again and raised the binoculars.

"Dane. When it gets light they'll send the CHP and search dogs and the fucking National Guard."

"Then we'll have to be far away when that happens."

He swept the ravine with the binoculars. Stopped and panned back. A large animal was moving through the trees.

"They have a horse."

Haugen adjusted the range finder on the binoculars. "Nine hundred meters, south-southwest. Maybe a hundred meters from the river." He jumped to his feet. "Get Von. We're going."

Gabe paused. The forest was thick, ponderosas standing close together on the steep slope. Jo and Peyton caught up with him. They were climbing slowly and with deliberate care, progressing cautiously so as to keep Peyton's heart rate from rising too high. The girl was pale and bent with pain. And silent — Jo didn't know whether she had run out of complaints, or out of breath, but either way she soldiered on. The moon had set. In the east, the stars had disappeared against a sky now perfused with purple and indigo. Dawn was coming.

Gabe stumbled on a rock and caught himself. Jo threw out an arm, like a crossing guard trying to catch a kid running into the street. Her eyes were gritty. Her head was humming. Her ears and face and hands were so numb she could barely close her fingers. She was beyond tired, into the range of exhaustion where reason ebbed and clumsiness took hold. The urge to sleep, the irritability of dead fatigue, became a constant, aching drumbeat. Every step, every breath, called out for them to rest.

But they had no food. No coffee, nothing hot to warm them. She took a swallow from a water bottle and passed it over. They had little choice but to keep going.

Where had Ratner taken Autumn and Lark and Noah? Would he keep moving or stash them somewhere? Would he keep all three of them alive?

In her mind's eye she saw Dustin, sprawled in the meadow with a hole blown in his back.

Stop that. She had to focus on their environment, had to keep an eye on Peyton, had to keep moving.

When the trees thinned and pale light rose in front of her, at first she didn't take it in. Then they stepped onto the logging road.

After their night in the gorge, it was like stumbling onto the Yellow Brick Road. Jo paused, overcome. Disbelieving.

Peyton said, "It's about time. This is good, isn't it?"

"It's beautiful. It's step one on our trip home," Jo said.

The sky overhead was clear and empty. The morning was silent. Heads swiveling, alert for errant noises in the forest, they edged their way downhill around a curve until they found a vantage point on the gorge. Their breath steamed the air. Below them, the river rampaged. Clouds drifted and clung to the ridge tops and stands of pine.

The river was already subsiding. Gray-brown and choppy in the first ashen twilight, it was retreating toward its bed. Along its banks, where the gorge narrowed, tree trunks and rocks piled up in a mass of debris.

Jo stopped. "Oh no."

Her last remaining energy drained away. A knot lodged in her throat.

The bridge had a long chunk ripped out of it.

"It's impassable," she said.

She felt an overwhelming heaviness. She swayed, hearing a hum in her ears. After so much time, so much effort, was this it?

"Dammit," she said.

Gabe looked around. "There has to be another way."

The cold seemed to pour through her damp clothes. "They have us in a pen. We're cut off."

"They've been trying to cut us off since last night. We've eluded them so far." His voice was wintry. "We'll continue to elude them. We'll get out of here."

He was at least as exhausted as she was, but he wasn't ready to relent. She pressed her thumb and forefinger into the corners of her eyes. His silence punched through her.

"Have I ever let you down?" he said.

She took a breath. "Never."

"We're getting out of here alive." He glanced at Peyton. "All of us."

Jo nodded. She took his hand and squeezed.

She barely felt a vibration in her pocket. "Oh my God."

She scrambled for her phone. "I have a signal."

She had just received a message. Brusquely she wiped her eyes and dialed 9-1-1. *Call failed*.

"No."

She ran back up the road, trying to regain the signal. No luck. While she spun around holding her phone up, begging the sky gods to answer her prayers, she opened the message.

It was from Evan Delaney. The first line was a name.

Dane Haugen.

She scrolled through the message.

DANGER. Ragnarok is number on Wylie's cell. Connected to Haugen & Sabine Jurgens. We think they abducted 21st birthday party, may have attacked a deputy. CALL 911 CONTACT ME.

Jo's heart swelled. She felt thrilled and amazed and grateful. How Evan had worked this out she didn't know, but it was a lifeline, the thinnest tether and thread of hope. And it scared the hell out of her.

365

Gabe walked up the road to her. She held out the phone. He read the message and his face hardened.

What did this information mean? Jo's brain felt sticky. She tried to clear her mind and put everything together.

Haugen. Sabine. Ragnarok.

Ragnarok's phone number was in the call register on Phelps Wylie's cell phone. So was Ruby Kyle Ratner's. Ratner had car-jacked Wylie and brought him up here. Up this road.

"Ruby Kyle Ratner — Kyle Ritter — killed Phelps Wylie," she said.

Gabe wiped cold sweat from his forehead. "I'm not going to doubt you. But how do you figure?"

"He's the voice on the cell phone recording. That puts him at the scene. Ratner killed Wylie and dumped him in the abandoned gold mine. And Ratner was working for Edge Adventures. This was his first gig. I'm guessing it was supposed to be a one-time deal — they hired him to play the Bad Cowboy, to 'help' Autumn confront her fears. Presumably they didn't realize he was dangerous."

They walked back toward Peyton. The light brightened in the east, above snow-dappled peaks that rose halfway to the sky.

"These other people are the hijackers. Dane and Sabine — those were names Friedrich mentioned before the Hummer crashed. I remember thinking — the Trapp Family Singers."

She shook her head. "None of this is coincidence. Us running into the Hummer was bad timing, but it wasn't random."

"Does Ratner tie in with the hijacking?" Gabe said.

"I don't know. But this abduction has been planned for a long time. And my investigation collided with it."

"Who's running the hijack — Dane Haugen?"

Peyton turned. "Haugen?"

Jo held up the phone. "The name of the man who may be behind the abduction."

"How do you know about him?"

"What do you mean?"

"Dane Haugen — he's the guy who hosted the party where the Bad Cowboy was working."

"Wait," Jo said. "Haugen hosted the Fourth of July party?"

"Haugen worked for Autumn's dad. He got fired a couple years ago. It was in the financial papers — Autumn couldn't help gloating. Said, 'The ass-clown who hired the Bad Cowboy got booted.' Like it was the least her dad could do."

Jo stood there, dumfounded. The walkie-talkie in her pocket came alive with static.

"Haugen? Yoo-hoo. You there?"

Sabine checked her gear. "It will not be simple to kill the Red Rattler."

"His name is Ratner."

She almost sneered. He could sense her disdain even in the twilight. He could also sense her inhaling, so the tattoo of the serpent swelled on her breast. *Provocateuse*.

She slung her backpack across her shoulders. "Mister Ratner is sneaky."

Same as you, sweetheart.

"You should have gotten rid of him long ago," she said.

"This turn of events could not have been predicted."

"Of course it could have," she said. "It was practically a certainty in any model you could have devised."

Haugen climbed to his feet. "I could not have foreseen that Edge would hire Ratner for this scenario. How could I? He is no longer in my employ."

"Are you stupid?" It came out as *styoo-pid*. "He never was in your employ. He was your enforcer. Your cleanup crew. But he's a coyote. A lone predator."

Haugen had to concede the point. "Peter Reiniger must have asked Edge to fine-tune Autumn's scenario so she could confront some specific fear. I couldn't know it would involve Ratner."

"And who hired him to begin with?" Sabine said.

"It was only after that party that I realized his skills extended beyond parking cars."

He didn't know what Ratner had done to terrify Autumn, except that it must have been effective. And, with his weight loss and prison haircut, Ruby Kyle Ratner looked completely different from the day Autumn would have formed her childhood impression of him. Ratner was twelve years older, and had shaved a

368

Zapata mustache, cut his Kemo Sabe ponytail, and lost sixty pounds.

Haugen credited himself for those changes. And he had given Ratner the chance to . . . let his natural instincts find fruition. Ratner had, for years, been a useful man to have at hand. Until he exceeded his remit.

Sabine stood blocking his path, arms akimbo. "What if Autumn recalls where she first met him? At a party thrown by an executive who worked for her father's firm? At the splendid former home of disgraced financial wizard Dane Haugen?"

His breath frosted the light. "It hardly matters now, does it?"

"It matters a great deal," she said.

She was testing him. He despised it.

Disgraced? No — betrayed. Haugen had been betrayed by Peter Reiniger, cut loose from Reiniger Capital over nothing — over trumped-up charges that he had slept with the wife of a major investor.

Insider trading, *heh-heh-heh*. Everybody did it. But Reiniger had used that as an excuse to dump him. Haugen, and everybody at Reiniger Capital, knew the real reason he had been fired: because of the incident at the Edge Adventures weekend.

The memory of the king snake, sliding from beneath the driver's seat of the car, climbing up his leg, onto his lap, gagged him. He forced himself to stay calm. He tried to suppress the memory of how he had screamed. He couldn't keep from hearing the engine rev, or from recalling the outcome: He had driven, out of control and shrieking, with a car full of his colleagues, across a lawn and into the revolving doors at the resort where the game was taking place. The crash trapped him in the car, battering at the windows, weeping, kicking, while a four-foot-long, legless muscle with a flicking tongue coiled around his haunches.

Peter Reiniger had special-ordered the snake to test Haugen's response to fear stimuli. But Terry Coates, Mr Edge Adventures, had put it beneath the seat. Coates, the son of a bitch who was now dying or dead in the back of a big rig. The image soothed him.

"Everything is manageable," Haugen said. "None of this should have happened, but we will recover."

"Really? You set all of this in motion. It was completely foreseeable. It has been, ever since you told the Red Rattler — excuse me, Ratner — to keep your lawyer on the leash."

"Phelps Wylie was a buffoon. I presented him with the opportunity of the century, and he botched it."

Wylie could easily have arranged everything Haugen requested, while keeping his hands clean. Or, at least, while keeping himself willfully ignorant of Haugen's intentions. It was a lawyer's duty to zealously represent his clients — not to question why they wanted so many shell companies incorporated and so many accounts linked together, most of them offshore, all of them hidden from the financial regulators.

Wylie. The prig. Having an attack of cowardice — or, as he'd called it, "conscience" — and daring to tell Haugen that he wished to withdraw as his attorney. Daring to say he knew Haugen's intended transactions were illegal. Worried about money laundering. Worried that his law firm might be tarnished. *Besmirched* was the word the toad had actually used, standing in his office wringing his hands.

Haugen had not stood for it.

"Wylie would have talked. He was on the verge of emotional collapse. He had no stomach for high-stakes finance."

"But telling Ratner to 'put the fear of God' into him was unwise. Dane, can you not finally admit that your choice of words gave Ratner undue leeway?"

Haugen had wanted to scare Wylie into shutting up. Ratner was adept at that sort of thing. But, as Sabine had so helpfully pointed out, Ratner was a psychopath. Instead of frightening Wylie into silence with a bit of carjacking, he killed him.

So, when Ratner phoned him from the road, saying *oops*, Haugen had found himself with no choice but to engineer Wylie's disappearance. He had already reconnoitered the mine while preparing for Autumn Reiniger's ascension to high priestess of abductees. He told Ratner to dispose of the body.

And now Ratner had captured Autumn and her friends. If he couldn't be brought down, this would become *his* big score.

Haugen zipped his coat. "Leeway ends. Now."

The walkie-talkie squawked. "Yoo-hoo. Dane? You there?"

CHAPTER
FIFTY-ONE

The Tuolumne County sheriff's cruiser eked its way up the highway. In the predawn twilight, Sheriff Walt Gilbert could only see as far as his headlights. What unfolded in front of his car was storm damage: rocks and mud washed across the road, trees down, one side of the tarmac undermined by wave action as gushing water had run off after the downpour. He eased through it, careful not to get snared by debris.

He reached the clearing. It was empty.

He parked, put on his hat, and got out and walked the perimeter of the clearing. It was a muddy washout. He hiked two hundred yards up the trail, and back, heels sinking in the wet earth. He returned to his cruiser and radioed it in.

"No sign of Ron or the hikers' pick-up — at all?" the dispatcher said.

"None."

He gazed up the gorge, where the logging road climbed out of sight into thick forest and steeper, more mountainous terrain.

"I'm going to drive up the road a ways and see if I can find them," he said.

He pulled out. His heart, his gut, all his instincts, were dark.

Ten minutes later, he swung the cruiser downhill to the bridge across the river. He stopped. The bridge was broken in two. The river gushed past, brown with mud, ferocious.

Jo turned up the volume on the walkie-talkie. Gabe and Peyton crowded round.

"Here, kitty-kitty . . ."

The voice was creepy, singsong, a timbre between tenor and alto.

"Here, Dane. Here, Sabine. You want your mice?"

Jo murmured, "It's Ratner."

A new voice. Male, deep, studied — actory. "I want to finish this in a professional manner. If you wish to participate, let's meet and we'll join forces."

Jo said, "Haugen?"

Ratner said: "Look at these mice. They're squirming. They're hungry. You know what happens to mice in the wild? They become food."

Another squawk. "Enough. Speak plainly."

The singsong voice didn't relent. "You doubt me. I'm crushed. Here, listen." Snuffling sounds. "Talk. Tell him."

A girl's voice came through clearly. "We're with Kyle. Me, Noah, and Lark."

Jo looked at Gabe, her heart rushing. They were all alive.

"Let me hear from each of them," Haugen said.

More static, then Lark said, "It's me." Finally, Noah. "Holloway."

Ratner's voice. "Ain't that a scream?"

There was a long pause. "Very well. Let's come to terms."

"Hee," Ratner said. "Here's your terms. Fifty-fifty, or Daddy Reiniger gets no proof of life. All he'll find is his baby girl and her buds, taking a dirt nap."

Jo put a hand to her forehead.

"Fine," Haugen said. "Let's rendezvous."

"Fifty-fifty?" Ratner said.

"Yes. I'm a realist."

"Ain't that nice. Sit tight. I'll get back to you on the when and where," Ratner said. "Over and out."

The walkie-talkie went quiet.

Gabe said, "He'll never turn them over alive. Not all three of them. Maybe he'll keep Autumn alive until she can talk to her father on the phone. But the others, forget it."

His voice was strained. Jo's stomach had knotted.

They could get out of here, she thought. With Haugen and Ratner maneuvering around the forest like pieces on a chessboard, it would be possible for her and Gabe to slip under their net and disappear.

Maybe.

But it would only be possible if it was just the two of them. Peyton was near the end of her rope, while they were hardy, healthy — sort of — and could travel quickly over the terrain. They could escape, but by leaving the others behind.

Jo's throat tightened. "I know where they are."

374

Gabe's eyes were grave. He had put on his game face. "The mine."

She nodded. "We don't have time to get out and then bring law enforcement back." She looked at the walkie-talkie. It didn't have a police band, no emergency frequencies. "Ratner or Haugen will kill them."

Peyton said, "Do something. I'm useless, but I can hide beneath those rocks. You'll know where I am but nobody can see me from the road, or from above."

Gabe's eyes didn't soften. But the look in them opened and went deeper. It almost became haunted. And Jo didn't need to hear him say it to know what was written in his conscience, his muscle memory, his life. It was his pledge, the motto of Pararescue: *So That Others May Live*.

She nodded — to him, to Peyton, to herself. They would not abandon Autumn and her friends.

And the odd, just-out-of-reach feeling finally stepped forward and came into focus. Jo knew what had been scratching at the back of her mind.

"I know where *we* are."

From the sports bag Gabe was using as a backpack she grabbed a map. Chilled stiff, her hands could barely unfold it.

"We're not far from the mine as the crow flies," she said. "We've been struggling to get away, hide, get back to the road. We haven't focused on the bigger picture — what the geography actually is."

Gabe tilted his head to orient himself to the map. "You're right."

The logging road ran essentially west-east into the high Sierras. But, because the terrain was so rugged, the road didn't run straight.

Jo tapped the map with an icy finger. "Here's the clearing, where we parked yesterday, and where the Hummer stopped."

She traced the footpath she and Gabe had hiked to the mine. It cut back and forth, up one ridge and down the other side, up again and down a second ridge — a journey of switchbacks and steep changes in elevation.

"We crossed the second ridge, zigzagged to the bottom, crossed the gully, turned east" — parallel to the logging road — "and hiked up the slope to the mine. It was at least three miles. But look here."

The logging road followed the contours of the river. From the clearing, it kept climbing. But Jo remembered the long, severe turn the limo had taken when they were barreling along before the crash. She remembered the light angling across the Hummer as they swung around hairpin curves and climbed ever higher.

She traced the road on the map. "It crossed the river, then crossed back again — two bridges. And a couple of miles after we left the clearing, the road made a broad, one-hundred-eighty-degree turn. It looped in a semicircle and kept climbing."

She traced the line on the map. Gabe saw what she was talking about.

"The road climbed over both ridges and doubled back," he said.

"We're now on the other side of the mine." She stood and pointed north. "It's directly that way. If we took the road it would be a six-or seven-mile drive. But if we cut straight across the hills, it's less than a mile. Maybe much less."

They had a shortcut.

She put a hand on Peyton's arm. "You sure you'll be okay by yourself, staying out of sight?"

Peyton nodded, quick and tight. Jo said, "All right."

She stabbed the map. "These two ridgelines here. That's where those power pylons are. And there's a bridge that links them."

Gabe looked at her. "Say what you're thinking."

"If we shortcut to the mine and get the kids, we can then use the catwalk to cross the ravine and keep going down to the clearing where I parked yesterday. The clearing's below the bridge that's out. That means the bad guys can't reach it via car. But the authorities can."

He looked like he was trying not to say the obvious. So she said it.

"I know it's a risk. I'll take it. I don't think these kids have time for anything else." She paused. "Neither do we."

He examined the map. His pulse was beating in his temple.

"We can do it," she said.

Gabe took out his knife. "Let's go get them."

CHAPTER
FIFTY-TWO

The Gulfstream 5 streaked over the runway threshold and touched down, wheels squealing. In the pre-dawn light of the high desert, the sky in the east was veined crimson. Peter Reiniger held on while the thrust reversers roared and the jet slowed. The air looked cold and clear. The lights of Reno were pallid and shimmering.

He unbuckled his seat belt and headed to the cockpit. Without knocking he opened the door.

"Park it. Refuel. Stay at the controls," he said.

Both pilots frowned, but the captain said, "Yes, Mr Reiniger."

He closed the door and, as the jet taxied, phoned the number his daughter's abductors had given him.

After a series of clicks and buzzes and delays — which told him the number was being forwarded through a series of exchanges to make it impossible to trace — it rang. A nasal double tone — *ring-ring* — like a European phone's.

The voice answered, disguised by the voice modulator, hob-gobliny. "Yes?"

"I'm on the ground at Reno."

"And the money?"

"After I speak to Autumn."

A beat. "You speak to Autumn when you send me evidence the transfer can be accomplished at the click of a button."

Reiniger's stomach tightened. The plane juddered over dips in the taxiway. "Nothing moves until I have proof of life."

"Phone again when you've carried out my instructions. Then we'll discuss speaking to your daughter."

The call cut off.

Shaking, so enraged and sick that he could barely focus on the keypad, Reiniger sat in one of the plush seats and phoned New York.

Sabine shook her head. "What a bastard. 'Proof of life.' Who uses that phrase about his own child?"

Haugen put away the satellite phone. "Mr Reiniger is one of a kind."

His acid reflux burned. Proof of life was the nut of the matter. He couldn't make Reiniger move the funds until Autumn cried to Daddy over the walkie-talkie. There was simply no way. Reiniger was too much of a hard case.

He and Sabine pulled on gloves and their final layers of clothing. He took a swig of lukewarm coffee from the thermos. Then he got the walkie-talkie.

He clicked the Transmit button, twice.

A moment later Von clicked back. *Understood*. He was in position, ready to close on Ratner when they flushed him from hiding.

Sabine checked her SIG Sauer. The weapon shone dully in the dawn. She shoved it beneath her waistband in the small of her back.

"How do you plan to get to the Reno airport?" she said.

"Really? You don't know?"

"Even if the bridge were not out, the swarm of cops looking for the deputy would stop us."

He smiled. "Know how far it is to Reno as the crow flies?"

"At least sixty miles. What are you planning?"

"An airlift. We just have to time it right." He pulled a backpack across his shoulders. "Let's go."

The sky was a polished blue, the mountains charcoal with shadow and deeply silent. Jo and Gabe eased their way through the trees, cold in the morning twilight, inching their way toward the top of the ridge above the abandoned gold mine. They had left Peyton well concealed amid a field of boulders, clenching one of the carved spears.

They dropped to their hands and knees and crept forward. Cautiously they peered over the lip of the hill at the ravine below.

It was rock strewn and glistening with dew. The night's manic rains had torn new channels in the hillside, claw marks where frantic water had scored the slope.

The entrance of the mine was about a hundred meters below them. Gabe lowered his head. So did Jo.

"Getting a direct vantage point on the entrance will be impossible," he murmured.

"We need to find out where Ratner is."

He nodded at the walkie-talkie. "Keep the volume low. If they're close, we don't want them to hear us overhearing them." He looked around. "Hopefully we're high enough on this ridge that we'll have a line of sight and can get radio reception without the hills blocking it."

They lay flat and eyed the scene below them. A bird chirped. In the chill morning, the sky in the east brightened to gold, etching the crest of the mountains.

They had come at the mine from behind, opposite the way they had approached the day before. Jo hoped that Ratner and Haugen — and his gang — would be approaching the entrance from the front, up the bottom of the ravine, and would not have the situational awareness to think about the high ground behind it.

The ground was cold and damp. The chill seeped through Jo's clothes into her already-cold body. She crept next to Gabe. He pulled her against his side and rested his arm across her back. Jo let something unwind inside her, an overloaded spring. Just for a moment, this was enough. Reassurance, sustenance, every right kind of warmth.

The walkie-talkie scratched. Two clicks. Then another.

Gabe swept the mountainside with his gaze. "They're getting into position." Nothing moved. Nothing rustled. No piece of metal or glass reflected light.

"They could still be a mile away," Jo said.

Gabe ducked.

Outside the mine, Ratner appeared, leading the horse.

He had removed its saddle and saddle blanket and was brushing its back and flanks with the flat of his hand gently. He propped the shotgun against the exterior wall of the mine entrance.

His shirt was off. Despite the chill, he was bare chested. His arms were covered with tattoos. Even from this distance, Jo could see their outline. Snakes.

A coiled rope hung from his shoulder. He turned, stroking the horse's neck, revealing his back. The pockets of his sagging jeans bore a walkie-talkie and a handgun. A tattoo Jo recognized as signature state prison technique, in sickly blue ink, covered his back: an iron cross from which hung a noose.

Gabe held motionless. Jo didn't want to breathe. They were under the trees, in a shadowed nook, but she didn't want to betray their presence.

"Gotta do something soon if we're going to do it," Gabe whispered. "Once Haugen and his gang get here, it'll be too late."

How? Jo thought. Ratner had a semiautomatic pistol, a twelve-gauge shotgun, and apparently the snake-action power of Hangman Christ. She and Gabe had a knife and a sharpened stick.

Then she grasped it. "He's not going to let Haugen come here. He's outgunned against Haugen and his gang. And he won't want them to know where the kids are stashed."

Below, Ratner stroked the horse's soft muzzle. From his pocket he took a granola bar. Unwrapping it, he fed it to the horse. He couldn't have looked more tender and content.

Gabe said, "He has to have the kids immobilized inside the mine. And not just because of injury and fear. He's too casual. He has them constrained physically."

They looked at each other. Jo said, "Which means he'll feel free to leave them here while he goes to meet Haugen."

"*If* he meets Haugen. He must want money. But Haugen doesn't have cash. Nobody's been up here delivering a ransom."

"He'll have to arrange getting paid. Getting cash or getting funds transferred into his account."

"Cash. If you were Ratner, would you trust Haugen to transfer a bunch of money sight unseen — when you're up a creek without any way to verify it? Besides, he's a greenback kind of guy."

"Haugen will demand a meeting. He won't take phone calls or even photos as proof that Autumn's alive. Ratner will take proof of life. But he'll leave the kids in the mine."

"If Ratner agrees to a meeting, he'll have to leave them. Anything else is suicide for him, literally."

They really couldn't know. They had to hope.

Ratner hitched up his jeans.

"We won't know how much time we'll have before he comes back," she said. "And we won't know whether Haugen's going to play straight, or whether he has somebody lurking out there, trying to track down Ratner's hiding spot."

"You can bet he does." Gabe locked eyes with her again. "Yes or no?"

"Yes. We'll just have to be quick."

Heart thudding, she rested her chin on the ground and kept Ratner in view.

Exhaustion swamped Jo like a wave, and drowsiness hummed in her ears. Just for a moment she shut her eyes. Just for a blissful instant.

The walkie-talkie bleated. She raised her head, powerfully and painfully alert.

"Ratner, come in," Haugen said.

Outside the mine, Ratner pulled the walkie-talkie from his back pocket. Jo and Gabe saw him put the device to his face and heard his singsong voice on the radio.

"Beautiful morning, ain't it? Shall we dance?"

"We meet. You bring Autumn, we arrange the division of funds."

"Nuh-uh. We meet, you give me something that *secures* your promise to pay me, and I'll bring you . . . a lock of the little princess's hair."

Long pause. "At the bottom of the ravine."

"On my way."

"I'll see you there."

"You'll see me there, *what?*" Ratner said.

The pause on Haugen's end seemed to virtually steam the walkie-talkies. "I'll see you there, *partner.*"

Laughing, Ratner clicked off. He pulled on a shirt and picked up the shotgun. He strode into the mine.

Jo and Gabe held their breath. A minute later Ratner came back out, tucking something into his pocket. He grabbed the horse's reins and a handful of its mane, and swung up onto its back. He turned it and, kicking its sides, headed down the vale of the ravine.

Jo and Gabe waited until he was out of sight. They stood and ran down the hill toward the mine.

CHAPTER
FIFTY-THREE

Gabe paused at the entrance to the mine. His buck knife was in his hand, low, the blade smooth in the rising light. He pressed himself against the rocky face of the hill and peered into the gloom inside.

He put a finger to his lips. Signaled for Jo to guard the entrance.

He ducked inside. Jo's pulse ticked like a watch about to blow its springs. A cold shaft of air funneled past her, drawn inside. She heard Gabe's feet scuff on the dirt as he edged back into the darkness. She watched the hills and shadowed depths of the ravine. The morning sky was calm, but even so, the trees wafted back and forth, squirrels jumping, birds taking flight. Her mouth was so dry she couldn't spit.

Inside, Gabe turned on the flashlight. She heard muffled crying. A girl, shouting from behind a gag.

"Jo, quick," Gabe said.

She ran inside. Gabe was around the bend, planted in the center of the tunnel, one hand out warning her to stop. His flashlight illuminated the exposed crossbeam in the crumbling ceiling of the tunnel.

Lark was strung up by her hands, swinging from it. Shocked, Jo said, "Oh God."

Lark's eyes glittered. She was gagged with a strip of fabric. Her arms stretched overhead. She looked to be in incredible pain. Behind her on the dirt, Noah slumped against the tunnel wall. His hands were bound and tied to his feet. Jo ran toward him.

From behind the gag Lark screamed, shaking her head and kicking frantically.

Gabe grabbed her. "It's not safe. Look."

Beneath Lark, a tarp had been laid across a hole in the floor of the mine and covered with a layer of dirt. Gabe pulled it aside. Lark wasn't hanging two inches off the dirt. She was hanging above a pit.

Jo and Gabe edged forward. He shone the flashlight down.

"That's what Ratner did with their spears," he said. "Turned them into punji sticks."

It was the flood runoff pit. At the bottom, four whittled spears pointed straight up. Anybody who walked up to Lark, intending to cut her down, would have plunged into the pit and been impaled.

Now she understood why Gabe needed her here and not standing guard at the mine entrance. It would take two people to get Lark down and Noah out.

"Hang on, we're going to cut you down," he said.

Lark nodded, but it was half relief, half terror. She cried something that, even gagged, was clear. *Hurry.*

Gabe looked around. "Ratner had to have climbed on something to get the rope knotted up there."

They found it: an ancient wooden crate. Beneath it was a pickax. Gabe handed Jo his knife. He set the crate next to the wall. Then he jumped across the pit, pulled Lark toward him by her belt, and said, "Cut the rope."

Jo climbed on the crate. She sliced through the rope. Lark dropped and Gabe yanked her backward toward him. They fell in a heap.

He pulled off the gag. She clutched him, crying. "Thank you. Oh God. Help Noah."

Jo jumped across the pit and sliced the ropes that bound the boy. He was deeply cold. She took his pulse: slow and regular, but far weaker than before. She tapped him hard on the cheek, twice. His eyes opened. He saw her, nodded, and said, "Yeah."

She turned to Lark. "Where's Autumn?"

"Deeper in the mine. He dragged her way back in there. This thing branches off in a bunch of directions. I don't know where she is."

"Come on, let's get you two out of here," Gabe said.

He grabbed Noah in a fireman's carry, which must have nearly killed both of them. Jo grabbed the pickax. She and Lark ran out first, checked the hillside, and motioned Gabe to come.

He lugged Noah into the daylight. "Lark, can one person reach Autumn by themselves?"

"Should be able to. She's fine, as far as I know."

Jo said, "Go. I'll get her. I'll hurry."

Gabe said, "Give Lark the pickax."

Jo kept the buck knife. Gabe and Lark struggled uphill and disappeared into the trees.

Jo dashed back to the mine. She ducked low and ran down the tunnel. The mine was cold and dank and ghostly.

"Autumn?" she said.

The only reply was darkness.

"Thank you, Sheriff Gilbert."

Tang slammed down the phone, grabbed Evan's elbow, and pulled her off the plastic desk chair.

"Come on. I need to get out of here for a minute."

Evan bumbled to her feet and followed her. "What's happened?"

Tang pushed the button for the elevator, then, fidgeting, headed for the stairs instead. She had a pack of cigarettes in her hand.

"Jo's truck is no longer parked at the roadside where the deputy found it," she said. "It's gone."

From Tang's tightly spun anger, Evan knew this did not mean Jo had driven down the canyon to hole up in some cozy motel overnight.

"It'll be light soon," Tang said. "And the weather's clearing. With luck, they'll get a helicopter airborne searching for them."

"With luck?"

"Roads are washed out. Other campers are stranded, and drivers got swept off the roads in the flash flood. It's a mess. The authorities are swamped."

They jogged down the stairs and hit the ground floor. Tang kept going, straight through the doors and outside into the clinging, twilight damp. She stopped on the sidewalk, cupped her hand, and lit her smoke.

"The deputy's still missing too, isn't he?" Evan said.

"No sign of him or his cruiser."

She snuffed her lighter, jammed it in her pocket, and squinted as she inhaled.

Not going to be a happy ending. The street was glum and empty. The roadside attractions included bail bondsmen and an auto body shop.

Tang glared at stoplights directing nothing, red and green and lonely, all the way toward the bay. "How do you figure this all fits together?"

"Dane Haugen ambushed Autumn Reiniger's group on its Edge Adventures weekend."

"What about the rest?"

"Ruben Kyle Ratner is working for Edge Adventures. And Ratner murdered Phelps Wylie. He carjacked him here in the city, forced him to drive to the Sierras, and then killed him and dumped his body in the mine."

"And Jo stumbled into it?"

"Yes. And no. Jo was at the wrong place at the wrong time. But it wasn't random."

It still didn't fit. Not completely.

Behind them the door banged open. Ferd ran out, panting. He was wearing a headset, and his eyes were wide.

"I got it. Ragnarok. I found the next iteration in their mythology," he said.

Tang looked, for a second, like she wanted to punch him. But then again, she looked in the mood to punch a brick wall.

"What, Ferd?" Evan said.

He danced on his toes. "Ragnarok — like I said, in Norse mythology it means the end of the world and ruin of the gods. Literally it translates as 'destruction of the powers.' I know you searched U.S. databases for information about it. I did some parallel processing."

Tang spun her hand. *Speed it up*.

"I do a lot of online gaming, and —"

"*Ferd*. Please," Tang said.

He stopped, abashed, almost dashed. Mr Peebles glared from the Baby Björn. Ferd rubbed the monkey's back, a quick, reassuring motion.

Tang shut her eyes. "What?"

"One of my online friends is in Oslo. I contacted him about Norse mythology. I asked him about mythological themes related to Ragnarok. He came up with a few."

Evan was skeptical. "I found summaries of Norse myth in online encyclopedias. It's not necessarily helpful."

"You don't understand. He knows this stuff inside out. He checked online for companies with related names. *Norwegian* companies. You said this series of shell companies was international, right? I heard you mention an Interpol flag. Didn't I?"

Did he have bat ears?

"Yes," Tang said.

"You've been checking American search engines and government databases. My friend checked Norwegian databases for corporations with dot-no Internet addresses. And he speaks Norwegian. He doesn't have to rely on online translation."

"And?"

"Asgard." Ferd squeezed his hands into fists. "Asgard is a kind of Norse god headquarters. And you have to be dead to get in. But it's also a hollow shell of a company with Norwegian roots, and a dot-no address. I checked its connections with Ragnarok. They're tenuous, but they're there."

"Ferd, I don't know. It seems awfully convenient that you found this information," Tang said. The rest was implied: *You're seeing what you want to see.*

But Evan felt an electric buzz. "Yeah, but Haugen seems full of hubris. Maybe he's the type to go for grand gestures, thinking he's always going to be a step ahead."

Ferd was nearly bouncing. "You've only heard part of it." He held out his phone. "Asgard-dot-no doesn't have offices in San Francisco. But they've leased a big rig. And they've parked it here."

Tang peered at his phone. A list of companies and contract information for a tractor-trailer depot were displayed on the screen.

"How on earth . . ."

"Don't ask. Please." He went as red as the stoplights down the street. "All you need to know is that Google doesn't own the only heavy-duty search algorithms in the Bay Area."

And they certainly didn't use password-cracking software to prioritize search results, Evan bet. Not openly.

"Why would Asgard need to rent a tractor-trailer? Why would they store it near Candlestick Park?" Ferd said.

Evan had her car keys out and was running toward the garage.

The sky was brightening above the bay. The stars had winked out. The dawn was cool and clammy. Ahead of the Mustang, Tang flashed her badge at the gate to the truck depot. The depot foreman, who had been rousted out of bed, unlocked the gate and rolled it open.

Ferd filled the passenger seat of the Mustang. Not physically — emotionally. It was his anxiety that practically turned the air in the car a jangly red. Behind him, perched on the back of the headrest, Mr Peebles kept watch.

"Think Jo's in there?" Ferd said.

"We'll see."

Tang drove through the gate. Evan goosed the Mustang and rumbled after her.

"You're really fond of Jo, aren't you?" Evan said.

"We're ad-hoc investigative partners." He crossed his fingers to show her: *like that*. "We have an intuitive connection. I think it's because Mr Peebles loves her so."

Evan glanced at the monkey. It glanced back. She thought it rolled its eyes.

"He's really sensitive," Ferd said. "I can tell he likes you. You're a pet person."

"I wouldn't have a pet if you paid me in gold bullion. However, I could see Mr Peebles being my butler. Does he mix cocktails?"

Ahead, Tang and the depot foreman pulled up behind a parked forty-foot trailer. It was painted white without any markings. Tang got out and gestured Evan and Ferd to stay put.

They were out of the Mustang before Tang finished glowering.

Tang shone her flashlight on the trailer. The double doors on the back were locked. She walked up to it.

"Blood," she said. "Come on, get this open."

The foreman used a crowbar and bolt cutters. When the lock snapped, he swung the doors open.

Evan ran forward, heedless of contaminating the scene or documenting it for her article. Inside the trailer, squinting under the beam of Tang's flashlight, were four men in Edge Adventures shirts. They were tied together with their feet shackled to a ring on the floor in the center of the trailer.

Evan boosted Tang up and hauled herself into the trailer after her. They rushed to a man who lay, barely conscious, near the doors. He had graying hair and brown skin. His clothes were dark with dried blood. Tang pulled off the gag and rolled him onto his back.

"Thank God," he croaked.

"Terry Coates?" Tang said.

"Yeah. Never thought you'd come. God bless the SFPD for ignoring everything I phoned in."

CHAPTER
FIFTY-FOUR

The paramedics prepared to load Terry Coates into the ambulance for transport to San Francisco General Hospital. He was strapped to a stretcher and had an IV line running. A gunshot had shattered his femur. Tang was trying to get as much information from him as she could before the ambulance drove away.

"Does the name Dane Haugen mean anything to you?" she said.

Though he was already lying down, Coates seemed to slump. "The Reiniger Capital weekend."

"You know him?" Tang said.

"Yeah. He's infamous."

Evan inched toward the stretcher. "Why?"

Coates had liquid eyes, brimming with pain. "He freaked out during a scenario. Found a snake in his car and had a panic attack. Afterward, Peter Reiniger fired him."

"Because of a snake?" Tang said.

"He's phobic. He went berserk. I mean *berserk*. I should have known better — that was the last time I agreed to use snakes in a scenario." His voice was dry. "So Haugen did this?"

"Very possibly."

"Then it's about more than money."

The EMTs loaded him in the ambulance. Tang and Evan exchanged a look.

Evan got her phone out and typed a message to Jo. She didn't know if it mattered, whether she was writing to the air.

Tang said, "Really?"

"You gotta have faith."

Or at the very least, you had to act as though you did — and you had to try, without evidence, proof, or promise of an answer, to get through. Perhaps, if you went through the motions with enough conviction, you could make it real. Wasn't that what hope meant?

Haugen and Sabine waited for the tattooed and tatty Ruben Kyle Ratner on a clear patch of hillside where sunlight flowed over the lip of the mountains. The light was cold but clarifying. At the edge of the clearing, a chunk of the mountain had washed away in the night's flood. The rock and dirt dropped twenty feet, a raw wound in the earth. It seemed, to Haugen, a fitting symbol of the nature of change. It was violent, and painful.

True transformation was agony. That's what Peter Reiniger hadn't yet grasped. That's why he thought Edge Adventures was a hero factory. But in fact Edge offered merely puerile diversion. Its moments of illumination were fake. Whereas this moment, here on the mountain — life and death, wealth beyond imagining — this was real. All or nothing. Reiniger didn't understand that. Nor did Terry Coates, the lackey who did Reiniger's bidding and forced people to confront their worst fears.

Face your demons. That was simply code for getting Peter Reiniger's employees to piss their pants.

Edge was fake. But by taking Autumn, Haugen had made things real. And her father was soon going to understand the true meaning of *all or nothing.*

Ratner stepped from the trees, leading a bay horse. His bandy stride was cocksure. He wore a sleeveless wife-beater shirt, shamelessly displaying the snake tattoos that coiled around his arms. Cheap prison tats, the mark of mediocrity. For years Ratner had been the go-to guy for Haugen's intimidation needs. But now Haugen saw him clearly: lying, unpredictable, uncontrollable. If only he had fired the loser before he killed Phelps Wylie.

Haugen and Sabine walked to the center of the clearing.

"Two against one," Ratner said. "It's fair I get fifty percent. I done all the work, rounding up your chicks after they escaped the coop."

Haugen remained composed. "Proof of life. Now."

Ratner showed Haugen a cell phone photo of him with Autumn. In the dark, someplace close. Then he tossed a hunk of Autumn's long brown curls, tied with a rubber band, on the dirt.

"The other two kids, I presume they can be set aside for now, or forever," Ratner said. "I want to know how you plan to boogie out of here. 'Cause you're taking me with you. How we getting out of this wondrous shithole wilderness?"

"In good time," Haugen said.

"Now's a good time," Ratner said, "because there's a trail out of here that meets the road down below the washed-out bridge. It comes out at the clearing where Von and Friedrich shot that kid Grier. If you don't think this place is going to be crawling with cops soon, you're dreaming."

"I have a plan," Haugen said.

"I want to see it put into motion before we go further," Ratner said.

"All right." Haugen waited a beat. "But a cell phone photo and a lock of hair aren't proof of life. I need to hear Autumn's voice in conversation with me."

This was the moment, the instant where everything was going to fall into place. If Autumn was alive, he was about to get her. Then the money would flow from Peter Reiniger's fingers into his own account. It would land in Bermuda, for a few minutes, before being broken up into smaller transactions and winging around the world, account-hopping: Dubai, Singapore, Guernsey, Honduras. It would turn into gold and platinum and back into cash. Its trail would dim with each hop, until eventually it faded out completely.

And what a surprise awaited Peter Reiniger. Because twenty million was just the start.

The ransom was only stage one of Haugen's payday, because Haugen knew there was only one way Peter Reiniger could get that much cash within the deadline. He had to raid the reserve account at Reiniger Capital.

Reiniger's investment pile, his hedge fund mini-empire totalling a billion dollars in assets, was heavily

398

leveraged. Reiniger Capital maintained a slim cash reserve, in the form of instantly accessible money market accounts — a mere 2 percent of funds under management. That reserve cash amounted to just over twenty million. To ransom Autumn, Reiniger would have to plunder it.

Leverage. It was about to become Haugen's doomsday device.

Because Reiniger Capital was structured so that, if its reserves dropped below 2 percent, it triggered a margin call. Reiniger would have to pony up extra cash. But Reiniger was going to be tapped out. So the only way to replenish the reserves would be for Reiniger's investors to pony up. Immediately.

The thing was, all of Reiniger Capital's investors were highly leveraged too. They'd have to call on their own banks, and on the institutional investors behind them, to raise the necessary funds. That meant that they'd have to conduct fire sales, all around the world.

Haugen knew this for a certainty, because he had enticed many of those investors to sink their money into Reiniger Capital. Not only that, but he had written their investment contracts.

To be sure, lawyers had read the contracts. But the contracts were sixty-five pages of fine print. And Haugen had, without any difficulty at all, added wording at the last moment, unnoticed, almost certainly unread — a short phrase about mutually assured liability. It looked like gobbledygook, boilerplate, but in fact it meant that if the hedge fund's cash reserves dropped below 2 percent of gross assets, each investor was obligated to provide additional cash immediately.

That wasn't the brilliant part. The brilliant part was that, thanks to Haugen's rewording, the contracts obligated each investor to make up the difference between the required reserve and the amount it was underwater.

Each of Reiniger's investors was on the hook for the entire twenty million.

There was going to be a massive scramble by all of them to come up with the cash.

And Haugen was going to profit from it.

Reiniger Capital's investors were multimillionaires and financial partnerships — people who had deep-pocket institutions behind them. When the investors dumped their assets to raise the cash — each of them racing to pull out twenty million by trashing positions they'd held for years — Haugen was going to make a mint. To raise so much cash so quickly, the investors would need to call on *their* backers — institutional investors, banks overseas, some of them unforgiving — at outrageous interest rates. And because the whole edifice was highly leveraged, all the way down, those deep backers would have to unwind positions at fire-sale prices. It was going to be a slaughter.

And Haugen had hedged his bets against those deep backers. He was short against all of them.

The twenty-million-dollar ransom was nothing. Haugen was set up to get bonus megabucks by his back-end investments. The second Peter Reiniger paid the ransom, massive amounts of money would start moving. He estimated that he stood to make up to two hundred million dollars in the next forty-eight hours.

And he would thereby send Reiniger down in flames.

It had taken him a year to set up the scheme. He'd first dreamed it up when he realized how much he loathed Peter Reiniger. His initial idea, in fact, had been to kidnap Reiniger. But then he'd been fired, and the timing was ruined. But that was all right. Autumn was an even better prize.

He simply needed to push Reiniger Capital past the tipping point. After that, the house of cards would collapse.

And when he landed in Brazil, he'd have decades to savor his victory.

He just needed to put a radio to Autumn's lips and let her sob for rescue, so she could melt her daddy's heart.

Ratner shifted. "I said, how we getting out of here ahead of the cops?"

Haugen got out the portable police-band radio Sabine had taken off the body of the dead deputy, D.V. Gilbert. He considered for a moment and handed the radio to Sabine.

"More dramatic if it's a woman."

She switched the radio on. Cleared her throat. Pushed the button.

"Hello?" She sounded cold and shaky. "Is anybody out there?"

She let go of the button. Waited. Called again. "Hello?" Static crackled. A voice, distant, official, said, "Come in. Who's this?"

"Oh my God. Thank God — I'm trapped on the mountain. There's been a wreck. I need help."

Haugen smiled. Sabine was pitch-perfect.

"We got lost hiking in the storm, but Deputy Gilbert found us. We were coming back toward Sonora on the gravel section of the logging road and a rockslide took us out." She let her voice crack. "The cruiser, it went over the side. And now the road . . . the bridge is washed out. I don't know how long we can last."

"How many of you are there?" the voice said.

"Three of us. Me, my boyfriend, and the deputy. He's hurt awfully bad. Can you send a helicopter?"

"Hang on. We'll get you help."

"He needs a medical evacuation. He's so weak . . . Please help us. Please."

"Just hold on, ma'am. We'll get a bird in the air as fast as we can. Where are you?"

Sabine looked at Haugen. He pointed at the top of the ridge, beyond the power pylons, where the trees thinned.

"Hold on . . . my map's wet . . . it's . . . we're southeast of the state logging road about three miles, way up in the mountains. There's a clearing on top of a crest above us, with power pylons. We'll get to a high spot and set up a signal for you."

"Can I talk to Deputy Gilbert?"

"He's unconscious. God, he's so cold. He lost a lot of blood."

"Roger that. You hang in there."

"Hurry. Please," she said, her voice breaking.

She let go of the button.

Haugen doffed an imaginary cap. "Brava."

Ratner smiled crookedly and said, "Take a bow. But where are we going to go in that rescue chopper — back down to the sheriff's office parking lot?"

Haugen said, "Reno. Peter Reiniger is waiting at the airport with a private jet that will fly us wherever we want to go. It's fueled and waiting."

Sabine said, "Let's go."

Ratner raised a hand. "Not so fast. I need a guarantee that I'm getting my fifty percent."

Haugen said, "Do you have your bank account number with you?"

Ratner scoffed. "You'll pay me in cash."

Haugen nodded without hesitation. What a buffoon. This was going to be far simpler than he had imagined.

"Fine. And as a guarantee of your safety, I'll walk ahead of you all the way to the chopper. Which will also be a guarantee of my safety. Because for you to get the money, I have to be alive to provide access codes and transfer information to my bankers. Sabine doesn't have that information. Only I do. I need to be conscious and talking. And none of that will take place until we get Peter Reiniger in front of us."

Ratner seemed to think about it. His heated gaze — those burning eyes that stared out from sunken sockets — was full of cunning. The white snake around his iris told more than he knew. He expected vipers in every basket. But he couldn't see any flaw, any chip in Haugen's reasoning.

"You should have brung me in on this gig from the get-go," Ratner said. "None a this would've happened.

We'd be sitting pretty on a yacht somewhere already, smoking cigars."

"Lesson learned," Haugen said. *Moron.* As soon as he got Autumn, Ratner could be disposed of. The fool didn't even know that Von was still alive.

"Now give me proof of life. Let me talk to Autumn," Haugen said.

Ratner nodded at the walkie-talkie in Haugen's hand. "Turn up the volume and listen in. She's broadcasting. Daddy's Little Princess, playing her Top Forty, nonstop."

CHAPTER
FIFTY-FIVE

Jo pushed deeper into the mine. In her left hand she held the flashlight, in her right the buck knife. She kept her eyes on the path ahead and counted footsteps. Anything to keep her mind focused on finding Autumn and not on her sense of suffocation, of being squeezed by the throat in the dark. She glanced back, at the now-distant square of sunlight at the entrance. Claustrophobia tingled along her skin. *No. Don't let it hit. Don't.*

She swept the flashlight along the ground. How she wished she had her climbing harness and ropes now. She hurried past the side shaft where Wylie's body had been dumped. As she neared the flood pit filled with punji sticks, she chopped her steps.

Taking a deep breath, she jumped it. Landed in dust, slid, and kept going.

"Autumn?" she said.

Her phone vibrated. Startled, she tucked the flashlight beneath her arm, pulled out the phone, and read a surprising message from Evan.

She heard a muffled cry.

"Autumn?"

She put away the phone and scurried around a curve. Her view back to the entrance vanished. Sweeping the flashlight, she spotted, fifty yards ahead, the split in the tunnel.

"Autumn?"

The muffled cry came from the left. She put a hand on the wall. Cold rock — but solid. She forced herself to keep going. All she could see was the narrow beam from the flashlight, hitting stone and thick soft dirt on the floor. A rat's eyes caught the light, tiny and fervid. It spun and fled.

"Autumn, where are you?"

Footprints, soft in the mounded dirt, tracked in and out. Again she heard the muffled cry.

The roof of the tunnel lowered. Crouching, she rounded another curve.

Bright eyes.

Caught in the flashlight, Autumn seemed stunned. Her gold sweater looked incongruously cheerful. She was gagged and hogtied against the dead-end of the tunnel. Facedown, hands tied behind her back, back arched, feet bent behind her.

On the dirt near her face, its Transmit button taped open, was a walkie-talkie.

Ratner was a clever bastard. That's how he planned to give Haugen proof of life without giving away Autumn's location: by letting Haugen hear her mumble over the radio. And in a tunnel alive with rats, she was not going to keep quiet. If, of course, the walkie-talkie would actually work this deep in the mine.

Jo grabbed it and pulled off the tape. If the walkie-talkie did work, she didn't want to broadcast her presence.

The rope that bound Autumn's feet behind her back ran up and around her neck in a noose. It was a torturer's method of binding: to keep slack in the rope, the victim had to arch her back, tip her head back, and keep her legs tightly bent. If she relaxed by even a few inches, the rope would tauten, the noose would constrict, and she would strangle.

Jo ran to her. "Hang on."

She set down the flashlight, raised the buck knife, and reached for the rope. Autumn screamed through the gag. Her eyes, crazed and gleaming, pleaded *no*.

Jo stopped. Ratner had booby-trapped the flood pit before stringing Lark above it. Had he done something similar with Autumn?

The rope around Autumn's neck, she saw, was not a simple noose. Thin gauge, 10 mm rope that looked like a fuse, it looped twice around the girl's throat and then ran down her back, beneath her sweater.

Tears were bright in Autumn's eyes. She was fighting mightily to hold still, but her trembling seemed uncontrollable.

"Can I cut off the gag?" Jo said.

Autumn blinked. *Yes.* Cautiously Jo slid the blade of the buck knife beneath the dirty strip of fabric, sliced it off, and pulled a wad of torn shirt from Autumn's mouth.

"Don't tug on the rope." Autumn gulped a lungful of air and fought against crying. "He put . . ."

Jo went cold. She looked at Autumn's sweater. The girl's back was arched, but that only made more room beneath her clothing.

Something was beneath her sweater. It was moving.

"Snake?" Jo said.

"Snakes."

Jo's skin shrank, crown to toes.

"Baby rattlers. In a burlap bag. He tied the end of the bag closed with the rope around my neck. Just a slipknot. If I straighten my legs the knot will come loose."

And so would the snakes. Nice and warm and awake, and agitated about being held captive so close to a terrified human being.

Jo aimed the flashlight down the back of Autumn's sweater. She cringed. "Oh."

The bag was writhing.

Baby rattlers. They had potent venom and no experience at striking prey. Baby rattlers often emptied their venom in one burst.

Jo resisted the visceral urge to pull her hands in and skitter away on her butt. If Autumn could hold it together, she damned well could too.

"First I'm going to cut the rope by your feet."

"Do it."

"Bend your legs harder."

Autumn forced another inch. Jo carefully grasped the rope above Autumn's ankles, braced her arm on her own knee, and sliced the binding. Autumn whimpered in relief and straightened her legs.

Jo cut the knot around her hands. Autumn carefully lay flat. She shuddered and bit back tears. The rope still wound around her neck and down her twisting sweater.

"Let's get that bag out of there," Jo said.

"Good, good, good," Autumn whispered. "It's not just a way to keep me quiet. It's a booby trap."

"What?"

"Kyle says it'll set off the guy in charge. 'Boom'."

"Haugen. I know."

Autumn's gaze slid abruptly toward Jo. "Dane Haugen?"

"He's behind the kidnapping."

"But — he's the one who held the party. Where the Bad Cowboy . . ."

"Peyton told me."

Autumn tensed. "Is she . . ."

"She's okay."

Relief swept over Autumn's face. Then confusion and fear. "This is revenge? Haugen grabbed us to get back at my dad for firing him?"

She tried to swallow. The noose tightened around her neck. She squeezed her eyes shut. "Tell me you can get the sack out."

"Working on it."

And Jo was thinking about how to work on Haugen. *It'll set off the guy in charge. Boom.*

And Evan's message had explained what *Boom* meant. It said, *Haugen has snake phobia. Berserk panic.*

In the sharp beam of the flashlight, Autumn's sweater virtually swam. Muscular forms eeled over one another. An unmistakable dry rattle emanated from the sack. Jo saw only one way to remove it without exposing Autumn — and herself — to multiple attacks. Once she pulled the bag out, she needed to put it inside another container. She flashed the light around. Kyle had left a backpack on the dirt six feet away. She grabbed it.

"Hurry," Autumn said. "Kyle's going to come back."

Steeling herself, Jo reached beneath Autumn's sweater and grasped the end of the sack where the rope wound around it. She gagged and forcibly held herself still.

"Here goes."

She pulled the sack out.

Autumn sagged on the dirt, facedown. She jammed a hand in her mouth to keep from crying too loud.

Jo lifted the squirming sack to the backpack, holding it like a bag of unstable nitroglycerine. She slid it in and worked the zipper all the way closed.

"Where did he catch baby rattlers?" Jo said. "A nest?"

Autumn clambered to her feet, wiping her eyes roughly. "He brought them with him. In his backpack. He planned all along to terrorize me. I don't think Edge Adventures knew that. And I hope my dad didn't."

Jo expected her face to crumple, but she looked flinty.

Jo wound up to toss the backpack as far away as possible, and stopped. *Berserk panic.*

410

She knew exactly how that felt and how completely it disabled the phobic person. Activate a panic trigger, and you might as well hit the person with a Taser.

She didn't think Evan had mentioned Haugen's phobia as an aside or as a colorful bit of background on him.

She got a piece of the 10 mm rope and threaded it through the zipper pulls, tied a knot, and secured it. She took a breath. Then she put the backpack on.

"What the hell? Are you an animal-rights activist?" Autumn said.

"Never waste a weapon. Especially a potent one."

"It's dangerous."

"That's the point. I don't want to use it. Hope we don't run into Haugen." She aimed the flashlight up the tunnel. "Let's get out of here."

Gabe lugged Noah a hundred yards up the slope before he got out of sight of the mine entrance. Legs burning, lungs burning. His ribs and shoulder screamed. He kept going and saw the power pylons towering above him. Near the base of the southern tower, he set Noah down on the ground.

Lark huddled by his side. "He's not doing great."

Gabe rubbed Noah's arms to warm him. Noah's eyes flickered open.

"Hold on, buddy," Gabe said. "We're getting out of here."

Gabe tried to get his breath. Telling Lark he'd be right back, he clambered back to a vantage point overlooking the mine. He dropped to his knees. He wondered if he'd have the energy to stand up again.

Come on, Jo.

His breath caught. Sneaking toward the mine from the bottom of the ravine was Von.

CHAPTER
FIFTY-SIX

Jo and Autumn scurried along the low tunnel. Their feet tossed up soft earth. The turn back to the main shaft was only twenty yards ahead. Jo trained the flashlight on the ground directly in front of her, watching for rats and traps and other tricks Ruby Kyle Ratner might have placed there.

They reached the spot where the punji sticks lined the flood pit. Jo said, "Take a running jump. Just go. You'll make it."

Autumn accelerated, cleared the shaft, and landed softly. Jo followed, leaping on exhausted legs, and wobbled to a landing.

They hurried on, following the long curve of the tunnel. Jo held out one hand, fingers touching the wall to keep herself anchored, flashlight low. She passed a gap, the long drop into the shaft where Phelps Wylie's body had fallen. She kept thinking, *A few more yards, and we'll see the exit. A few more yards, and we'll see sunlight.*

The walkie-talkie in her pocket squawked. She grabbed it and turned the volume down. Her mouth was chalk dry.

They heard a man's voice. "I'm there."

It was Von. And worse, though they heard him through the walkie-talkie, they also heard his voice echo from the other end of the tunnel. He was at the entrance to the mine.

Haugen heard Von over the walkie-talkie. Ratner did too. His hot-cigarette eyes looked uphill, toward the mine, surprised, aware, full of enmity and the realization he'd been outmaneuvered. That Von was still alive.

Merely by looking in the direction of the mine, Ratner gave himself away. Haugen knew all he needed to know about where Ratner had stashed Autumn.

Ratner swung around and faced him. But not fast enough.

Jo felt cold and sizzling all at once. For a second, her mind felt blank — bleached clean by bubbling desperation.

"Come on." Grabbing Autumn, she ran back deeper into the mine.

"No. He'll find us," Autumn said.

Jo held her arm. "Here."

They reached the shaft where Wylie had been dumped. It was about three feet in diameter. The airshaft went up into gloomy light — all the way to the surface. But they weren't going to climb.

"Hide in here. We can chimney."

Jo demonstrated: back against one wall, feet against the other, pressing against both sides of the shaft like a spring.

"We only have to hide for a minute. Once he passes us, we'll run for the entrance."

They shimmied into the shaft. It was even colder than the main tunnel. The wind fingered over them. Jo turned off the flashlight.

A few seconds later, she heard scuffling. A dark figure, hunched and breathing hard, crept past them, headed deeper into the mine.

Autumn clamped her jaw tight. Jo held her breath, listening for him to recede down the tunnel. They had to wait until he turned the corner. But, to her horror, she heard him turn around and come back. She tried not to breathe. Autumn's legs were shaking. Von walked by so close they could smell him.

He's giving up, she thought. *He's leaving.*

A rat crawled from a cleft in the rock above Autumn's head. Its tail swept around and clipped her in the face. She squeaked.

Jo heard Von turn.

Only one thing she could think to do. "Run."

She jumped out of the shaft into the main tunnel. Autumn, screaming through her teeth, was a moment behind.

Von was blocking their path to the exit, a black bulk, pumpkin headed and menacing. Jo grabbed Autumn and ran deeper into the mine. They pounded through the soft dirt, breathless. They heard Von coming behind them.

He yelled into his walkie-talkie. "Boss, Autumn's here. She's running."

Gabe was already on his feet, sliding down the hill toward the mine, when he heard the distant report of gunfire. Hard sounds popped and echoed in the morning air. Crows lifted from the trees into the sky. The firefight was down the ravine, in the direction Ratner had ridden the horse.

He kept running.

If they could only get past the bend, they could make it. Jo struggled, sure she could feel Von's breath on her neck. They reached the bend and pummeled around it. Jo aimed the flashlight ahead in the tunnel, just for a fraction of a second.

"See it?" she said breathlessly.

"Yeah," Autumn said.

Jo turned off the flashlight. She gasped. "Five, four, three, two . . ."

They leapt over the punji-stick pit. And kept running.

A moment later they heard Von bash the wall as he hit the bend. Jo flashed the light on the roof of the tunnel, wildly, wanting to be sure he saw it. Wanting his eyes pinned on them.

She glanced back and watched him run straight into the pit.

His thick form disappeared with a yelp. They heard a thud. He screamed.

Jo stopped. Autumn grabbed on to her. Von kept screaming, loud and long and freaked out.

"We're out of here," Jo said.

416

They jumped back over the pit. Jo kept running, but Autumn stopped and leaned over the pit.

"This place is full of rats. They drop on you like shit. Have fun, you bastard."

"You *bitches*," Von screamed.

Autumn turned, eyes wide, grabbed Jo, and ran for the exit. The last sound they heard was Von firing his gun wildly from the bottom of the pit, and then bullets hitting the walls.

Misty sunshine fizzed off the hood of the Mustang. Through the windshield Evan saw Tang pacing by the big rig, directing the detectives and uniforms and forensics techs who had swarmed to the truck depot. A cup of coffee was growing cold in her hands. Evan drove past the rig and parked. She had dropped Ferd home and rushed back. She hoped Tang wouldn't count the minutes she'd been gone and compare them to the speed limit.

As she climbed out of the car, Tang's phone rang. The lieutenant grabbed it. Distantly, Evan heard her say, "Yes?"

Tang listened for a minute. Evan's stomach was tight. Tang hung up and jogged toward the Mustang.

"Tuolumne. They got a call from a woman saying she was in an accident in the forest where Jo's missing."

"It was Jo?" Evan said.

"Could be. Said she was with her boyfriend and the missing deputy. Deputy's hurt, needs medevac."

"And?"

"County rescue up there's swamped. They have a helicopter, but it's in use, pulling a family out of a station wagon that got swept into the river. The roads are a mess too. Nobody from their SAR people can get up to the area."

Evan ran her hands through her hair. "What are they going to do?"

"They've called the Air National Guard. The PJs are on their way."

CHAPTER
FIFTY-SEVEN

Jo and Autumn left Von's screams behind them and ran from the mine. They lugged themselves up the eroded and slippery hillside outside the mine shaft. Autumn's hands trembled as she grabbed roots and rocks to pull herself up.

The walkie-talkie scritched. Von's voice came through. "Help me."

Nobody responded. Von called again. "I'm in the mine, with my leg impaled on a fucking spear. Get me out of here."

Jo kept going. Nobody replied to Von's cries for help.

"Don't they hear him?" Autumn said.

"Maybe not."

They pulled themselves farther up the hill and over the lip of a gully, to a small crest in the trees. Above them, Jo saw the power pylons that bookended the ravine. On the near side, beside the steps that led up to the catwalk, Lark knelt by Noah's side. Jo couldn't see Gabe.

From the mine, Von screamed over the walkie-talkie. "Don't leave me here. I'm stuck like a pig. Get me out of here."

Haugen radioed: "Shut up."

419

Von screamed again. "Ratner's gonna come back. You gotta get me out."

"Von, close your mouth and pay attention. Ratner is not after you. He's gone."

"Gone where?"

"He went over the side of a washout with a bullet in his back."

Jo and Autumn exchanged a glance. Ratner, *gone*. A wave of relief hit Jo.

"Is Autumn secure?" Haugen said.

"Are you going to get me out?" Von said.

"Did Autumn elude you?"

Von hesitated. "No. But she will if you don't hurry and pull me out of this pit."

Jo's relief waned. Von was a terrible liar. Haugen had to realize Autumn had escaped — and that she couldn't have gotten far.

Haugen's voice cooled. "Don't fret. We've arranged rescue. The police are sending a helicopter."

"You better not be goddamned lying, Dane."

"They're en route. They think Sabine is that Beckett character, here in dire straits with the missing deputy. You'll be out of there in no time."

"And then?"

"Then we fly to Reno in their chopper. And from there, off into the great nowhere. Hold on, my friend."

"How are we gonna fly away — Alaska Airlines? I have a fucking *branch* in my leg. Am I supposed to ask the stewardess for a cup of ice to control arterial bleeding?"

420

Sabine came on. "The chopper is medevac search and rescue. And a private jet is waiting for us in Reno. Now get off the radio."

"They'd better be waiting. If they aren't, I'll —" He screamed again. "The fuck is . . . Oh God, rats —"

His shriek nearly caused feedback from the walkie-talkie. A shot blared, and a second.

Then the walkie-talkie feed went dead. Jo and Autumn gaped at the radio.

Jo said, "I think Von just got hit with a ricochet."

Autumn eyed her, hard. "I told him rats would get him. Panic is self-sustaining. Fear will kill you."

Downhill, something moved. Autumn peered toward the mine. Jo ducked and pulled the girl down below the crumbling dirt lip of the gully. She put a finger to her lips.

Was it Haugen? Sabine? They had to be nearby in the forest. She listened and heard rocks slide down the hillside — pebbles, ticking and tumbling — as if kicked loose by a person walking on the slope below them.

She and Autumn needed to move, but not if standing up would expose their position. She got out her phone. She thumbed the controls until she found ringtone options. She selected *Alarm*. She put the phone to the walkie-talkie, pushed the Transmit button, and set off the phone's alarm.

Smothered in her hand, the sound from the phone was barely audible. But the walkie-talkie sent it out strong. It sounded like a Klaxon.

Beyond the eroded lip of the gully above them, echoing through the pines, amplified and distorted by cheap electronics, the sound blared from another walkie-talkie.

Three feet away.

Jo's hair stood on end. She looked up. From the top of the gully, Sabine reared up and grabbed for her.

Jo leapt back but Sabine snagged a handful of her hair. They fell together into the gully. They rolled in the dirt, grunting, and as Jo went over and over, she saw the pistol in Sabine's hand. They slid across wet rocks to the edge of an eroded drop-off and lurched to a stop against a fallen log, with Jo on her back and Sabine on top of her. Sabine brought up the gun.

The pickax came from the side, over Jo's head, whirling end over end. With a blunt crack it hit Sabine full in the face.

She toppled backward and slid down the drop-off onto mossy rocks six feet below.

Jo spun. Gabe ran past her, grabbed the pickax again, and jumped over the log toward Sabine.

Jo crawled to her knees and looked over the log. "Is she dead?"

He lifted Sabine's head by the hair. Her eyes were vacant, but she was breathing. He dropped her head, careless of the rock beneath it. Jo had never seen him act so heartless. She thought she'd never loved him more.

He looked for the pistol. "Fell between the rocks. There's a cleft — damn."

He knelt to try to retrieve it. Jo and Autumn clambered down to help.

"It's lodged five feet down there in the cleft," Jo said. "We'll never reach it."

He stood. "Then let's go."

Sabine moaned. Jo grabbed the walkie-talkie from her, flipped Sabine onto her stomach, pulled off Sabine's pack, and unzipped it.

Jackpot. Ropes.

"Gabe, get going. I'm going to tie her up."

He hesitated until she said, "No. I don't trust this bitch as far as you can throw her."

He nodded and darted back up the hill for Lark and Noah.

Jo pulled out a thin length of rope and a roll of electrical tape. She tossed the tape to Autumn. "Gag her."

Autumn wound the tape around Sabine's head five times, tore it with her teeth, and slapped her palm against the woman's mouth to seal the adhesive. Jo whipped the rope around Sabine's hands and feet. They left her roped like a steer and climbed the hill after Gabe.

In the cold air and golden sunlight, Jo saw clearly. The next few minutes would go very right or very wrong. They had choices to make.

"Autumn, I want you to listen to me. We may have to separate."

"What are you talking about?"

"I have to help Gabe get Noah across the catwalk. Then we have to get Peyton. That'll take time. If I get caught, if Haugen gets me and Gabe, you have to get away. You'll have to take the long way out of here."

"Alone — leave you guys?"

"You'd have to. If Haugen sees you, you're toast." Jo grabbed her arm and pointed back down the hillside, past the Jeffrey pines and crimson dogwoods. "Below the mine there's a trail. It winds through the ravine and eventually ends at the clearing by the logging road where we ran into you yesterday."

"That's where we're going, right?" Autumn said.

"Yes. The trail is longer — it'll take you a couple hours. I know you're spent. But if things go bad, you have to go for it. You'll get there, and the cops will too."

Autumn froze, her face a welter of fear and remorse and longing. "No."

Jo's eyes welled. Was Autumn serious? "You can escape. That's what we've been aiming for this whole time."

"I won't leave without my friends," she said.

Jo knew something Autumn might not be considering: Autumn was her only bargaining chip. Should she herself be captured by Haugen, the only way she could possibly buy her own freedom was by turning Autumn over to him.

"You sure?" she said.

"Completely."

Jo squeezed her shoulders. Autumn did look like Tina. She saw it now.

"We only have a couple of minutes," she said. "Whatever you have left in the tank, we're going to spend it."

They crept uphill again. Through the trees Jo glimpsed Gabe and Lark. They were at the base of the south power pylon. The pylon was still considerably above Jo and Autumn, a few minutes' hike away. Gabe was preparing to cross the bridge.

The power-pylon shortcut was a scanty catwalk almost a hundred yards long. It crossed high above the ravine. Gabe climbed the rickety stairs to the bridge and hoisted himself around a locked chain-link gate designed to keep unauthorized people out. He had a couple of ropes, Jo saw. He began tying them to the bridge. He didn't think Lark could get across safely, and he didn't want to risk losing his balance while carrying Noah. It was sound procedure but was costing him time.

Jo and Autumn fought their way farther uphill, breathing hard, cold and frightened. The trees closed in and blocked their view. The scent of pine and clean air seemed, all at once, cloying. Jo kept going until the trees thinned and she got another clear view of the bridge.

Lark had climbed around the chain-link gate and was on the catwalk. Gabe was preparing to follow. He had rigged a piggyback sling from a piece of the tarp they'd found in the mine. Noah was strapped to Gabe's back, holding on with what nominal strength he had. Gabe was going to climb around the gate, carrying him. Jo's head went incurably dizzy. If Gabe lost his grip, the drop from the bridge into the ravine would kill them both.

Then she saw that he wasn't free-soloing. He had roped up: one end tied to his belt, the other secured to the railing of the catwalk. Holding tight, his face grim, muscles straining, he climbed around the gate.

Noah looked like a rag doll. But once they'd swung around the gate and set foot on the bridge, the group got going. Lark led the way, gripping the rails like death. Gabe untied the rope and followed slowly, his legs working hard under the strain.

Jo and Autumn continued to climb. They ducked through the trees and once more lost sight of the bridge. Then Jo rounded a boulder, got a clear view, and felt a moment of jubilation. The threesome on the bridge was halfway to the gate at the far end.

And, fifty meters above Jo on the hillside, Dane Haugen rode the horse out of the trees.

He kicked its sides and urged it up the slope to the power pylon. He dismounted and climbed the steps to the bridge. He stopped at the chain-link gate. He was smiling. He had a gun, and it was smiling too in the morning sun.

The gun was aimed at Gabe's back. Haugen cocked the hammer, sighted down the barrel through the gate, and fired.

CHAPTER
FIFTY-EIGHT

The shot from Haugen's revolver boomed in the mountain air.

On the bridge, Gabe reflexively ducked. Lark dropped to her knees.

Haugen continued to aim his revolver through the gate. "Stop right there."

From their vantage point in the trees fifty yards back, Jo and Autumn held painfully still. Jo's eyes were stinging. A wail, inhuman and demanding, began in her head. *Do something.*

Gabe urged Lark forward. Jo barely heard him say, "Keep going."

Lark regained her footing and they struggled onward, toward the far gate at the north end of the bridge. Noah, clinging to Gabe's back, turned and looked at Haugen. His eyes were ghostly. He seemed almost gone, nearly on the other side already, as though he were only looking back to see what was behind him.

Everything.

Haugen held his aim through the gate and fired again.

The shot ricocheted off the railing of the bridge. Lark cried out but kept pacing along the rickety metal surface. Gabe was right behind her. Haugen fired a third time.

"Stop," he shouted.

They ignored him. Gabe knew he had to get to the far side of the ravine. They had no options.

Haugen shoved the gun in his back pocket, clawed his fingers into the chain link of the gate, climbed on the rail, and swung around. He dropped onto the catwalk and stalked toward the trio.

Do something. Do it now.

"I have an idea," Jo said. "Quick."

She pulled Autumn behind the boulder and took off her jacket. "You too."

Thirty seconds later she and Autumn crept back around the boulder. Lark and Gabe were closing the distance to the north gate, but Haugen was gaining on them.

"Stop, right there," he shouted. "This time I can't miss."

He was close. He couldn't miss. Gabe and Lark stopped.

Haugen inched forward, his gun arm extended, sighting on Noah and from him straight through to Gabe. His revolver was huge, blue steel, shining in the morning sun.

He kept back, taking care to stay out of Gabe's reach on the swaying catwalk. He looked around, scanned the mountainside, and called out, "Turn Autumn over, right now, or they die."

Crouched by Jo's side beside the boulder, Autumn moaned.

A breath of wind brushed Jo's face and whispered past. *When you can't change a situation, and can't get out of it, you have to go forward.*

Jo didn't look at Autumn. There was no time, nothing more to be said. She cupped her hands to her face. "All right."

Autumn said, "No."

Haugen kept the gun aimed at Gabe but turned his head. "Now. Get out here."

"Okay," Jo yelled.

Autumn shook her head. "Don't. Jo, no."

The important thing is not to be afraid. Even when you know what's coming.

Jo looked at her. "Yes." She called again to Haugen: "Let them go."

She swept an arm around Autumn's waist. Holding her tight, she walked into the open.

They walked to the foot of the stairs. Autumn tried to pull Jo back. Quietly, desperately, Autumn said, "Don't do this. There must be another way."

Gabe and Lark and Noah had no other way.

Haugen continued to hold the revolver on Gabe. When he saw Jo and Autumn, his chest swelled.

"On the bridge, right now, both of you. Or I'll shoot your friends," he called.

Jo clung to Autumn's hand. Together they climbed the stairs.

Autumn murmured, "I can't believe you're doing this."

"Shh."

"*Jo . . .*"

Whispering, viciously, Jo said, "Don't fight. Do not."

Haugen shouted: "Get out here. Both of you. Move it."

He wanted them contained, with nowhere to run. Jo got to the gate. She saw Gabe's carabiner there, tied to the rope he'd fixed.

Autumn looked at her, beyond desperate. Pleading.

"This is it," Jo said.

Autumn shut her eyes tight. She nodded. Jo clipped the carabiner to the girl's belt.

Autumn grabbed the gate. Shaking, she climbed up on the rail. "Oh my God."

It was a long drop.

"Hang on to the gate. Dig your fingers in. Hold on and swing around to the other side."

Wobbling, Autumn clenched her jaw and slid her foot along the rail, an inch at a time. She got her leg around the gate, jabbed one arm around and grabbed hold of the gate on the far side, and in a burst of panicked bravery, swung all the way around and clattered down onto the bridge.

She unhooked the carabiner from her belt and stood holding the rail.

Jo reached and got the 'biner, clipped it to her own belt, and dug her fingers through the chain link. She clambered up onto the railing and swung around the gate, carefully, aware of her exhaustion and hunger and cold hands, clearly aware of the drop into shadow and crumbling boulders that lay below the bridge.

430

Fingers clawing into the chain link, stinging with cold, she swung around on the slippery wet railing and got her body weight over the catwalk. She slid down, heard the chintzy aluminum ring, and planted her feet on the bridge.

She unhooked the 'biner and grabbed hold of Autumn. "Let's go."

Together they inched forward toward Haugen along the catwalk.

Autumn swallowed. "I don't want to fall."

"Don't make any sudden moves." Jo glanced down. The railing wasn't really that high. And the catwalk was swaying. Falling would be easy.

Haugen watched them come. "That's it. All the way."

Autumn whimpered. And stopped.

The bridge swayed. Pinned under Noah's near-dead weight, Gabe held on to both railings, fighting to keep his legs under him. If he lost his balance it would be too easy for both of them to go over. Ahead of him, Lark trembled. She half turned to see what was happening behind them on the catwalk. Gabe didn't dare shift his center of gravity to look back. But he sensed the barrel of Haugen's gun aiming for a bull's-eye on his center of mass.

He knew Haugen had no plans to free him. Perhaps Haugen would be satisfied to abandon Lark and Noah to the elements after capturing Autumn, but the man would never leave him and Jo alive to come after him — on the mountain or a witness stand.

"Lark, what do you see?" he said.

431

She gripped the railing and crouched low and peered around him to see behind down the rickety length of the catwalk.

"Oh my God. Jo . . ."

She blinked and pushed her index finger up along the bridge of her nose. It was an automatic gesture — as if trying to adjust the eyeglasses that weren't there.

"Jo's forcing Autumn onto the bridge."

It hit Gabe like the sound of broken glass. "That makes no sense."

Haugen shouted, "Don't stop. Come here. All the way. Pick it up."

"They're fighting," Lark said.

The wind gusted. Gabe dared not turn.

"She's got hold of Autumn and she's dragging her toward the middle of the bridge." Lark gasped. Her chest began to heave. "I don't believe this. Oh God."

Haugen yelled, "Bring her here, dammit."

"Autumn's stuck. She won't move." Lark's mouth widened. "Jo's running away."

Gabe heard footsteps retreating. He felt them through the surface of the catwalk. Then he heard Haugen turn and run back toward the middle of the bridge.

He nodded to Lark. "Run. *Run.*"

Jo felt the surface of the catwalk judder beneath her boots. The aluminum bridge rang with the pounding of footsteps. She was close, so close, to the south gate — and close enough to Autumn that she hoped — prayed — Haugen wouldn't risk shooting for fear of hitting the girl. His prize was nearly within reach. He needed Autumn alive.

She had to gamble everything. *Gabe, forgive me for what I'm doing*, she thought. *Autumn, please . . . I hope you'll be okay.*

Her heart thundered. In the distance, above the rushing of the wind, she thought she heard a deeper sound: the *thwap* of helicopter rotor blades. The catwalk vibrated again, and harder. Haugen was coming for her.

He eked his way along the catwalk, tense and single-minded. He gripped the rail and checked his footing. He glanced at Jo and smiled like a jackal. He looked back down at his footing.

He didn't really see her. He hadn't seen her at all. He had only seen his payday.

He kept coming, step by step, eyes on the catwalk. When he was fifty yards away, Jo turned and ran.

Autumn was already way ahead of her, rushing back toward the gate.

Gabe reached the north gate and grabbed hold. Finally anchored, he looked over his shoulder and back at the bridge.

What the hell was Jo doing?

She was rushing the other way, toward the south gate. And she was wearing Autumn's clothing.

Autumn was ahead of her. She was dressed in Jo's jacket and hiking boots. They had swapped clothes.

And Haugen hadn't seen it.

Far away, eyes only on the gold-as-sunlight sweater and shining riding boots and the long brown curls that flowed from beneath the Marine Corps utility cap, he had taken Jo for Autumn.

He was after the wrong woman. He was trying to grab Jo. If he did, Autumn would escape.

If he did, Jo would be trapped with him on the bridge, with no way out.

Jo pounded along the swaying catwalk. She heard Haugen behind her, gaining. He was running full tilt. He still thought she was Autumn.

Ahead of her, Autumn reached the gate. She crashed into it and hesitated. She had no time to rope up. She simply had to go. She held tight and climbed onto the rail.

Haugen's footsteps closed on Jo. She heard him breathing. He grunted and his fingertips scraped the backpack and slid off. She kept going.

Now, she thought. *The helo's coming. I have to risk it.*

She reached around with one hand and unzipped the backpack. Haugen was right there. She felt him. His form, his hot breath. He grabbed her. She saw his gun — it swung up as he struggled to control her. He was going to fire at the girl climbing around the gate. He thought he was aiming at Jo Beckett.

Get here quick, she prayed.

Jo spun. As she did, she pulled the burlap sack from the backpack. She grabbed Haugen's coat and yanked him toward her, off balance. He was still, incredibly, focused on Autumn.

Until he looked at Jo at last. His face blanked with shock.

Then his confusion cleared into rage. He remembered the gun in his hand.

She looked him in the eye. "For you."

She dumped the sack on him. Rattlesnakes poured out. And she heard, beneath the *thwap* of helicopter blades, the distinctive and deadly *chirr* of a rattle.

CHAPTER
FIFTY-NINE

Gabe swung around the north gate, fingers aching, chain link rattling. He fought to hold on against Noah's added weight, jumped down, and staggered down the stairs. He labored to his knees and unhooked Noah from the piggyback sling. With Lark's help, he laid the young man on the ground. Then he looked back up at the bridge.

Jo, brightly clad in Autumn's gold sweater, was at the far end of the bridge, up on the rail, climbing around the south gate. Autumn had already climbed around and run down the stairs to the hillside. She streaked into the trees on the other side of the ravine, a blur of movement Gabe registered and ignored, because Jo was in trouble.

Haugen had her. He was trying to haul her down from the railing. She dug her fingers into the chain link and held on for her life. Gabe heard screams. Jo was completely above the rail, one foot on its slippery surface, one foot kicking Haugen.

And Gabe realized it was Haugen who was screaming, in hysteria.

Haugen jerked away from Jo, slapping at himself, swiping and flailing. He had dropped his gun. He spun in a circle. He moved as if he were on fire and trying to douse the flames.

Jo sagged on the gate. She looked woozy. But she tried to use whatever was happening to Haugen to get away. She dragged herself back up and tried to swing around to the far side.

Haugen shrieked like a banshee.

Gabe struggled to his feet and stumbled back toward the bridge. The sound of heavy-duty rotor blades beat the sky. A helicopter was coming.

"Lark, get to high ground," he said. "Signal them. Take off your coat and wave it in the air."

Lark ran up the hill. Gabe turned back to the bridge.

Jo was still up on the rail and halfway around the gate, poised above the ravine. Haugen lunged for her, roaring.

Gabe ran up the slope.

Haugen grabbed Jo's legs and pulled her feet from the slippery rail. She hung on to the gate, kicking. Haugen leaned out beyond the railing, trying to pry her loose and dump her.

She cried out. Haugen wrenched her hands loose from the gate.

Completely exposed in midair, falling, she clawed for Haugen's coat. She got a handful of his collar. Her momentum pulled Haugen off balance and over the rail. He swiped for the gate and missed. Then he fell.

Jo dropped with him, out of sight. Gabe didn't see the rest.

CHAPTER
SIXTY

Evan stood next to Tang's car. The sunlight seemed to sting. Her eyes were gritty. Her nerves felt scoured. The phone was on speaker.

"Anything?" Tang said.

"Connecting."

The SFPD switchboard patched through the call, and all at once they heard the radio conversation between the SAR helicopter and the Tuolumne County Sheriff's Office. The droning engines and beating rotors nearly overcame the electronic sinkhole of the pilot's voice.

". . . over the site now. People on both sides of the bridge. Two over the railing."

Evan rubbed her forehead. Tang leaned against the car and listened with her eyes shut.

". . . survivors. A woman's on the top of the hill, waving her coat to signal us. But a body is visible in the ravine." Static. Engine noise. A new voice, also from the helo: "Guy just climbed onto the bridge — he's headed to the point on the span where the man and woman fell over."

The pilot said: "It's Quintana."

"What the hell's he doing here? Where's he . . ."

More static. "Power lines — can't fly any lower. Going to pick up survivors."

The radio clicked off.

The *thump* of the rotors echoed painfully across the hillside. It bounced off the slopes of the ravine and moaned through air and pine and metal. The sky had brightened to azure, a pure vision of blue. Gabe was leaning over the rail, his voice swallowed by the roar of the chopper above him. Its blades beat the air, the downdraft flattening grass on the hillside and causing the pines to sway. Gabe stretched over the rail, yelling, but his words were gone.

Jo hung by the 10 mm rope that was secured to the railing of the bridge. It was tied to Gabe's carabiner, which she'd clipped to her belt. The belt was barely holding. She looked up at the bridge. It glared in the dawn sunlight, a painful metallic sheen. Gabe grabbed the rope and struggled to keep her from swinging.

She swiped for the rope, but her arm was numb and couldn't move. The pain burned her.

She had been bitten by a rattler. She reminded herself to keep the bite below the level of her heart and to hold still. She lowered her arm but continued looking up. Her heart was up there. He was holding the rope.

"Rattler strike . . . ," she said, and knew Gabe didn't hear. The helicopter, she saw, was a Pave Hawk. It was the goddamned 129th.

She looked at the hillside. Lark and Noah were on the north side of the bridge. They were safe. She looked down. At the bottom of the ravine lay Haugen. She felt dizzy, heard a new hum in her ears, high pitched and squealing.

She turned her face to the sky. On the bridge above her, Autumn climbed around the gate and joined Gabe in hauling on the rope. Jo felt herself being lugged up toward them, a few inches at a time.

Autumn hadn't wanted her to risk duping Haugen. Autumn had tried to stop her, because she feared it was dangerous. Autumn was a damned smart kid. She'd been right.

The pain was incredible. Her arm throbbed and she felt nauseated.

She reached up with her uninjured arm and heard the thunder of her blood in her head.

Haugen had been covered in rattlers. They had poured out of the sack onto him. Angry, basic, fight-or-die Mojave greens. How many times they had struck she couldn't imagine. She looked down again. His face was a mass of swollen bites.

The helicopter hovered above. Its loud and ugly rotors sounded like salvation. She had heard Haugen say it was inbound. She had gambled that even if she got bitten, they'd be here in time. She didn't know yet if she'd won the wager.

Hurry, she thought. And closed her eyes.

When she opened her eyes, she was in the Pave Hawk.

"Hold on. We're going to get you to the hospital," a PJ said.

440

Her vision was blurred but she could see that they were still on the ground. She saw the mountains outside. Granite peaks patched with snow. She was on a litter. The rotors were cycling up.

The PJ's green flight suit looked reassuring. She felt the needle prick, but compared to the rattler strike it was nothing.

"Antivenom?" she said.

"Yes, ma'am."

She felt like she was on fire. She felt blurry and sick. Noah lay nearby her on a litter in the Pave Hawk. Another PJ was working on him. He had an IV line in.

"Peyton?" she said.

"She's being treated." A hand touched her shoulder. "Lie still. You're going to be okay."

"You guys have a reassuring bedside manner," she said.

Outside the helicopter, hands over her ears, Lark stared in at her. Jo tried to give her a thumbs-up.

Behind Lark, Gabe stood as still as a totem pole, his face grave. Sunlight kicked from the dial of his watch. Jo closed her eyes.

When she opened them again, the rotors had cycled up to a high whine. The grass outside lay beaten flat and the trees swayed in the downdraft. Lark was leaning in the door, hands still covering her ears. She looked at Noah and mouthed, *Love you.*

Gabe put a hand on Lark's shoulder and gently pulled her back from the door. Behind him in the trees, pale shadows moved. Jo caught his eye. She tried to tell him, *Love you too, Sergeant,* but the noise was too loud.

The PJ turned to the door and grabbed the handle. Jo's eyes began to drift shut. Behind Gabe on the hillside, Ruby Kyle Ratner stepped out of the tree line.

When Jo opened her eyes, the Pave Hawk's door was sliding shut. Gabe raised a hand, wishing her a safe flight. Ratner was closer. His eyes were blazing, his lips blue with cold. His left side was caked red with blood.

Jo raised her head. "Gabe —"

Ratner's right arm came up. It rippled with blue snakes. A pistol shone in his hand.

"Everybody in the chopper," he said.

Gabe turned. The Pave Hawk shuddered.

"You're taking me to Reno," Ratner said.

The sound of the gunshot was muffled by the rotors. Ratner dropped where he stood. His knees hit the ground and he slumped and toppled forward. His chest hit the grass. The round had caught him in the side of the head.

Autumn walked toward him from the far side of the helicopter. Haugen's revolver was steady in her hand.

CHAPTER
SIXTY-ONE

The media beat Peter Reiniger to the airport in Sonora. The flash flood — and the rockslides, the station wagon that washed into the river, and a school bus that had nearly swept away — had brought news crews to the Sierra foothills. Through the window of the G5, Reiniger saw reporters and photographers and a TV crew from Sacramento, with its television cameras, its microphones, its van with the microwave dish on top. His private jet was the most exciting thing to land in the pine-covered hills for at least half an hour.

The plane eased to a stop. Reiniger opened the door himself while the engines were still screaming. Waiting outside the terminal building was Autumn.

The steps came down. Reiniger climbed out and ran across the wet runway. Autumn stood solemnly, her curls rising in the wind like a corona. The morning sun reflected from the rainwater on the ground, blinding gold. She was wearing a jean jacket and hiking boots he didn't recognize. She was pale. She had dark circles under her eyes.

Where was Dustin? Reiniger would have expected to see him holding Autumn up. Instead, Lark was beside his daughter. Autumn hugged the chubby girl, said something to her, quietly. Lark squeezed her back. Autumn turned and strode toward him.

He crossed the distance in seconds. The jet's engines wound down behind him. He grasped Autumn by the shoulders, fighting emotion. The media was watching.

"Thank God." He embraced her. "You're safe. It's over." He squeezed her hard. She felt edgy and exhausted and resistant.

She pulled back. "I'm safe."

Her eyes were dry. She stood as stiff as a door. Was she still terrified?

"It's okay. You don't have to be afraid anymore," he said.

He glanced at the crowd outside the terminal. Lark was sensible and grounded. If Autumn lost it, Lark could pick up the pieces. Lark could get Autumn to hold it together.

"Where is everybody?" he said.

"Didn't you hear?"

He smiled. "Hear what?"

She looked astonished. "Don't you know? Dustin's dead. Grier's dead."

Reiniger felt all the heat in his body evaporate.

"It was Dane Haugen," she said.

Reiniger's hands wouldn't seem to work. Or his tongue. He tried to take Autumn's hand and couldn't raise his arm. He felt frozen.

"You knew it was Haugen, didn't you?" she said.

Her gaze felt like raw heat. He nodded. "He wanted me to ransom you."

444

"It was revenge, wasn't it? Because you fired him. Because he freaked out on an Edge Adventures weekend."

"Autumn, not here."

"You'd been letting him do whatever he wanted until then. But he couldn't cut it in your playground, so you cut him loose."

"*Not here*," he said, glancing at the news crews. But she wouldn't move. Finally, Reiniger said, "He's a bad man."

"He's dead too. And so is the Bad Cowboy. I killed him."

Reiniger felt the words go through him. They made no sense. "What do you mean, killed him? Like, a game? You got him out of your system?"

"I shot him with Haugen's three-fifty-seven revolver." She waited, frosty and implacable. "We have to call Grier's family. And Dustin's."

He rubbed his forehead. "Right."

"You didn't pay him the money, did you?" she said.

"No. I didn't."

"What did he want you to do?"

He didn't want to discuss this. "It's irrelevant. It's done now. You're safe."

"He was going to make a killing in the market, wasn't he?"

"Autumn. Enough. You're out of it. You don't know what you're saying."

"But you were willing to pull all kinds of dirty tricks to buy my way out of there, right? And let Haugen fly off in your jet?"

"I'm your father. I'd do anything to save you. Anything."

"That's the problem."

She turned and headed toward the small terminal. Cameras and microphones perked up and swung their way. Reiniger hurried after her.

"Where are you going?" he said.

"Leaving."

"So get on the jet."

"No. We're driving back to the hospital to see Noah and Peyton. Then we're going to talk about your money."

"Autumn —"

She turned, slowly, with great deliberation. "Did you pull cash out of Reiniger Capital?"

"Yes." He was hot now. "It can't be undone. I'm on the line for all of it."

"Good. Because you're going to take the proceeds and put them toward Noah's recuperation, and Peyton's. And money for scholarships in Grier's and Dustin's names. And we'll find out from the sheriff's office what they need, and you'll set up a trust fund in memory of the deputy who died last night. And another for the family of the rancher who was killed."

Autumn stood in front of him, dirty and exhausted, and wearing it like a badge of honor and rage and friendship. Lark watched her with open pride in her eyes.

Reiniger hesitated, incredulous. His daughter was steel.

"Have the Edge game runners been found?" she said.

He nodded. "They're all alive."

"Great." She looked relieved. "That's wonderful. Put them on the payroll at Reiniger Capital."

"Excuse me?"

"They're going to need new jobs."

He paused. "I think you're confused —"

"They'll need new jobs, because you're going to pay whatever it takes to buy Edge Adventures. And shut it down."

"Autumn. Get real."

Her smile was chilly. "Right. Real. In that case, you buy Edge. And *I'll* shut it down."

She put an arm around Lark. Reiniger stood on the runway like he'd been struck by lightning. He watched Autumn walk away.

CHAPTER
SIXTY-TWO

When Jo walked out of the hospital, she had her arm in a sling. The day was burnished, the best San Francisco had to offer. Tina paced along slowly at her side, carrying her things. Jo's forearm was immobilized in a cast. She had suffered nerve damage from the bite of the Mojave green. She faced months of rehabilitation and physical therapy. But her prognosis was good. She had been lucky.

Outside, Amy Tang was waiting, leaning against the side of an unmarked Crown Vic. Spike haired, dressed in goth black, chewing gum, she somehow had a Buddha's calm. From behind her sunglasses, she said, "I'm still counting those lives, cat."

"It's all about statistics with you, isn't it?" Jo said.

Tang smiled.

Tina hefted the flowers Ferd had sent. They were so lavish that they looked like a stage prop for *Little Shop of Horrors*.

"I need to load these in the car before they eat me," she said.

As she headed off, Jo moseyed over to the Crown Vic. Mosey was her top speed at the moment. Leaning against the car next to Tang, like they were bandmates in a rock video, was Evan Delaney.

She looked calm and bright-eyed, her toffee-colored hair flicking in the breeze. And she looked strangely melancholic at seeing Jo. Perhaps it was the sight of Jo's lingering injuries and knowledge of the chaos wrought by Haugen and Ratner.

Noah had been released from the hospital. His recovery was going to be painful but straightforward, thanks to youth, fitness, and good luck. He had months of grueling rehabilitation ahead, but he could look forward to a full recovery. So could Terry Coates. His shattered femur had been pinned back together, and with work, he should return eventually to full strength. Peyton had not been quite so lucky. The broken clavicle was healing, but she too had suffered nerve damage from the snake bite. The doctors didn't yet know if she would recover full use of her arm.

Jo approached the Crown Vic. "I can't look that bad, can I?"

Evan said, "You look ready for your close-up. In a zombie movie." Then she smiled. "No, you look sunny. But you gave us a scare."

"And you got the story," Jo said.

"Bigger story than even I could have imagined. And I have a gargantuan imagination." The smile softened. "But you got more than anybody bargained for."

"Thank you for your help. You were a lifeline. Both of you."

Jo held out her hand. Evan squeezed it. Jo held on for an extra second. "I'm going to archive all your text messages. I'll never erase them."

Tang glanced across the road. Gabe's 4Runner was parked across the street. Gabe was waiting behind the wheel, elbow propped on the open window.

"Got energy for the debrief?" Tang said.

"Not really."

Jo knew most of it already. Haugen had died from the fall from the catwalk. But if he hadn't fallen, he would only have lived a few hours. He'd sustained enough bites from the nest of baby rattlers to kill five people.

Von was also dead. His body had been found in the pit in the mine. A punji stick had impaled his thigh, but he had died from the ricochet of a bullet fired from his own gun.

Sabine Jurgens alone had survived. Now she was talking, at length, to the Tuolumne County sheriffs and the FBI, in the hopes of leniency. She wouldn't get it.

Jo had no interest in hearing about Sabine's attempts to spin excuses for herself. The only thing she found pertinent was Sabine's admission that she had shot and wounded Ruben Kyle Ratner as he fled from her and Haugen during their negotiation on the mountain — and that she had erred in assuming Ratner was dead. She and Haugen had seen him lying bloody and motionless at the bottom of a gully. Impatient, Haugen had left the scene and gone after Autumn. But Ratner regained consciousness and was able to drag himself up the ravine and nearly hijack the Pave Hawk.

Tang raised her hands in surrender. She'd wait to talk until Jo was ready.

Then Jo mellowed. "Give me the short version."

"The sheriffs rescued the horse," Tang said.

Jo felt the beginnings of a smile. "Great. Has anybody told Autumn she's a hero?"

"I don't know," Tang said. "But I'm going to tell her to apply to the SFPD. That kid has a spine."

"No kidding."

Evan looked tart. "I'll give you the short version. Peter Reiniger planned a dream birthday for his daughter. Haugen turned it into a nightmare. But you stole the show."

Jo smiled at her. "Call me the nightmare thief."

She walked past the Crown Vic and stepped into the sunlight. The hospital looked out across the hillsides of the city, past the white towers of St. Ignatius Church, over the rolling green forest of the Presidio, to the iron red towers of the Golden Gate Bridge. She inhaled air tinged with salt. For a while, she had wondered if she would ever see this view again.

She ambled slowly toward the 4Runner. Tang and Evan flanked her.

"So what did you get up to while I was gone?" she said.

Evan said, "This and that. Tang and I did each other's hair. And she showed me her scrapbooks, all those pony club ribbons for dressage. Tina taught me how to count cards."

Jo gave her a crooked stare.

"Then Ferd entertained us with selected songs from *The Mikado*. In costume," she said. "Did you know Mr Peebles mixes a wicked cosmopolitan?"

"What the hell are you talking about?"

"You have a good bunch here."

They reached the 4Runner. Evan paused. "Up there on that bridge — you threw the dice hard, Jo."

Gabe glanced over.

"It was a calculated gamble," Jo said.

"I have to know — what gave you the nerve to try?" Evan said.

Jo hesitated. "Something a friend said to me. That when you can't change a situation, and can't get out of it, you have to go forward. Call it a hard fact of life."

Evan looked, all at once, like she'd turned to smooth stone. Her eyes were hot, confused, and longing, all at the same time.

"He told you that, didn't he?" she said.

Jo held poised. She sensed that Evan was on the lip of something — a change, a breakthrough, a crash. Light. She waited, and Evan said it.

"Jesse."

"He's the one."

Evan flushed, and her eyes shimmered. Jo lowered her voice to a murmur.

"Jesse told me about your father's disappearance, and — the rest. I'm sorry."

"I don't . . . I want . . ."

Jo thought about shaking her hand, then pulled her into a hug. She said, "Waiting's no good. Jesse's out there."

452

Evan held still, tightly knotted. After a moment she inhaled and stepped back. Her eyes gleamed. "Right."

Gabe got out of the 4Runner and walked around to open the passenger door for Jo. She smiled once more at her friends and got in.

Gabe got behind the wheel and pulled out carefully. They drove quietly for a block. His mind was elsewhere. Jo suspected he was evaluating what she had said to Evan about the calculated gamble.

She turned to him. "I saw my chance and took it. I knew the chopper was coming."

"I know you did."

"I'm sorry that I worried you."

"Don't apologize."

She felt, all at once, a swell of emotion. Everything swept over her: relief, happiness to be going home, sadness at the loss of innocent lives, elation that Gabe was alive and unharmed and there with her. Her vision swam.

He pulled over. "Jo."

She raised a hand. "It's okay. Rogue emotional wave. I'm fine."

He unhooked his seat belt and pulled her against him. "Let's not think about everything right now. I know you're okay. It's just that . . . the risks you take —"

She felt a cold thread of worry. "Don't tell me you're breaking up with me."

"What? No. Christ, no."

She looked up. "Then what?"

"You scare me sometimes. So kick my butt. Keep me onside. Sometimes I'm stupid."

"What are you saying?" she said.

"That I know I can trust you. You're not reckless. But you are going to live at high pitch, and go to the wall. I just have to roll with it."

She shook her head, baffled. "You're losing me."

"That's what I don't want to do. I want to keep you. I want you to be with me. Always. I want Sophie to have a good role model. Jo, stay with me. Move in. Let's make a life. Crazy as it is. Let's keep each other alive. When I'm with you I *am* alive. I don't want to lose that."

She leaned back. "Wow."

"I talk about my emotions once every five years, and when I do, I empty the clip." He looked at her. "Think about it."

"You bet I will."

She pulled him to her and kissed him. He put his hands to her face. She tightened her arm around him and held on. He was smiling. The phone rang. He kissed her again.

The phone continued to ring. She ignored it until he said, "Answer it."

Reluctantly she sat back, brushed her hair from her eyes, and answered.

A woman said, "Dr Beckett? It's the Quest Network."

Her lipstick had smeared Gabe's mouth. She wiped it off. She was smiling.

"Excuse me?" she said.

"We're calling about Edge Adventures."

Jo hesitated. "Quest — the television channel?"

"We're developing the premise into a television show. We'd like to talk to you about being a consultant."

"No."

"There's enormous interest in the concept."

Jo pulled the phone from her ear and stared at it. "No."

The woman kept talking as if Jo hadn't spoken. "It's a hot property. And you're the hottest property of all."

"Hot? You bet I am."

"All right . . . there's also the possibility that we can discuss hosting the show."

"Really? *Dr Jo's Disaster Camp?*"

"Well, we'd have to negotiate the title."

"In that case, listen closely." She waited. The woman listened. "*No.* As in never."

"But Dr Beckett —"

Jo hung up and tossed the phone in the backseat. She pointed at the road. Gabe put the truck in gear.

Acknowledgments

For their advice, support, and encouragement, my thanks go to Ben Sevier at Dutton and Patrick Janson-Smith at Blue Door. An author couldn't ask for better editors, and I'm privileged to work with them. Thanks as well to everyone at my U.S. and UK publishers, including Jessica Horvath, Stephanie Kelly, and Jamie McDonald at Dutton, and Laura Deacon at Blue Door. My gratitude also goes to my agents, Sheila Crowley and Deborah Schneider. I'm lucky to have them on my team. And for their knowledge and advice on subjects ranging from emergency medicine to auto mechanics, I am indebted to Sara Gardiner, M.D.; John Plombon, Ph.D.; and Dan Kotwasinski. Thanks as well to my first readers: Mary Albanese, Adrienne Dines, Kelly Gerrard, Susan Graunke, Kathy Montgomery, Betsy Speer, and David Wolfe. And, as ever, for everything, thanks go to my husband, Paul Shreve.

Also available in ISIS Large Print:

The Bone Yard

Jefferson Bass

The onset of summer brings predictably steamy weather to the Body Farm, Dr Bill Brockton's human-decomposition research facility at the University of Tennessee. But when Angie St Claire, a forensic analyst with the Florida Department of Law Enforcement, asks him to help prove that her sister's death was murder, things get a lot more uncomfortable.

Brockton's quick consulting trip takes a harrowing turn when he discovers bones buried amid the forests of Florida. Two adolescent skulls, bearing the telltale signs of lethal fractures. The evidence leads him to the ruins of the North Florida Boys' Reformatory, where Brockton's team find a cluster of shallow graves, all containing the bones of boys who met violent deaths. As the investigation expands, it encounters opposition from the local sheriff, who's less than delighted to find forensic experts digging up dirt in his county.

ISBN 978-0-7531-8952-8 (hb)
ISBN 978-0-7531-8953-5 (pb)

Fifth Victim

Zoë Sharp

Bodyguard and ex-Special Forces soldier Charlie Fox would do anything to take her mind off her partner: shot and lying in a coma. A new assignment seems like the perfect opportunity. The job: to protect the daughter of an investment banker from a gang of kidnappers who prey on the children of the wealthy. Usually those who disappear are returned unharmed — except this syndicate likes to take a piece of the victim as part of the pay-off.

Still, it all looks simple at first. A round of charity auctions and luxurious parties — few risks for an experienced operative. But Charlie soon finds out that defending a young woman determined to put herself in danger is far from easy. And when her instincts lead her to suspect an inside job, she discovers that not everyone who mingles with the jet-set is what they seem . . .

ISBN 978-0-7531-8912-2 (hb)
ISBN 978-0-7531-8913-9 (pb)